D1418195

FRONTIER JUSTICE

Center Point
Large Print

Also by Bill Brooks and available from Center Point Large Print:

Vengeance Trail

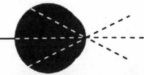

This Large Print Book carries the Seal of Approval of N.A.V.H.

FRONTIER JUSTICE

A JOHN HENRY COLE STORY

Bill Brooks

CENTER POINT LARGE PRINT
THORNDIKE, MAINE

This Center Point Large Print edition is published
in the year 2016 by arrangement with
Golden West Literary Agency.

The text of this Large Print edition is unabridged.
In other aspects, this book may vary
from the original edition.
Printed in the United States of America
on permanent paper.
Set in 16-point Times New Roman type.

ISBN: 978-1-68324-046-4 (hardcover)
ISBN: 978-1-68324-050-1 (paperback)

Library of Congress Cataloging-in-Publication Data

Names: Brooks, Bill, 1943– author.
Title: Frontier justice : a John Henry Cole story / Bill Brooks.
Description: Center Point Large Print edition. | Thorndike, Maine :
Center Point Large Print, 2016. | ©2012
Identifiers: LCCN 2016014683| ISBN 9781683240464 (hardcover : alk.
paper) | ISBN 9781683240501 (pbk. : alk. paper)
Subjects: LCSH: Private investigators—Fiction. | Murder—
Investigation—Fiction. | Large type books. | GSAFD: Mystery fiction. |
Western stories.
Classification: LCC PS3552.R65863 F76 2016 | DDC 813/.54—dc23
LC record available at http://lccn.loc.gov/2016014683

CHAPTER ONE

It had been a long hard ride from Deadwood. John Henry Cole stepped from the Deadwood to Cheyenne stagecoach feeling like he had gone twenty rounds with John L. Sullivan—and lost. He waited for the driver to hand him down his Dunn Brothers saddle and his Winchester rifle. He'd made up his mind that he was going to tell Ike Kelly that he was resigning as an operative of The Ike Kelly Detective Agency, Cheyenne, W.T. He'd only been in the detective business a couple of months, since coming north from Texas. Ike Kelly had been kind enough to offer him a job when he'd had none. Kelly had needed a man, and Cole had needed to clear out of Del Rio. They'd both hoped it would work out. But Cole's last assignment in Deadwood had nearly killed him, and even though he'd been lucky enough to survive and solve the case, he'd also broken the trust of his friend and boss.

Kelly and Cole had been friends ever since their misspent youth when they'd both worked for old José Chisholm, punching cattle, and later driving them north to the railheads in Kansas. It was there that Ike and Cole had learned the rear-end of a cow from the front, and how to ride and rope and shoot pistols. And at the end of the cattle drives, they'd learned how to drink raw whiskey and gamble a bit, and the pleasures of a woman. Just a pair of fuzz-cheeked boys learning to grow up and become men. That's what old José Chisholm and his cattle operation had done for them. In between the first time and the second time they'd worked for that good man, they'd fought in the War Between the States. Kelly had got shot three different times and Cole twice. They'd both come out of it all right except for the bad dreams. After the war and their second go around with punching cattle, Kelly and Cole had drifted their separate ways. They'd both ended up getting married, and they'd both had sons. And they'd both seen their wives and sons die long before they should have.

Over the intervening years, Kelly and Cole had crossed paths and stayed in touch with one another because good friends weren't something that fell out of the sky every time it rained. So it was a hard decision for Cole to return to Cheyenne and tell Kelly he was quitting, and the reason why. On the ride back from Deadwood, he'd had plenty of time to think about everything that had happened to him. For one thing, he'd fallen in love with a woman—the wrong woman. And as much as he tried not to, Cole was still carrying a small craziness inside of him—like a bullet too close to the heart. But the real problem was the woman Cole had fallen in love with was also the woman Kelly had once fallen in love with. That was the thing that he'd come back to tell Ike Kelly and the reason he was going to quit. He felt like he'd broken Kelly's trust in him.

There were some other reasons for Cole's decision as well. He didn't care much for getting shot at or threatened or beaten up. All of which had happened to him in Deadwood. He was still sore and hurting in places he wouldn't speak about in decent company. By the time Cole climbed down off the Concord stage, he felt like he'd been ridden hard and put away wet. And when he looked at his reflection in the big plate-glass window of the telegraph office, he saw a weary man who needed a shave, a hot bath, and a bottle of good Tennessee whiskey. That is exactly what he planned to do before he saw Ike Kelly.

The weather was damp and gray, threatening rain, as he started toward Sun Lee's where he had a rented room in the back of the ancient Celestial's laundry. He hitched his saddle over his shoulder and carried the heavy Winchester in his right hand. It struck him that old drifters were always carrying their saddles and rifles to one place or another—drifting, like the wind. A good horse and a good home were hard luxuries to come by, and harder still to keep. But Cole had plans that as soon as he finished settling up with Kelly, the first order of business was to purchase a good horse. He was tired of carrying the saddle. Beyond that—well, beyond that he had no plans.

It began to drizzle. A light cold rain pelted the brim of his Stetson. It was just one more inducement to hurry up and find that hot bath and the comfort of some Jack Daniels. Cole hadn't gone a block when he heard a brass band start to play the first strains of a mournful dirge. Farther up the street, he could see cadaverous Karl Cavandish riding high up top of his new glass-sided hearse that was being pulled by a pair of dappled grays. Cavandish wore a stovepipe hat and a claw-hammer coat over a boiled shirt. His young Mexican assistant, José Hernandez, sat next to him, looking cold and miserable from the drizzle. A six-piece band trooped along behind the hearse, playing a funeral march.

Cole stopped under the eaves of the White Elephant Saloon and waited and watched as the procession passed. He made a cigarette and smoked it and wondered who the unlucky soul was inside the black crêpe-draped coffin. A few of the town's citizens followed along on foot and in buggies behind the band. The men all wore suit coats, the women black dresses and hats with veils. Cole watched as they headed up the street, turned the corner at the north end of town, and headed for the city cemetery, what some called boothill. A number of people watched the procession from doorways—mostly saloon doorways—having taken a break from their normal activities. Funerals, fires, shootings, and cuttings always drew the curious, and even gamblers and whoremongers would take time out from their activities to witness such events.

Cole stubbed his cigarette and hefted his saddle once more. Only this time, a familiar voice stopped him.

"Too bad about your friend, John Henry."

Cole didn't have to turn around to recognize who it was: Leo Foxx, Cheyenne's city marshal.

"What was that?" Cole said, turning to face a man he didn't like.

Foxx looked at Cole with the flat, pushed-in features of a pug fighter, the dull eyes that could read a card or leer at a woman but could not express even the remotest amount of compassion. Leo Foxx, gambler, pistoleer, man-killer, and lawman was just the sort of man a lot of town councils hired as their marshal. The thinking generally went—it took a desperado to tame a desperado.

"I said, it's too bad about Kelly," Foxx repeated. He wasn't alone; he never was. He had two of his deputies with him, men that were better at getting him a beer or a woman than they were at understanding the law. The one Cole recognized was Bill Longly, a Texas gunfighter sometimes called Long Bill. Longly's reputation included several dubious shootings while serving as a city marshal in places like Big Springs and Tascosa and other one-horse towns, trying to rid themselves of the bad element by hiring the same.

The Longlys and the Foxxes usually didn't last long before they were fired. But there was always another town looking for a gun tough to do their dirty work, so such men were never long without jobs—unless someone killed them first. It was apparent that no one had killed Longly yet. Foxx probably enjoyed the idea of having a man like Longly working for him; it was akin to keeping a mean dog around just to see who he would bite next. But it wasn't Longly that troubled Cole; it was what Foxx had said.

"What about Ike?" Cole asked.

"That's him that passed by in that meat wagon," Foxx said, picking at his back teeth with the nail of his little finger. "Somebody murdered him."

Cole dropped the saddle. His self-cocker was in easy reach, resting on his left hip in a cross-draw holster. He was prepared to pull it, more than prepared.

"Who killed him?" he asked, feeling the hot anger race through his blood like a prairie fire.

Foxx, for all his deficiencies as a man, was a skilled gunfighter and he knew a man ready to fight him when he saw one. He took an instinctive step backward nearly bumping into Longly. "Hold the hell on before you pull that piece, Cole!"

"Tell me who killed Ike?" Cole repeated.

"Not me, god damn it!"

Cole kept his eye on all three of them. The third man, whose name he didn't know, was short, squarely built like Foxx, same black mustaches only not as well trimmed and cared for as Foxx's. Cole could tell by the way Foxx shifted his gaze that he wasn't up to a fight unless he was forced into one.

"I'll ask you one more time, Foxx, then I won't ask again."

"It happened two nights ago. Me and the boys were in the Blue Star when someone ran in and yelled . . . 'Fire.' We ran outside, saw the blaze. Whoever did it, burned him up in the fire. We found what was left after the ashes cooled. There wasn't much. Old man Cavandish said he'd bury the remains regardless . . . him and Kelly were friends. That's all I know about it. That's all anyone knows."

"I don't believe you."

"Hell, go down and see if his office ain't burned to the ground. Burned up Ella Mims's millinery shop next door, too. Town fire department had a hell of a time keeping half the damn' town from burning down. Lucky it rained that night or it would have."

Maybe it was that Cole just didn't want to believe that Ike Kelly had been murdered. Maybe he just wanted to take it out on Foxx because he was the one who had told him. Whatever it was, Cole knew he had to get it under control. He stood waiting, looking into their faces, challenging them to make something happen. And when it didn't, Cole again picked up his saddle and walked away.

Sun Lee looked up from his bowl of soup. Some of the soup still clung to his long thin chin whiskers like yellow dew. "Mistah John Henly . . . you back!"

Cole dropped the saddle on the floor and laid the Winchester on the counter without bothering to take them back to his room.

"How about taking care of these for me, Sun?" he asked. "I've got to go see about something."

Sun Lee looked sad, sad as an old hound. "I sorry Mistah John Henly about what happened to Mistah Ike."

"Me, too," Cole said. Hearing Sun Lee confirm it, made it real for Cole, Ike's death. It put knots in his stomach and something painful pressed against the sides of his temples. He thought he'd left the killing back in Deadwood, but now he was right back in the middle of it again.

Sun Lee stared at Cole with those sad-hound eyes. Cole wondered how much tragedy a man like him had seen in his lifetime to have given him such sad eyes—probably a lot more than anyone suspected.

"Poor, poor Mistah Ike," Sun muttered, shaking his bony skull.

"I'll be back in a while, Sun."

The two burned-out lots between the other buildings that showed the scorch of the fire along their walls looked like rotted black gaps between teeth. The charred remains of a few thick timber posts were all that was left, that and the burned smell. Cole headed for the cemetery.

By the time he arrived, the mourners were just leaving, heading back for town. Some raced; a burial was cause for celebration, a reason to get drunk and raise a little hell because you never knew when your time was coming. Only Karl Cavandish and his Mexican assistant, José, remained behind to fill in the grave.

Cole asked Cavandish if he might take over the shoveling from him, and Cavandish allowed he could. Cavandish's face was sweaty and his hands shook. It took twenty minutes for Cole and the boy to fill in the grave. It had stopped raining by the time they finished. Cole made a cigarette and offered the boy one that he gladly took.

"What can you tell me about this?" Cole asked Cavandish.

He was a tall, cadaverous man with deep-set eyes and a dark beard. He could have passed for the twin brother of the late President Lincoln. He was checking the harnesses of his team. His tall stovepipe hat was beaded with raindrops.

"I know as little or as much as anyone," he said. "Our dear friend was . . . obviously murdered, perhaps shot, his office set afire with him still in it. Whoever did it certainly must have had . . . some deep anger against him. That, or just plain crazy . . ." Cavandish's voice seemed to catch on the rising wind and get carried off.

"That's it . . . you don't know anything more?"

Cavandish shook his head.

"No. Me and José did the best we could, considering . . . ah . . . the situation. Ike was my friend, you know. I gave him a good coffin. It's the best I could do."

"I'll be glad to pay the expenses," Cole offered.

"No. It's not necessary. Do you want a ride back to town?"

Cole told him no. Cavandish was wise and experienced enough to understand a person's need to grieve alone. He and José climbed atop the hearse, and he snapped the reins over the haunches of the grays and started back down the hill, keeping the hearse's wheels in the same set of muddy tracks they'd cut earlier.

The cemetery was surrounded by a black, wrought-iron fence with a gate and a high arch. The gray tombstones were stained dark from the earlier rain. Some were tilted, their epitaphs worn away by time. They were cold reminders of the fragile mortality of good men and bad alike, the strong and the weak. It seemed odd to Cole that it was the one way he'd never thought about Ike— in death. He'd always been such a solid, enduring man, a man who'd outlived his wife and child and many of his friends as well as enemies. For Cole he hadn't been the sort of man to whom he would attach the fragility of dying. They weren't that much different in age, yet, somehow, Ike had seemed much older and wiser.

Ike Kelly had been there for Cole when Zee Cole and Cole's infant son Samuel had died. He had gotten drunk with Cole and let Cole raise hell and cry about it and feel sad because of it. And when he said he understood, Cole had known Ike had meant it, because he'd lost a wife and a son, too. And after Cole'd shot that Mexican bandit, Francisco Guzman, and had had to leave Texas, it had been Ike who'd offered him a job. Cole felt he owed Ike Kelly a lot, and now he wasn't going to have the chance to repay him, unless he could find the man who had killed Ike.

CHAPTER TWO

Cole didn't know where to begin to find Ike's killer. By the time he had walked back from the cemetery, afternoon had turned to evening under the sunless sky and the on and off rain only added to his bad mood. He needed a bottle of mash whiskey and a bath now, to try and sweat out some of the anger he was feeling and set his thinking straight again. He went back to Sun Lee's. The old man had left a lantern lit for Cole and the door unlocked. He was nowhere around.

Cole pulled the only clean shirt he had from his

15

saddlebags and headed to Ed Harris's bathhouse. Wayback Cotton, Harris's assistant, if you could call him that, was curled up on the floor asleep with his hands between his knees. The old man claimed to have been a fur trapper and Indian fighter in his youth, but he didn't look like much of either, lying there on the floor with his hands between his knees. He simply looked old and broken-down, a man waiting for the last beaver hunt.

Cole looked around for Ed Harris, didn't see him, so he rang the bell on the counter. In a few seconds, Harris appeared from behind a curtain, a napkin stuck down the front of his shirt, a piece of fried chicken in his right hand.

"John Henry," he said, his voice full of surprise. "You back from Deadwood?"

"What's it look like, Ed?"

He grinned, showing some of his missing teeth. Then he saw Wayback Cotton curled up on the floor asleep and the grin fell off his face. "Hey there, you old alky!" Harris shouted. But Cotton didn't so much as wiggle a toe.

"Lord, I'm going to fire that old fool someday," Harris declared, coming from behind the counter and kicking Cotton on the soles of his boots until the old man started, and sat up. "I'm docking you fifteen cents for sleeping on the job!"

"I wasn't sleepin'," Cotton argued. "I was just contemplatin' what work I was goin' to do next."

16

"Where I come from they call laying down with your eyes closed sleeping, you crazy old coot!"

"Well, you must come from the moon then . . ."

"I came to get a bath and a bottle," Cole interrupted. He was in no mood to listen to the two of them bicker back and forth like washerwomen.

Cotton said—"I'll get ya a bottle."—as he worked his way up off the floor. He rubbed his eyes and licked his sunk-in lips that no longer had any teeth behind them for support.

Cole gave him $1 for the bottle and 50¢ extra for his trouble. Cotton looked like he might weep at the blessing.

Harris worked at his piece of chicken as he poured into the zinc tub several buckets of hot water he maintained on a big iron stove. "I suppose you done heard what happened to Ike?" Harris said around a mouthful of the chicken.

"I came here for a bath and a little peace," Cole said.

"It's a bad thing," Harris continued. "Ike shouldn't have had to die like that."

"Nobody should," Cole said, taking off his clothes. Some of the wounds and bruises he'd received in Deadwood were beginning to heal.

Harris looked at him and said: "Looks like you took a beating and then some."

"You have a bar of soap I could use to scrub with?" Cole asked, choosing to ignore Harris's curiosity.

Harris said: "What's this world coming to, that somebody would burn up a man like Ike Kelly right in his own office?"

Cole didn't know.

When Harris finished fixing the bath, Cole climbed in. It had the shock of a thousand needles piercing his flesh. "You want to go check on that old Indian fighter?" he asked. "I could sure use that bottle." Harris didn't look any too happy about leaving the comfort of his living quarters to go out into a cold damp night, but business was business, so he agreed to do it.

"He's probably drunk up that fifty cents you gave him and is working on your dollar," Harris grumbled as he pulled on his coat. "Didn't I tell you once before not to give that old man money before he finishes the job? Hell, he's liable to have run off to Nebraska with some whore now that he's got a little money."

"I don't think a man could get all the way to Nebraska on just a dollar and fifty cents."

"You don't know Wayback, then," Harris muttered as he went out the door.

The silence of being alone in the room was welcome to Cole. The bath water was plenty hot and he closed his eyes and welcomed its relief to his bruised and battered body. Somehow, even knowing what he knew, Ike's death still didn't seem real. It was as if Ike would come through the door any minute and ask Cole how he'd made out in Deadwood and how was Lydia Winslow, the woman both had fallen in love with at different times. The woman over whom Cole had broken Ike Kelly's trust. But the door didn't open and Ike didn't walk through it. And Cole knew he never would.

Cole had lost his wife and son to the milk sickness several years before. And along the way, he'd lost more than one or two friends to drownings and knives and gunshots. And now he'd lost another friend. The plain truth was, Cole felt, that you never do get used to losing people you love, and you never get over it. And of all the faces that flooded his memory just then, not a one deserved the fate they were given.

Wayback Cotton's grand and sudden entrance broke the spell that had set Cole to visiting with ghosts. "Sweet Jesus!" Cotton announced, charging into the room, slamming the door shut behind him. "Gettin' cold as a well digger's nuts outside!"

"Did you bring that bottle of Jack Daniels I sent you for?"

Cotton grinned. It was like looking into a wound, that mouth without any teeth. "Got 'er right hyar!" He pulled the bottle from his coat pocket and handed it to Cole, then stood there, staring like a dog watching its master eat a ham.

Cole pulled the cork and took a long tug. "Ed thought maybe you'd met some whore and run off to Nebraska with her."

Cotton clucked his tongue. "Ed's imagination is the only thing that could run off to Nebraska on a night cold like this." He smacked his lips. It was a strange, debilitating sound.

"Grab a glass and I'll give you a taste," Cole said. "Then, I want my privacy."

Cotton was gone and back before Cole could finish a second pull on the bottle. He filled Cotton's glass. His eyes grew moist. "You understand, don't you?" he said.

"Understand what?"

"About how it is for men like you and me."

"Tell me," Cole said.

Wayback Cotton held the glass inches from his mouth, his eyes fixed on it like a cat watching a mouse that it was getting ready to pounce on. "Me 'n' you," he said, peering over the glass, "we understand about the Big Lonely."

Cole didn't say anything.

"Ed, he don't understand. Citified. Never been nowhere, never done nothin'. Most men is like Ed," Cotton said, bringing the glass an inch closer to his mouth. "They got their warm beds and fat wives to rut around with. They got their work-adaddy jobs and their Sunday suit clothes. They got their mean little bastard kids who run around screamin' and hollerin' if they don't get their way. They got ever'thin' but they don't got what me and you has got, do they, John Henry?"

"What have we got, Wayback?"

20

"We got ourselves, boy! We got our damn' freedom. We been places, seen things, done things them talleywackers could only dream about. We knowed women of the wildest variety, and set down to poker games with some of the meanest most notorious bandits in the West. We've crossed wild rivers and seen the ocean! We drank likker outta a whore's slipper and been rich and been busted. Hell, they ain't none of them ever done some o' the things we done!"

"It's not all been good times, Wayback. Lest you forget."

Cotton looked at Cole then, his eyes narrowing to the seriousness of a man who was near to seeing his last season. "No, it sure by God ain't! That's the part I'm talkin' about, you 'n' me bein' the same . . . we both knowed the Big Lonely, all that space in between the good times, di'n't we?"

"Yeah, maybe so," Cole said, not wanting to admit that Wayback Cotton knew a lot more about the true state of Cole's soul than he was comfortable with.

"God damn' right!" Cotton declared, and tossed the glass of whiskey down his gullet in one great gulp. "See," he said, wiping his soft, caved-in lips with the back of his hand. "Men like me 'n' you 'n' . . . God rest his soul . . . Ike, we done what we done 'cause there wasn't any other way for us to live. Men like us is just like a bunch of wild horses that goes where they want, does what they want."

Cotton held out his glass again. Cole pointed to his pants that were lying across the chair. "Take a dollar and buy your own bottle, Wayback. I'll need the rest of this."

He winked, slapped his leg, retrieved $1 from Cole's pants, and headed for the door. Pausing, he turned, his eyes red and rheumy, struggling to hold the light of old fires now burning out in his soul. "Thing is, John Henry, a man does all that livin', what's he end up with? Can't ever get it back, can't ever find it again. Nothin' left but the Big Lonely. Sometimes it feels like its goin' to swallow me whole. . . ." Then he closed the door behind him and the room was quiet again.

Ed Harris, and some of the other men who knew Wayback Cotton, claimed he was a fraud, that he never did hunt beaver up in the stony mountains, that he had never fought Indians, or done any of the things he claimed to have done. Cole thought maybe they were wrong about Wayback. He thought Wayback knew more about the human condition than a roomful of physicians. He hoisted his glass in the old man's honor, then drank the rest of the whiskey just to numb his senses.

By the time Cole had finished the bottle and the bath water had grown tepid, he was ready for a warm bed and a long night's sleep. Anything to keep him from thinking about what Wayback had called the Big Lonely. *Sleep tonight,* he told

22

himself through the heavy haze in his brain, *and tomorrow will take care of itself.*

He climbed out of the tub on unsteady legs and dried himself with a rough towel, then dressed. He laid $1 on the counter for the bath, tugged his Stetson down on his head, and headed for his room at Sun's.

As he sprawled across the small bed in the back room of the laundry and listened to rain peck at the window, he thought of how life had a way of changing one's plans without one willing it. How it sometimes takes you where you really don't want to go, but to a place where you need to go in order to find yourself.

He closed his eyes, listening to the rain dancing against the glass and wondering what fates were at work that would bring him back from the killing of innocent women in Deadwood to the murder of his friend. And would those same fates lead him to Ike's killer, or perhaps to his own death?

Chapter Three

John Henry Cole got lucky. That night he didn't dream. He wasn't visited by the haunting images that were usually awaiting him: the faces of the dead, the clatter of musketry in some wilderness with men dressed in blue and gray mingled together on the ground, their wounds spilling out their life's blood, the crying sounds of his son Samuel.

When he heard someone calling his name from out of the distance, he opened his eyes to the glare of sunlight coming through a sooty window opposite the bed. Sun Lee was standing in the doorway, calling his name.

"Mistah John Henly. You wake?"

Cole rolled over, sat up, took a deep breath, and let it out. The realization that he'd made it through a night without dreaming was like a small gift. Then he remembered about Ike, and the good feeling went away.

"You want some tea, Mistah John Henly?" Sun asked. He was wearing a red silk jacket and red silk pants and black slippers. He stood barely five feet tall and weighed maybe ninety pounds wet. And when he moved, the silk of his clothes whispered.

"I appreciate the offer, Sun, but tea won't get the job done this morning."

Cole didn't know if Sun Lee understood his need for bone-jarring thick black coffee so bitter and vile it either wakes you up or kills you, but that was what he needed to get all his vital parts working again. He doubted Sun had ever spent time on a cow outfit; if he had, he would know that old drovers don't drink tea first thing in the morning, if they drink it at all. Maybe tea and whiskey mixed together, but never just tea by itself.

"What you do now, Mistah John Henly?" Sun asked as Cole slowly got dressed. The hot bath and whiskey the night before had done wonders, but they hadn't cured everything. He was still very stiff and sore.

"You mean about Ike?" Cole asked.

Sun nodded.

When Cole looked in Sun's aged face, he saw mysteries that would never be solved. "I don't know exactly, Sun. I'll ask around. Somebody had to have seen something. Someone didn't just walk into Ike's office, kill him, then set fire to the place and walk away again without anybody seeing anything."

"T'llible thing," Sun muttered. "Very t'llible thing."

"Yeah." Cole had seen men killed in lots of ways in his time, but it took someone special to kill a man the way Ike had been killed.

Cole walked over to Shorty Blaine's Diner and took a seat near the window. Then he remembered the last time he had tried to eat breakfast sitting in front of a window. King Fisher had tried to shoot him through the glass and nearly succeeded. It'd been just one more reason why he had been glad to leave Deadwood.

Shorty Blaine saw him, came around from behind the counter, limping from an old busted leg and hip he'd got when a horse fell on him.

The bones had never healed right, and that was his last time on a trail drive. He brought a pot of coffee and two tin cups and sat down across from Cole. Smoke from a cigarette dangling from his lips curled up into his craggy face and caused his right eye to squint.

"You heard about Ike?" he asked.

"Yes."

Shorty Blaine had one of those old cowhand faces that, if you looked into it long enough, you could see deserts, the great plains, the Llano Estacado, and a thousand head of cattle being driven up by a dozen dusty riders all rolled into one. He had watery blue eyes that were permanently squinted from too much sun and wind and tobacco smoke. And when he poured the coffee, you couldn't help but notice how his hands were scarred and rough with large knuckles and crooked fingers.

When Cole said that he'd heard what happened to Ike, Shorty just looked at him for a long time without saying anything. "He was my friend," Shorty finally said.

"He was my friend, too."

"It ain't how a man like him should end up," Shorty said, stubbing out the cigarette he was smoking, then rolling another shuck and lighting it.

"No, it's not," Cole said, tasting the coffee, spooning in an extra load of sugar.

"You know what's worse than anything?" Shorty asked.

"What?"

"Nobody even knows who done it." He shook his head, looked through the window at nothing in particular, just looked.

"Somebody knows," Cole said.

Shorty turned his head, looked at Cole like he was a wide river that Shorty had to cross with a herd of Mexican cattle and a crew of greenhorns. "Who'd know that?" he asked.

"The man who killed him."

"Shit! I'll bet he ain't talking."

"He will when I find him."

Shorty squinted through the blue haze of his cigarette. "Let me go with you."

"I know you want to," Cole said. "But maybe it's better you stick around here and keep your ears and eyes open. Just in case whoever did it is still hanging around."

"What about you?"

"I'll go where the trail leads me."

Shorty looked out the window again. "Ike was in eating breakfast the day he was killed," he muttered. "He always liked the same thing . . . burned bacon, eggs, grits with lots of lick poured over 'em." Shorty was now staring through the blue smoke. "I just couldn't bring myself to go up the hill and see him put in the ground. Seen too many of my boys put in the ground. Couldn't

27

stand the thought of seeing another one. Not Ike, anyway."

"Ike would have understood."

"Sure. He'd 'a' known."

Cole drank some more of the coffee.

"God damn cattle!" Shorty cursed, as though he was back there on one of those drives instead of looking through blue smoke out the window at nothing at all.

"We drove a lot of them north," Cole said.

Shorty focused again at Cole. "Yeah, we sure as hell did, didn't we?" He had a smile that lifted the corner of his mouth where the cigarette was dangling.

The door opened and a woman with honey-colored hair came in and took a seat at one of the tables.

Cole watched as she removed her gray gloves and put them in the reticule she carried. She was a good-looking woman with fair skin, tall by most standards, with light gray eyes. She wore a tie-back dress and a wool capote. Her hair was pinned with combs. Her hair looked like it would fall to her waist if she unpinned it.

Shorty hadn't seemed to notice her; his mind was still somewhere else, in a place that was no more. Then he mashed out his cigarette, stood, and said: "I hope you find him, John Henry. Find him and kill him and be done with it. That's all I hope. No trial, no anything. Just like he done Ike. That's the way it ought to be."

"Who's that woman?" Cole asked.

Shorty looked around. "Oh, that's Ella Mims. It was her shop that got burned down in the fire. Sweet disposition." Then he gave Cole a knowing look and added: "Single, too."

Cole watched as he limped back to the kitchen. He thought: *An old busted cowboy the good earth is waiting to reclaim. Just like the rest of us.* Then he went over to Ella Mims's table. She looked up. "We haven't met," Cole said.

"No."

"My name's Cole. John Henry Cole. I was a friend of Ike Kelly."

"Oh. Ike. Poor dear man, how awful."

"Do you mind if I ask you a few questions about the night of the fire?"

She had the rarest gray eyes of any woman Cole had ever met, gray but clear as glass.

"No. Please, sit down, Mister Cole."

He took the chair opposite her. She introduced herself. Cole told her he already knew who she was. She seemed surprised. Then he told her how he knew.

"I guess in a small town like Cheyenne," she said, "no one is a stranger."

"I've seen you before. Once or twice on the sidewalks."

"Funny I didn't notice you." Her gray eyes took stock of him. "I would think I would have noticed you, Mister Cole."

29

"Well, I'm usually dusty and hollow-eyed. I had the good fortune to have a bath and a shave last evening."

She tilted her head slightly. "What is it you wanted to ask me?"

"Did you notice anything unusual that day of the fire, any strangers hanging around?"

She spent a minute thinking about it. It gave Cole time to notice that she was even more attractive close up.

"No," she said. "I didn't see anyone around that day that I didn't know."

"I'm told the fire started sometime in the evening. How late were you in your shop?"

Again she thought about it, then shifted her gaze back to Cole. "I usually leave around five-thirty," she said. "But I had to stay over that afternoon. I was trying to get a special order ready for Missus Teague. She needed it the next day. So, I'd say I left around closer to seven." She gave a slight shrug of her shoulders. "Does that help you in any way?"

"But it would have been dark by then. Maybe not long before the fire was started."

"Yes, I suppose so. As a matter of fact, I remember hearing the fire brigade shortly after I got home. The men were running around, shouting. Then I saw the flames." The sadness showed on her face. Her lips trembled slightly.

"I'm sorry for your loss," Cole said.

"It was everything I owned, Mister Cole. I am forced to leave Cheyenne now. That's the worst of it."

"You've given up on starting over again?"

She shook her head. "I've no money to start again."

She hadn't been the first woman Cole'd met lately who'd had to start over. He felt sorry for her, only this time he was in no position to help. "Well, I won't trouble you further. Enjoy your breakfast, Miss Mims. And I wish you well."

He started to rise from the table. Her eyes followed him.

"I'm very sorry for you," she said. "It was a terrible tragedy. I wish I could have been more helpful. . . ."

The gray eyes searched Cole's. He thought he saw something in them that went beyond sympathy, but it wasn't the time or the place to explore what might be behind that look.

He stepped outside. The sun was glancing off the tin roofs of the buildings, but the air was noticeable in its chill. Winter would arrive soon. Winter up in the high country was something you could feel coming just by taking a deep breath. He leaned against a post and made himself a shuck. *No one had seen anything.* He struck a match and touched it to the end of the cigarette. It seemed curious to him that a cautious man like Ike could be murdered and there were no witnesses to anything. He wasn't buying it.

He saw Bill Longly step out onto the balcony of the Blue Star Saloon. He yawned and stretched his arms. He was wearing just his drawers, his galluses undone, his hair tousled. Then Cole saw one of the Blue Star's employees, a working girl who went by the name of Cimarron Cindy, join Long Bill on the balcony. She tried to wrap her arms around his neck. He said something, then pushed her away, and, when she tried wrapping her arms around his neck again, he slapped her. Then a few seconds later, they both went back inside the room they'd come from.

Longly was rough trade. Cole felt sorry for the woman. In fact, he felt sorry for all the women who had to earn their living like Cimarron Cindy. Then he heard laughter drifting down from an open window of the same room Longly and Cindy had gone into. It made him wonder if his concern wasn't sometimes misplaced. He let go of the thought just in time to see a lone man riding a big, chesty Morgan down the center of the street. He led a pack mule, but it was plain to see he was no prospector on his way to the Black Hills. He was a manhunter.

John Henry Cole watched as he reined in at the White Elephant Saloon and tied up his animals. Then he watched him jerk the brass-fitted shotgun from his saddle boot and take it inside the drinking den. Normally he wouldn't have given it any more thought than that. He'd seen manhunters before, plenty of them. But this one was different. He knew this one.

He crossed the street, stepped into the dim confines of the bar. The manhunter was there, leaning against the bar, his hands atop the long sweep of mahogany, a pair of silver dollars resting next to a bottle and a glass. The shotgun leaned against the bar at his side.

"Will," Cole said. "Will Harper."

Harper stiffened. When a man gets called by his name in a strange town, he gets himself ready for a fight. Only Cole hadn't come to fight.

"Relax, Will. I'm not here to do you harm."

Harper turned slowly, and, when he did, Cole could see the pearl handles of his revolvers showing from his waistband. He squinted through the dim light.

Cole told him who he was before he had a chance to think about it.

"John Henry Cole?" Then Harper remembered, but still didn't come away from the bar, or show any signs he wouldn't pull one or both of his pistols if the mood struck him.

"Been a long time," Cole said. "Where was it, El Paso?"

"Tombstone."

"Yeah. Tombstone." Cole remembered then. In that rough little hell hole of a town Will had served as its city marshal for less than three

33

months. Right up until the time he shot a woman he had been living with. Even Tombstone wouldn't stand for such an outrage and fired him.

"How's Flora?" Cole asked.

Even in the poor light, Cole could see him smile, the large teeth flashing beneath the shaggy mustaches. "Hell, Flora's fine. Married and got three little screamers. Lives up in Montana last I heard."

"You mind if I buy you a drink?"

"No, I don't mind," he said. "Come right ahead."

That time of day, the bar was nearly empty except for the two of them, the barman, and Wayback Cotton sleeping on the billiard table.

"You know that was an accident," he said, "that thing that happened between Flora and me. I never meant to shoot her."

Cole half thought about asking him why, if he hadn't meant to, he had shot Flora. He remembered her as having been a working girl out of the Crystal Palace. Will and she had been some sort of married, but marriage in a place like Tombstone could mean a lot of things other than a legal ceremony. Cole decided to forgo the subject of Will's shooting Flora. "You on the dodge? Or, are you looking for someone?"

"Looking."

He was well-built, not very tall, and, when he spoke, he had a slight lisp that lent a feminine quality to his voice. But if you watched him long enough, watched the cautious way he carried himself, the way everything was deliberate about him, then you would know that he was a thoroughly dangerous man. Cole was about to ask him who he was looking for when he said: "I heard you killed Francisco Guzman down along the border. That true?"

"It is."

"Well, you did the world a favor."

"Maybe so. But none of his relatives thought so."

Harper leaned on the bar, lifted another glass of liquor, stared at it for a moment, then swallowed it, and set the glass down again, deliberate in his movements.

"You didn't say who it was you were looking for," Cole prompted.

"Real bad actor," he said. "A colored. A freedman from down in the Indian Territory. Name's Leviticus Book."

"What'd he do to get you after him?"

"Killed some people. Said to have killed two or three down in the Settlement, down around Eufala. Then he killed two or three more in Texas. Shot a man in Colorado as well. Killed 'em every way there is to kill a man. Shot some, knifed some, even strangled one man, they say. Hell, they say he even burned that fellow in Colorado. Shot him full of lead and burned him in his cabin."

35

That got Cole's attention. "You want to tell me more about that part?"

Harper waited until he poured himself another glass of whiskey. He did it with the same great care and deliberation. "Which part?"

"About his burning the man in Colorado."

Harper studied the whiskey before drinking it, just like the previous glass and the one before that. Then he set the empty shot glass down on the bar again. "They believe he did it because the fellow was supposed to have a cache of gold buried on his property. That's about all of it I know."

"That the only one he burned?"

"Far as I know. There could be others. The marshals say he's killed fourteen men. But it could be more, it could be less. Who the hell knows? He's got half a dozen rewards posted on him. Adds up to a little over eight thousand dollars. Now you know why I'm looking for him."

"What makes you think he's come this way?"

He eyed the bottle, started to pour, set it back down again, put the cork in it. "I've been tracking him for a month. I figure he's heading north, to the border."

"Why north, why not south?"

"Why anything, John Henry? You ever see a smart criminal, one that thinks things through?"

"A friend of mine was killed the other night," Cole said. "Shot, then burned."

Harper studied Cole. "That's too bad."

"It sounds like it could be this Book fellow."

"Could be."

"Then I want to go along."

"I don't share reward money, Cole. It's not in my nature."

"I'm not asking you to share."

"What are you asking me, then?"

"To go along, like I said."

"This one, I have to bring in alive in order to collect on," he said. "You along, that might not happen."

"I can go after him on my own," Cole said. "That means I catch him first, and you're out the reward money."

"I drink too damn' much," Harper said. "Why else would I shoot off my mouth and tell my business to you?"

"You'll get your reward money, Will. I just want to make sure my friend gets justice."

"Damn' mighty noble principles. Why don't you just stay here and let me catch Mister Leviticus Book for you? He'll get hanged, I'll get my money, and your friend will get justice. Everybody will be happy . . . except Mister Book, of course."

"Then I'll go alone. Thanks for the tip."

"Ah, Jesus, John Henry!"

CHAPTER FOUR

Cole left Will Harper standing at the bar in the White Elephant while he went to get his things and find a place to buy a horse. He stopped by the diner to ask Shorty Blaine if he knew where a man could buy a good horse and he said there was a man named Simms west of town who had some good stock. Blaine offered to take Cole out there in his wagon.

"You leaving town so soon, John Henry?"

"I maybe got a line on who killed Ike."

"Ike must have turned you into a better detective than I thought."

"No, I just got lucky."

"How'd that happen?"

"You remember an old Colt name of Will Harper?"

Shorty Blaine looked at Cole. "Yeah, I remember him. What about him?"

"I ran into him over in the White Elephant. He's been trailing a fugitive. A man wanted for murder. This man murdered and burned one of his victims."

"Son-of-a-bitch, that *is* a lucky break."

"Yeah, it seems to be."

They reached Simms's spread less than an hour later. A lodge-pole corral appeared to be the main attraction. There were several waddies riding the rails, and several more inside trying to stick to some rough-looking stock.

"That's Simms standing there in the beaver hat," Shorty said as they pulled up.

Simms looked more like a whiskey peddler than a horse trader, wearing a beaver hat, an old Army jacket, and checked pants. Underneath the jacket, he wore a paper vest but no shirt. His belly bulged over his belt; it looked like the head of a balding man.

"He's a rarified individual, Simms is," Shorty said.

"How so?"

"Hell, just look at him." Shorty snorted.

"I don't care how he dresses," Cole said. "I just care about whether he has a decent horse I can buy."

Shorty checked the reins of the bay pulling the wagon, then called to Simms who turned around and came their way.

"Shorty Blaine," Simms said as he walked up to the wagon. He needed a shave and a little bath water wouldn't have hurt his appearance any, either.

"This is John Henry Cole," Shorty said. "He needs to purchase a saddle horse."

Simms extended his hand and Cole shook it.

"Tall man like you needs a tall horse," Simms said, appraising Cole as he climbed down from the wagon.

"I prefer them that way," Cole said.

"Got one you might be interested in. Over there." He ran his tongue across his bottom teeth, then spat.

The horse he indicated was a line-back buckskin with a nicely formed head and hindquarters.

"Have to warn you," Simms said. "I won't take less than fifty dollars for that gelding."

"I don't have fifty dollars, Mister Simms."

"That's too bad. It'd make you a good animal." Then he looked around, leaned and spat, and said: "Got another over yonder in that little corral . . . speckled bird, rough as a cob. Bites on occasion. But overall, she's a sound horse. Ain't for the faint of heart, you understand. I'd take thirty for her."

Cole walked over and looked at Mr. Simms's speckled bird. She had spotted hindquarters and the rest of her was the color of rust with flecks of white dappled in. She had some mustang in her, some thoroughbred, too, it appeared. She stood there, alert at their approach, her ears pricked and her eyes dark and wet. Her nostrils flared as she tested their scent.

"She ain't as big and tall as that buckskin," Simms said. "But the price is right."

Cole crawled between the rails and the mare pawed the ground and snorted as she watched him. Cole talked a little Spanish to her. One thing he'd learned from Francisco Guzman, the bandit he'd shot down in Del Rio, was that horses love to be talked to as much as women. And there is no better lingo than Spanish to talk to them, either. The mare's ears flicked to the sounds of his voice as she continued to keep a sharp eye on him. Cole figured if he made the wrong move on her, she would either try and kick him to death or bolt right over the rails. He asked Simms to hand him a rope, then let out a wide loop and made his approach, the whole while talking Spanish to her. She did a little dance with her hind feet, but he let fly the loop and it dropped over her neck and she gave a toss of her head, but didn't try to run out from under it.

"Watch her close!" Simms called. "She's liable to think you're a carrot or an apple and take a chunk outta you!"

Cole got up close enough to put his hands on her. "Look," he said in Spanish, "I've only got thirty dollars to buy a horse and you're the only thirty-dollar horse around here. One way or another, you and me have to get along. Let's just do it the way that's easiest for us both, eh, *amiga*?"

Then he walked her over to the rail, took one of the saddle blankets, and laid it gently across her back. Then he dropped the saddle on and cinched it. He asked Shorty to hand him the hackamore hanging on a post and slipped that over the mare's nose.

"What ya sayin' to that beast?" Simms asked.

"Just love talk. Sometimes it works."

41

"Oh," Simms said, as if that was all he needed to know about speaking Spanish sweet talk to a horse.

Cole climbed aboard and she threw him in three jumps, then stood there, staring at him, challenging him to try again.

"I guess that love talk didn't work." Simms grinned, seeming to enjoy the show more than Cole thought was necessary.

Cole climbed aboard again, and again she threw him, only this time it took five jumps.

Simms was trying hard not to bust the belly-band on his paper vest. Shorty Blaine just rolled his eyes. It had been a long time since Cole had tried his hand at busting broncos. And every time he hit the ground, he remembered why he'd quit the profession. It wasn't bad pay if you didn't mind getting your brains kicked in and your bones busted and landing on your head in the dirt. After a couple of seasons of trying his hand at it, he had decided it was undignified—getting half killed by hammerheads.

The third time he took the saddle proved to be a charm, if you could call it that. He got her settled down to a trot around the ring and she only tried to scrape him off twice. But she finally understood he only had $30 and she only cost $30 and Cole wasn't getting off—that was just the way it was going to be.

"Damn' fine-lookin' animal, Mister Cole!"

42

Simms declared. "Lookit her trot. Maybe I set the price too low."

"Here's your thirty dollars, Mister Simms," Cole said after he was satisfied the speckled bird would do. He just had to be careful not to turn his back on her and let her take a bite out of him. Other than that, he figured they'd get along fine.

Simms took the money and stuffed it in his pocket while Cole unsaddled her and tied the speckled bird to the back of Shorty's wagon.

"Anything else I can do you for today, Mister Cole?" Simms asked.

"No, sir. I don't believe there is."

Shorty grinned all the way back to Cheyenne. "I think he was a sorry son-of-a-gun to have let that ugly horse go so easily," he said.

Cole looked back at the bird, trotting along behind the wagon. "She's not all that ugly, do you think?"

Shorty grinned harder and said: "She is."

Cole led the speckled bird down to the local livery and told the liveryman to put a new set of shoes on her and throw an extra ration of grain in her feedbag. Then he walked over to the White Elephant where Will Harper was still standing at the bar, drinking in a deliberate way.

"Well," Harper said, "I hope you have come to tell me that you've changed your mind about going with me." When Cole said he hadn't, Will simply turned the shot glass between his fingers and said he was leaving first light and asked Cole if he knew of any good whores in town. Cole told him he wasn't familiar with the local trade but that Will might try a prostitute named Cimarron Cindy, over at the Blue Star. Cole figured, if nothing else, it would cut into Long Bill's time and that in itself would be doing Cindy a favor.

After Cole left the White Elephant, he headed back to his room behind Sun Lee's laundry. He didn't have a lot to pack, but he put an extra shirt and a pair of socks into his saddlebags along with a bar of soap, a razor, and extra loads for the self-cocker and the Winchester. The last thing he put in was a leather-bound book Lydia Winslow had given him the day he had left Deadwood. It was by a fellow named Cervantes, and the book was titled *Don Quixote.*

"You should read this," she had said. "He reminds me a little of you."

Cole hadn't gotten around to reading it yet, but thought someday soon he might. There was a knock at his door. He thought it was probably Sun Lee, asking if he should hold Cole's room until Cole got back. But it wasn't Sun Lee; it was Ella Mims.

"I remembered something about that day," she said.

"Do you want to come in?"

"Is it proper for a woman to come into the room of a gentleman stranger?"

"Well, we're not exactly strangers. And I've never been accused of being a gentleman, Miss Mims, but if you'd rather not."

She stepped into the room, looked around without being obvious about it.

"So this is where you live," she said.

"It's a temporary home."

She smiled. "Don't you feel a little closed in?"

"I mostly just sleep here when I'm in Cheyenne. Only lately I haven't been in Cheyenne. It's not much, but then I don't require much."

"Bachelors," she said, the amusement evident in her voice.

Cole looked around, too, and thought she was right. A bed, a chair, a single small dresser with pitcher and pan, and a mirror were hardly what most folks would consider home. "Yeah, we're a poor lot as human beings go, bachelors are."

"I didn't mean it that way. I just find it funny how single men live such temporary lives, while we women seem to be in constant search of permanency."

"It wasn't always like this for me."

She studied his face for a moment. "How was it for you, Mister Cole?"

"You wanted to tell me what it was you remembered about the day Ike was killed?" Cole wanted to change the subject.

Ella Mims was a wise enough woman to have seen it in his expression, his unwillingness to share the intimacy of what he once had been. She walked over to the small window that looked out on an alley lined with barrels and busted wagon wheels. All the refuse didn't stop the sun from shining, however. It shone brightly through the window, and became trapped in her honey-colored hair. She turned and looked at Cole once more. She could have been a painting, hanging on some rich man's wall.

"Yes," she said, "I'm sorry I didn't remember it earlier when you first asked me, but there was something that occurred just before I left my shop that evening Ike was . . ."

He waited for her to tell him.

"I remember that just before I left my shop, I heard what sounded like an argument coming from Ike's office." She shrugged her shoulders. "It was hard to tell for certain. Even though our buildings shared an adjoining wall, the sounds were very muted."

"So you can't say whose voice it might have been that was in the room with Ike that afternoon?"

"No."

"You didn't see who it might have been? You didn't see someone coming out of his office after that?"

Again she shrugged. "I left my shop shortly afterward. I had to deliver the special order hat I'd been working on that day to Missus Teague.

I'd promised to have the hat ready for her by no later than eight o'clock that day. She wanted to wear it at the opera house that evening. That's all I know." She looked at him apologetically. "It isn't much, I know. But you seemed so determined, I thought I would just tell you what I remembered after I'd had some time to think about it."

"Well, it probably was nothing," he said. "Ike had lots of clients from what I knew. Maybe one of them was unhappy with the bill for his services."

She nodded. "I see you're packing. Are you leaving?"

"Yes. First thing in the morning. I might have a lead on who killed Ike."

She blinked. "You already know something?"

"Possibly."

She looked relieved. "So you will be gone for a time?"

Cole sensed that he was about to say or do something that he shouldn't. It wasn't just that she was an attractive woman physically. It had to do with the way she talked, the way she looked him directly in the eyes as she spoke. She had a way of tilting her head slightly when she listened. Maybe it was just the way the sun was coming through the window and catching in her hair. He didn't know exactly what it was about her, but he was getting a feeling. He barely knew Ella

Mims, and he hadn't yet put out all the flames that once had burned so hotly for Liddy Winslow. He chalked his idiot urge up to the fact he had once more lost someone he had cared about and was feeling a little alone. He opened the door for her. That's what a sane man would do.

"Yes, Miss Mims, I'll be gone for a time. Thank you for coming by."

"Well, I wish you well in finding this person, whoever he is," she said. Then she started for the door, and Cole moved aside to let her exit.

She started to, then stopped. "If this man is as . . . as cruel as he seems, then I fear for you, if you *do* catch up with him."

"I appreciate your concern, Miss Mims. And believe me, I'll keep in mind his talents."

She started to say something else, changed her mind, then paused and said: "Maybe, when you return, you can come and see me and tell me if you were successful in your search, Mister Cole."

"Maybe." Their eyes met and held for a full few seconds longer than they should have. And then she turned and left.

Cole waited a minute or two, then left the room himself. The sunlight was banking off the metal rooftops, casting long shadows of horses and men down the wide dusty street. He watched Ella Mims as she walked north. He drew up a chair and rolled himself a cigarette and smoked it and watched the shadows of late afternoon grow longer.

Maybe if he got lucky, Will and he would catch Leviticus Book and that would put an end to it. Then maybe he could find whatever in the hell it was he had been looking for such a long time. It seemed to him, there had to be some place out there in those mountains and meadows where an old drifter could go and put himself up a regular house and sit on the front porch and watch the sun rise and set while he had his coffee and tobacco. There just *had* to be, and he was intent on finding it as soon as he caught Ike's killer. He was still thinking of those things when Bill Longly shot the Mexican kid, José Hernandez, over a 10¢ glass of beer.

CHAPTER FIVE

The pistol shots were like whip cracks. They came from the direction of the Blue Star Saloon, three doors down and across the street from where Cole was sitting. He saw the kid stagger through the doors of the Blue Star, holding his side. The same youth who had earlier helped Cole bury Ike Kelly. He was just a boy, really— young, straight black hair, skin as brown as the desert. He had a wide-eyed look, like he'd been surprised, or maybe had seen something that didn't exist for others.

Long Bill followed him into the street; a pistol in his left hand trailed blue smoke. The kid seemed lost, staggering this way and that, blood soaking the bottom half of his shirt, spilling through his hands.

Several more people came out of the Blue Star behind Long Bill; they were holding their whiskey glasses and beer mugs. One of them was Leo Foxx, the city marshal, Long Bill's boss.

Longly continued to follow the kid outside as he staggered into the street, trying to find some direction of escape. A teamster driving his freight down the center of the street had to jerk hard on the reins of his team to avoid running over the boy. José took two more stumbling steps, then fell to his knees. He was muttering in Spanish, asking for his mother, asking for God to save him, praying for his life.

Cole didn't think it was any of his business, and really it wasn't, but that didn't stop him from wanting to put a few rounds into Bill Longly. He was standing over the kid, watching him die. So was Leo Foxx and the others, like it was some sort of stage play or a circus they'd paid money to see.

Maybe Longly was surprised that Cole was interfering with his entertainment. "Why'd you shoot this boy?" he asked.

Longly snorted, looked at Cole much the same way he'd looked at Cimarron Cindy on the balcony of the Blue Star that morning just before he'd slapped her. "Mind your own business, Cole!"

Cole looked at the crowd. "Somebody take this boy to Doc Price's," he said. Everyone seemed nearly as disappointed that Cole had interfered as Long Bill did. Then to his credit, Leo Foxx ordered a couple of the bummers to carry José over to Dr. Price's office. José moaned when they picked him up, moaned and leaked blood all over their boots.

"I'll ask you again," Cole said, having never taken his attention from Long Bill. "Why'd you shoot that boy?"

"Go to hell, Cole!"

"One of us is about to."

Leo Foxx drew an amused look on his fry-pan face. "Better watch it, John Henry. Long Bill's a fast man with a gun, or didn't you know that?"

"First him, then you, Foxx."

He lost the smile. "That a threat? You threatening to take on the entire Cheyenne police department? 'Cause that's what it'll be if that's the way you want it."

"What the hell kind of law is it that would shoot an unarmed boy?"

"He was stealing a glass of beer . . . Long Bill's beer!" Foxx said, as if that justified anything.

"A ten-cent beer and you shot him for that?"

"Yeah, and I'd shoot the little greaser again if he was to try it again. I hate god-damn' greasers! I had my fill of 'em in Texas!" Longly cursed.

Foxx had moved out to the side of Long Bill,

51

the other deputy had taken a similar position to their right. The rest of the crowd figured they might get their money's worth after all. Cole didn't much care. There were just some things he couldn't walk away from. This was one of them.

"We'll bury you next to your pard, Ike Kelly," Foxx said. "How'll that be, Cole?"

Long Bill was a gun hand, and so was Leo Foxx. The deputy Cole couldn't be sure of. He'd concentrate on Longly and Foxx and worry about the remainder of Cheyenne's police force if he was still standing at the end. Longly already had his gun in his hand, but Cole could see it in his eyes. He wasn't entirely sure that Cole wasn't fast enough to kill him.

That was the thing about a pistol fight. Few were willing to be the first one to take a bullet. Cole could see it in Longly's face that he was hoping Leo Foxx would make the first play, and Foxx was waiting for Longly to be the one. Cole supposed the deputy was waiting for both of them, hoping they'd kill Cole in the process so he wouldn't have to be tested. Time seemed to stand still.

Just then a loud voice from back of the crowd caused it to separate down the center and allow a new player to enter the act. Will Harper was carrying a shotgun with sawed-off barrels. He had it aimed directly at the guts of Longly, but if he pulled the triggers, some of the buckshot would hit Foxx and the deputy and maybe one or two others standing near them.

"I use dimes in my loads," Will said. "You boys ever seen what a load of dimes will do to a body?"

The three didn't seem to know exactly how much damage a shotgun loaded with dimes could do. If they did, they weren't saying. Suddenly it was as quiet as a graveyard.

"Something like this will tear a man up real bad," Will said. "I know, I seen it done."

Foxx studied him for a long hard second. "Who the hell are you?"

"Does it really matter?"

Longly started to speak, but Will cut him off with a short wave of the twin barrels.

"Naw, don't waste your breath, mister. Either get to it, or get the hell on down the street."

"These men are deputized officers of the law," Foxx managed to say, though his heart wasn't any longer in the argument. "And I'm the city marshal."

"Well, I guess they can put that in tomorrow's newspaper and on your gravestones so everyone will know," Will said. "Go on, make your play, my beer's getting warm."

Cole could see it in Will's eyes. Harper was thoroughly drunk, but his hands didn't shake, and Cole didn't think he much cared if there was more blood to be shed or not, even if it ended up being his own. He was set for a fight. The others could see it, too, that Will didn't care, and seeing it cost them their will.

"Come on, Bill," Foxx mumbled. "We got a poker game to finish. Fred, you go on over to Cavandish's and tell him his gravedigger's been in a accident and is over to Doc's getting taken care of."

Will waited until they dispersed before cradling the shotgun in the crook of his arm.

"Thanks for the help," Cole said.

"You change your mind about going with me yet?"

"No."

"Well, I'm through drinking now. I reckon I'll go see that whore you told me about . . . what was her name again?"

"Cimarron Cindy," Cole said. "But I'd keep that shotgun handy next to the bed if I were you."

"Why's that?"

"That tall gentleman you just threatened to deposit that double load of dimes in is Cindy's common-law husband."

"Well, now, I'll just see if I can't talk her into getting a divorce." Will grinned. Even drunk, he could be scary.

Cole walked over to Dr. Price's to see how José was. Cavandish was there when he arrived.

"I'm told you stopped Bill Longly from finishing him," Cavandish said. "For that, I am grateful. I think of José as my own son."

"How bad is he?" Cole asked Dr. Price.

"How bad would you be if you got shot twice in the body?" Doc said, without interrupting his treatment.

"I wish I could have stopped it sooner," Cole told Cavandish. José moaned even though the doctor had put him under with a sponge soaked in ether.

"Why did this happen?" Cavandish's cadaverous features were stricken with the grief he felt for the boy. His head was full of questions no one could answer, or, if they did, none of the answers would have made any sense.

Cole couldn't bring himself to tell Cavandish the boy had been shot over the theft of a 10¢ glass of beer. He didn't need to remind Cavandish of how cheap life had become on the frontier. He'd buried enough men to know that already.

"I wish the boy good luck," Cole said.

Cavandish looked up from where he'd been staring at his hands. There wasn't any more words they could tell each other that would change anything, so they didn't try.

Cole walked over to Shorty's Diner, intending to have supper before checking on the speckled bird, then going back to his room. But halfway there, he decided that wasn't what he really wanted to do.

Shorty was standing at the counter with a cup of coffee in one hand and a cigarette dangling from the corner of his mouth. His left eye squinted against the smoke.

"John Henry," he said, "I heard you, Foxx, and Long Bill almost rubbed each other out."

"If it hadn't been for Will Harper," Cole said, "we probably would have."

"Longly shot that kid who was Cavandish's helper? José Hernandez?"

"Yes."

"For what?"

"For a glass of beer."

Without changing expressions, Shorty said: "Why ain't I surprised?"

He poured Cole a cup of coffee.

"Let me ask you," Cole said. "Do you know where Ella Mims lives?"

He squinted through the smoke. "North end of town. A little clapboard house with flower boxes under the winders. Hard to miss. The only place that end of town with flowers under the winders."

"Thanks."

"None of my business."

"Then don't ask."

"I won't."

Then as Cole got ready to leave, Shorty said: "She's a nice lady from what I know."

"Thanks for the coffee. Next time, leave out the arsenic."

"Next time leave a nickel on the counter."

Cole figured the speckled bird might like a

chance to throw him in the dirt again, or show him how fast she could run if given her head. He stopped by the livery and put his Dunn Brothers saddle on her, then spurred her into a dog trot before putting her into an easy lope. When they both got comfortable with that, he let her have her head. The wind almost took off his hat. She was quick and she was fast, and, if Cole had let her, she might have run clear to the mountains.

"You sure don't act like any thirty-dollar horse," Cole told her as he slowed her to a walk on the way back to the town. Of course, she hadn't taken a bite out of him yet to prove she actually *was* just a $30 horse. But it wasn't the speckled bird he was thinking about as the little clapboard house with the flower boxes under the windows came into view.

Cole reined in, dismounted, and tied the bird to the picket fence out front. "Don't eat the lady's flowers," he instructed. The bird simply eyed him like it was he she'd rather try eating.

Cole knocked on the door, and, when it opened, Miss Mims didn't seem all that surprised to see him. She didn't say anything, but stepped back to allow him to enter. He remembered to take off his hat. She just looked at him.

"I didn't really want to spend the evening alone," Cole said.

"I'll hang your hat up," she said.

Cole viewed three-dimensional photographs

through a stereoscope in the parlor while she fixed dinner. They ate at a small table sitting across from each other. Cole couldn't really say what it was she'd fixed; his mind was not on the meal.

Later, they went into the parlor and drank sherry, and he asked her to tell him about herself, and she did. And then she asked him to tell her about himself, and he did, or at least as much as he was able to without revisiting the old places of the heart that still brought too much pain.

The hours went by, and she had to light a lamp, but Cole asked if they could go into the other room, where the fireplace was, and they did, and he built a fire and that was all the light the room needed as far as he was concerned.

They sat on the floor in front of the fireplace, and he told her how, the first time he had seen her, he had thought she was attractive, and she blushed slightly, but he could tell that she knew already, before he'd even said it, what he thought of her.

They talked until the fire burned nearly down, and he offered to go outside and bring in some more wood, and she said that it wasn't necessary. Then he offered that maybe he should leave.

"I thought you didn't want to be alone tonight?" she said.

"I don't."

"Then why do you want to leave?"

"I just thought . . ."

She placed the tips of her fingers on his mouth.

"I don't want to be alone tonight, either," she said.

The kiss was like something they'd both been waiting for all their lives. Her mouth was sweet, flavored by the sherry. Her hair smelled of soap, and, when he unpinned it, it fell over his hands like strands of silk. And when he pulled his hands away to unbutton her blouse, she kissed them first. He took her face and held it and kissed her mouth again. She made a sound that made him want to kiss her harder.

He felt the coolness of her fingers race over his chest, and he felt her smooth bare skin under the tips of his fingers, velvety and warm in a way that made him weak and hungry for her all at once. And there, in the muted light of a dying fire, he lifted her to him, her hair cascading over his face, her breasts brushing his chest, her bare legs entwining his, and no words were needed to explain or confess their desires. Only the burning coals, only the long sweet night, only the lonely wind outside the door, were to witness their truth.

CHAPTER SIX

Old habit woke Cole early. The light outside the windows was shaded somewhere between darkness and dawn. Cole felt her there beside him, Ella Mims, her hair soft and silky on his shoulder and chest, her face close to his. He didn't want to disturb her, but Will Harper had said he was leaving at first light and Cole wanted to be leaving with him.

"Ella," he whispered.

She stirred.

"Ella, I have to be going."

She opened her eyes, looked at him in the dim gray twilight. Sometime during the night, she had gone into the bedroom and brought back a blanket and they had wrapped up in it. It had felt good to have her there next to him under that blanket. The kind of good that made a man want never to leave. Her fingers traced the curve of his jaw.

"I have to leave," he said again.

She was a woman who spoke openly with her eyes. "Kiss me before you go," she said.

He did, a long lingering kiss that sent heat through his veins.

Cole got dressed while she watched him from the warmth of the blanket. The room was cold, the fire long extinguished. He could hear the wind scratching along the outer walls of the house. Outside, it looked cold and dark and uninviting. It seemed he was always leaving what he wanted for what he didn't want, always moving away from the warm places of the heart to the cold places of the unknown.

"How long do you think you'll be gone?" Ella asked.

"Hard to say. Will Harper has been chasing this

60

man for more than a month and he's still chasing him. Will's the best manhunter I know of, that means the man he's chasing is going to be hard to catch." He saw the look in her eyes. "Maybe with two of us, we'll catch him sooner rather than later."

"I may be gone by the time you get back," she said. "That is if you were intending to come back."

He was reminded of what she had said yesterday about having to leave Cheyenne because of losing everything she owned in the fire. "Where will you go?" This time it was his turn to feel disappointment.

"I have an aunt who lives in Nebraska," she said. "Perhaps I'll go there first."

"I have a friend in Nebraska," Cole said. "His name is Bill Cody. He lives near North Platte." He went on to explain that Bill often ran a touring company of actors and did stage plays throughout the country, and in between engagements he led hunting parties for the rich and famous. He also explained that Bill had a jealous wife and plenty of admirers, many of whom were young actresses.

"He sounds like a very interesting man," she said.

"A lot of people think he is. There's even been some dime novels written about him."

"North Platte is not that far from Ogallala," she said. "My aunt lives in Ogallala."

"In case you get around to North Platte," Cole

said, "you might stop in and see Bill and tell him you're a friend of mine. I'm sure if you still need work, Bill would give you a job."

"As an actress in one of his stage plays?" She smiled.

"Why not, Ella, you're attractive enough. More than attractive enough."

"You don't think that Missus Cody would be jealous," she teased.

"Probably so."

"Why do I get the feeling you have lived quite an untamed life?" she said. "You and your friends."

"You wouldn't be that far wrong."

"Do you suppose you could tell me more about it someday? Your untamed life?"

"Maybe someday."

He rubbed frost from the glass and looked out the window after he pulled on his boots. A blood-red sun was peeking over a slate-gray horizon.

"What are you looking at?" she asked.

"I just hope that thirty-dollar horse of mine hasn't eaten up all your flowers."

She laughed. "It wouldn't matter," she said. "The frost will have killed them anyway."

He walked over to where she was, reached beneath the blankets, and took her in his arms again. He could feel the heat of her, the warm sweet scent of her causing him not to want to let go. "You're an uncommon woman, Ella. I just wanted to tell you that."

Cole looked into those clear-as-glass gray eyes and knew he'd miss her before he got as far as the town's limits. But it couldn't be helped. Will wouldn't wait for Jesus.

"I have this feeling," she said, "that I will never see you again. Why do I have this feeling?"

"I think you're wrong about that."

She smiled. "I hope that I am."

He kissed her and walked out into air so cold and brittle you could almost hear it cracking as you passed through it. The speckled bird stood there, asleep, oblivious it seemed to the cold night. But as he came up to her, her ears pricked up, and she rolled those big dark eyes in his direction.

"Don't ruin the last few good hours of my life by trying to bite a chunk out of me," he warned. He swung up in the saddle, making sure he kept the bird's head in check, just in case she was hungry after having spent the night eyeing Ella's flowers.

Will Harper was adjusting his gear on the pack mule in front of the Inter-Ocean Hotel when Cole rode up. He looked first at Cole, then at the speckled bird.

"Never seen a horse with quite that coloration," he muttered. "Exactly what color would you call that?"

"Don't know that there's a name for it."

He tightened a knot on his pack. "I seen a dog once in a Comanche camp that was about that color." He moved around to the opposite side of the mule in order to tighten another knot. "It had a real sweet taste to it, that dog did, when me and those Comanches ate it. 'Course that was before the Comanches started fighting the white man and you could go into their camps and eat dog with them. You can't do that any more."

When Will was satisfied the pack was well set, he walked over to have a better look at the speckled bird.

"I wouldn't get too close to her, Will."

"Why not?"

"I'm told this mare bites."

He stopped his advance and simply gazed at her. "Look at her eyes," he said. "I wouldn't be surprised if that horse won't someday fall over on you first chance she gets, or kick out your brains. She looks like she hates white people as much as the Comanches do. If you paid more'n ten dollars for her, you paid too much."

"I paid thirty."

He simply shook his head and said: "Let's get going."

They followed the road northwest toward the Blue Mountains. Even from a long way off, you could see the Blue Mountains had fresh snow on their peaks. Ella had been right. The cold weather would kill her flowers.

Clouds the color of cannon smoke drifted against a light blue sky. Even though it was so late in the year, they could feel the heat from the sun on their backs. A broad plain of silvery sage spread before them, clear to the mountains, and you could smell the sweet scent of the sage whenever the wind came from the right direction.

They rode most of the morning without conversation, then stopped around noon by a small tributary whose waters flowed from high up in the mountains, clear and cold as metal. They built a small smokeless fire, and Will set a pot of coffee on to boil and a pan of bacon to fry.

"I was wondering if we were going to take time to eat lunch," Cole said.

"I take it you worked up quite an appetite last night," he said, looking at Cole across the fire like some little devil was whispering in his ear.

"What would you know about where I was last night?"

"Ran into Shorty over to the White Elephant around ten or eleven. He was drinking peach schnapps. He told me you went to see some woman."

Cole rolled himself a cigarette, waiting for the chuck to be done. He figured he wasn't interested in holding a conversation about Ella, or what they had done last night.

Wind swept down from the mountains and they ate their lunch in the great silence of that country before mounting up again.

They rode the rest of the afternoon in the same

general silence, their gazes fixed on the distant range ahead of them and the Blue Mountains that never seemed to get any closer. Cole figured Will Harper was still recovering from his bout of drinking and maybe his honeymoon with Long Bill's woman. Cole meant to ask him about that when they stopped for the evening, sort of as a payback for his asking Shorty about where Cole had spent his night.

They found a spot along the same meandering stream they'd been following as it cut through a stand of cottonwoods where the banks had washed away, exposing the roots of some of the trees. Cole tended to the horses while Will prepared the meal. Then, after they finished eating, Cole made himself a cigarette and offered the makings to Will.

Harper took out a pipe instead and smoked that while they sat around the fire, watching the night crawl over them and the little camp. The sky turned from a silvery blue to a soft rose, then to black velvet that began to fill up with stars.

"How far behind Leviticus Book do you reckon we are?" Cole asked.

"Three, maybe four days," Will said, sucking on the stem of his clay pipe. "Been three, four days behind him for the better part of two weeks. He's like those Blue Mountains. It don't seem I ever get any closer, no matter how much traveling I do."

"He must be a hard man to catch if you haven't caught him yet."

"We'll catch him, just a matter of when."

"It takes a lot of patience to trail a man," Cole said.

Will nodded. "Takes the patience of an Apache," he said. "Ain't nobody that's got the patience of an Apache. But I do my best."

"There's got to be easier ways to make a living, Will, for a man your age."

"I suppose there is. I've even tried some of 'em. I tried selling Bibles door to door once in Saint Louis. I didn't sell many Bibles, but you'd be surprised how many lonely wives just sit around the house all day wishing they had someone to talk to and maybe a few other things as well."

"Well, I wouldn't think even a good salesman could get rich selling Bibles."

"No. But after meeting all those lonely women, I can see why some of those drummers do what they do. It may not be good money, but there sure is a lot of potential for having fun." He grinned like a coyote. "But it won't do for me, selling Bibles . . . or most of that other stuff you have to do in the cities to make a go of it. I guess a hard bark like me can't change much. Hunting men is what I'm best at. 'Sides, it gives me a real good chance to see some real pleasant country."

"Sleeping on hard ground and eating fried pork would seem to me to get old at some point, Will."

"Anything can get old."

"What happens when you run out of desperados to chase?"

He looked at Cole like Cole had just fallen out of a tree. "You think that day's ever going to come . . . that there ain't going to be any desperados to chase?"

"No, but the day may come when you're not able to chase them any more."

"Then I'll chase whores instead." He laughed. "They're slower than desperados and a only half as dangerous."

"Speaking of which . . ."

"Long Bill's woman," he said, tapping the ashes out of his pipe against the heel of his boot. "I was wondering when you were going to ask me about that. Let me tell you, John Henry, she was worth every red cent. Damned voluptuous woman. Lusty, you might say."

"Did you keep that shotgun handy the whole time?"

"That and other things." He grinned.

A wolf howled somewhere far off in the great black emptiness, then was answered by another. Pretty soon a chorus of howls raised from the valley floor, and just that quick they stopped, and the sudden silence almost hurt your ears to listen to it.

It snowed sometime during the night and they awoke under white blankets.

Will jumped up and ran to a tree and relieved

himself, then ran back and set up a pot of coffee, and began frying bacon.

"Can't wait until I can get back to Texas," he said, rubbing his hands. "It ain't nearly this cold in Texas, 'cept up around Dallas where they get ice storms. Sometimes the ice storms get so bad, a horse can't stand up and will slide right out from under you. Seen ice so heavy on trees, it'd break 'em. I don't care much for Dallas when there's ice there. I prefer a little farther south."

They got started on the trail as soon as they had finished their meager breakfast. For the first hour of the ride the air was still cold enough that the breath from the men and horses came out like train steam. But by midmorning, the sun had climbed high enough in the sky that they could feel its warmth on the backs of their hands and necks and they ended up having a pleasant ride all the way to a small town named Broken Wheel.

It was just a collection of log huts, whiskey dens mostly.

"How about stopping for a drink?" Will suggested.

"A little something to oil the bones," Cole replied.

Will nodded. They reined in, tied the horses to the rail, and went inside a low-slung log affair you had to duck down to keep from bumping your head. The light was so dim inside you couldn't see the other customers, but you could smell a good many of them. Will and Cole stepped up to the bar, a raw plank resting atop two whiskey barrels.

A bulldog wobbled from behind the bar on short thick legs and sniffed at their boots.

"Don't mind Petey," the man behind the bar said. "He's just checkin' to see if either of you is a bitch."

"Your dog can't tell a human from another dog?" Will asked.

"Naw, he's blind. Happened when he was a pup and I was carrying him around in my knapsack in the war."

"What war?" Will said.

"How many wars has been fought in the last twelve years?" the barman said.

"You talking the War Between the States?"

"That's right. Pea Ridge," the man said. "That's where Petey got blinded. A Yankee cannon shell blew up half the troop and blinded my dog."

"That's a hard story to believe," Will said.

"Petey's going to be eighty-four years old come Christmas day," the man said. "In dog years, that is."

"Mister, give us a drink and quit fooling around, huh?" Will demanded.

The man rolled his eyes, and Will shook his head. "An eighty-four-year-old blind bulldog," he said. "I've heard everything."

They drank the whiskey without spilling any of it—the true sign of men who appreciate the scarcity of drinking liquor on the frontier. Then Will asked the barman if he'd seen a black man any time recently.

"The Double X out east of here's got two or three Negro cowboys," the man said.

"I don't mean cowboys," Will replied. "I mean a lone black man who you ain't ever seen before, someone like that."

The man rubbed his knuckles in one eye. "I don't know, mister. Them colored people all look pretty much the same to me."

"Like Indians all look the same," Cole said.

"Yeah, like Indians," he agreed.

"Mister, maybe that Yankee shell screwed up more than just your dog's eyes," Will replied sarcastically.

"Did you see a black stranger or not?" Cole said, beginning to lose his own patience with the man.

"Might have been a colored man through here a few days ago," he confessed, seeing that neither customer appreciated his stalling or his blind dog sniffing at their heels. "Anyone would know would be Miss Haversham. She runs a cat-house down the street. Got a colored whore works for her. Girl named Jilly Sweet. Guess they named her right, 'cause she's sweet as sugar."

"I guess they don't all look the same to you, then, do they?" Cole said, but the man didn't get it.

Will took hold of Cole's elbow and steered him

to the door. "That man's dumber than a knob," he said.

They found the brothel easily enough. It was between two whiskey dens and had a red-painted front door. Miss Haversham was a heavy-set woman with powdered cheeks and a gap between her two front teeth when she smiled. Will asked her about Leviticus Book and described him. She confirmed that a man fitting Book's description had visited her house three nights back.

"Could we talk to the girl he was with that night?" Cole asked.

"She's busy right this minute," Miss Haversham said. "You boys can wait for her to finish her present business, or you could have your pick of another gal, though I only got one other, not counting me who is indisposed at the present. Monthlies, you know."

"No, I had me a good whore couple nights back and am still recovering from it," Will said. "I think I'll just wait here in the parlor if you don't mind."

"How about you, lanky?" she asked, turning to Cole.

"No thanks. I'll wait in the parlor with Will."

"Well, you two are the first men that's ever come in here just wanting conversation," Miss Haversham said. "You boys ain't clever, are you?"

"What do you mean, clever?" Will asked.

"You know, the type of men that don't like

girls? The type that likes other men instead?"

"I like girls plenty!" Will growled. "Didn't I just say I was with a whore two nights back?"

"Well, I don't mean nothing by it," she assured. "Just that I know there are some men is clever is all."

"Well *we* ain't like that," Will declared. "Now, if you'll inform your girl we're waiting to talk to her, it'll be much appreciated."

After Miss Haversham left them sitting alone in the parlor, Will said: "You imagine that? Her thinking you and me are *clever?*"

"Takes all kinds."

"I don't much care for this burg," Will opined. "Blind bulldogs and a big jolly whore that thinks any man who don't want to buy a whore is clever. I'll be damned."

They sat with their hats resting on their knees until the Negro girl, Jilly Sweet, came into the room. She was waif-thin, wearing a cotton shift, pretty, with dark freckles across her nose.

"Miss Haversham said you gents wants to see me?"

Will told her the reason.

She sighed, languished on the horsehair settee across from them, and said: "Yas, I remember Leviticus Book. How could a gal forget? He was like a wild stallion." She sighed again and rolled her eyes.

Will said: "So you got a good look at him?"

Jilly Sweet stopped her swooning long enough to say: "Why, yas, I surely did. I seen more of that man than his mama did the day he was born."

"Well, then, I guess you got a *real* good look at him," Will ventured.

"Why you be wantin' to know 'bout Leviticus for anyhow?" Jilly asked, one bare leg crossed over the other, her small brown foot swinging back and forth.

"Because he has killed several men and is wanted by the law," Will told her. "And you're lucky he took a liking to you, or who is to say you might not have ended up being his next victim."

Jilly Sweet's eyes grew large and white, then she giggled. "Oh, no, suh, the only thing that man'd be killin' is a poor gal's heart."

"I don't suppose he said anything to you about his future plans?" Will asked. "I don't suppose this heartbreaker told you which direction he was headed?"

"No, but I shore 'nough wished he had," Jilly Sweet said.

"Why is that?"

" 'Cause, if I knowed which way he went, I'd go catch up with him and become his reg'lar gal."

"Then you must have mush for brains, young lady," Will said.

Jilly Sweet rolled her eyes and said: "Jus' ain't no way I can explain his powers over a female."

"Powers," Will grumped as he headed for the door. "I've seen and heard enough in this town to last me two lifetimes."

He was still grumbling as they walked back down the street.

"Blind dogs and lovesick whores. I guess I've seen and heard everything. Let's get riding before a pink elephant comes trotting down the street."

CHAPTER SEVEN

Will was all for quitting the town then and there, but Cole persuaded him that they ought to stay long enough to buy a hot meal. They found a place that advertised itself as MA'S RESTAURANT and grabbed up a couple of chairs at a table near the kitchen.

Will sniffed the air. "Smell's like that Comanche camp where I ate the dog."

"It beats trail grub," Cole reasoned.

"I ain't so sure." Will squinted at the chalkboard where the menu was scrawled.

It proved out that the restaurant was run by a German couple. The man cooked and the wife washed dishes and served the meals. The man was short and as thin as a stick. The wife was stout as a dray horse and taller than her husband and wore a dark dress that showed sweat stains. There was something else about her that didn't fail to get Will's attention.

"You ever see bosoms that large on a woman before?" Will asked as soon as the woman had taken their order and walked back to the kitchen.

"Once, in San Francisco."

Will was easily fascinated by the unusual and could be downright single-minded about any subject that caught his interest. "Well, I ain't never seen any that large. Those big bosoms were to fall on a man's head, they'd likely break his skull."

"Well, there is probably not much chance they'll fall on your head and break it. So I guess you're safe."

Will grinned. "Biggest ones I ever seen was on a gal in Ulvade," he continued, not content to let the subject drop as a matter of conversation. "Tits so big you couldn't hold a whole one in your hand. But nothing like that German lady's."

"Will, you have a way of wearing a subject plum out."

That made him laugh and stomp his feet.

"Is dere someting wrong?" the woman's husband asked, coming out from the kitchen upon hearing Will stomp his feet.

"No, we was just killing the roaches." Will laughed.

The man looked at the floor but didn't see any dead roaches. Then he looked at Will and Cole as though they had escaped from a loony bin.

"Oh, I see," the man said, then went back to his kitchen, shaking his head and muttering.

In a few minutes, the woman brought out two plates of beef and beans and set them down in front of them, almost hitting Will in the head with her bosoms as she set the plates down. Will ducked out of the way, waited until she'd left again, then smiled so broadly it caused his ears to lift. The beef was tough and stringy and the beans were overly sweet.

"This is poor grub," Will said. "These beans got sugar in them. I ain't never liked sweet beans. We should have gone some place else to eat our supper."

"It's the way German people cook their food," Cole said. "They like to use lots of sugar. Besides, this is the only restaurant we've seen in this town. And even if there was another restaurant, you would have missed seeing those big bosoms."

"That's probably true," Will replied. "But right now, I'd rather be eating beans that weren't so sugary and beef that wasn't so stringy rather than look at big bosoms."

Cole ate his sugary beans in silence, but the beef was beyond redemption.

"How about we stop off and get us a bottle to take with us on the trail?" Will said. "I got a feeling, it's going to get mighty damn' cold tonight."

"I've no objections, Will."

He set his knife and fork down beside his unfinished meal.

"I'm done," he said. "Maybe the next cowboy that comes in can finish this ol' steer. I hope he's got sound teeth and a good stomach whoever he is."

They paid the bill and walked next door to a whiskey tent and bought a bottle of whiskey.

"This ain't snakehead whiskey, is it?" Will asked the barman. "This ain't something you brewed up yourself out back and dumped snake heads into, is it?"

The man said he had sent all the way to St. Louis for his liquor, and that Will could read the label if he didn't believe him.

"Well, don't get insulted," Will said to the man. "But I've drunk snakehead whiskey before and don't ever want to drink it again. Just 'cause it's got a Saint Louis label on it don't mean jack shit to me."

It was already dark by the time they mounted their horses and rode out of town. They topped a ridge and looked back at the distant yellow lights.

"Maybe we should have found us a hotel room back there," Will said as a blast of icy wind rattled through their clothes.

"In the mood you were in, you would have probably've ended up shooting the desk clerk if we had. It's better we make camp out here where you can't shoot anybody."

"Aw, hell, John Henry," Will said, already

working on the bottle. "My nerves are up, that's all."

"Well, maybe that Saint Louis whiskey will help to calm them down."

Will laughed, offered Cole the bottle, which Cole took for no other real reason than to ward off the cold. Cole no longer had the need to drink the way he once had. With the night so clear and full of stars, the air was freezing.

They found a sheltering stand of pines and made camp. Cole built a fire while Will took care of the animals. He had just settled in front of the fire with his palms held out to relieve the numbness when he heard Will howl.

"Gol dang!" he yelped, and walked over to the fire holding his shoulder. "That damn' crow bait of yours just took a bite outta me!"

Cole made Will sit down where the light was good and looked at his shoulder. The skin was barely broken beneath the heavy coat and shirt he was wearing. The clothing had prevented the speckled bird from doing too much damage.

"You're lucky, Will. That mare hardly clipped you. I tried to warn you not to turn your back on her."

Will rubbed his shoulder and looked glum. "Bit by an ugly horse . . . ," he muttered as he lifted the bottle of whiskey. "Ugly horses, blind bulldogs, lovesick whores, and women with giant bosoms. I believe I haven't had such an eventful day since I camped on the Nueces River with Mister Pester's twin daughters."

Will hooked the neck of the bottle, took another swallow, then grinned at the thought of Mr. Pester's twin daughters and the day he had camped with them.

They sat around the fire, watching the flames dance against the black air and passed the bottle back and forth until it made its own sort of fire in their bellies and veins.

As Cole sat there in the mute stillness, surrounded by deep shadows and a sky that was awash with stars, he began to get that bone-deep feeling of what Wayback called the Big Lonely. He'd felt it plenty of times before. It always had a habit of sneaking up on you at night when whatever home you may have had sometime in your life seemed like a thousand miles away. He looked across the fire at Will, a man much like him in certain respects: a drifter, a man who got by on his wits and pistols and instinct, a man who, like himself, had no one waiting for him to come home to, no one worried he wouldn't. Something swooped through the air just above the fire—perhaps an owl—and the cold solitary flight of the creature seemed to flap its wings against Cole's soul.

Will sat wrapped in his blanket, staring vacantly into the flames, remembering, Cole supposed, the precious moments of his life—a pair of pretty girls camped with him on a Texas river, a good horse he once had owned, his first whore, and his first taste of whiskey. That's what the Big Lonely did. It made you remember the sweet places in your life and realize the cold places you'd come to. For Wayback it was the beaver he'd hunted and the Indians he'd fought and loved, and maybe even a woman he'd come close to marrying.

"Tell me about the time you were camped on the Nueces River with Mister Pester's daughters," Cole said to Will.

Will didn't seem to hear him, and Cole didn't ask him again to tell the story. He imagined he was too busy enjoying it himself.

He pulled his blanket up and put his feet closer to the fire and settled in for another night on the prairie. One more night on a trail to nowhere— that's the way it seemed. The wind blew cold down from the Blue Mountains.

"How can it be so damn' cold when there ain't even any snow on the ground?" Will said suddenly.

Cole guessed the cold wind had caused him to come back from the Big Lonely. "Not much of a life, is it?" he said.

"Ain't we had this discussion once before?" Will muttered.

Cole rolled a cigarette and tried his best to keep the wind from blowing all the tobacco out of the paper. He thought of Ella Mims in that spare moment. He wondered if she'd packed her belongings and was on her way to Nebraska. Then that thought led him to a second—Bill Cody.

He was probably this very night sitting in that big house he'd built on the North Platte with a bunch of his cronies and several adoring young actresses nestled at his feet while he recounted stories of his stage acting or his buffalo hunts with dignitaries and royalty. Maybe after Will and he had caught Leviticus Book, Cole would ride over to Nebraska and stop in and see Cody. In spite of his bloated fame, Bill was still a good man at heart—once you got him out of the company of actresses and Ned Buntline.

In the old days, Bill and Cole liked to drink—a lot. Bill would get drunk and maudlin and relive the old days of his youth, before anyone but his closest friends knew who he was. Cole had asked him once why he just didn't take his wife Louisa and settle down and live a quiet life. When Cole had asked him that, Cody had simply looked at Cole and said: "John Henry, once you've become famous, you can't never be anything else but that."

"Well, what's so terrible about being famous?" Cole had asked.

"Nothing," he'd said. "And everything." Then he had looked at Cole with his clear blue eyes, handsome as a racehorse in all his fine buckskins and polished riding boots and silver spurs, and said: "Fame is the worst kind of disease a man can get, John Henry. It's worse than ten cases of the clap or the yellow fever. It's worse than dope or whiskey or sexual urge. It's worse than any kind

82

of sin because there ain't no redemption. Once you've experienced it, you can't ever get enough of it. God damn if you can!" Then his sweet blue eyes had narrowed and he added: "But do you want to know the worst part about all of it? It scares hell out of me is what it does."

Cole tossed his cigarette into the fire and looked over at Will. He was asleep, sitting up, hugging the nearly empty bottle of whiskey that had come all the way from St. Louis. Cole laid back and tugged his hat brim down over his eyes and listened to the rhythm of the horses, cropping grass. He hoped Ella would find Nebraska to her liking, and he hoped Bill Cody was swappin lies with some sweet young actress, and he hoped Ike was resting in peace, and that soon he would catch his killer.

CHAPTER EIGHT

Will woke with a hoot. "Hey, damn!"

Cole came up with the self-cocker in his hand, thinking there was trouble, that maybe they were under attack by road agents or renegade Indians. It was nothing as dramatic as that. Will was bucking out of his blankets along with the young prostitute, Jilly Sweet.

"What the devil you doing here?" Will cawed.

She stood there, shivering in the cold dawn.

"I want to go with you to find Leviticus," she said through chattering teeth. She wore an old Army campaign coat and a flop-brimmed hat and loose trousers that fluttered about her ankles. She looked for all the world like some poor sodbuster, standing there in a pair of run-down brogans.

"Find Leviticus!" Will swallowed several times in exasperation over the surprise package.

"Yas, suh," Jilly Sweet said, chattering like a squirrel.

"Do you intend on arresting him and collecting the reward money, too?" Will asked, not at all happy with the unexpected turn of events.

"No, suh," Jilly Sweet said. "I want to find him 'cause I's in love with him. There ain't never been no man make me feel like Leviticus do."

"What does this look like?" Will declared, flinging his arms out. "An expedition for the lovelorn?"

Jilly Sweet just stood there shivering, the whites of her eyes showing little fear from under the soft brim of her hat.

"And what were you doing in my bedroll?" Will demanded.

"Trying to get warm . . . it mighty cold out here, or ain't you noticed?"

The wind was whistling through the holey parts of Will's drawers, and a big Colt pistol now in his hand. Will Harper ought to have been a man embarrassed, but he wasn't. "Well, who said you could climb in my bedroll anyhow? Why didn't you climb in John Henry's bedroll, instead?"

The girl looked at Cole. "I would have, if I'd known you was goin' to be such an ol' grump about it. Most mens wouldn't mind if I's to climb in their bedrolls wid 'em. I remember now, Miss Haversham sayin' how she thought maybe you was a clever man."

"Don't say that!" Will warned. "I ain't clever!"

"Will, maybe you ought to get some clothes on," Cole suggested. "The girl's right, it's mighty cold. You're liable to freeze off some of your vital parts."

Will looked down at his condition and said—"Oh."—then quickly started putting on his clothes. Jilly Sweet giggled when Will tried to get his pants on, having put his boots on first, and this caused him to stumble and fall over his saddle. He gave her a fearsome look because of the giggle.

Will finally got on his clothes and said: "You go on back to town now, child, and leave us alone."

"No, suh, I ain't goin' back to town. I come to find Leviticus."

"Well, do you see him anywhere around here?" Will scowled.

"No," Jilly Sweet said, "but I know you is lookin' for him, and I aim to follow you until you find him."

"Follow me?"

"Yas, suh."

"You can't follow me," Will argued.

"Why not? It's a free country, ain't it?"

Will walked around in tight little circles, tugging and pulling on his hat, taking it off, and putting it back on again. "I won't allow it. And that's that."

"Can't stop it nohow," Jilly said. "I ride where I wants, goes where I wants, same as you."

Will walked a little way from camp, then walked back again. "Jesus, John Henry, can't you do something here? Can't you try talking to her?"

"I don't know what I can say that you haven't already. I guess, if she wants to ride all the way to the Blue Mountains, she can. But I figure she'll go just a little way, then turn back. What else can be done?"

Will rolled his eyes, shook his head, and walked over to his gear and started packing it on the mule, muttering the whole while.

"He say he goin' try to stop me?" Jilly Sweet asked.

"No," Cole said, "but I don't think you're going to be welcomed with open arms in his camp. You sure you don't want to ride back to town?"

"No," she said, watching Will pack his mule. "I'll just tag along back yonder a ways. Don't want to be in his ol' camp, anyhow. Grumpy ol' man."

"You probably just gave him a start, waking

up and finding you there in his blankets, is all."

"Humph!" Jilly grunted, and with that she marched to a little sorrel staked out on a long rope and climbed aboard, prepared to go wherever Will and Cole went.

Cole looked at Will, who was tying knots in his ropes. He was paying no attention to either of them. Cole went over to Jilly Sweet.

"You know, it's not safe out here for a woman alone. Hell, there's every kind of sorrow and danger."

"I won't exactly be alone."

"I don't think Will is going to slow down just so you can keep up, Miss Sweet. In fact, he'll probably travel a little faster just because of you."

"He won't have to do no slowin' down for me. Me and little Cheater here can keep right up wid anywhere that big ol' sassy man wants to go."

Cole gave up, and walked back over to Will.

"I guess we don't have much choice," Cole stated.

"Lovesick whores . . . ," Will muttered. "What next?"

Finally he finished his packing, then turned to Cole and said irritably: "Do you know how to make coffee? Because I sure could use some coffee on a cold dreadful morning like this."

Will refused to budge from camp until after he had drunk three cups of black coffee and eaten several strips of burned bacon. Cole fixed Jilly

Sweet some of the coffee and bacon and carried them over to her. Will stared off at the Blue Mountains, refusing to acknowledge her presence in camp.

"This sure is some good grub," Jilly Sweet said. "Good coffee, too."

It just seemed to irritate Will all the more to hear Jilly Sweet compliment Cole on the coffee and bacon.

Finally Will was prepared to leave. Jilly Sweet mounted her little sorrel. Will acted like she wasn't there. Cole gave the girl his blanket to wrap over her shoulders.

"Thank you kindly," she said, and took the blanket.

"There's a lot of empty country out there," Cole told her, "and all of it's cold. Least back in town, you'd be warm."

"I don't reckon I would, seein' as how I told Miss Haversham I quit last night," she announced stubbornly. "Miss Haversham don't like her girls quittin' on her. Ever' girl that quits, means Miss Haversham got to take up the slack for her. Miss Haversham said she gettin' old and her back be hurtin' her from all them cowboys ridin' her. I thinks maybe it's jus' 'cause she's fat and can't get her wind and move around like them young rascals want. Either way, Miss Haversham don't take kindly to her girls leavin' her. Reckon I won't be goin' back there, even if I wanted to."

Will, paying no attention to the girl or Cole, set out toward the Blue Mountains at a quick pace. Jilly Sweet put her little sorrel into a choppy trot.

Cole spurred the speckled bird ahead until he caught up with Will.

Later, after several miles without bothering to turn around to look for himself, breaking the silence between them, he growled: "She still back there?"

"She is, Will."

He rode along glumly for several more miles. Occasionally he would ask Cole for a report on the girl's location, and, when Cole would tell him that she was still on their heels, he would grunt and knee his mount to a little faster pace.

"You're going to wear out your horse," Cole said at one point.

"It wouldn't be no great loss to the world if that flea bag you're riding was to wear out," Will declared.

But the speckled bird was doing just fine. In fact, she seemed to enjoy the quick pace and the clear cold air of the high country. Cole couldn't say the same for Will.

The sun followed them and the air turned pleasantly warm, and they stopped by a small creek for their noon meal. Jilly Sweet halted her little sorrel a hundred yards from the resting spot. She dismounted and sat on the ground, watching them.

"We can't just ignore her, Will," Cole said as he unwrapped some beef jerky and hardtack.

"Why can't we? Feed her and it'd be just like feeding a stray cat. I don't want to encourage her. I want to *discourage* her."

"Well, she can have my portion," Cole said.

"That's up to you," Will snapped. "You keep feeding that gal your food and pretty soon you'll end up looking as flea-bitten as that ugly horse of yours."

"Careful, Will, I think the speckled bird understands human talk."

Will tossed Cole a look, then settled into making himself a sandwich of jerky and hardtack, what Cole once heard a captured young Rebel call 'possum cake.

Cole walked out to where Jilly Sweet sat on the ground and gave her his portion of the beef jerky along with the hardtack. She took it without a word and chewed it.

"He still bein' mean about my comin' along?" she said after a few minutes of chewing her 'possum cake.

"He's still not happy that you're following us."

"Why's he so mean an' contrary, and you so nice?"

"He's not so mean. He's just got his ways."

"He really goin' to take Leviticus back to get hung?"

"Yes."

"Why?"

"Because Book is wanted for murder. In fact, the reason I'm riding with Will is that one of the people Leviticus Book murdered is a friend of mine."

She shook her head. Will was sitting with his back to them, facing the Blue Mountains. "Leviticus ain't never killed no mens except maybe one that was trying to kill him furst."

"How would you know that?"

"Mans got such tender hands an' a tender heart. Couldn't be no way a mans wid such tender hands and heart be killin' nobody."

"Well, I'm afraid you're wrong, Miss Sweet."

She quickly turned her attention to Cole, her large dark brown eyes flashing with determination. "No, suh. I ain't. I's a woman, and womens knows about mens. An' me, I seen all kinds of mens. Been wid all kinds . . . good an' bad. Womens know. *I know*."

"Well, that may be. But I know Will well enough to know he wouldn't be wasting his time chasing after an innocent man."

"Jus' cause that mean ol' boot say Leviticus guilty, don't mean he is."

"It's not just him that says Book is guilty," Cole reminded her.

"Who else say he is?"

"The law."

"*Huuuh!* Law don't know more'n I know. Law

ain't never felt those tender hands o' Leviticus's. The law ain't never looked into his sweet brown eyes or heard the tender way he talks."

Jilly Sweet stopped chewing on her jerky and was just sitting there, her eyes big and round, remembering.

"Well, I'm sure the law doesn't care much about those things, Miss Sweet. I know Will doesn't, and to be honest with you, I don't, either."

"Leviticus ain't what you think he is," she said, staring up at Cole like an awe-struck child.

Cole walked back to where Will was sitting, cross-legged, staring at the Blue Mountains. "You talk her into going back to Broken Wheel yet?" he asked.

"No."

"Damn' fool girl. Well, let's get going."

"It'd make sense to allow her into camp," Cole suggested as they mounted their horses. "She could cook and clean the plates as payment for her meals."

"Next thing you'll want me to do is stop at the nearest town and buy a fiddle so we can have dances every night," Will growled.

"It might not be a bad way to pass the evenings," Cole said, only this time Will wasn't in the mood to be humored.

They arrived in Laramie, a rugged frontier town seated on a high plateau near the Snowy Range, just at dusk. They could see the lights twinkling against the rosy glow of distant sky.

"We'll check around here," Will said, reining his horse and mule in front of a saloon. "I'll ask around and see if anyone's seen Book."

"What about her?" Cole asked.

Will looked around. Jilly Sweet was sitting astride her tired little sorrel half a block distant.

"Aw, hell, John Henry, go and see if you can get a couple of rooms for the evening. Meet me back here."

Cole went back to where Jilly Sweet was sitting her horse and said: "I think you're starting to grow on him."

"I hope I ain't," she answered.

Cole asked a man, standing out front of a billiard parlor, where he could find a hotel. The man looked at Cole, but mostly he looked at Jilly Sweet.

"Up 'at way." He pointed with his nose after he'd gotten a good enough look at the girl.

They tied up out front and went inside.

"Need to rent a couple of rooms," Cole said to a pocked-face kid sitting behind the desk. He was reading the latest issue of the *Police Gazette*. His feet were propped up on a crate and he hadn't noticed their arrival. He had carrot-red hair that was wild and uncombed. All that wild red hair and a sharp bony beak made him look like a rooster.

When Cole told him about needing rooms, he

looked up, but right away his attention went to the girl. "Huh?"

"I said we'll need a couple of rooms for the night." Cole couldn't be certain he had heard him the second time because his attention stayed on Jilly Sweet.

She leaned over the desk and smiled brightly at him. "You see somethin' you like, child?"

Cole thought the boy might swallow his tongue. "Rooms," he said a third time, now with a little more force. "Two of them."

The kid fumbled getting a set of keys from a box, while Cole scratched the name *Billy Cody* on the register with a nib pen.

"You wait here in the room," he said to Jilly when they got inside one of the rooms. Then he tossed her one of the keys. "I'm going to go scout up Will, then we'll all go get some supper together."

She said: "You want rest there on the bed for a little bit first?"

"Why?"

Then she laid her hand on Cole's forearm and said: "Jus' wonderin' if maybe you wasn't lonely for a gal. You was awful nice to talk ol' grumpy into not runnin' me off and bringin' me food and gettin' me this room. . . ."

"No, Jilly. I'm not lonely for a gal."

She looked half disappointed, half relieved. "You sure?"

"I'm sure."

"Well, if you change your mind later, jus' give a little knock, OK?"

Another time, another place, Cole thought as he went back down the stairs, he might have taken Jilly up on her offer. But fortunately he was no longer a man that lonely, or that young.

CHAPTER NINE

After Cole had left Jilly Sweet, he walked back to the saloon where Will had gone. The horse and mule were tied up outside. The windows were yellow smudges of light. The place seemed to have a life of its own, its belly full of laughter—carousing men and shrill women. Someone was pounding the keys of a piano—a woman was singing in high falsetto voice.

Cole stepped through the double doors. The air was close, smoke-filled, like every saloon Cole'd ever been in. Some things you can count on, like the smell of a whiskey parlor. Blue haze from cigars and hand-rolled shucks hung in the air like mist over a bayou. There was a smell of sweat and cheap perfume and stale beer so thick you could almost cut it with a knife, the clink of glass and poker chips falling in between the laughter. Each voice sounded a little louder than the next. It could have been Saturday night, maybe Friday.

Cole had lost track of the exact day, but then it didn't matter. Whatever night it was, it was hell-raising time. The good folks, if there were any, were all at home, sitting around a supper table. The rest were in this place. The name of the place didn't matter. They were just names for the same thing.

Cole undid the bottom two buttons of his sheepskin coat as he pushed his way through the crowd. Close as it was, it didn't hurt for a man to be prepared for whatever trouble might break out. With the bottom two buttons undone, he could reach the self-cocker riding on his left hip. He worked inward till he reached the bar. He had kept an eye out for Will but failed to catch sight of him.

A barman wearing a towel and carrying a pair of empty mugs with flecks of beer foam still clinging to them asked Cole what he'd have to drink. He ordered a whiskey and waited for the barman to return with it.

While he waited, he got a better look at the woman standing next to the professor at the piano. She was tall and her hair was platinum and she wore a blue velveteen dress. She couldn't sing very well, but she was giving it her best. Most of the rowdies who were paying attention didn't seem much interested in her singing. They were mostly fuzz-faced cowboys, and a few old bachelors.

She finished her song just as Cole's whiskey

arrived and some of the men up front clapped and hooted and stomped their feet.

"Sing us another, Lily!" someone shouted. She smiled without conviction and nodded to the professor, a tubercular man with garters on his sleeves who immediately began clinking the keys.

"Fifty cents," the barman said as he slid the drink across to Cole. He laid the money on the bar and took the drink in hand. His funds were low, so he took his time enjoying the simple luxury of manufactured whiskey.

The woman began singing "Old Folks at Home", a sentimental song that was guaranteed to bring tears to the eyes of maudlin men made even more maudlin by heavy drink and lonely places. Already some of the men up front were bowing their heads and shaking them sadly.

"That Lily," the barman said, wiping up a wet spot from the bar with the towel. "She knows how to make those gents cry in their beers, even if she can't sing a lick."

Cole held off finishing the rest of the whiskey in his glass a few moments longer, until the woman finished her song to a great outburst of emotional applause as several of the cowboys and old bachelors pushed forward and dropped money into a mason jar atop the piano. Cole lifted his glass in salute, not so much for her rendition, but for her instincts of knowing how to survive in an otherwise difficult world. She deserved what she got—the silver out of those thirsty men's pockets.

He swallowed the last of the whiskey and it barely seemed to touch the weariness of an all day ride, so he ordered one more. While he was waiting, the blonde diva pushed in beside him and said: "That was very nice of you."

He looked at her. "What was very nice?"

"To raise your glass to me."

"I didn't think you'd be watching."

"My eyes are used to the poor light," she said. "And used to the normal crowd of faces. Yours is new. Would you care to buy a lady a drink?"

"Sure, why not," Cole said. How could he refuse, even though his pockets were nearly empty? "What exactly do you drink?" She told the barman to bring her a peach brandy.

"My name's Lily," she said. "I was named after Lily Langtry, the actress. Have you heard of her?"

"No. But then, I don't go to very many plays."

She smiled and tasted her brandy.

"Neither do I," she said. "Laramie doesn't even have an opera house."

"Well, it must be a great loss for all who live here."

It took her a moment, then she laughed. "You didn't say what your name was."

"John Henry Cole."

Her face brightened. "I have a brother named John Henry," she said. "He lives in New York."

"Here's to names," Cole said, touching his shot glass to hers.

"So, John Henry," she said, some of the peach brandy still glistening on her upper lip. "Are you a cowboy?"

"No. I was once, but not any more."

She had a small mole just to the right of her mouth. Somehow it seemed to fit her smile. He caught the look she gave him as he drained his glass. In spite of his instincts, he didn't mind it so much, the way Lily was looking at him. Maybe he should have, considering a lot of his thoughts were still back with Ella Mims. He tried to push the look out of his mind and concentrate on locating Will.

Several men tried to buy her drinks while they were standing there, having small talk. She graciously turned them down. Most of them took it well, but a few looked glum.

"I'm all for some place quieter," she said. "How about you?"

"I'm here looking for a friend." Her look turned to mild disappointment. It was something Cole could feel as well as see.

"That's too bad," she sighed, tipping up the brandy glass.

"I need to see him."

"Then what, after you see him?" she wondered.

"I guess it depends on what he has to tell me, if anything."

"How long do you think all that will take?"

"Not long."

"I have a room not far from here," she said. "A girl gets lonely for the company of a gentleman."

Cole looked around. "There doesn't seem to be any shortage."

"Not if a girl's not choosy. I'm choosy."

"Give me a minute," he said, then asked himself what the hell was he doing as he looked around for Will.

Leaving Lily standing at the bar, he made his way through the crowd until he spotted Will. He was at a table with three other men, playing stud poker. From the winnings in front of him, he wasn't doing too badly. Cole figured whatever scouting he had done so far in the way of finding Leviticus Book had been put on hold. Hell, he should go back to the hotel and wait for Will to show up. But he didn't.

"Did you find your friend?" Lily asked when Cole returned to where she had been standing at the bar. A cowboy wearing angora chaps was trying to buy her a drink.

"Yes, I found him," Cole said. "But right now, it looks like he's busy."

"Good," she replied. She hooked her arm through Cole's.

"I don't think this is such a good idea."

"Walk me to my place, give yourself time to

decide. You don't want to come in when we get there, I won't force you."

They went out into the chill air. Lily had wrapped a heavy wool capote over her shoulders. "It's not far, my room," she said.

It was a small dwelling at the end of the street, behind a butcher shop. They went in. There was a bed along one wall, a small travel trunk at the foot of it. There were curtains hanging in the window and a small wood burner in the corner. Several tintypes rested atop an armoire, images of her family Cole knew once she pointed them out while she removed her cloak.

"That one's my brother, John Henry," she said. "The one who has your name. He's a typesetter's apprentice for one of the newspapers in New York." She identified a mother and father and two younger sisters from among the other portraits, all still living in the East, New York and New Jersey.

She built a fire in the wood stove and the room quickly grew warm. She produced a bottle of peach brandy and a set of glasses and poured them each a drink. They sat on the side of the bed, the only place there was to sit, and Cole listened while she told him more about her family and how she had joined an acting troupe touring the West.

"By the time we arrived in Laramie, we were broke," she said, pouring herself a second brandy and unlacing her shoes. "Some of us took what work we could. Others booked passage back to

New York. That was last summer." She sipped her brandy. "As you can see, I'm still here."

"Why didn't you go back to New York with the others?"

She tilted her head just enough to show Cole a smile that didn't come from happiness. "The director of the troupe convinced me to stay here with him. He had a weakness for cards and the obscure, and I had a weakness for him. He ended up leaving in the middle of the night with an eighteen-year-old chippie named Millicent, and I've not seen or heard from him since." She stared at the wallpaper for a time, her teeth biting the edge of her lower lip. "I thought I was old enough and wise enough not to be fooled by a man. I was wrong."

"That still doesn't explain why you stayed on instead of going back home," Cole said, thinking there were no words adequate when a woman tells you a story like that.

"Maybe I'm still waiting for him to come back." She sighed. "Maybe I've not learned just how much a fool I am."

Sitting there close together like they were on the side of the bed, Cole could see she was not as young as she had first appeared to be back in the saloon. He could see, too, that she had watery brown eyes that were looking into some pretty faraway and awful places of her past.

"I was married once," she added after a long

pause, "to a banker. We lived in a large white house with shutters and rolling lawns. For a time I thought it was all I would ever want or need, that big house and a rich husband."

"But it wasn't."

She looked sharply at Cole. "It was until a handsome, sweet-talking, young dentist who was better at poker than pulling teeth came along and convinced me it wasn't."

"So he divorced you," Cole said, "the banker?"

"No. He shot the dentist and went to jail."

"Love makes some men desperate," Cole sympathized.

"It wasn't love," she said. "Not on George's part. For him, it was more like stealing to have this other man come into his life and try and take something that belonged to him. A matter of embarrassment, not of love."

"A lot of men might have done the same thing," Cole suggested.

"Of that, John Henry, I have no doubt." Then, without bothering to set her glass down, she gave him a long and full kiss.

Cole wasn't sure this was something he wanted to happen, but he didn't do anything to stop it, either.

"There's just some nights I don't want to be alone," she said. "This is one of them."

"Why me, Lily? You could have had your choice of men?"

"I told you, I'm choosy. You don't look like the kind of man who will hurt me, lie to me, or ask me to marry him. You know how long it's been since I had a man like that?"

Cole didn't know.

"I don't want your life," she said. "I just want some of your time."

Cole touched her hair. She kissed him again. Her mouth tasted like the peach brandy; her breath was warm against his neck. Maybe he wasn't being as honest with himself as he could have been. Maybe he didn't give Ella Mims as much consideration as he should have there in that wanting moment. But he told himself that Ella was an uncertainty, like all the other uncertainties in his life, and Lily was here and now and professing her need for him. There is something powerful about a woman's needing you. So, Cole didn't try any harder than that to stop it.

Without bothering to turn down the flame in the oil lamp, she undressed.

"I'm not as young or pretty as I once was," she said.

Cole reached for her, pulled her down to him. Her hands unbuttoned his shirt, her lips fluttered over his chest, the tips of her fingers trailed down his ribs. She paused, drew away, looked at the scars her fingers had found welted in his flesh.

"What are these?"

"Nothing. Just the marks of living an eventful life."

"Do they still hurt?"

"Not in ways I can explain."

She kissed the scars and whatever doubts he had about being there with her began to abandon him. Her breasts were small and soft in his hands and she shuddered when he touched them. "Like that . . . ," she whispered.

"Like this . . . ?"

She moaned. She reached for him and held him in ways that caused his breath to come up short. He closed his eyes and drifted through the pleasures of her hands and kisses, through the soft warmth of her flesh and womanly scent until he felt himself being drawn into her, felt her strong hips moving against him, and felt himself becoming one with her. And her loneliness and his found each other as they suffered the heat of each other's passion.

Sometime later, Cole awoke in the cold stillness of the room. The fire in the small stove had gone out and the lamp had extinguished itself. Lily lay there beside him, asleep and unmoving. It took several seconds for him to regain his bearings. When he finally did, he left the bed as quietly as he could and found his clothes and dressed.

"You don't have to leave at this hour . . . ," she said, mumbling, still half asleep.

"I was hoping I wouldn't wake you."

"I was dreaming," she said, "of a beautiful white horse. I was riding through a meadow of pretty wildflowers on a beautiful white horse."

"I have to go and meet up with my friend," Cole explained, pulling on his boots.

"I was young again, just a girl," Lily said, her voice as soft as a girl's. "I've had the same dream before. It always makes me feel good when I dream it."

"Will you be all right?"

She lifted herself to one elbow. "Yes, I'll be OK."

"I'm sorry about this, having to leave like this."

"Don't be," she said.

He finished pulling his boots on, and then slipped into his coat, and took his hat from the back of a chair. "Do you think you'll ever go back home to see your people, Lily?"

"Someday," she said. "When I get tired of waiting for Freddy to return."

He kissed her cheek.

She said: "Thank you."

He had no words to give her back, but he knew she probably didn't expect any, either. He stepped out into a night as black and cold as a cheater's heart. The sky glittered with stars that were beyond a man's reach, but not beyond his dreams. Most of the whiskey dens and gambling houses

106

still operated and their lights glowed like the eyes of alley cats.

He walked back to the log saloon where he'd last seen Will playing stud poker. He wanted a cigarette but waited until after he got there and stepped inside.

The whiskey parlor wasn't as lively as it had been earlier. Probably a lot of the cowboys had drifted back to the scattered outlying ranches, to their lonely bunks where they thought about women like Lily, or a lost sweetheart. The poker game was still in progress, and Will Harper was still having a good turn of luck, judging by the chips stacked in front of him. The man behind the bar asked Cole what he wanted to drink, and Cole told him coffee, if he had any. He grumbled, but said he'd fix some. Cole waited and watched the game and tried hard not to think about Lily or Ella Mims.

He made himself a cigarette and smoked it while waiting for the coffee. He turned his attention away from the table only long enough to strike a match, but in that fleet second something happened, and, when he turned back, Will and another man were facing each other—the other two players having scrambled out of the way. The room became so quiet Cole could hear the cigarette paper of his shuck burning.

"What'll it be, mister?" Will asked the other man.

"Don't know, but you've been winning hands all night."

"Luck and skill," Will said. "That's what poker is, or ain't you heard that?"

"I heard," the man said.

The man was not large or unusual in appearance in any way. He wore a straw sombrero but otherwise dressed plainly. There was nothing about him to attract attention unless you knew a *pistolero* when you saw one. A man who makes pistols his business will have a way of standing with his good side turned slightly to you. He makes a small target.

"You accusing me of cheating?" Will asked.

"Ain't accusing you of anything," the man said. "But it's awful damn' strange you winning 'most every hand."

Cole circled to get a better look at the man, to see him under the light from the twin lights hanging over the table. And when he got around to where the light was better, he saw just who it was Will was confronting.

"Will," Cole said.

Will didn't turn his attention away from the man, but said: "What, John Henry?"

"Time we got going."

"Can't you see I'm in a situation here?"

"It doesn't have to be a situation, Will. Fact is, it's damned late and we've got an early start ahead of us in the morning."

The man standing across from Will, the one Cole had moved around to get a better look at, turned his head enough to see who was talking.

"You this man's friend?" he asked.

"Will's a partner," Cole said.

"Then you better get him home before he gets himself killed. All those winnings aren't going to do him any good where I'm about to send him."

Will stiffened at the challenge, but Cole couldn't allow it to happen, not with this man, he couldn't. Will was a pistol fighter in his own right, but no match for the man across the table from him.

"Will, I need to talk to you about something," Cole said.

"We'll talk later, John Henry!"

"No, we need to talk now!"

For an instant, Cole thought Will would pull his Colt, but his warning must have pierced Will's mule mind, for he slowly turned his attention to Cole. "Can't this wait?"

"No, Will. It can't."

Still, Will was in a precarious situation. He naturally did not want to turn his back on the man, and yet he knew there had to be a good reason why Cole was interfering. There was.

"Let me take my friend home, Hardin," Cole said. "He's not a card cheat . . . he's just lucky."

Cole saw the recognition come into Will's face at Cole's mention of the man's name. But it wasn't fear or anything akin to it. Will wasn't the

109

type to be afraid, not even of the devil or John Wesley Hardin.

"He's awful damn' lucky," Hardin declared.

"Let me put it to you this way, Wes," Cole said. "If you draw on him, you'll need to be fast enough to shoot us both, and I don't think you are. Maybe you can see some reason for some of us to die here tonight, but you'd be the only one who would."

Anyone who knew anything knew of the reputation of John Wesley Hardin. He was not known as a generous man when it came to a gunfight. But he wasn't stupid, either. Two against one, spread out as they were, there just wasn't any way he was going to get them both. Either Will would kill him, or Cole would.

Hardin let another few seconds pass—just long enough to maintain his sense of honor, then said: "I'm going to walk over to the bar and have a drink. After that, if you boys are still present, there just ain't no telling what might happen next. I'm damned nerved up."

Will started to say something, but Cole said something first. "It's not worth dying over, Will."

Will was mad as hell when they hit the street.

"What was that all about, John Henry?"

"He would have killed you," Cole said. "Or me."

"What makes you think it wouldn't have been him that would have gotten killed?"

"It would have been him, too. But he would still have killed one of us, Will. And to tell you the truth, I wasn't planning on dying in some damned dirty saloon over a hand of cards."

"You didn't have to butt in, you know."

"Yeah, Will, I did have to butt in, god damn it."

"No, you're wrong."

"Look at you, Will. You're drunk and in the wind. Killing you would have been as easy as killing a blind mule. Hardin wouldn't have thought twice about it."

Will swallowed then, because Cole had spoken the truth. He was drunk even though he walked a straight line, and, while the whiskey made him braver than he ought to have been, it also made him slower, too. John Wesley Hardin didn't need any extra advantage.

"I got us rooms at the hotel," Cole said to Will's sullen silence. Maybe he was thinking how close he came to dying. If he was, Cole thought, all the better. Maybe next time he decided to get in a poker game with someone as quick and ill-tempered as John Wesley Hardin, he would refrain from the whiskey.

They arrived at the hotel only to find several guests standing outside in their nightclothes.

"What is it, a fire?" Cole asked one of them—a balding man in a long nightshirt.

He rolled his eyes and said: "A man's been killed up there!"

"Up where?" Will asked.

"In one of them rooms!"

It was more a feeling than anything else, the sense that Jilly Sweet was somehow involved. Cole looked around but didn't see her among any of the shivering guests. "Let's go!" he said to Will as he rushed inside.

Cole found the door to her room wide open. He also found the pock-faced desk clerk with his drawers down around his ankles, squatting beside the bed. It looked like he had washed in blood. He was dead as a man can get.

"What the hell!" Will said.

The kid was the only one in the room. Jilly Sweet was gone. Cole went down the hall, saw the back door had been kicked in, saw the stairway that led to an alleyway.

"Who would have done this?" Will said when Cole got back to the room.

"Guess."

"Book?"

"Who else would come to steal that girl in the middle of the night?"

"God damn!" Will declared. "Here we been chasing him, and he's been following us!" Then Will noticed the boy and said: "Who's he?"

"Just a randy kid who knocked on the wrong door."

Will swallowed hard. "You think Book did him because of the girl?"

"I don't know why else."

"You want to leave tonight, or first light?" Will asked.

"There's no point in trying to trail them tonight, Will. You know that as well as I do. Besides, you're drunk enough that you might fall off your horse and break your neck."

"I rode two hundred miles once across the Llano Estacado drunk as a 'coon and never one time fell off my horse," Will argued.

"How would you know if you had?"

Will looked at Cole and said: "I'm going to bed before something else up and bites me in the ass."

Cole considered the abilities of a man who could cut the trail of Will Harper without Will's knowledge as he slipped the big self-cocker under his pillow that night. It was cold comfort, that big three-pound pistol under his head. If Leviticus Book could murder a man like Ike Kelly and steal the colored whore right out from under their noses, then there was no telling just what else he could do, if and when he was ready.

CHAPTER TEN

The next morning, as soon as it was light enough to cut sign, Will and Cole followed a double set of tracks leading from the alleyway in back of the hotel to the south road.

"You see that?" Will declared, through bleary eyes. "He's turned around and is now heading south."

"I see."

"But why south? Why ain't he still heading north?"

"Maybe he's changed his mind as to which border he wants to cross."

"Damn' son-of-a-bitch," Will moaned. "Gonna make me chase him all the way to the Mexican border if he can."

"Warmer that direction," Cole offered.

"Farther, too."

As they followed the tracks through the back alley, Cole saw Lily standing in the doorway of her little cabin, a tin cup of coffee in her hand. Their eyes met, but they didn't speak. Will noticed her as well.

"Fine-looking woman," he said. "You know that gal?"

"We've met," Cole said.

He twisted his neck in order to keep looking at her as they rode past.

"Pretty hair," he said.

Cole allowed himself a few moments of the previous night's memory, then let Lily slip away from his thoughts. Lily's memory wasn't something he wanted to carry with him the rest of the trip. "We push hard," he said to Will, "we might catch Book in three, four days."

Will was still nursing a sore head from all the hard liquor from the night before. His eyes were rimmed red and he kept swiping at his mustaches. "That is, if he ain't behind us somewheres." He groaned.

It was something Cole had considered as well— that Leviticus Book was tracking them instead of the other way around.

"You think he maybe killed the girl?" Will asked.

"No. It wouldn't make sense to kidnap her if he was just going to kill her."

"A man would have to be damn' sweet on a gal to take such risks as he took last night," Will said.

"Maybe there was more to it than that."

"How so?"

"Maybe he wanted to prove to us he could do it, steal the girl out from under us."

"Crazy son-of-a-bitch then," Will said, swiping his mustaches again.

"Maybe not so crazy as we might think."

Will rode on for the next few hours without further comment. His head must have felt like an anvil from all that bust-head whiskey he'd soaked up. Cole had learned one thing in his own drinking days. It was not to put cheap liquor in you. Good Tennessee mash, that was another thing.

The day was cloudy and looked as though it would either rain or snow. They crossed several tributaries, and in every one the water appeared black under the dull gray sky. A stiff wind blew out of the northwest and pushed tumbleweeds across their path. Once, a jack rabbit broke from the cover of a greasewood bush, and Will tried to shoot it with his Colt but missed. It was as big as a dog, and, when Will's big pistol went off, the jack bolted behind a clump of sagebrush and was out of sight before Will could pull the trigger a second time.

"I could almost taste that rabbit roasted on a stick," Will said in a forlorn voice.

"Did you really think you'd hit it with that big iron?" Cole wondered.

They stopped at noon for a lunch of hardtack and beef jerky and canteen water and gave the horses a blow. Off to the west, they could still see the Blue Mountains, only now their peaks were obscured by a bank of clouds so gray and heavy you could almost smell the snow in them.

"It's damn' well gonna come a storm," Will declared. "I can feel it in my feet."

"How does a man know from his feet whether it's going to snow or not?" Cole asked, enjoying a cigarette.

"You remember Gettysburg, don't you?"

"It would be hard to forget."

"Got both my feet broke when a caisson rolled over 'em trying to get to the top of Little Round Top. Hurt like hell. Hadn't been for my feet getting broken, though, I might have been killed . . . 'most everybody I knew got killed that day. My feet got broke by that caisson and I lay in the grass a long time. Never did make it up Little Round Top. So I guess, in a way, it was lucky my feet got broken . . . except now, whenever it's going to come a storm, they ache like blue blazes."

"We all got hurt in that war, one way or another."

"Don't I know it." Will moaned as he pulled off his boots and began rubbing his feet. "I sure wish I'd've been far-sighted enough to have bought an extra bottle of mash in Laramie. I could use a little taste of medicine on account of these feet of mine."

"I would think maybe you had put enough medicine in you last night that your feet wouldn't be troubling you for at least a week or two. I doubt if Wes Hardin *had* shot you last night, that you would have even felt the bullet."

Will stopped rubbing his feet long enough to give Cole the eye. "Well, getting shot by Wes Hardin couldn't have hurt much more than these feet of mine are hurting me now." He grinned at John Henry as he rubbed his feet. "Unless you've had your feet run over by something as heavy as a caisson, you can't begin to know what it feels like."

"I wish I had a drink to give you, Will. Hell, I almost wish I had one for myself."

"Everything was going along smooth for me

until I ran into you back at Cheyenne," he grumbled. "Ever since that unlucky day, it's been one setback after another. And now my feet are aching."

"Well, I'm sorry about your sore feet, Will. But running into me doesn't have anything to do with your suffering."

Will pulled his boots back on with much agony, then hobbled to his horse and rode off at a quick pace like he was trying to outrun the pain in his feet. Or, maybe it was just Cole's company.

They followed the double set of tracks the rest of the afternoon, Will complaining every so often about how bad the pain in his feet was and saying how it was going to snow sometime soon. The gray sky seemed to lower itself just over their heads and the wind tried to push its way up under their coats and to steal their hats.

Every passing hour, the sky grew darker and settled in all around them so that by late afternoon they not only could reach up and touch it, they were riding in it. It was cold traveling and uneventful until they saw a man sitting on the carcass of a dead mule that was still harnessed to a bright blue-and-yellow wagon.

The man looked up as they approached. "How do," he said. His clothes were dusty, especially the knees of his pants. He wore a claw-hammer coat with satin trim and a battered plug hat that was tied on by a long wool scarf.

"What are you doing sitting on a dead mule out here in the middle of nowhere?" Will asked.

"Waiting for someone to come along, sir," the man replied.

"Well, that's plain enough a blind man could see," Will said. "But that wasn't quite my point."

The man brushed the dirt off the knees of his pants, then stood. "I'm Bart Bledsoe," he said, then touched the brim of his hat in a formal and gentlemanly way. "I sell patent medicines, as you can plainly see by my wagon."

Written on the side of the wagon in large black letters were the words:

BLEDSOE'S PATENT
MEDICINES & BITTERS,
BART BLEDSOE, PROP.
CERTIFIED PHRENOLOGIST—DENVER

"What's that last part mean?" Will asked. "That freenologist?"

"In quite simple terms it means, sir, that I am practiced in the science of reading the bumps on a person's head in order to determine his character."

"Reading the bumps on a person's head?" Will repeated.

"That is correct, sir."

Will turned and looked at Cole. "Well, I guess I ain't seen everything like I thought I had."

"I guess not," Cole said.

"That still don't explain you sitting out here in

the middle of nowhere on a dead mule," Will said. "Even if you can read a person's head bumps."

"I had the misfortune of buying a colicky mule in Laramie yesterday," Bledsoe explained. "My previous beast came up lame and I traded him, along with ten gold dollars, for this colicky mule. I also had to throw in two bottles of my patent medicine which will cure everything known to man . . . but, alas, not to mules, at least not to mules that are colicky."

"Well maybe you should invent a patent medicine that would help a colicky mule," Will suggested. "Then you wouldn't be in such a poor situation as you are now."

"Believe me," Bledsoe said, "I couldn't agree with you more."

"Say, you didn't see a big black cuss riding by with a little bitty colored girl with him, did you?" Will asked.

"No, sir, I did not see such a man."

"Oh," Will said, the disappointment plain in his voice.

"But," Bledsoe added, "there were one or two riders that went by here late last night. Unfortunately they did not bother to stop. They seemed in quite a hurry, judging by the sounds of how fast their horses were running. It might have been the party you are looking for."

"Well, maybe so," Will said. "But if it was

them, it is lucky for you that they didn't stop, or you might be just as dead as your mule."

Bledsoe swallowed hard and his eyes got a little buggy. "Surely you can't be serious."

"I'm as serious as a tax collector," Will said, then added: "Say, does that patent medicine of yours cure feet pain?"

It took Bledsoe a few seconds to find his voice. "I . . . believe I should have something in my wagon that will relieve the discomfort of painful limbs."

Will pulled out his watch and looked at it. "It is just about suppertime," he said to Cole. "Maybe we ought to just make camp here and get an early start."

Cole didn't quarrel with the decision. If Will was right about a storm coming and they pushed on past dark and got caught out in it, they would probably end up lost. Cole took care of the horses this time while Will and Bart Bledsoe scouted around in Bledsoe's wagon for the right pain remedy.

"This ought to do," Bledsoe said, handing Will an amber bottle with a cork stopper. Will held it out at arm's length and read the label before taking a taste.

Will licked his lips and said: "It's a bit bitey, but it warms you."

Bart Bledsoe said: "Give it a chance to work. I think you'll see that taste isn't everything."

Will plopped himself down on his saddle and

pulled off his boots and wrapped his feet in one of his blankets while Cole built a fire.

"How did you come by your affliction, sir?" Bledsoe asked him.

Will explained how his feet had been run over during the battle of Gettysburg and how they'd troubled him on and off ever since. "Whenever there's going to come a big storm, or any change in the weather, that's when they start barking. Like now. If my feet ain't failed me, it's one hell of a storm on the way. Ought to hit us anytime."

Bart Bledsoe looked all around him, in every direction. It was cold and dark and getting more so by the minute. "I would admit," he said, "that the conditions do seem ripe for some sort of change in the weather. A little snow perhaps, but I see nothing to indicate a storm."

"You will," Will said. "A big one, too."

Will continued to work on the bottle of bitters that Bledsoe had given him while Cole unpacked the mule and brought to the fire enough supplies for supper.

"May I contribute something to the repast?" Bledsoe asked when he saw Cole slicing bacon into the black frying pan.

Will looked at him from across the fire. "Repast?"

"I've a fruit cake in the wagon . . . a gift from a woman I know back in Duluth."

"Fruit cake!" Will tipped the bottle up, then brought it down again. "Well, hell, I ain't et a fruit cake in twenty years . . . bring her out. And I'll make us a pan of biscuits if someone will fetch my Dutch oven outta my pack."

"What do you think?" Will asked when Bledsoe went into the wagon to get his fruit cake.

"About what?"

"Him!"

"What about him?"

"You really think he can read a person's head bumps?"

"I've heard tell there are people who can." Cole didn't know what was in the medicine bottle Will was sampling, but it seemed to be doing the job on him, judging by the unsteady look in his eyes and the happy look on his face. "That helping your feet?"

Will looked down at the outlines of his feet beneath the blanket. "Don't hardly feel them. Come to think of it, I don't hardly feel my legs, either." Then he snorted a laugh and held up the bottle. "Damn' stuff makes you feel good, John Henry. You ought to try a little."

"Not tonight, Will. One of us should probably stay on the alert."

"You think Book will double back and try to kill us in our sleep?" Will asked without the least bit of concern.

"Anything's possible," Cole replied, not feeling quite as confident as Will about the matter. But then Cole wasn't tossing down whatever balm was in that bottle. "To tell the truth, Will, it's a possibility that Book could double back on us."

"Who might kill us in our sleep?" Bart Bledsoe interjected, walking into the light of the fire carrying a gaily decorated cake tin and a can of peaches.

"You don't have to worry there, Mister Bledsoe," Will said. "I ain't gonna allow nothing to happen to you and these wonderful patent medicines of yours. You got another bottle of this? It's working miracles on my sore feet."

Bledsoe looked at Cole with owl-like eyes. He had an unusually large head for such a small man. "Not to worry," Cole said. "There's not much chance anyone's going to come and kill us in our sleep, especially if there's a big storm brewing out there."

Bledsoe looked uncertain.

"And after you get me another bottle of medicine, Mister Bledsoe," Will said, "maybe you could read my head bumps."

By the time they had finished eating, they could almost feel the storm without actually seeing it, as if it were waiting just at the edge of their camp, just beyond the firelight. The night sky had a blood red quality to it.

Will forewent eating very much supper, choosing instead to concentrate on the small amber bottle Bledsoe had given him. "It makes me feel sorta like I'm floating," he said.

"What'd you put in that medicine bottle?" Cole asked Bledsoe.

Bledsoe offered him a weak smile. "I always mash in one or two opium pills. The rest of the formula is a secret." The opium pills explained Will's happy mood.

"You reckon you are ready to read the bumps on my head?" Will asked. "My feet are feeling much better and I feel like having my head bumps read."

"Certainly, sir," Bart Bledsoe said.

"What'll I have to do?" Will asked.

"Simply remove your hat, close your eyes, and be very relaxed."

"Oh, I'm real relaxed," Will said. "Thanks to this wonderful curative of yours."

Will closed his eyes while Bart Bledsoe felt around his head. Bledsoe's bony fingers searched and felt their way through the dark tangles of Will's long, uncombed hair. Cole rolled himself a cigarette and watched the show while he kept an ear toward the night.

"Ah . . . here at the occipital area, I can feel a ridge that indicates you are a man of truthful character," Bledsoe said after a few minutes of probing around in Will's hair. "And this bump here at the parietal region speaks of a man who is highly determined." Will looked pleased with the interpretation while Bledsoe continued his search for more bumps. "And these, here in the frontal portions," Bledsoe continued, his eyes closed, his chin lifted, "these show a man who . . . who . . ." Bledsoe lost his voice again.

"Who what?" Will asked, opening his eyes, wanting to know exactly what it was Bledsoe had discovered in the nest of his hair.

"These bumps . . . show a man much given to a violent nature . . . I'm afraid. . . ."

"Oh," Will said, settling down once more. "I thought you were going to tell me my bumps said I was clever, or something like that."

"Clever?" Bart Bledsoe said.

"It's not what you think it means, Mister Bledsoe," Cole said, enjoying his cigarette and the bump-reading display.

"It's something a dang' jolly whore called me," Will said, sipping from the patent medicine bottle. "Of course, what does a jolly whore know about anything?"

"Indeed," Bledsoe said.

Then, it started to snow, just as Will had predicted.

"Look at the size of those flakes!" Bledsoe cried. "They are nearly as big as fancy belt buckles."

"I told you it was going to snow big," Will said, closing his eyes and letting the snowflakes collect on his face.

"Well, what if we are snowed in come the morning?" Bart Bledsoe asked. "What will we do then?"

"Seeing as how your mule is dead," Will said, "I don't know why you're so worried about being snowed in. That dead mule of yours sure ain't going to take you anywhere whether it snows or not."

Bledsoe swallowed like he had an apple stuck in his throat.

"Don't worry about it, Mister Bledsoe," Cole offered. "Tomorrow, we'll hitch up one of the horses to your wagon and escort you into the next town so that you can buy yourself another mule."

"Only this time," Will said, his face nearly covered under the big snowflakes, "don't buy a mule that's colicky."

CHAPTER ELEVEN

Sometime during the night John Henry Cole dreamed of bayous and Spanish moss hanging from cypress trees and the blackened smoke of burning plantations. He dreamed of dead horses still in their traces, lying bloated along the road, their legs stiff, their bodies black with rot. And marching along the road were long columns of men in dusty blue tunics, heading straight into the blaze of a setting sun like they were marching to their final fiery death. But something troubled him awake, something that seemed to go right through his flesh and gnaw on his bones. He opened his eyes and saw by morning's light that he was surrounded by a world of white. In spite of his blankets, his teeth were chattering. The snow that had begun the evening before had continued throughout the night and by now Bledsoe's dead mule was buried except for one ear sticking up. The air felt so cold, Cole thought, if someone fired a pistol, it would shatter.

Will and Cole had been smart enough to move their bedrolls under the medicine wagon before going to sleep the previous night. It was lucky they had or they might have been as buried as Bledsoe's mule.

Will stirred from his sleep about the same time Cole did. He sat up and nearly hit his head on the bottom of the wagon as he did. Instead, he caved in the crown of his hat. He removed it and looked at it before punching it up again and settling it back on his head. He blew breath into his hands as he surveyed the wintery scene.

"Well, it is a good thing we stayed here last night and didn't keep going . . . else, we'd be out there somewhere under all this snow, maybe fallen down in some arroyo with our legs broke."

"We'll play hell picking up Book's trail now," Cole said, feeling like his bones were broken as he tried to climb out from under the wagon.

"Maybe that murdering devil himself is laying at the bottom of some arroyo," Will said. "Who's to say he could find his way any better in a snowstorm than we could?"

"Well, maybe the storm will have at least slowed him down," Cole said.

They could hear Bart Bledsoe moving around in his wagon above them.

"I wonder if Bledsoe has any more of that foot medicine," Will said. "Only it ain't my feet that hurt as much now as it is my head. Them bitters's got a kick to them."

Cole was trying hard to get his parts in working order when he noticed what was wrong. "Will, our horses are gone."

"What!"

They swept away the snowdrifts surrounding the wagon and climbed out into the sharp glare of sun coming off the snow.

"Maybe they laid down to go to sleep and got covered up," Will suggested, but they both knew that wasn't the case.

They saw a line of shallow depressions leading toward the Blue Mountains.

"Well, at least we know they didn't run off of their own accord," Cole said after a quick study of the tracks. The tracks had nearly been covered up with snow, but there was still the slight cupping of footprints alongside those of the horses leading off in single file.

"Indians must have come and stole them!" Will said.

"Possibly."

"I don't know who else but an Indian would

129

come out in a blizzard and steal horses," Will stated. "Indians love to steal horses more than they love to hunt or screw their women."

"Does it really matter whether it was Indians or not?" Cole asked.

"No, I guess it don't," Will replied glumly.

Bart Bledsoe appeared from inside his wagon; he had a long woolen scarf wrapped around his neck and was wearing heavy mittens on his hands.

"My, oh, my," he declared, looking at all the snow. "You were right, Mister Harper, about the storm being a big one."

"Our horses have been stolen!" Will announced.

"Stolen!" Bledsoe yelped. "But how can that be?"

"They just come in the middle of the night and stole 'em, is how," Will declared.

"Who would come during a snowstorm and steal your horses?" Bledsoe asked.

"Indians, most likely," Will said. "They went off toward those Blue Mountains." He pointed toward the jagged line of peaks in the far distance with his grizzled chin.

"Well, what will we do now without any horses?" Bledsoe said, stamping his feet and slapping warmth into his hands.

"We'll have to go after 'em," Will said.

Bart Bledsoe stared hard at the white emptiness but did not see either the horses or whoever had taken them. "But how will you go after them with your sore feet, Mister Harper?" he asked, his voice filling with distress as he stood with his gaze fixed on the vast open horizon.

"My feet are only half sore," Will replied. "It's my dang' head that hurts."

"You stay, I'll go," Cole said.

"I'll go, too," Will said.

"With your bad feet, you'd only slow me down, Will. Stay here in camp with Mister Bledsoe."

Will looked unpleasant about it, but he and Cole both knew that, if Harper went along, they would never stand a chance of catching up with whomever had taken their horses. "You don't catch up with them by tomorrow noon," Will advised, "it means they got too good a jump on us . . . you might just as well turn around and come back."

At least the thieves hadn't stolen their supplies along with the horses and mule. Cole made himself a small pack of food and took both canteens of water. Then he took one of the coals from last night's fire and smudged his cheeks under his eyes to cut down the glare of the snow. Finally he made sure he had enough loads for his self-cocker.

"Ain't you taking that big Winchester?" Will asked.

"Too heavy to carry if I'm going to travel fast."

"Well, what if you get a chance to shoot them thieving sons-a-bitches?"

"I'll just have to shoot them with my self-cocker, Will. I don't suppose it will matter all that much to them what they get shot with if I have to shoot them."

"Well, shoot 'em even if you *don't* have to for putting us through all this inconvenience," Will growled.

Cole was already walking away from camp, following the shallow depressions in the snow. Once he got out of sight of the camp, the land seemed as lonely as any he'd ever been in. It struck him that a man could die out in this great emptiness and no one might ever know it; a man could die and his bones could turn to dust and be carried away by the wind and that would simply be the end of his existence. The sad truth of the matter was plenty of men had died just that way.

He walked all that day with the great silence broken only by the crunching of his boots upon the snow and the sound of his labored breath. His mustaches turned to ice, but the rest of him stayed warm because of the pace he'd set. His one advantage over whoever had stolen the horses could be that they might not consider the possibility that anyone would follow them on foot through the deep snow, and therefore might not be in any great hurry. It was about all the hope he had, that and the fact that most of the criminals he'd ever dealt with were not very smart to begin with.

Cole rested for only a few minutes at a time, long enough to catch his breath, sip some water, and have a smoke. He was counting on the horse thieves taking a lot of long rests. Once or twice, he had to force himself back to his feet again. Trudging through the deep snow took a lot more energy than he was used to. There hadn't been much of his life he could recall not doing his work from the back of a horse. All day he forced himself to keep going, following that single line of tracks toward the Blue Mountains. Gradually the tracks started to become a little fresher.

By late in the day he decided to take a prolonged rest. The sun was beginning to set just over the mountains, casting long shadows of distant pines across the snow. He rested near a meandering tributary that cut through the snow like a wet black snake. He refilled the canteens and boiled a little water for coffee. At least the wind wasn't blowing like it normally did in that country and that made his rest a little easier. He rolled a cigarette and smoked it while having his coffee. It made him wish he was back in Shorty's Diner in Cheyenne, having a slice of pie to go along with his coffee before setting out to visit Ella Mims. He'd been thinking about Ella Mims a lot more than he'd planned on. Maybe it was squatting there all alone in a valley of snow with the Blue Mountains off in the distance and the unending silence pressing in on him that caused him to think of Ella again. Hadn't Wayback Cotton said that one thing about the Big Lonely was that it made a man think about women—the ones he'd known, and the ones he wished he'd known?

Cole closed his eyes against the ache of tired burning muscles. He felt as exhausted as he'd ever been and it was tempting to shallow a place in the snow and just let sleep take over. When he had closed his eyes against the sting of sun glare and when he did it now, white flashes of light burst inside his skull and his arms and legs throbbed with the pain of a thousand needles. He snorted at the thought, but it felt like he had been carrying a horse across his back all day, tired as he felt.

With one great effort, he managed to get back to his feet. The sun had by now gone behind the mountains and a moon as round as a fancy silver buckle had risen in the deepening blue of the sky. In another hour there would be enough moonlight reflecting off the snow so that following the tracks wouldn't be a problem. If he was right, and the horse thieves didn't believe they were being followed, they would be in camp somewhere not far ahead of him. If he was wrong—well, he didn't want to think about if he was wrong.

Cole stopped only long enough to catch his breath, and then would move on again. The thought of catching the horse thieves was all he needed to keep putting one foot in front of the other every time he thought about quitting, that and the thought of maybe someday riding to Nebraska to see Ella Mims again.

After what seemed forever, dawn finally broke behind him over the eastern horizon—a red ball of shimmering sun balanced atop the glaze of icy earth. He stopped just long enough to watch it. It gave him a good feeling, seeing the sun come up again. He moved on.

Finally he reached a point where his legs felt too heavy to take another step. He rested against the base of a bluff and leaned his back against the incline. The fiery pain shot through his legs and into his groin. He caught his breath and tried rubbing life back into his legs and thought of Will and the way he'd tried to rub the pain out of his feet. With the sunrise came a wind that began to blow stiffly, kicking up snow dust. He was somewhat protected by the bluff as he rested, trying to feel the sun's warmth on his face and hands. It wasn't much comfort, but it was some. He remembered Will warning that, if he didn't catch the thieves by noon this day, he should give up and turn back. The question that nagged him now was whether or not he had enough left to make it back to the camp. He didn't know how far he'd traveled in the last twenty-four hours, but, considering the pace he'd set, it was a greater distance than what he wanted to think about doing again on foot.

He rolled himself a shuck with the last of his makings and took his time smoking it, enjoying the moment. He didn't know if he'd have that many more moments in his life to enjoy. Being afoot on the frontier, he was at the mercy of just about anyone on a horse, including renegades and road agents. It had been foolish of him not to have carried more firepower. In fact, the thought of carrying that big Winchester rifle didn't seem like such a burden to him now.

He finished the cigarette and forced himself up the slick rise to the top of the bluff. That was when he saw it. Down below sat a small, weathered cabin with a tin roof that shone dully under the morning light. A crooked stovepipe spewed black smoke. But the thing that really drew his attention was the six horses and one mule bunched together in the corral twenty feet from the cabin. You'd have to have been blind not to spot the speckled bird among the bunch.

He dropped to the ground, hoping no one inside the cabin had spotted him. There was no way of knowing how many were inside the cabin. Between the bluff and the cabin, there was just a lot of open ground. Cole thought for a moment about taking his chances trying to cross that coverless patch of ground, but if someone were sitting in the window of the cabin, he'd be a dead man before he made it halfway. He eased himself back below the brow of the bluff and settled in. He thought about what Will had said regarding the patience of Apaches. If he wanted to steal back their livestock, he'd have to wait until dark to do it.

CHAPTER TWELVE

There is nothing so slow as time, when you're just waiting for it to pass. Every few minutes, Cole would make his way back to the top of the bluff and check for signs of activity down in the cabin. He remembered the book that Lydia Winslow had given him. He'd carried it in an inside pocket of his coat, thinking that someday he'd find time to read it. Now it looked like that day had come. It had a soft leather cover and the paper was of good stock, the print on the fly leaf fancy. It felt good just to hold it in his hands, feel its weight, know that he didn't have to spend the day just staring at the sky or over the top of the windswept bluff. *Don Quixote.* He wondered if *Señor* Quixote was anything like Francisco Guzman, the Mexican bandit he'd shot in Del Rio. He'd been friends with Francisco Guzman up until the evening Guzman became insanely jealous over the affections of a sloe-eyed Mexican whore they both had taken an interest in. It wasn't one of the proudest things he'd ever done in his life—shooting Francisco Guzman. But Francisco had been a man with a wild lust and an impatient heart, and sooner or later someone was going to kill him. It just happened to be John Henry Cole. It was too late now to think about that. The pages were thin, the print small.

In a village of La Mancha, the name of which I have no desire to recall, there lived not so long ago one of those gentlemen who always have a lance in the rack, an ancient buckler, a skinny nag, and a greyhound runner.

Every now and then, Cole stopped reading long enough to take a peek over the top of the bluff. The sun rose higher in the sky and started to bring with it some real warmth. Along toward noon, the only thing that kept it from being a pleasant day for him was a cup of coffee and a shuck to go with it, that and nailing those horse thieves down in the cabin.

It was when he heard a door open and close on a set of rusty hinges that he put the book away and looked again over the top of the bluff. He couldn't tell if it was a man or a woman bundled up in heavy clothes carrying a water bucket. He watched as the figure went to a rain barrel at the side of the cabin, shattered the plate of ice formed atop the barrel, and filled the bucket. Then he watched as the person carried the bucket of rain water back inside the cabin. A few minutes later, unmistakably a man came out and raced for the nearby privy. Seconds after that, another man and a boy came out of the cabin and walked to the corral. From where Cole was kneeling, they didn't look so much like horse thieves as they did a family of poor squatters.

A few minutes passed while the man and the boy pitched some apples from a bucket over the fence to the horses. The speckled bird was the first one to get in line for the eats, pushing and biting her way to the front.

"Lookit that ugly mare, Pa!" the boy shouted. "She the one tried to bite One-Eye on his arse?"

The man laughed. "Yeah, Son, she nearly did, too. Your Uncle One-Eye jumped three feet high off the ground."

The man came out of the privy, pulling up his galluses, and casually strolled over to the corral.

"Teeter asked me if that scratchy mare was the one nearly bit your arse clean off," the man with the boy said. He wore a floppy-brim hat that fell halfway over his eyes.

"Damn' near put a bullet in her ugly hammer head," the man with the galluses said.

"I wonder, does she like eatin' them winter apples as much as she does humans?" the man with the big hat said with a broad grin.

The boy laughed and scratched his haunches. The man with the galluses didn't seem to share in their humor.

A woman came to the door of the cabin and shouted: "Biscuits are ready, come eat!"

Two men, a boy, and a woman. It made Cole's decision easier. When he kicked open the door and pointed the self-cocker at the men, the woman said: "Henry, we got company."

"Mister, you come to rob us, you rode a long way for nothin'," said the man the woman called Henry. He was still wearing his flop-brimmed hat and Cole could only see some of his eyes as he tilted his head back.

"Please don't shoot my pa, mister!" the boy cried. His face was peppered with freckles and his front teeth were crooked.

The other man sat there with his palms atop the table, his head half turned as though he was afraid to look at Cole directly but was still curious to see who had come to rob him. The woman was moon-faced; her hair was pulled straight back and tied in a bun so tight it looked like it had to hurt. She had small nervous eyes that looked at Cole.

"Henry's serious as the plague," she said. "We ain't got a chamber pot or hardly a window to throw it out of. Can't you see that?"

"I didn't come here to rob anybody," Cole said. "I came for that speckled horse out in your corral, and the others you stole."

The other man, the one wearing his galluses down, shifted his gaze fully in Cole's direction. His left eye turned inward toward his nose. " 'Fraid not, mister. Didn't steal them animals, bought 'em."

Cole looked at the woman, then at the two men. "Like she said, don't look like you have a pot. I'd be curious as to how you bought a pair of good horses and a sound pack mule."

"Bought 'em for a jug of likker, a sack full of corn dodgers, and a pair of blankets. That's how," the man with the bad eye said.

"I walked a long way to get those animals back," Cole said. "Lies are the last thing I want to hear right now."

"He's tellin' you the truth," the woman said. "Christ if he ain't."

"Stealing horses is a hanging offense," Cole said. "I was to hang you boys, wouldn't anyone blame me."

"Well, you can hang One-Eye there," the woman said. "He ain't much good fer nothin', 'cept eatin' and layin' around sippin' likker. So him, I don't mind so much you hangin' . . . though he didn't steal them horses or that mule, neither."

"Shut yer trap, Sis!" the man with the galluses and bad eye cawed.

"Henry," she continued, ignoring her brother, "me and him's wed. You was to hang him, you'd be leavin' me a widow, and this young 'un an orphan. I won't sit here an' swear to you he ain't never done nothin' wrong in his day, but he's tellin' the truth about tradin' dodgers and blankets fer them animals."

Cole's gaze switched to the boy.

He nodded, swallowed hard. "Swear to God, mister."

"Renegades," Cole said. "Is that what they were . . . the ones who traded horses for a meal of

141

corn dodgers and whiskey and a pair of blankets?"

The man wearing the hat shook his head, causing the brim to flap up and down. "Wan't no Injuns. It was a big black cuss and a little scrawny colored gal. Come through late last evenin', leadin' them horses and that mule. Said he'd trade 'em fer somethin' to drink and somethin' to eat and somethin' to keep warm with. I looked at those horses and said to myself . . . 'This ol' boy's either crazy or desperate.' Hell, I seen me a deal and took it. Wouldn't you?"

"If I hang you from that tree out yonder," Cole said, "I guess it might not be as good a deal as you figured on."

"I guess not," the man said, then swallowed.

The woman said: "Ain't I always said little comes of little, Henry?"

"Yes you have, Minnie. But I thought this was one of those times when some good fortune had fell my way."

She crossed her arms and stared at him.

Cole looked at the man with the bad eye. "You want to go out and tie a rope around those horses and that mule and bring them around?"

He shifted his weight in the chair.

"I'm still thinking about hanging you," Cole said. "Hanging you wouldn't leave this woman a widow nor that boy an orphan, but it might just make me feel better for the long walk I've had."

He pushed himself away from the table, gave

the woman a hard look. Then he stood and pulled up his galluses with a hard snap over each shoulder, and went outside.

"You want somethin' to eat, mister?" the woman asked. "You look gant."

Cole shoved the self-cocker back into the cross-draw holster he wore on his left hip, and sat down. "Some of those corn dodgers and that ham and maybe a little of that coffee," he said. She gave her man a look and he gave her one back that told her to go ahead and fix a plate. Cole kept his eyes on the man and the boy until she brought him the food.

"Got no sugar fer yer coffee," she said. "Sugar costs money."

"I can do without sugar in my coffee," Cole said, trying hard not to cram the food into his mouth all at once. The ham was salty and the dodgers hard and the coffee hot and tasteless, but it was one of the best meals he'd eaten in a while and it kept his spirit from departing to the hereafter.

By the time he'd finished the coffee, Bad-Eye stepped back into the cabin. His face was red from the raw wind, and no doubt the effort of trying to put a rope around the speckled bird while at the same time trying to keep her from taking a bite out of him.

"Your hosses is ready," he said unhappily as he walked over and stood in front of the cook stove and rubbed the palms of his hands together.

"Did that mare try and bite you on the arse again, One-Eye?" the man wearing the hat said, trying hard to keep any sign of a smile off his face.

The man, One-Eye, never took his bad eye from Cole. "Don't know why anybody'd want to steal that ill-tempered ol' cayuse anyhow," he grumbled. "An' don't know why a man'd walk all the way out here in the tules to get her back, neither."

"There's just some things that can't be explained," Cole said. "Which way did the colored man and the girl go when they left here?"

"Couldn't say," the man wearing the hat said.

"Why not?"

"It was dark."

"It wasn't that dark, besides, there was a moon out. Moon on snow," Cole said. "Easy for a man to see which way the man and girl were headed."

"They went south, mister," the woman said, chewing a piece of ham. "Henry and One-Eye feels like it's a wrong thing to do, give up a man that's on the dodge. But not me. I don't want no horse thieves or cut-throats hangin' around here nohow. They went south."

Cole started to leave.

"That buck," Henry said. "He wan't no common thief. Treated that gal special, took good care of her. Christ, his hands was bleeding from the cold. I guess, if he wanted to, he could've raised all sorts of hell 'round here. But he didn't. He just took them corn dodgers and that jug and blankets

144

and thanked us for 'em and went on his way."

"Well, that makes me feel a whole lot better," Cole returned. "The fact that he stole my horse and traded it for some damn' corn dodgers."

The boy rolled his eyes and giggled and the woman tossed him a hard look.

"What's south of here?" Cole asked.

The woman's husband spat and said: "Cañons, rocks, and one little ol' town called Buffalo Tongue. It ain't much, but it's got a whore stands over six feet tall and a one-eyed lawman named Moses Boss. The thing they say about going to Buffalo Tongue is, if one don't get you, the other will."

"Have a good day," Cole said. "And next time you think fortune has smiled on you, ask for sale papers. It might save you from getting hanged."

"I'll do it," the woman said, "even if Henry and One-Eye is too lazy to ask."

One-Eye kept his bad eye on Cole while he put his foot in the stirrup and swung aboard the speckled bird.

"That's one bad-blooded hoss, mister. Someday you might regret having walked all this way just to get her back."

Cole turned the bird's head without bothering to look back. He figured with the way the mare could eat up ground, he'd be back in camp before midnight. It felt good not to have to walk, not to have to face the prospect of it. The thing that bothered him, though, was just how easily Leviticus Book had come into camp and stolen their animals. He could just as easily have slit their throats or fired a bullet into their brains. The question was: why hadn't he?

CHAPTER THIRTEEN

"Well, I see you found my horse and mule," Will Harper said as John Henry Cole rode into camp. "But why'd you have to bring that snapping turtle you call a horse back with you? Couldn't you've swapped her for something that was better natured?"

Cole ignored Will's comments and went directly to the fire and poured himself some coffee. "You have any tobacco?" he asked.

When Will proffered his makings, Cole rolled a cigarette and said: "You'll never guess who stole our horses."

"Who?"

"Book."

Will looked like he'd been hit between the eyes. "That's one bodacious son-of-a-bitch, then!"

"I don't know if we're chasing him, or he's chasing us . . . but I do know I'm getting tired of playing these games with him." The coffee tasted dark and bitter like it had been brewing over the fire for a long time.

Bart Bledsoe walked into the light of the campfire.

"Here," he said, handing Cole a plate of beans and a large roasted turkey leg. "Mister Harper shot a wild turkey this afternoon. I'm not much of a cook, but I did the best I could."

"Book's got at least a two day jump on us," Will said. Then, shifting his gaze to the surrounding darkness: "Unless he happens to be sitting out there right now watching us, that is. You think maybe he could be out there somewheres, John Henry?"

"Well if he's not, I know where he might be headed," Cole said. "This is wonderful turkey, Mister Bledsoe."

"Thank you, sir. I did the best I could under these crude conditions."

"Where's he headed?" Will asked.

"South, and the nearest town that direction is a place called Buffalo Tongue. I figure from the condition he and the girl are reported to be in, they'll have to stop there and get resupplied."

"We'll be slowed down if we have to hitch up the horses to Bledsoe's wagon," Will said.

"Will." The look on Bart Bledsoe's face said it all.

"I know, we can't just leave him here," Will said.

Bledsoe looked relieved.

"We can start tonight," Cole said.

The speckled bird was not too happy about being hitched to the wagon and she tried to bite Will and Cole several times in the process of putting the harness on her. But she had to learn that, if she were going to remain Cole's horse, she'd do what he asked of her. And once hitched, she got along just fine.

They rode throughout the night. Cole snatched a few hours' rest in the back of the wagon, while Will and Bledsoe rode up front. It was the first real sleep he'd had in the last thirty-six hours, and even at that it was a fitful sleep, full of dreams that made little sense. In one dream, he dreamed of Francisco Guzman. In the dream, Francisco and Ella Mims were riding a white horse across a shallow river while Cole stood on shore and watched. The water splashed up around them like handfuls of diamonds tossed against the sun while Francisco grinned through his dark mustaches and Ella clung to him tightly. It gave Cole a sad feeling, like he was losing both of them and would never see them again. He awoke feeling sad, lying in the back of the wagon alone like that.

They reached Buffalo Tongue late in the afternoon of the following day. It was a squalid collection of log huts and whiskey tents grown up on either side of a wide muddy street. Judging by the size, there were maybe three or four hundred souls living in Buffalo Tongue. Why they stayed was another question.

It didn't take them long to see or smell how the town had come by its name. Just as they rode up to the first set of buildings, there was a twenty-foot-high mound of buffalo bones: skulls, ribs, and leg bones large enough to cover an entire city lot.

"My word," Bart Bledsoe said. "It looks as though every one of the great beasts that ever roamed the plains has ended up here."

"What in the hell would they want to collect buffalo bones for?" Will asked.

Cole had noticed a railroad spur line running just north of the pile of bones. "No doubt a shipping point."

Bledsoe was looking hopeful as they pulled into the heart of the town itself. "I see a great opportunity here for my patent medicines," he said. "I have been in outposts such as this before. There hardly ever is a physician or an infirmary to be had. The poor residents are suffering from just about every sort of illness and malady. Dropsy, female problems, memory loss, stuttering, melancholy, unwanted hair, and digestive interference, just to name the more common ills. Yes, indeed. I should be able to sell enough medicines and bitters here to buy myself a new mule and perhaps even a suit of clothes." The little man was alive with excitement over his prospects.

"I wish you well, Doc," Will said. "This place looks like it could use all the patent medicines you got and then some. Your medicines might be the only thing that could save a place like this. That, or be burned plum to the ground."

"Let's look up the local law," Cole suggested. "If Book and Jilly Sweet did pass through here, maybe the law would know about it."

They stopped a fat woman with a fat youngster in tow and asked her if she knew where the city marshal's office was.

"Try looking in the beds of harlots or in the bottom of the nearest whiskey bottle," she said, her voice full of scorn. "That is where you will most likely find Marshal Boss." Then she stamped away, pulling the youngster behind her as she went.

"Well, that is sure some clue," Will grumbled. "I'm ready for a drink of liquor myself."

"Why don't you see if you can find a livery, Mister Bledsoe," Cole suggested to Bart, "and see if they have a healthy mule to sell you. I'll swing by later and unhitch the speckled bird."

"Thank you, gentlemen, for your kindness in bringing me out of the wilderness. Who knows what may have become of me if the two of you had not come along."

"Just make sure before you buy another mule," Will said, "that he ain't colicky, or you might end up stranded again and not be so lucky that two fine gents like me and John Henry will come along and save you."

"I will, sir. Indeed, I will."

The two went inside the nearest saloon and straight to the bar. Will ordered whiskey; Cole settled for a glass of beer. "Where's your city marshal?" Will asked the barman.

"Boss?" the man said.

"That what you call him, boss?" Will asked.

"His name's Boss," the man said.

"Well then, where's Boss?"

"Don't know, not right this minute I don't," the man said.

"Where's he usually?" Cole asked.

"Usually he's either gambling or spending his time with Miss Pearl Mae."

"Miss Pearl Mae?" Will said, pricking up his ears. Women and whiskey always made Will's ears prick up at the mention of them.

The barman nodded; he had a large nose, fat on the end, full of black pores. "Yes, sir, gents. Pearl Mae, tallest whore west of the Mississippi."

"How would you know she's the tallest whore?" Will asked. "You met all the whores west of the Mississippi?"

"No, but I've met Miss Pearl Mae and she's taller than any whore I ever seen," the barman argued. "She's taller than most men I ever seen. Except for Broke Toe Bob."

"Who's Broke Toe Bob?"

"Man I knew back in Blue Lick, Kentucky."

"Oh," said Will as though that were enough to

satisfy his curiosity. Then tapping his glass atop the bar, he said: "Give us another." And when the barman poured him out two more fingers' worth of whiskey, Will looked him straight in the eyes and said: "I'll bet there's at least one whore west of the Mississippi that is taller than the one you got here in this town."

"I'd like to see her if there was," the barman said.

"Look," Cole put in before Will and the barman could get into a full-blown argument about the tallest whore in the West, "we want to find this Marshal Boss and talk to him. And if he is with this Pearl Mae, we want to find her. Can you tell us where she does her business from?"

The man said: "Sure. Back on Revelation Alley. Go out the door, turn down Laredo Street, cross the spur line, and you're there . . . Revelation Alley. Can't miss it because the air smells like perfume."

"Which place is hers?"

"First red light you come to," the barman said.

"Let's go, Will."

"What's that awful stink?" Will said, once they stepped back outside.

"Hides," Cole said. "Buffalo hides. I saw them right after I saw the pile of bones. This must be a northern terminus to ship the hides from. Did you notice that rail spur?"

"That's what I thought it was," Will said,

wrinkling his nose. "Nothing stinks worse than a pile of buffalo hides, unless it would be a roomful of buffalo hunters."

They followed the barman's directions, turned down Laredo Street, crossed the tracks, and came to a row of crib houses with red lights in the windows. Will sniffed the air and declared that he didn't smell anything but the stink of buffalo hides. "I reckon that barman don't know the difference between perfume and rotting hides," he added irritably.

Cole knocked on the first door they came to, then waited and knocked a second time. Finally the door opened and a tall, big-boned woman stood in the frame.

"You gents come right in," she said. She wore a faded silk rose in her hair.

"You the one they call Miss Pearl Mae?" Will asked.

"I'm her, honey . . . the one and only! You all want to go at it together, or just one at a time? Two at a time costs more but twice the fun, don't you know."

"We didn't come here for that," Will said.

"Well, then what did you come for?" Pearl Mae asked. " 'Cause *that's* what I do. I don't do nothing else but that!"

"We're looking for the city marshal," Cole said.

"Boss?"

"Yeah, Boss," Cole echoed.

"Boss ain't here," she said. "I ain't seen Boss since early this morning when he was trying to pull his pants on over his poor sore little pecker." She laughed until you could see her back teeth.

"Do you know where he might be now?" Cole asked.

"Well, if he ain't with me, he's usually over to the Red Beaver playing with the pasteboards, honey. You-all sure you don't want to come in? I can give you a group discount, if you just want to go one at a time. Sunday morning is slow around here."

"Group discount?" Will said.

"Don't even think about it, Will. We've got business to attend to," Cole warned him.

"Maybe some other time," Will said, making sure he got an eyeful before leaving.

"No time like the present," she said with a wink.

As Will and Cole walked back to the center of town, Will said: "You know, if you weren't so damn' impatient, I could have screwed the tallest whore west of the Mississippi."

"How do you know she's the tallest?"

"I don't, but who's to say she's not?"

"You are sometimes too easily distracted."

"Well, a tall gal like that is something that don't come along every day. Or every other day for that matter."

They found the Red Beaver.

"That must be him," Cole said to Will, pointing

toward a table of men, one of whom was wearing a patch over his left eye.

"How do you know that?"

"Because I was told by the man I got our horses back from that the lawman here was one-eyed. I don't see any other one-eyed men in here, do you?"

"Let's go ask him."

"You Marshal Boss?" Will said as soon as the last hand was finished being played and before the next one could be dealt.

The man looked up. He had a broad, deeply lined face and one glassy blue eye shining forth, with a heavy black patch over the other.

"Who's askin'?" His voice sounded like ground glass.

"We are," Will said.

"Who is we?"

Will looked at Cole and said: "Nobody gives an answer to a question in this town. Everybody always asks a question to a question."

Boss had a cud in his cheek. Now he took the opportunity to lean and spit into a coffee can near his feet. Then he straightened and stared some more with his one blue eye.

"We're looking for a man," Cole said. "A black man. He's got a young colored girl with him."

"And I'm looking for an inside straight," Boss growled. "Everybody's looking for something."

"Why does this have to be hard, Marshal?" Cole queried.

"You in or out, Boss?" the dealer asked, holding a worn deck of cards in his left hand and staring at the kitty.

"Deal!" Boss said. "I didn't come here to chat about darkies."

"This man we're looking for," Will said. "He's killed some folks, and he might kill some more. If he's come this way, he might just kill some folks right here in your town. That any concern to you?"

Boss's one blue eye moved from the cards dealt in front of him to Will. "You're interrupting my game."

Before Cole could stop him, Will pulled one of his ivory-handled Colts at the same instant he stepped next to Marshal Boss and placed the muzzle against his ear. "I don't know what makes a man like you hard to get along with," Will said. "Maybe it's 'cause you lost an eye. Or maybe it's 'cause your girlfriend is so tall. Or, maybe, it's just because you are a no-good son-of-a-bitch. But one way or the other, you're going to say whether or not you've seen a black man with a young gal come through here."

Cole saw one of the players slip his hand below the table. "Don't!" he ordered. "This doesn't have to get bloody unless you want it to." The player's hand came back up and rested atop the table.

Boss had lost some of his color. "Ain't seen no darkies through here . . . lately," he managed to say.

156

"You sure about that?" Will said. "Because the word I got is that this fellow we're looking for was headed this way. Now how could he be headed this way, and not come through here?"

"Don't you think if I'd seen him, I would have noticed?" Boss objected, his voice rising as Will wormed the barrel of his revolver a little farther into Boss's ear.

"Let him go, Will. I don't think he's seen Book."

Will reached inside the man's coat and brought out a policeman's model Colt pistol and held it in his left hand before letting the hammer down on his ivory-handle Colt Peacemaker. "This is a nasty little piece of iron," Will said as he bucked open the cylinder of the smaller gun and let the shells spill to the floor. "Good for shooting men in their spleens, I suppose."

Boss looked mad enough to chew nails; his blue eye was fixed and glaring.

Will and Cole backed out of the room.

"What the hell was that all about?" Cole asked as soon as they were outside.

Will dropped Boss's pistol in a water trough. "My patience is running low. I was hoping this would be the place we'd catch Book. Hell, it don't sound like he's even passed through here. What with the snow covering his tracks, he could be anywhere. Behind us, in front of us, who knows? On top of which, my head hurts and my feet ache. How come that black rascal can find us whenever he wants, but we can't find him?"

"He's smart, for one thing," Cole said. "That's the worst of it, that he's smart."

Will shook his head and muttered: "Smart killers and tall whores . . . I thought I'd seen and heard everything. I guess I ain't."

"I'm going down to the livery and unhitch my horse," Cole said.

"You'd be best off to let Mister Bledsoe keep that ornery beast," Will responded, "and go buy yourself another."

"I spent the last good money I had on that horse. I guess she'll have to do."

"A fool and his money are soon parted," Will said sourly. "I'm going to see about buying a few extra supplies."

Cole told Will he'd meet with him in twenty minutes in front of the livery.

"Yeah, yeah," Will said, and went off down the street.

Cole found Bart dickering with the stable man over a jack mule. The man wanted $40.

"But how do I know your mule isn't colicky?" Bart wanted to know.

"You can see he ain't," the man insisted. "Look at how clear his eyes are. A colicky mule don't have clear eyes. They're like children . . . when they get sick, their eyes get cloudy. Look at his eyes, mister."

Cole checked out the mule and found it to be

sound. He told Bart to offer the man $30 for the mule. The man had black chin whiskers that he pulled on as he walked around in small circles, contemplating the offered price. "Thirty dollars is less than I wanted," he said.

"I'll throw in a bottle of my Joint Fever Medicine," Bart proposed.

"But I don't have no joint fever," the man declared.

"You might someday," Bart said, "living up here in this cold climate. And if you do, you'll wish you had the medicine."

The man seemed to consider the possibility that someday he might come down with joint fever and need a bottle of the medicine.

"It's awful painful," Bart added, "joint fever is."

"OK," the man said. "But I want two bottles of that fever medicine, not just one."

"Why two bottles?" Bart asked.

"Case my wife was to come down with joint fever, too." They agreed and shook hands.

Cole unhitched the speckled bird from the wagon. She looked grateful and snorted. "Well, I guess that's it," he said to Bart, offering his hand.

Bart Bledsoe seemed as grateful as the speckled bird. "I think I can earn enough money here to get me to Texas," he said.

"Why Texas?" Cole asked.

He smiled and said: "I hear there is a lot of dropsy in Texas."

"Well, I wish you well, Mister Bledsoe. I think you have bought yourself a good mule this time."

Bart looked very pleased with the mule, but he said—"Wait."—as Cole was taking his saddle from the back of the wagon to put it on the speckled bird. Bart walked over and handed Cole a small brown bottle. "Give this to Mister Harper. It'll help relieve the pain in his feet."

"I'm sure he'll appreciate it," Cole said, and slipped it into his pocket.

"Maybe we'll run into each other again sometime," Bart said with a wave as Cole mounted the bird and brought her head around.

"You never know what the future might hold, Mister Bledsoe," Cole said, and headed down the street to find Will rather than hang around waiting for Will to find him.

"That's right," he heard Bart say as he rode away. "You never know what the future does hold."

Cole rode past the dry-goods store and saw a *Closed* sign in the window. Will's horse and mule weren't out front, either. Cole speculated on where he could have gone and figured maybe to one of the saloons. He rode up the main street, looking for his animals without luck. Then he thought of the one other place he might have gone—Miss Pearl Mae's. That was just before he heard the gunshots from over across the tracks where the red lights hung in the doorways and windows.

CHAPTER FOURTEEN

There were three shots, then two more. The bird was skittish about stepping across the tracks; the sudden gunfire made her even more skittish, but Cole spurred her across.

Miss Pearl Mae came running out the front door, clutching her side just as Cole reached Revelation Alley.

"I've been shot! I've been shot!" she cried, a red stain flowering her yellow dress just below the arm.

"Who?" Cole shouted, dismounting the bird and drawing the self-cocker at the same time.

"Boss! Boss and that other man!" She sat straight down on the sidewalk, her lower lip quivering. "Oh, Lordy, I've been shot!"

Cole took a quick look. The bullet had scored a red path through the ample flesh but had done no real damage other than ruining her dress. She was lucky. "It's not as bad as you think," Cole said.

"Will I die?" she squealed, her face crumpled under tears and black eye kohl.

"Someday you will," Cole said. "But not from that scratch."

She blew a hot breath of relief and touched the back of her wrist to her forehead as she examined the flesh wound.

Then Will came through the front door. His

shirt tail was out and his hat was missing, and he was limping. He said: "Boss came in and started shooting up the place. I killed him!"

"Ten minutes alone and this is what happens?" Cole asked.

"It wasn't the reason I came here," Will said. "Not to get shot. I can't help it that Johnny Law was a jealous man."

"I don't know why that would surprise you."

Will looked at Pearl Mae and said: "You all right, sweets?"

She squinted through tear-stained eyes and said: "No thanks to you."

"He shot me in the hip," Will said, calmly looking down at a bloody patch near his front pocket. "I think the bullet's still in there, smashed flat against the bone. Least it feels that way."

Cole went inside Pearl's crib and followed a narrow hallway to a back bedroom. There was City Marshal Boss, lying across the bed, face up, his one blue eye staring at the ceiling. He had a neat dark hole directly in the middle of his forehead. A halo of bright red blood soaked the sheets beneath him. A Smith & Wesson .44-40 hung from the forefinger of his right hand. It wasn't the same pocket pistol that Will had taken off him earlier and dropped in the water trough. Cole guessed that like most men of his type he had owned more than one pistol. He went back outside.

"He's dead," Cole confirmed.

"I'm not surprised," Will said. "Never knew anyone that could survive a bullet through the brain."

"You should have known a thing like this might happen, Will."

"It all sort of went off at once," Will said, taking his bandanna from around his neck and plugging the hole in his hip with it. "Me and Miss Pearl Mae was just getting around to negotiating a fair price for her services when Boss showed up, waving a big six-shooter. She tried to calm him down, but he wasn't having any of it. He went into a rage, cussing and swearing oaths. I was trying to get my guns when he shot me. He would most likely have killed me except some of his loads were bad and didn't fire. I got my iron and put a round in him. But not before he jumped out of the way of the first one. I got Boss with the second round. Wonder we weren't both killed." Will paused long enough to look at Pearl Mae. "You know I didn't mean to shoot you," he insisted.

She tried hard to smile, but her heart wasn't fully in it. "I've been done every way a man can do a woman," she muttered, "but you are the first man to shoot a hole through me."

"Accident, hon." Will looked sheepish.

"She'll live," Cole told Will. "But you might not, if Boss's friends get a lynch party together and hang you."

163

"We better git," Will said. "Though I don't think I can sit a horse with my shot hip."

"Grip onto the horn of my saddle," Cole said, taking the reins and leading Will and the speckled bird down a back street.

"You expect me to walk to the next town?" Will said. "If so, just leave me here where I am and I'll take my chances. This damn' hip of mine hurts too much."

"Not to the next town," Cole said. "Just till we clear the main section. And stop your complaining."

Will limped alongside the bird, holding onto the saddle horn, as Cole led them through the back streets and alleys of Buffalo Tongue. They finally got to the place Cole wanted to be—Bart Bledsoe's medicine wagon. It was parked out front of a saloon called *The Goodnight Cattleman's Club*. Cole opened the rear door of the wagon and told Will to crawl inside. When he didn't move fast enough, Cole shoved him the rest of the way in. "Stay there and be quiet until I come for you."

"What about my hip?"

"Drink some of Bledsoe's bitters. Hell, drink all of it, if it'll keep you from complaining." He closed the door before Will could drag him into a long conversation that would end up going nowhere.

Bart was inside the saloon, passing out flyers advertising his patent medicines and his gift for reading heads. "Big medicine show tomorrow, ladies and gents!" he was announcing as he handed out the flyers. "Come and learn about the miraculous benefits of Doctor Bledsoe's patent medicines. You gentlemen who are experiencing waning desire for your wives. You women who wish to rid yourselves of unwanted hair. Hear handwritten testimony from former sufferers of such troublesome and disturbing ailments as the rickets, dyspepsia, constipation, and catarrh . . . all cured with just a few doses of Bledsoe's Miracle Cure!"

Bart was laying it on thick and the crowd was eager to have their internal organs invigorated and their sex lives rejuvenated, judging by the way they were snapping up the flyers.

"What time tomorrow you having this medicine show, Doc?" a toothless man with a bent back asked. "Couldn't I just buy one bottle tonight? My back hurts like the dickens."

"Noon, my dear sir . . . be there. No early sales. I only have a limited supply of these fine patent medicines, ladies and gentlemen, and they will be sold on a first-come, first-served basis. Do not miss out on this golden opportunity. And for those who would like to see into the future, I will be doing readings of the head as well."

Bart had them champing at the bit to buy his patent medicines and get their skulls read. After listening to him, Cole was almost ready to buy a bottle of the stuff himself. It was hard to believe that this was the same frightened little man Will and he had found sitting on a dead mule in the middle of nowhere, looking so forlorn. But he was in his element now.

"Bart," Cole said as soon as he had passed out his last flyer.

"Mister Cole. What a surprise to see you. I thought you and Mister Harper would have left town by now."

"We would have, Bart, but there's been some trouble."

"Oh, dear."

"I need your help . . . Will and me both."

"Yes, yes, anything. What can I do?"

Cole walked him outside where they had some privacy. "Will's inside your wagon, Bart. He's been shot."

Bart's eyes jerked at hearing the news. "Shouldn't we find him a doctor?"

"If this was any other place or time, we would. But in this case, it's not wise. Will shot and killed the city marshal."

Bart pursed his lips, but, instead of saying anything, he simply whistled.

Cole saw a group of armed men crossing the far end of the street, heading for the red-light district. They were carrying torches that bobbed like lanterns on a black sea. "I think those may be some of Boss's pals," he said, lowering his voice as he led Bart closer to the wagon. "Once Pearl Mae tells them what happened, they'll be looking to invite Will to a necktie party."

"Fact?" Bart said.

"Fact. Even a hardcase like Boss has his friends. It doesn't help any that he was the town's lawman. That alone will get you hanged in nine places out of ten."

"What shall we do?"

"We need to clear out of the country, Bart. Now."

Bledsoe was eager to help, but Cole had to be honest with him about the price he might have to pay for his loyalty. "If they do find Will in the back of your wagon, Bart, they'll be in the mood to hang you as well."

Bart looked at Cole with mournful eyes. "He saved my life, as did you, sir. What sort of man would I be if I didn't try and repay the debt?"

"Just wanted you to be aware of the consequences, Bart."

"Well, aware I am."

"I'm going to lead that lynch party on a little bit of a chase, Bart. I want you to take the south road and keep going. I'll catch up with you later."

Cole climbed aboard the speckled bird and put her into a dog trot down toward the tracks and the red-light district. He came close enough to see that the torches had stopped in front of Pearl Mae's crib. He heard the sputtering details of how she and her lover had been shot by Will Harper, how it was she who had tried to defend Marshal Boss. Then she cut loose a wail like a scalded cat and every last man in that drunken crowd was ready to take up the cause and defend her honor and avenge the death of their friend.

Cole felt she had given a performance that would have caused Bill Cody to sign her to a stage contract. He fired his self-cocker into the air and shouted: "I'm here for any son-of-a-bitch that wants to hang me!" He made a big show of it by firing one or two more rounds as he jumped the bird across the tracks, all the while praying a wild round from one of the rifles wouldn't find him in the darkness and split his skull open. But by the time the lynch party did open fire, he was already gone.

He knew those that were determined would first have to hoof it back to their horses before they could give chase. He was more worried that the bird would step into a gopher hole than he was of anyone catching him. He had known a kid on the Bandera Trail who broke his neck when he was pitched from his cow pony during a midnight stampede. He remembered at the time thinking it wasn't a way he'd care to die. He was still thinking that as he rode out a mile from town and slowed the bird to an easy lope.

He got far enough away that the lights of the town looked no bigger than stars lying on the ground and reined up long enough to listen for voices or the thunder of hoofs behind him. There weren't any, so he rolled a shuck, lit it, and kept moving. The bird seemed to know she had the game beat and just set herself into an easy rhythm that felt like sitting in a rocking chair. She was the best $30-horse Cole had ever known.

He figured to ride a wide loop around the town and catch up with Bart and the medicine wagon in a few hours, but a fresh snow began falling sometime shortly after the lights of the town faded out of sight. He stayed to his plan and rode until nearly dawn before realizing something wasn't right. He still hadn't cut sign of Bart's wagon. He considered the possibility that he'd ridden a smaller loop around the town than he'd intended. If they were still ahead of him, the snow would have covered whatever tracks they might have left. Still, it didn't feel right. He traveled several more miles without coming on them. Then another thought came to mind, one not as acceptable as the first. He wondered if it was possible that a second lynch party had followed them from town and caught up with them. It didn't seem likely, but he couldn't take the chance. If Bart and his wagon were not ahead of him, then they had to be somewhere behind him. He turned the bird back toward town. Only he didn't make it back to Buffalo Tongue before he found the wagon. Bart's new mule was gone, and so was he. Cole found

Will tied to one of the wheels. He looked half frozen with the snow clinging to his beard and eyelashes. His flesh was as pale as moonlight.

Cole considered the strong possibility that he was dead. Dismounting, Cole kneeled in front of Harper and tapped him on the cheeks. "Will?"

Harper didn't move at first, but when Cole tried to untie his wrists, he moaned.

"Easy! My limbs is froze. You move 'em . . . too fast . . . they're liable to just break clean off!" His face knotted up in pain and he said: "I'm about to piss my britches from being so cold!"

"Where's Bart?" he asked.

Will groaned when Cole tried to lift him. "My hip! Is it still there?"

"Bart?" Cole repeated. "What happened to him?"

"You ain't . . . gonna believe . . . John Henry. You ain't . . . gonna believe." Will was chattering so hard Cole thought his teeth would chip off.

Chapter Fifteen

Cole helped Will back inside the wagon and warmed him with blankets until the color came back into his face and he could stop his teeth from knocking together long enough to tell him what had happened.

"We were going along just fine," Will said.

170

"Then all of a sudden I feel the wagon stop and I hear some voices outside. I figured it to be a lynch party. But before I could look out and see who it was, the back door throws open and standing there, big as you please, is Leviticus Book. His face looked like a black moon and he was pointing the biggest damned Sharps buffalo gun at me I ever seen." Will motioned toward one of the bottles Bart kept in a wooden crate. "You mind?"

Cole pulled the cork on one and gave it to him. He took a good swallow, then leaned back again. "Damn if this ain't the coldest I ever been." Then he took another drink, and licked the dew from his lips. "I looked him straight in his god-damn' eye and said . . . 'You are just the man I'm looking for. You might just as well put that Big Fifty down and give yourself up.' "

"Well, that must have made him sweat like hell, Will."

"It was worth a try, John Henry."

"I take it he didn't abide by your order."

"He laughed is what he did and said . . . 'Mister, why you tryin' to catch me anyway?' I told him why. Then he laughed some more and said . . . 'First off, ain't nobody can catch Leviticus Book iffen he don't want to be caught. Second, I ain't never kilt no innocent men, so I ain't guilty of nothin'. And third, if I was ever plannin' on killin' a man, you just might be the first, the way you been houndin' me around.' " Will shook his head. "I came close, John Henry. I could see it in his eyes. All he had to do was pull the trigger and I'd have been dog scraps."

"Why didn't he?"

"That's a hell of a good question, why didn't he? Instead, he just made me get out of the wagon so he could tie me to the wheel. Maybe he thought it would be more painful for me to freeze to death than to eat a bullet."

"What about Bart? What happened to Bart?"

"They took him, John Henry. Book and that young whore, Jilly Sweet. They unhitched the mule and set him on it and took him."

"Hostage?"

"Most likely."

"Doesn't make sense, Will."

"It might not, but what does any more?" Will sipped some more from the bottle. "What now?" he asked.

"Well, I can't go after them and just leave you here," Cole conceded. "The nearest town that's safe for me to take you to is back to Cheyenne. I figure it to be about a hundred miles from here."

"Ain't that where we started from in the first place? Or am I confused?"

"You have a better idea, Will?"

"This has been a long haul for nothing," he grumbled.

"Is it just the pain in your hip, or have you gone back to complaining just for complaining's sake?"

172

"We've been defeated," Will said sourly. "Been beat by a damn' killer and a lovesick whore."

"You want me to take you back to Cheyenne, or leave you here?"

Will was still muttering when Cole went around to the front of the wagon. He walked over to the speckled bird and said: "You're not going to like this very much." Then he took off her saddle. She rolled back her eyes as he hitched her in the traces.

Will was right, Cole thought, as he tied his saddle to the top of the wagon and took up the reins. They had been defeated by the killer and it wasn't setting with him any better than it was with Will. Cole climbed down from the wagon seat and went around to the back again and opened the door.

"What now?" Cole growled.

"Toss me a bottle of that cure-all," Will said. "I think I'm going to need it."

It took them three days to arrive back in Cheyenne. To their good fortune the weather had cleared, and Will had not bled to death, although he wasn't in the best shape by the time they reached the town's limits.

Leo Foxx and Long Bill Longly and the other deputy were walking near Shorty's Diner when Cole drove the wagon past them.

"You take up a new profession?" Foxx called. "Peddling snake oil?" Longly and the other man seemed to enjoy Foxx's humor the way dull men will enjoy something stupid.

Cole continued on down the street without bothering to acknowledge the jibes of the Cheyenne police force. He pulled up in front of Dr. Price's house and climbed down from the wagon. He helped Will out of the back. He was thoroughly intoxicated, lying among several empty bottles of Bledsoe's patent medicines and unhappy about having to move.

"Well, at least you didn't suffer," Cole said as he helped Will to walk.

"I suffered aplenty," Will muttered. "In ways you wouldn't understand. Did you miss any damn' big rocks on the way here that we ought to go back and run over again?"

"I can see that Bledsoe's medicines are good for everything but good temperament," Cole concluded as he tackled the steps to the front door.

Dr. Price answered his knock. He was wiping his hands on a towel. He looked first at Will, then at Cole. "Is it your mission in life to bring me every shot-up son-of-a-bitch in the territory?" he asked.

"Just the ones who can't defend themselves, Doc. Where do you want me to put him?"

The doctor directed Cole to the same back room and table where he had taken the young Mexican gravedigger that Long Bill had shot over a 10¢ beer.

"How did that kid make out?" Cole asked Dr.

Price as he helped Will up onto the table and began stripping off his boots and pants.

"He's alive, but he'll be a cripple the rest of his life." He asked Will: "Did you shoot yourself in the hip, or did someone do it for you?"

Will looked at him through unsteady eyes. "What does it look like?"

"A man in your condition, I wouldn't be surprised you shot yourself. It happens all the time. Only most of you drunkards shoot yourself in the foot, or shoot your peckers off trying to show what a fast-draw artist you are with a gun. It takes a special talent to be able to shoot yourself squarely in the hip."

"I didn't shoot myself in the hip or the foot, or nowhere else for that matter," Will declared. "Someone else did it for me."

"Why doesn't that surprise me?" Dr. Price wondered. "A man with your disposition. Now just shut up for a minute and let me see what we have here."

Will looked at Cole and said: "All the places in the territory, you had to bring me here?"

Dr. Price did something with his metal probe that made Will yelp. "If you cannot be quiet and remain still," he warned, "then this is going to end up hurting a lot more than it has to." Cole headed for the front door. "Don't bring me any more patients," the doctor called after him, "especially grumpy ones!"

Cole walked down the street to Cavandish's Funeral Parlor. Karl Cavandish was sitting at an expansive oak desk with a pile of papers in front of him. He wore gold-rim spectacles that were perched on the bridge of his bony nose. He looked up when Cole entered.

"John Henry," he said, "yours was a short trip. Were you able to find Ike's killer?"

"Not yet," Cole said. "We ran into some bad luck."

Cavandish looked disappointed, removed the spectacles, and pinched the place on his nose where they had been resting. "That's too bad. I was hoping for justice to be done."

"It will be," Cole promised. "It's just going to take a little longer than planned."

"Can I get you something, a drink perhaps?"

"Coffee, if you have it."

"I keep some going," he said. "Back here."

They went to a rear apartment that had a bed and a potbelly stove throwing off heat. Cavandish took a tin cup from a hook and poured Cole a cup of hot black coffee. Cole wished he had a cigarette to go with it, but he'd run out of tobacco several days back.

"How's the boy?" he asked.

Cavandish had small grayish eyes, and, when Cole asked him about the Mexican kid, the eyes watered. "An invalid . . . poor José."

Cole had seen kids maimed during the war, kids

without arms and legs, kids missing an eye, or both eyes, or a foot. Flesh and bone were no match for lead and steel.

"Where's he at, Karl?"

"In the back. I fixed up the summer kitchen into a room to better accommodate him, and I pay a local woman to come in twice a day to care for him. The rest I do myself."

"He's lucky, then."

"Not so lucky," Cavandish said.

"He's got you to take care of him. That's more than a lot of kids like him would have."

"But what happens when I'm not around any more? Who's going to take care of him then?"

"Doesn't he have family?"

"He has an uncle in Sonora, but he doesn't know where in Sonora. That's it. I'm his family. But I'm not a young man any more. I've got a few years left, if I'm lucky. I was counting on José to dig my grave and put me in it and take over the business."

"You do what you can," Cole said. "Let tomorrow worry about tomorrow."

"I guess so."

"It's a good thing you're doing here, Karl."

For a long time he didn't reply. "The really sad irony of it is," he finally said, "if Longly had killed José, perhaps some charges could be brought against him for murder. But with José alive, there isn't even a legal recourse for what he did."

"I know. But I'm a real firm believer in what goes around comes around, Karl. And I think Bill Longly will pay the price for his sins someday. Men like him always do."

"That's little consolation to that boy in there, the fact that his shooter is up walking around every day, enjoying himself, and José needs help just to go to the toilet."

"Bill Longly won't always be walking around, enjoying himself. Someday he'll know what it's like to be on the other end of a bullet."

Cavandish tried rubbing the weariness from his face with his bony fingers. "I'd like to believe that, John Henry, I truly would. Fact is, every time I see Longly out on the street, I want to kill him myself." His words were as tired as his eyes. "You really think there's any justice left in this world?"

"I have to believe so, Karl. Why else would any of us keep going if we didn't believe there was still some justice to be had?"

"Maybe the only true justice is what each of us takes into our own hands."

"Sometimes that's true, Karl. But let the thing with Longly go."

He looked at Cole and sniffed.

"It's not your way to kill a man, Karl . . . that's one thing. The other is, he'd most likely kill you in the trying. That kid in there needs you, like you said. Let it go with Longly, he'll get his some other way."

They shook hands and Cole left.

He walked to the house Ella Mims had rented. He knocked on the door and waited, then knocked again. A man wearing a paper-collar shirt answered the door. He had heavy dark mustaches and was holding a newspaper in his hand.

"Ya," he said.

"I'm looking for Ella."

"No Ella here," he said. He had a German accent.

"Ella Mims."

He shook his head. Then his eyes showed he recognized who it was Cole was asking for. "Oh dat *voman!* No, she's gone away, mister. Me and my *vife* live here now! Since last *veek.*"

"Did she say where she was going?"

He shook his head. "Sorry, she didn't say notting."

Cole thanked him for his trouble and then headed for Shorty's Diner.

Shorty was wearing an apron and waiting on tables when Cole walked in. He nodded his head and told Cole to take a seat and he would be with him as soon as he finished waiting tables.

Cole sat by the window so he could watch the street.

In a few minutes Shorty came over. "Did you catch Ike's killer?"

"No. Not yet."

He seemed as disappointed as Cavandish had. "Trail gone cold?" he asked.

"Worse than that," Cole admitted. "Will Harper

was shot in the hip and I had to bring him back here to get patched by Doc Price."

"That colored do it?"

"No, but the difference is slim." Then Cole told Shorty about Book stealing Bart Bledsoe.

"You want some coffee?"

"That and tobacco, if you've got any."

"My waitress, Mary, she didn't show up for work today. That's why I'm wearing this apron."

"It looks good on you."

"Please," he said, and went off to get the coffee. Cole saw Bill Longly going into the Blue Star Saloon across the street. No one was with him. The sudden thought came over him that if he got up now, walked over there, and shot him, what was the worst that could happen to him? He thought of the kid, José, lying in his bed all day not able to move, thought of how many years he would be like that before he just gave up and died. Maybe the only true justice was what you took into your own hands sometimes. The thought that Long Bill was walking around free, going into the saloon to take a little pleasure from the bottle and from the woman he enjoyed slapping around just made the urge in Cole all that much stronger. Somehow, life seemed about as twisted as it could get.

Shorty returned with two coffees and some tobacco and papers and sat down across from him. "You want to tell me how that colored stole a friend of yours?" he said. "Or do I have to guess?"

Cole explained what had happened. Shorty sat there, drinking his coffee, listening like he'd heard it all before, the smoke from his cigarette curling up into his squinting eyes.

"So the thing is," Shorty said, after Cole had finished, "this Book fellow can find you anytime he wants, but you ain't able to find him. That what you're telling me?"

"Pretty much."

Shorty shook his head in disbelief. "And he's traveling with a young gal to boot?"

Cole nodded by way of explanation.

"Well, if you and Will Harper can't find him, I doubt anyone can. What now?"

"Soon as Will's able, we'll go looking for him again."

"Maybe he's just too smart to be caught, John Henry."

"I don't believe that."

"Well, if you're going out again, so am I."

"No, Shorty, that's not necessary."

"I know it ain't necessary," Shorty protested. "But look at me. I'm wearing a damn' apron."

"You've also got a bum leg, Shorty."

"Well, from what you tell me, Will's going to have one, too. So being a little crippled up ain't no excuse for you not to let me go along. 'Sides, I used to be a damn' good tracker. And the way it sounds, the two of you could stand to have a damn' good tracker along next time."

"What about your business, Shorty? You just going to close up?"

"What the hell kind a business is it for a man to be wearing an apron, anyhow?"

"Beats starving, ending up in an old soldier's home back East somewhere."

"Hell, I can always get a job burning eggs and cowboy hash if I have to."

"I know. Let tomorrow worry about tomorrow, right?"

"Right."

"I'll have to run it past Will."

"You do that, John Henry."

Another customer came in, and Cole watched as Shorty hobbled off to wait the table. He concluded that Shorty was a good man in a world where there weren't many good men to be found. He saw Bill Longly exit the Blue Star and knew, in spite of what he'd just been thinking about doing, that he wasn't going to walk up to him and put a bullet in him just because he knew Longly deserved it. A little part of him still wanted to believe that he, too, fell into that category of good men, men like Shorty and Ike Kelly and Karl Cavandish. What he was going to do, now that he had a couple of weeks to wait around until Will could recover enough to travel again, was take a trip over to Nebraska and see an old friend, and maybe in the process he might find Ella Mims.

CHAPTER SIXTEEN

John Henry Cole caught the stage east to North Platte, then rented a horse, and rode to Bill Cody's ranch. Through the stands of leafless trees lining its banks, he could see the waters of the Platte, slipping along like a fat gray snake under the sunless sky. Patches of snow lay in the dead brown grass, making a patchwork quilt of the land. Several times pheasants exploded from the winter grass and startled the rented sorrel he was riding. And twice, Cole saw small herds of whitetail deer foraging through the brittle cover.

Nebraska was like a lot of places Cole had been. It had its own kind of beauty and its own kind of loneliness. When he thought of Bill Cody living out here, he thought it was a long way from New York or Denver, and farther still from London, England. In those places Cody was a celebrity, a man recognized. Out here, he was as common as the deer and pheasant and wild turkey. Cole wondered how long at a time Cody could stay so far removed from his audience and not begin to miss it. He wondered, too, as he rode along, if he would find Ella Mims. He wasn't exactly sure what he truly felt toward her. The thought of her had been buzzing around in his mind since that first and last night they had spent together. He'd been with his share of women since Zee Cole's death. Most times, it had been simply a matter of need, a matter of being with someone when the Big Lonely got too big to carry around inside. There were only two had stayed with him long after he'd left their beds. Lydia Winslow back in Deadwood had been one of them, but Liddy's hands had been covered with innocent blood, and that ultimately muddied her memory for him. Ella Mims was probably the other one. With Ella, it felt different. For one thing, they hadn't met or been introduced under similar circumstances, but still, if it hadn't been for a case of murder—Ike's—she and Cole might not have met at all.

His wife Zee Cole had been his one true love in life (and he knew they say, you only get one). When he had buried her, he had buried a lot of himself with her. For a long time after the funeral, he hadn't been much good for anything but drifting, getting in and out of trouble, the bottle, and the beds of widows and whores. And for a lot longer than may have been practicable, it had been enough. But in the last few years, he'd begun to need more than just to hang his hat on some woman's chair and leave his boots by her front door and his horse tied up at her gate. He had begun to tell himself it was just that he was growing older and tired of drifting, and he was beginning to believe it half the time. Now Ella Mims's honey hair and the way she raised herself up on that last cold morning was an image he saw riding around with him everywhere he went. He felt he needed to see her one more time just to make sure of what he was feeling, one way or the other.

You could see Bill Cody's big house from a long way off. It stood out in that open country, large and square and white as a wedding cake with a porch running all the way around it. Cole imagined Bill could stand on his porch and shoot quail and not even put on his boots. He could just bang away there in his stocking feet and whistle and his hounds would bring him the quail so Louisa could fry them up for breakfast along with his eggs. The pack of dogs Cody always kept about started barking as he approached the house. Several long-legged hounds came trotting out to greet him, their barks crackling through the cold clear air.

He was about a hundred yards from the house when he saw Bill Cody step out onto the porch. You would have to be blind not to recognize him. He was dressed in a bright red shirt and black trousers and knee-high leather boots. He had that same long hair that Custer had had, only darker than Custer's, and he sported a fine black Vandyke beard. The only thing Cole could see that was unusual about him was that he was standing there alone without a crowd around him. The dogs gathered around the sorrel Cole was riding, then fell in behind, barking and baying as he rode up to the porch. Cody stood there watching Cole, trying to figure out who he was. It had been a long time since they'd last crossed paths. Cole supposed Cody had met a lot of people in between, any one of which might come visiting him on a crisp winter day.

"You hounds git!" Cody called to the pack of dogs. As though God himself commanded it, they scattered.

"Bill," Cole said, "it's been a time."

Cody looked intently for a moment, then smiled broadly. He had fine teeth. "Damn, John Henry Cole, I didn't recognize you with all that brush on your face. You've aged some."

"A lot," Cole said. "You mind if I get down?"

"No, of course not, son," he said, coming down the steps to shake Cole's hand. He had put on a small amount of weight around his middle, but it hadn't hurt his appearance any. His grip was firm; the handshake of a man well schooled in the art of giving firm handshakes. "You know," he said, clapping Cole on the shoulder as he led the way back up the steps to the porch, "you're not going to believe this, but I was just this morning thinking about the past, about some of the friends I hadn't seen in years and you and Ike Kelly came to mind. And damn, here you are!"

"I've been thinking about you some lately, too, Bill. Fact is, I sent a lady friend of mine to see you. She has an aunt that lives near Ogallala."

Cody blinked, then offered Cole a wink. "Pretty gal, is she?"

"Yes."

"You know me and pretty gals," Cody said. He smiled like a prince. "They are always welcome here." Then, looking over his shoulder: "Of course, it ain't exactly always tea and roses when they're about, you understand. Louisa still hasn't gotten over her jealousy . . . especially of actresses. She thinks they're all tawdry by nature. Whatever in the hell that means." He laughed.

"I warned my lady friend about you, Bill. How you had an eye for the ladies. I warned her to watch out for Louisa, too."

Cody guided Cole to a set of chairs a little farther down the porch and away from the front door. "You know I'm just like a papa to the young ladies," he said with a look of sincerity on his face. "They all like to kiss me and call me papa. It's just their way of showing affection for me. It doesn't mean a thing."

"Sure, Bill, I understand."

He grinned slyly. "The God's truth!" he declared, raising his left hand and placing his right over his heart.

Cody took a pair of cheroots from his pocket and handed Cole one. "Smoke?"

They sat there, smoking and reminiscing about old times and about friends, the ones they'd lost and the ones that were still alive. Cole told Cody about Ike and he seemed genuinely saddened by the news.

"I guess this has been the worst for me, this last year," Cody said. "First Georgie went down on the Little Big Horn, then Bill Hickok got killed up in Deadwood a couple of months after that. Now Ike. They were good pards . . . though Georgie was a bit of a vain and foolish son-of-a-buck at times. I am not at all surprised that he came to the end he did. You chase an Indian long enough, he's going to sneak around behind you and lift your hair."

"Hazards of the profession," Cole said.

"True enough," Cody replied. "I truly am sorry to hear about Ike," he added with a sigh. Then after several moments of quiet reflection: "We're dying fast as roses in winter, ain't we, John Henry?"

Cole agreed and blew rings of smoke from his cigar and studied them as they lifted toward the overhang.

"But the year hasn't been entirely bad," Cody resumed. "We've performed a number of stage plays in the East . . . Buffalo and New York City. Fact is, Wild Bill was with us for last spring. Him and Texas Jack . . . you remember Texas Jack?"

"Yes."

"Now there is a natural stage actor, that Texas Jack." Cody's eyes twinkled. "Handsome son-of-a-buck, too. All the ladies love Texas Jack. Me,

I'm not as natural an actor as Texas Jack. But Bill Hickok . . . whew! That man could not act worth a hill of beans. Terrible! Never seen such stage fright in a man . . . had to get good and drunk before every performance. Least that's the reason he gave for getting good and drunk. A condition Ned Buntline himself is an advocate of . . . except Ned has no compunction about exhibiting himself on stage. Shameless ham! I believe the man would walk naked through Central Park and not think a thing of it."

Cody sat there, smoking his cigar and smiling broadly as he told Cole about various plays and actors and actresses, and about the big cities they had performed in that past season and all the hell they had raised, and how different that life was compared to the one he led here at the ranch. "You know," he said, "if Hickok hadn't been so frightful of the stage, he'd probably still be alive today. He got scared and ran back to the frontier and straight into the arms of death. Of all the dangers he faced, the war and Indians and being a lawman in those rough cow towns, it was his fear of standing in front of strangers who admired him that ended up getting him killed. . . ." Cody's voice trailed off as he stared out toward the quiet land. "If he'd stayed with me and Jack and Ned, he'd've been a rich man today. Rich and famous and alive. . . ."

"He didn't know," Cole said. "None of us do."

Cody flicked the ashes from his cigar, looked at it, then said: "My friends are growing few in number."

"You've still got plenty of friends, Bill. I can't ever imagine you without a lot of friends."

He smiled warmly. "Sometimes it's hard to tell exactly who your friends are, John Henry. If I was broke and busting sod for a living, do you think I'd have all these people coming out to the house, or wanting me to have my photograph taken with them?"

"I think you know the answer to that, Bill."

"Well," he said, stubbing out his cigar butt, "I think not . . . unless it was Ned Buntline and he knew I had a bottle of sour mash in the cupboard." Cody's laughter caused several of the hounds to lift their heads. "Now, what was this about a lady friend of yours coming to see me?"

Cole explained about Ella Mims, the reason he'd suggested she come to see him.

"Well, I wish she had," he said. "I would give her a job as an actress. Can she shoot a gun?"

"That's a skill I never got around to asking her about, Bill, whether or not she could shoot a gun."

"I'm thinking about putting together a traveling show," he said. "One with Indians and buffalo and trick shooters. I've not worked out every last detail yet, but I am considering it. Maybe, if your lady friend could shoot glass balls out of the air, I could hire her to be in my traveling show."

"Well, that's something you would have to ask her if she comes around."

"I will. Let's go inside and say hello to Louisa. We'll see if Texas Jack has climbed out of bed yet. No use to bother with Ned, that man don't get up before noon, even on a good day."

Cody's wife was cordial, but not overly friendly toward Cole. She probably thought he was just another old pal, down on his luck, coming to ask her husband for a hand-out. She wasn't far from wrong. Cody kept almost as many old pals around as he did animals. Cole was sure it had to be hard on their marriage—Bill's never being alone with her, or her house never being completely her own. The real delights of the household were Cody's young daughters, dark and curly-haired and more rambunctious than his entire pack of hounds. Their laughter brightened everything in the house and it was plain to see Cody loved them dearly.

After greeting Louisa and the girls, Cody and Cole walked into the large formal dining room. There, sitting at the far end of the table, was Texas Jack Omohundro, his dark curly hair hanging down over his forehead and part way into his eyes.

"Look who's come for a visit!" Cody announced.

Jack smiled and said: "Excuse me for not getting right up, my head feels like broken glass from all the hard liquor last night."

Cody looked sheepish. "I guess we did sort of overdo things."

They sat and had coffee with Texas Jack and soon several young women came down to the dining room and joined them. Cody introduced each by name, then stated they were all actresses in the play company. Cole could see why Cody was in Dutch with Louisa a lot of the time. Cody kept everyone entertained as he told stories of the old days, including Cole in any number of his tall tales. Cole felt foolish listening to it, but remained seated out of respect for his old friend. It went like that for better than an hour before Cole realized that maybe he had made a mistake by coming.

Cole figured it was time he said good bye to his old friend. He had his world and Cole had his. Things weren't ever going to be what they once were between them—too much had changed in both their lives. He excused himself and went outside. He thought maybe he'd ride over to Ogallala and see if he could locate Ella, or her aunt. It would be at least another week or two before Will was ready to travel again; there was no point, sitting around wasting it. If he was lucky, finding Ella would turn out better than finding Bill Cody. He waited around long enough for Cody to take leave of his audience. Cole was adjusting the cinch strap on the sorrel, when Cody came up and ran his hand along the flank.

"What are you doing out here all alone, John

Henry?" he asked. "I don't even recall you leaving the table."

"Just needed some air, Bill."

He looked at Cole with a knowing gaze. "Got to be too much for you inside, didn't it? With all them folks, all those tall stories. I understand. Gets to be too much for me, too, at times."

"Not your fault they like you, Bill."

Cody placed his hand on the mane of the sorrel, twined it through his fingers. "It's hard for me to say no to them, John Henry. They expect me to entertain them, to be papa to them."

"I know, Bill. We'll always be friends."

"I know we will," he said. "I don't want to lose any more of the few good friends I have left. You take care of yourself."

They shook hands.

"Where to now?" Cody asked as Cole swung up into the saddle.

"I think I'll go and see if I can find that lady friend of mine. Spend a little time with her. Maybe ask her, can she shoot glass balls out of the air with a pistol."

He smiled. "You still miss your wife, don't you?"

"Yeah, Bill, I do."

Then he ran his hand along the muscled neck of the horse and patted its shoulder. "You take care, John Henry."

"I will, Bill."

"Your lady friend still needs work, you send

her along to see me. I'll make sure she gets work."

"Thanks, Bill."

Cole rode away knowing, without looking back, that Cody was still standing there in front of that big house filled with people who wanted his company. And Cole knew, too, there was a part of Cody wishing he was the one who was riding away.

CHAPTER SEVENTEEN

Cole arrived in Ogallala in midmorning. He wondered why the town seemed so quiet until he heard a church bell ringing and realized it was Sunday morning.

He figured on finding the local lawman. Maybe he would know something about Ella Mims. An old man crossed the street in front of him. He was wearing a black coat and a boiled shirt and was bent halfway over at the waist. It looked like he was carrying an invisible load on his back.

"Mister, can you tell me where to find John Law?" Cole asked him.

He paused, shaded his eyes with one hand, tilted his head as far back as he could, and looked at Cole. "That'd be Freddie Buck," the old man said. Then, pointing with his nose, he added: "Down the street."

Cole thanked the old-timer and touched his

spurs to the sorrel's flanks. The old man watched him until he rode past.

He found the city marshal's office easily enough. He tied the sorrel and went inside. He didn't bother to knock before opening the door.

Freddie Buck was standing in front of an oval mirror, waxing his mustaches. He turned around when Cole came in.

"Yes, sir, can I help you?"

He was maybe forty, heavy, with a belly that hung over his belt. He had small round eyes and florid cheeks and a drinker's nose that was wormed with busted veins. He wore a six-point star pinned to his vest.

"My name's John Henry Cole. I'm looking for an Ella Mims who was coming here from Cheyenne. Do you know any Mimses hereabouts?"

Maybe it was too much for him all at once. He blinked and said: "Huh?"

Again Cole told him what he wanted to know.

"Sure, the widow Mims lives about four miles out. North. Big white house, can't miss it."

Cole walked back outside and mounted the sorrel.

He rode north until he came to the white house. A woman was in the side yard, hanging bed sheets on a clothesline strung between two large cottonwood trees. The wind caught in the sheets and billowed them out like sails.

Cole stood by the gate of the wrought-iron fence that ran along the front of the house. He didn't have to see her face to know who the woman was. He didn't say anything at first. He just wanted to take a minute to look at her. She must have sensed it, for in a few seconds she stopped what she was doing, and turned to look at him.

"You ride all this way just to watch me hang sheets?" she asked.

Cole thought the wind had done something nice to her skin. Her cheeks had an apple glow to them and her hair had come loose in places from where she'd pinned it up.

"There wasn't much to do in Cheyenne," he said. "So I thought I would ride up this way and watch you hang laundry."

"Well, don't just stand there, come and lend a hand, if you've nothing better to do with your time, Mister John Henry Cole."

He looped the sorrel's reins through the fence, pushed through the gate, and took one end of a damp bed sheet.

"Like this?" he said.

"You look like you've had experience." Her smile was prettier than he remembered it.

They finished hanging the sheets, and she said: "Well, are you going to get on your horse and ride back to Wyoming, or did you plan on staying for supper?"

"Depends on what's for supper."

She put her arm through his and said: "Come and meet my Aunt Laura."

It was a big warm house with several large and bright rooms downstairs and what looked to be several more like them on the second level. Ella's aunt was in the kitchen, baking. Ella introduced them and Cole could smell the sweetness of bread on her.

"Saw you ride up on your horse," Aunt Laura said. "Saw you from 'way out." Her kitchen window looked toward the road. It was the kind of country you could see someone coming from far away. "You must be fond of this girl to come all the way from Wyoming to see her."

"Wyoming's not so far," Cole said, feeling a bit foolish about the situation.

"Far enough a man would have a special reason for coming," Aunt Laura said.

Cole looked at Ella. This time it was her turn to feel a bit foolish. "Aunty," she protested.

"Do you drink coffee, John Henry?" Aunt Laura asked.

"I do when I can get it."

"Good. I have some brewing. If you want to wash up, you can . . . out in the summer kitchen."

It was kind of her not to mention the trail dust he'd collected. He excused himself and went to wash up.

A minute later, Ella came out to the summer kitchen with a cup of coffee on a tray and several small cookies.

"Do you take it black, or would you like some sugar?" she asked.

There was just something about the moment for Cole, of Ella standing there, the way the strands of her honey hair had come free from the combs, the grayness of her eyes. He set the coffee aside and kissed her. She smelled fresh as wind-blown sheets, her hair scented and soft, her mouth sweet as apples.

He held her for a long time after the kiss. It felt good to hold her, to feel the firmness of her body against his, the way it curved into him.

"I think now I know why you rode all the way here from Wyoming," she whispered.

"That's not the only reason."

"But it is one of the reasons."

"Yes, it's one of the reasons."

"Tell me," she said. "What's the other?"

"This," he said. "I missed holding you like this, seeing your smile, hearing your voice."

She put the tips of her fingers to his lips. "Careful, cowboy, you could make a girl's heart go weak. Aunty Laura hears all your sweet talk, she's liable to call a preacher man."

"Maybe that's not such a bad thought."

Ella pushed up on her toes and kissed him, long and sweetly. Then, lowering herself again, she said: "Maybe it's not such a bad thought. But I know a drifting man when I see one. You're not up for preachers just yet."

"Maybe we should spend some time finding out how much drifting I've got left in me."

"Maybe." Then, in a more serious manner, she asked: "John Henry, did you find the man who killed your friend?"

"No, not yet we haven't."

"I'm sorry," she said. The light coming through the summer kitchen window seemed to dance in her hair. Then, pulling back, she looked at him with all the gravity in the world. "You say you came here to see me, to spend a little time getting to know each other. But that's not what I think is going to happen."

"What do you think is going to happen?"

"I think you will be gone come morning, back to looking for your friend's killer. And I think I will start to miss you all over again."

Cole couldn't lie to her. He still had to find Ike's killer. And if he wasn't gone in the morning, it would be the next day, or the one after that. "I think it's something I would like to do," he said. "Get to know you better, spend some time with you . . . afterward."

"I'd like it, too," she said. "Come, let's sit out on the porch, while you have your coffee."

They sat there and talked. He told her all that had happened since leaving Cheyenne with Will Harper that last morning they'd been together. He told her how Leviticus Book had outsmarted them, and how he had stolen Jilly Sweet and their horses. He told her about Will's getting shot in the hip, but skipped the particulars as to

199

why. Ella listened quietly. Sometimes she closed her eyes, and Cole wondered what it was she was thinking. "I always thought of criminals as not being too smart," he concluded. "But this Book is about as smart as they come. He's led Will and me on a merry chase."

"The one good thing about what happened," she said, "is it's given you time to come see me. I wasn't sure that you would take the trouble to look me up again." She gave a soft laugh, then bit the lower part of her lip and trained her gray eyes on him. "I thought for a time right after you'd left me that morning that I'd given myself too easily to you. That you might not have respected me. Funny what a girl will allow herself to believe about a man she's fond of."

He touched her hand, felt its smoothness against his own rough and calloused fingers. "I always knew I would come just to see you again," he said. "That ought to tell you something."

She blinked, looked off toward the river that you couldn't see because it lay beyond a rise and beyond the bare black trees of winter. "It tells me something," she said. Then she touched the corner of her eyes as though the raw wind had caused them to tear.

"I wanted to see you again, Ella. That's why I've come."

"We could have just kept the memory," she said.

"We could have, but to tell you the truth, I have enough memories already. All the memories I carry around inside me have just about worn me out from the carrying."

She was about to say something when they both noticed a buggy coming toward the house.

"Oh, my word!" she declared. "I can't believe it!"

"Someone you know?" Cole asked.

"Tom Feathers!"

"Who is Tom Feathers?"

"A cattleman and a neighbor. He and his father own all that land you see to the west. Aunty says he's the most eligible bachelor in all of Keith County."

"Maybe aunty invited him for supper," Cole said. "Why do you suppose?"

Ella tossed him a quick glance. He couldn't say exactly how it made him feel, that a bachelor cattleman was coming to call on Ella. She didn't act like she cared for it much, but then perhaps she was just trying to be kind to him for having come all the way from Wyoming to visit her unannounced like he had.

"Maybe I should go," he suggested.

Ella looked at him sternly. "No. You should not go." She could see he was uncomfortable with the situation, so she tried to assure him. "Tom Feathers is a nice enough man. He's wealthy and handsome. He has charm and is well traveled and well read. What else can I tell you? He would make the perfect husband for the right woman. I'm just not the right woman."

"Do you think your aunt has enough plates to set out for all of us?" Cole asked.

"If not, you can share mine," Ella said with a sly smile as Tom Feathers pulled up in his horse-drawn buggy.

Cole was downcast inside. It hadn't turned out like he'd planned it, his trip to Nebraska. First Bill Cody, now this.

CHAPTER EIGHTEEN

Tom Feathers was driving a nice bay with a white blaze face and four white stockings. You didn't have to be a horse trader to see it was an expensive horse. So was the buggy. He wore a greatcoat over a good suit of dark clothes with a white shirt and paper collar and a necktie. Perched on his head was a little sugar-loaf hat and he wore kidskin gloves that looked as soft as butter.

"Ella," he said as he checked the bay's reins, then tipped his hat without really tipping it at all. He made all the right formal gestures of a man that had come calling on a lady friend, but the whole time his gaze stayed on the stranger.

"Tom," Ella said. "I'd like you to meet my friend, John Henry Cole."

Tom Feathers stepped from the buggy and came up the steps, his right hand extended. Cole took it and said—"Howdy."—and felt him put a little extra into the grip. He was as tall as Cole, a little lighter built, and had keen blue eyes. He was freshly shaven and smelled of bay rum.

"Don't believe I've seen you around Ogallala," he said.

Cole opined that he wanted to know just exactly where this stranger was from and what he was doing in Ogallala. "I came up from Cheyenne," Cole said, not wanting to pussyfoot around for the next ten minutes in useless conversation with a man he already knew he didn't like.

"Cheyenne . . ." He said the name as though trying to think exactly how many miles away it was from the front porch. "That's quite some distance," he concluded.

"Yes, it is," Cole assured him. "But I figured it was worth the trip to see Ella again."

That caused Feathers's left eye to twitch. "Well," he said, turning his attention to Ella, "it must have been quite a surprise to have your friend suddenly show up all the way from Cheyenne."

"Oh, in a way, I suppose it was," she said. "But I honestly expected him before now." She gave Cole a smile as if she knew something Feathers didn't. Cole gave her one back.

Without so much as missing a beat, Tom Feathers said: "Your aunt was kind enough to invite me to Sunday dinner, Ella. How could I refuse an opportunity to share the company of two beautiful women and fried chicken?"

Ella smiled like the cat that ate the canary as she put her hand through the crook of his arm and said: "Let's go tell Aunt Laura that you're here, then, Tom."

Feathers removed his sugar-loaf hat before stepping through the door.

Cole thought it was damned gentlemanly of him to do so, and then cooled his heels by taking the saddle off the sorrel and letting him graze at the end of a picket rope. He checked the sorrel's shoes to make sure they were in good order. Afterward he walked off a little distance from the house and made himself a cigarette and smoked it.

Sunday and chicken dinner, he thought, company and conversation, sitting around a big table. Civil folks, talking about civil matters—the weather, crops, politics. He thought of Bill Cody, the life he was leading, and Ike Kelly, and the life he'd been trying to lead before he was killed. He thought of old Wayback, talking about the Big Lonely, and Will Harper, a man more likely to die from a bullet than old age. He'd probably end up like Wild Bill, dead before he reached forty. These were men who didn't care to sit around on a Sunday afternoon and talk politics and the weather and wipe chicken grease from the fingers onto a cloth napkin. Cole wondered what sort of life awaited a man between an early grave and talking politics and eating chicken around a big table on a Sunday afternoon.

Ella came out of the house and walked to where he was standing with the last of the shuck burning down between his fingers.

"John Henry, don't you want to come inside? Dinner will be ready soon."

"I feel out of place, Ella."

"Don't," she said. "You are as welcome here as anyone."

"I wasn't invited."

"You don't require an invitation. I meant what I said earlier to Tom Feathers . . . I was expecting you to come before now. In fact, I waited every day for you to show up. And every day you didn't come riding up to the house, I found myself disappointed in a way I didn't fully understand. So now that you have finally arrived, don't feel out of place. I want you here."

Cole and Ella ate dinner with Aunt Laura and Tom Feathers doing most of the talking. Tom told about the shorthorn cattle he and his father were raising.

"Not like those tick-fevered longhorn cows they used to drive up here from Texas," he said pointedly as he looked in Cole's direction. He held a drumstick in one hand and orchestrated his conversation with it. "What bad times those used to be, when the wild and woolly cowboys would ride north with their sick cattle, raising all sorts of hell, if you'll pardon my expression, ladies. How we ever survived either those men or their diseased animals, I'll never know."

"No one seemed to mind that we spent our money, as I recall," Cole said.

Feathers looked amused that Cole had joined the conversation. "We? Were you a drover, Mister Cole? One of those Texican cowboys?"

"We got called a lot of things, Mister Feathers. Cowboy was one of them. Working men was another."

"I see," Feathers said, satisfied that Cole had admitted to whatever sins he believed Cole was guilty of for having been a Texas drover. "Well, point of fact is, Mister Cole, that all the money spent by the Texican cowhands hardly made up for the troubles brought on by their wild behavior. Most of the money spent by the wild Texas gentlemen was spent in the gambling dens and on Cyprians and cheap liquor. Hardly of any benefit to the decent citizens, wouldn't you say?"

Ella placed her hand on Cole's knee beneath the table. She knew without Cole telling her what he thought of Tom Feathers.

"You are right in one respect, Mister Feathers . . . the liquor was mostly of a cheap variety. Watered down."

Feathers studied Cole for a long moment, his drumstick held aloft, the grease shiny on his fingertips. He seemed frustrated that he couldn't say more about what he really felt about the presence of John Henry Cole in the same room with him.

Out of respect for Ella, Cole changed the subject. "I notice you wear a Deane-Adams, Mister Feathers."

His smile was slow in coming, and it looked like it hurt him to have to do so. "Yes. I prefer it over the Colt."

"If you wouldn't mind, I'd like to take a closer look at it after dinner."

"Indeed," he said. "Perhaps we could even have a little shooting match. How would that be?"

Normally Cole would have turned down the invitation, but there was something about Feathers's smugness that wouldn't allow him to do that. "Why not?"

"Good," he said.

After the chicken, Ella's aunt brought out a peach cobbler that she served in small blue bowls. The cobbler was still warm and Cole poured a little milk over his.

Following the complimenting of Aunt Laura on her cooking skills, Feathers and Cole excused themselves and went outside. They walked a short distance from the house.

"What shall it be, fast draw and fire, or simply target?" Feathers asked with all the confidence of a pistoleer.

"How about that fence post sticking up there," Cole said, pointing toward the rotting stump of an old post protruding from the dead brown grass. The distance was about twenty paces.

Feathers drew and fired five times, fanning the hammer back with the edge of his left hand. Three times Cole saw the wood splinter from the post.

Drawing his self-cocker, Cole took his time, thumbed the hammer back, and fired. He did that four more times. Five times his round chewed up bark.

"That is very good marksmanship," Feathers acknowledged. "But as slow as you were, had that post been an adversary, you would well have been killed, I believe."

"Maybe," Cole said, "but I didn't miss."

Feathers looked doubtful. "I would submit that it is the man who gets off the first shot who wins the day."

"Only if he hits his target, Mister Feathers. You can kill all the air you want to, but it's not the air that's going to kill you back. Two of your rounds missed the mark."

"I have to disagree with you, Mister Cole," he said, pointing toward the post with his chin. "My first round did find its mark, even if two missed. Had that been a man standing out there, he would have well been dead if he drew and fired his weapon as slowly as you just did."

"I guess there's no way of proving it unless you

want to put it to the real test," Cole said. "Do you want a real test, Mister Feathers, or is this just a game you're enjoying playing . . . shooting at targets that don't shoot back?"

It was out there in front of them now, their common dislike of one another. Cole could see the truth knotting up in Feathers's face.

"Because my family has wealth and holdings, you don't believe that I know what it is to pistol fight a man, isn't that it?"

"It doesn't matter what I think, Mister Feathers. All I know is, that shooting at a fence post doesn't count for much in this world. Staying alive does."

"Why'd you come here?" he asked, knocking the empty shells from his Deane-Adams.

"It's personal, Feathers, keep out of it."

"She won't have you," he said. "Not in the end, she won't." He was deliberate in reloading, the sun glinting off the brass cartridges. "Ella's a fine woman. Any man can see that. She's too fine a woman to be taken in by a man without means. What could you offer her?"

He waited to see if Cole would rise to the bait. He didn't.

"Look out there, Mister Cole. As far as you can see, that is land my family holds. A woman needs a nest, Cole, and that is the biggest damned nest you'll ever see."

"What's your point, Feathers?"

"My point, Cole, is you should ride out. Say

your sentimental good byes and ride away. Why make it hard on everybody by hanging around here? Ella's too damned polite to ask you to go, but I'm not. Do you really think you stand a chance with her?"

"I don't think you have."

"Have what?"

"Ever been in a gunfight. I don't think you know what it's like to stand in front of another man's pistol." As he said this, Cole turned to walk away.

"Cole!" Feathers called when Cole had gone about fifteen feet.

Cole turned. The Deane-Adams was aimed at him.

"You forgot to reload your weapon," Feathers said. "I didn't."

"You think so?" Cole said.

He looked uncertain but said: "Everyone knows a man only keeps five shells in his piece. Everyone knows a man doesn't keep his hammer on a loaded chamber. I counted. You shot five times at that post. That means you're carrying an empty gun."

"Put your piece away, Feathers, before something really bad takes place here."

He blinked. He was wondering if Cole really did have one more shell left in the self-cocker or if he was riding on empty. He was wondering something else, too. He was wondering even if Cole did have a round left in his gun whether or not Cole was fast enough to pull it and shoot him before he could pull the trigger on Cole. A man with true nerve didn't have such thoughts. Any other man, any other time or place, Cole wouldn't have warned him first. Too much talk in a fight just gets you killed. But he was thinking of the woman inside the house, how he'd come all this way just to see her. He didn't want to be part of a senseless killing on a pleasant Sunday afternoon. He didn't want her to see him like that. "You've got one chance, Feathers. Put it away and walk back to the house."

Feathers blinked again, like the wind had stung his eyes, then his arm sagged to his side, the Deane-Adams dangled against his right leg.

"Next time," Cole warned, "there'll be no talk."

The color was gone from Feathers's face and his right hand shook, causing the sunlight to dance off the nickel-plated barrel of the Deane-Adams.

"I think you bluffed me," he said as once more Cole started back toward the house.

Ella greeted them when they reached the porch. She could see the discord on their faces.

"Aunty says the gunfire hurts her ears."

"I must be leaving now, Ella," Tom Feathers said. "Please tell your aunt I had to leave and thank her again for me for the wonderful meal."

After Tom Feathers climbed into his buggy and drove away, Ella turned to Cole and asked: "What was that all about?"

"I think you already know."

"Men," she said.

"Yeah, it usually has to do with a woman."

"It wasn't necessary in this case, John Henry. You must know that already. I have little interest in Tom Feathers as a suitor, or anything else for that matter."

"I know it, but I don't think Tom Feathers knows it."

"So you quarreled over me?"

"No, not exactly quarreled, Ella."

For a long moment she stood there, looking at him. "Let's go back inside."

CHAPTER NINETEEN

John Henry Cole stayed on two more days at the house where Ella Mims and her Aunt Laura lived. He was provided a spare room, but most nights he and Ella managed to find their way into each other's bed. On the last day, Ella and Cole spent the morning lying in each other's arms and watched the rain just outside her bedroom window.

"We've become decadent, John Henry, you and I."

"I don't mind, if you don't."

The rain danced on the metal slope of the overhang just outside the window and sounded like the drumming of a thousand heartbeats.

"This has been such a wonderful time for me," Ella said, turning her face toward the window, the light the color of pearl against the glass.

"And for me," Cole said, fully meaning it. The last few days had been some of the most pleasant of his life—the long languorous hours they'd spent together, the walks across the fields, seeing the flights of geese on their southward trek, the dark V of their flight cut against molten skies, the sound of a dry wind stirring through the brittle winter grass beneath their footsteps. And Ella, her honey-colored hair long and falling past her shoulders as she walked alongside him, holding his hand. It all seemed so right.

"Why not stay?" she said suddenly, turning to look directly into his eyes.

"You know why not," he said.

"I know Ike was your friend. I know you feel you need to avenge his death, John Henry. But will that bring him back? Will it change anything in the long run?" Before he could say anything, she turned once more to stare out the window as though already knowing what his answer would be and not wanting to hear it. "What about us?" she asked softly. "How many chances will we have to find happiness? And if we don't take what is left to us now, when it's right here, will what we have still be there later on . . . after you've done what is *necessary* to avenge Ike's murder?"

"I don't know the answer to that, Ella."

In the time they'd spent together, he'd told her about his late wife and son. He'd told her about the war and what it had done to him, to the very marrow of him. He told her about friends of his who had died before their time. He even ended up telling her about Lydia Winslow. He told her everything. But he didn't feel he had to tell her why he couldn't stay with her. Not this time.

"Then you will go and take the risks involved in finding Ike's killer," she said, the pearl light falling over her bare shoulders.

"It's not a matter of choice with me, Ella. If you've learned anything about me in these last few days, you at least know that much."

"He means more to you than I do. . . ." Her voice was barely audible against the drumming song of rain.

"Ike was my friend, Ella."

"Then you'll go, even if it means the end of us?"

"That's a separate issue."

"No, it isn't. Not really, it isn't."

"I think it is."

"Then we disagree."

"If that's how you see it."

A bad feeling was crawling over Cole. The conversation was going down a road he didn't want it to, but there didn't seem any way to stop it. Might there be a reason Ella didn't want him to find Ike's killer? Something like what had ultimately poisoned his love for Lydia Winslow?

Ella sighed, turned toward Cole again, looked into his face, her eyes seeking something he wasn't offering. The disappointment in her gaze was as sodden as the weather. "Why did you come and find me," she asked, "if it was only to get me to love you and then leave me again?"

"I didn't mean for it to end up this way, Ella."

Her hand reached out and touched his cheek. "You are a dear sweet man, John Henry Cole, and one I will always love. But I can't wait for a man who will only ride in long enough to break my heart and then ride away again. This time it is because of Ike Kelly, but next time it will be because of someone or something else. I know that much about you as surely as I know anything in this life. I need more."

Cole kissed her lightly on the mouth and she didn't protest, but she didn't kiss him back.

"I will be leaving when the rain stops."

"Yes," she said. "When the rain stops."

The rain stopped that afternoon and a patch of blue sky broke through the slate sky, sending a long shaft of sunlight crawling over the wet grass. Cole had saddled the sorrel and was preparing to ride back to North Platte when Ella came from the house and stood on the porch. It was one of the hardest things Cole had ever had to do, not to go over and tell her that he'd changed his mind and that he was staying.

He put a foot in the stirrup, gave it one more second of thought, then swung up in the saddle, and rode the sorrel up to the porch.

"I'm sorry it has to be this way, Ella."

Her smile was lacking, her eyes brimmed with tears, but she would not let herself cry. "I hope you find the man you're looking for, John Henry. I truly do."

"And after I do?"

She brushed the heel of her hand against the corner of one eye because a single teardrop was threatening to spill down her cheek. "And afterward, I hope you find whatever else you're looking for."

Cole knew they had reached the end of the line; there was nothing more to offer.

"Good bye, Ella."

She may have spoken his name as he rode away, but the only thing he heard was the wind.

CHAPTER TWENTY

John Henry Cole avoided Bill Cody's place on the return trip and rode straight to North Platte and turned in the rented horse. He took the next stage to Cheyenne.

On the way, he tried hard not to think about Ella

Mims, but hard as he tried, thoughts of her kept creeping into his mind. He didn't want to think that maybe this very night Tom Feathers was sitting with her in the parlor, sharing spiced wine and intimate conversation, but he did and it gave him a tight, wrenching feeling. So, instead, he tried to concentrate on getting back to Cheyenne and seeing the job done that Will Harper and he had started—catching Leviticus Book and taking him to trial if he gave them that chance. If he didn't, well, it didn't much matter to Cole. If he wanted to put up a fight and maybe save them the trouble of escorting him to jail, so be it.

The worst thing was, Cole couldn't figure the man. He had outsmarted Will and him, and he had led them on a merry chase. He'd stolen Jilly Sweet, their horses, and finally Bart Bledsoe right out from under them. He could have saved himself the trouble and run, but he hadn't. That was the most puzzling part—why he didn't run and keep running. All in all he was in a foul mood the whole way.

Back in Cheyenne, Dr. Price looked disappointed to see Cole, standing at his door again. He looked beyond Cole's shoulder.

"You bring any more shooting victims for me to patch up?" he asked.

"Not a single one this time, Doc."

"Then you can come in."

Dr. Price stepped aside. The room smelled of mineral spirits.

"How's the last patient I brought you?" Cole asked.

"Limping. But then, I'm not surprised. The bullet chipped off a piece of his hip bone. Things like that will cause a man to limp permanently."

"The big question is, will it interfere with his dancing?" Cole said.

"Only if he's dancing with a big fat woman and she falls on him. You want a shot of bourbon?"

"Is it recommended?"

He looked into Cole's eyes without a glint of humor. "From what I can observe, it is."

"What's your diagnosis, Doc?"

"Death, son. You and Will and the others like you. I look into the eyes of you boys and I see nothing but death. You're surrounded by it, have been all your lives. Guns, knives, horses falling on you, whatever it takes. A hundred ways for a man to die and you boys know them all. Men like you and Will . . ."

He shook his head, walked to a medicine cabinet, and pulled out a bottle and two shot glasses, and poured them each a drink.

"Is Will up to riding yet?" Cole asked.

"If he doesn't mind a little pain," Dr. Price answered, testing the bourbon with tentative lips.

"How's the Mexican kid, José?"

"Same as he was the last time you asked me," he

said sourly. "He'll always be the same clear up till he takes his last breath. And that may not be for a while, poor little fellow."

Dr. Price closed his eyes, tossed down his bourbon, then licked his lips and blinked. "Same thing could happen to you or Will the next time you catch a slug. Did you ever imagine what that'd be like, paralyzed like that, lying in a bed all day, staring at the ceiling, counting fly specks, waiting for somebody to come in and turn you so the bed sores didn't eat through to your bones?"

"No, Doc, I don't ever think of it in that way."

"Why not?" He said it almost angrily, his gray watery eyes challenging Cole for an answer. "It happens. Bullets can do a lot worse than kill you."

"I know it happens, Doc . . . we both do."

Dr. Price poured himself a second glass of the whiskey, said—"Cheers."—and tossed it down. He stood there for a time, staring at his empty glass before putting the bottle back in the cabinet. "Forget what I said," he muttered. "Just sometimes it gets to me . . . the destruction of the human flesh. I should have taken my old mother's advice and become a lawyer. Relieving men of their money and holdings is a lot easier than relieving them of their pain and misery."

"It's good work you do, Doc."

"Yes, I suppose some days it is. Other days, I'm not so certain."

"I've been reading this book," Cole said, "about an old man who rides out to fight windmills. He believes they are giants and that flocks of sheep are invading armies."

"*Don Quixote*," Dr. Price said with a half smile that showed his big front teeth. "I'm familiar with the work."

"I just wonder if sometimes we're not like that," Cole said, "believing we're doing the right and good thing, when it's all just windmills and flocks of sheep in front of us."

"Everyone is as God made him," Dr. Price quoted from memory, "and much worse."

"All we can do is try, Doc."

He nodded. "Go collect your friend and get him the hell out of here. He's sitting out back, restless as a pimp in church. He just can't wait to go out and get himself shot again."

"Thanks for everything, Doc."

"Do me a favor, will you?"

"What's that?"

"Watch your backs."

Will Harper was sitting in a wheelchair, trying to roll a cigarette.

"Doc said you're up to riding," Cole said.

"About time you got back."

"I was only gone six days."

"Seven. And I've been ready to ride since day before yesterday."

"It doesn't look it."

"Aw, hell, I don't need this," he said, standing up. "I was just sitting in it, waiting for you to come back. I planned on leaving tomorrow whether you came back or not."

"Well, I'm here now."

He had a little hitch to his step as he crossed the porch and asked Cole for a match with which to light his shuck. "Shot off a piece of my hip bone. Now my damn' leg's about an inch or two shorter than the other one," he growled around the blue smoke of the cigarette.

"Tennessee Bob had one leg shorter than the other," Cole said. "You remember Tennessee Bob, don't you?"

Will Harper tugged the brim of his hat a little lower over his eyes and started off toward the livery. Cole fell in alongside him.

"I figured you got married, or something," Will said.

"Why'd you figure that?"

"The way you looked all moon-eyed when you left here."

"Went up to see Bill Cody," Cole said.

"Bullshit, you went to see that woman, what's her name . . . ?"

"Ella, you mean?"

"Yeah, Ella. Hell, I was you, I'd have married her and not come back. I'd be laying up in a nice featherbed right now with her in there with me. Wouldn't get up till Christmas, and maybe not

221

even then, I had a looker like her. Why'd you come back?"

"You know why? And, besides, I doubt you'd just lay around in a bed all day even if there was a good-looking woman in it with you."

"You don't know."

"Let's stop a minute and see Shorty."

Shorty Blaine was waiting on a man and woman and three children who were all sitting around a table in the middle of the dining room. They were eating fried chicken and butter beans. Shorty saw them and hobbled over.

"You walk like I do," he said when he saw Will.

"I'd have to have both hips shot up to walk like you," Will said. "Both hips shot and a horse fall on me."

"You boys want some coffee?"

"No," Will said. "We don't have time for coffee."

"Don't mind him, Shorty, he's just irritable," Cole said.

"From what?"

"From not lying in a featherbed with a pretty woman."

"Hell, who wouldn't like to be lying in a featherbed with a pretty woman?" Shorty said with a crooked grin.

"We got riding to do," Will grumbled, acting as though he was ignoring both of them.

Shorty said: "Did you ask him?"

"Ask me what?" Will said.

"Shorty wants to ride with us to go after Book," Cole said.

Will gave Cole a look. "Ain't we lost enough time already?"

"That's the whole point," Shorty interjected. "The trail's gone colder than a storekeeper's heart by now. Anybody around here knows about tracking a man, it's me."

"Tracker," Will declared. "What the hell do we need another tracker for? Any time Book decides we ain't been doing a good enough job, *he* tracks us."

"That's true," Cole said, "but if anyone can find him, it would be Shorty. He hunted half the Apaches in Arizona before becoming a cowhand on the Chisholm."

"Aw, hell, do what you want," Will growled. "But I ain't sharing the reward money, tracker or no tracker."

"That's fine with me," Shorty said, yanking off his apron. "I'd almost pay to go with you."

"Say!" the man sitting at the table with his family called out. "Can we have some more chicken and some extra butter beans?"

"You can, if you'll go in the kitchen and get 'em," Shorty said. "And when you and them young 'uns are finished stuffing your beaks, lock the door when you leave, and put the closed sign in the winda."

Will said: "If you're giving away fried chicken, I wouldn't mind having a little myself."

"I'll bring a sack of it along," Shorty said.

Cole told Shorty they'd meet him at the stables. "I should have brought it up sooner about Shorty wanting to go with us," he said to Will as they left the diner.

"I guess it could be worse," Will said.

"How so?"

"Shorty could have offered just to bring along a sack of butter beans instead of his fried chicken. I never was big on butter beans."

They rode out of Cheyenne within an hour.

The next day, they arrived at the place where Leviticus Book had stolen Bart Bledsoe and his mule. The wagon was still there, but all the patent medicines inside were missing.

"Lookit that," Will said, peering into the back of the wagon. "Damn' thieves come along and stole all Bart's patent medicines. What the hell is this country coming to?"

"Well, they didn't steal the wagon," Shorty said.

"Wonder they didn't," Will muttered. "A wicked place like this, folks steal everything . . . including whores!"

Shorty had dismounted and was searching the ground for sign of tracks.

"How's he going to find any good sign?" Will finally wondered, watching him. "It's been more'n a week since that black devil stole Bart."

"I don't know, Will. But if anybody can cut sign, it'd be Shorty. He's got a knack for tracking."

Will offered Cole a doubtful roll of his eyes.

Shorty hobbled over to where they were sitting their horses and said: "They went thataway." He pointed toward the Blue Mountains with a finger as gnarled as an old twig.

"That means he's changed direction again," Will said. "First north, then south, now west. You sure it's the ones we're after that's made them tracks, Shorty?"

"You said they had a mule with them," Shorty said. "That set of tracks shows up as two horses and a mule. The mule is unshod and the tracks are shallow. You said that this Bart fella wasn't too big a man. That means he was sitting that mule. The big man was riding a horse of about sixteen hands, judging by the length of the stride. The girl was on a shorter horse. They're heading west."

"I'll be god damned," Will said. "Can I please have a piece of your chicken now, Mister Blaine?"

"You may."

CHAPTER TWENTY-ONE

Once more the trail was leading toward the Blue Mountains. Will rode along contentedly, eating several pieces of Shorty's fried chicken.

"This is mighty good chicken, Mister Blaine,"

he commented. "I think I'll save the leg bones and make whistles out of them."

"Whistles?"

"That's right. A little music wouldn't hurt this expedition any."

"I never heard of making a musical instrument out of a chicken bone," Shorty said.

"Well, you can," Will said. "I learned how from a Sioux woman."

"That's interesting."

Will produced a bottle of mash whiskey from his saddlebags and passed it to Shorty. Shorty took a long pull and said: "God damn but that tastes pretty good."

"How'd you end up with your leg all bent?" Will asked him.

"Horse fell on me. I was riding along pretty as you please and the son-of-a-buck just went over on me. Rode for years, all up and down the trails . . . the Bozeman, the Goodnight-Loving, the Bandera, the Chisholm . . . never once had a horse fall over on me. Had horses shot out from under me or drop dead of the staggers when being chased by Apaches and Comanches, but never had one fall on me until that day."

"That is a stroke of bad luck," Will said.

"Worst part of it was," Shorty said, taking liberty with Will's bottle. "I was on my way to see my sweetheart that very day. I was going to ask her to marry me. It was a Sunday. I remember it was a nice pleasant day like this one. I was just riding along, going to see my sweetheart when it happened. Her name was Josephine Dart. Tall gal, pretty as you please."

"You never made it, then?" Will asked, his curiosity now up as he gnawed on a drumstick. "You never got to ask your sweetheart to marry you?"

Shorty shook his head sadly and took another pull on the bottle of mash. "No, that horse fell on me and crushed my leg and pelvis and squashed my insides. They thought they was going to have to bury me that very evening. The pain was so bad, I was wishing they'd just get their shovels and bury me without waiting for me to die. Then I begged them to shoot me in the head, but no one would. Then a doctor rode all the way from Tascosa and gave me a bottle of laudanum and asked if I was a Christian man and said he would pray with me till my time came. The laudanum helped more than the praying."

"Well, wasn't that doctor able to set your leg straight once he seen you were going to live?" Will asked, tossing the drumstick bone over his shoulder.

"I thought you was going to make a whistle out of that bone," Shorty said.

Will reached into the sack and pulled out another drumstick and said: "I forgot. I'll just have to eat another chicken leg and save the next bone for my whistle."

"I don't believe you can make a whistle out of a chicken's leg bone," Shorty said skeptically.

Will went on chewing the drumstick, ignoring the comment. "You never did say why that medico wasn't able to set your leg straight after that horse fell on you, Mister Blaine."

"He wasn't much of a doctor for one thing," Shorty said. "He mostly treated sick animals and took care of burying the dead. I think that's why he rode all the way out from Tascosa in the first place. He figured the boys would take up a nice collection to have me buried. I found out later that, when he wasn't treating sick animals or burying folks, he gave haircuts and only charged twenty-five cents and was considered to be the best barber in the Panhandle."

"Well, I hope he was better at cutting hair than setting people's bones," Will said. "Your leg's as crooked as a cottonwood branch."

"I don't know," Shorty replied. "I never went to him for a haircut."

"I'd say you saved yourself a good two bits, then."

"It was my poor luck to have my horse fall on me in a country where the only doctor was a man whose best talent was hair cutting."

"That is poor luck," Will said. "All the way around."

"The great sadness was, I never did make it out to Josephine's that day. And by the time I was able to get around well enough to ride a horse again, Jo had run off and got married to a goat rancher."

"A goat rancher!" Will seemed incredulous. "Who in their right mind would ranch goats?"

"This man that Josephine married," Shorty said, "that's who."

"That would be a hard one to swallow, Mister Blaine," Will commented dryly, "to have your leg busted and set by a quack then find out your best gal run off and married a man that ranched goats."

"It wasn't the best year I ever had, I can tell you that."

They passed the bottle between them as they rode along, all the while commenting on the deficiencies of doctors and women in general, and goat ranching in particular. Cole's thoughts were of Ella Mims, so he didn't have a lot to contribute to the conversation of his companions.

Their journey remained uneventful for the remainder of the day, and that night they made camp near a clump of cottonwoods along a sweet spring that trickled water cold and clear. Shorty said he would cook their supper if the other two would gather firewood.

"My leg is aching something terrible," Will responded. "Gathering firewood ain't in my book."

Cole offered to gather the wood while Will

made himself a comfortable place to sit and nurse a fresh bottle of mash.

Shorty made biscuits for supper that night along with some extra for their breakfast the next morning. They ate the remainder of the fried chicken and washed it down with coffee, except for Will who preferred to wash his supper down with the mash whiskey. It was a good meal and afterward they sat around and smoked and shared some of Will's whiskey and talked about the old days, the places they'd been, the times they'd had—both the good and the bad. And gradually, as the conversation wound down, they were all left to their private thoughts as they lay, looking up at the stars.

That was the best and the worst time of night— when conversation ended and sleep hadn't yet begun. Cole pulled his blankets up tight and kept his feet pointed toward the fire. It was a cold night and getting colder. Lying there, thinking about it, some nagging doubts came into his mind, doubts about the man they were chasing. Leviticus Book had outsmarted them so far. That in itself was troubling. Will was a professional manhunter, yet he'd been outfoxed and Cole had been outfoxed along with him. That combined with the fact of how easily Book had murdered a man like Ike Kelly didn't exactly cause Cole to want to close both eyes at night, knowing the man was still out there in the dark somewhere. So far, Book had cost him a good friend and probably the love of a good woman. He wanted to get it over with, to end the business. Maybe when it was ended, he could ride back to Nebraska and see if Ella was still a free woman. He heard the call of a gray wolf and felt the heat of the fire against the soles of his boots. Those things and the mash whiskey finally forced him into a fitful sleep.

The next morning, they were awakened by a hard, icy rain. It fell out of the sky like a bucket of cold nickels and seemed to freeze as it hit the ground.

"Look's like breakfast is out," Will grumbled.

"Unless you want me to sit around in this frozen rain and cook," Shorty said, his own mood sour because of the nasty weather.

"There's bound to be a town somewhere along this road," Cole suggested. "Maybe, if we leave off with the griping and get a move on, we'll come to it."

No one argued.

"How come it ain't snow, I wonder?" Shorty said after they had ridden for a time in the ice storm. "It's cold enough to be snow. Why's it have to be ice? All the damned luck!"

"It's just one more thing," Will grumbled, his mustaches heavy with ice particles. "It's been my poor luck ever since I stopped in Cheyenne that first time and ran into John Henry." Will looked at Cole from under the brim of his wet hat.

"Nothing against you," he assured. "Just that, if I'd never stopped to wet my beak that day, I probably already would have captured Book and had him halfway back to Fort Smith by now."

Cole didn't bother to contradict Harper on the subject. He saw no point in discussing what might have been. Then he saw them coming through the glittering ice storm—the band of Indians.

"We've got company," he said.

Will and Shorty jerked up their drooping heads. The ice seemed to crackle off their slickers when they did.

"What the hell do you think they're up to?" Shorty said.

Before anyone could offer a reason, the forelegs of Will's horse buckled and sent him sprawling. Then Cole heard the crack of a rifle. He swung the speckled bird around and offered his hand to Will at the same time as he kicked his right foot free from the stirrup. "Get on!"

Will was still half stunned from the tumble he'd taken, but he grabbed Cole's hand and with a struggle pulled himself onto the back of the bird. She didn't care for it much, having to haul two big men, but she responded to Cole's command as he drove his heels into her flanks.

"Where?" shouted Shorty.

"Anywhere but here!"

Shorty tried to grab the lead rope of the pack mule.

"Leave it!" Cole yelled, and Shorty did.

They raced their horses across a sage-covered valley coated with a thin layer of ice that shattered like glass under the hoofs of their mounts. Cole looked back in time to see that one of the renegades had caught the pack mule, but the others were still on their heels. With the speckled bird having to carry both Cole and Will, the race would not be a long one. Several times bullets went whistling past their heads. Cole thought they were all holding their breaths, waiting for one of the bullets to find its mark.

After a mile, the bird started to labor under the load. Shorty's roan passed her and with every second opened a wider distance between them. Cole looked back again and saw the renegades on their swift mustangs were gaining. Shorty and his roan were several hundred yards ahead of them, then Cole saw Shorty's horse top a rise and disappear over the other side. The bird was doing her best, but her best wasn't going to be good enough, not with two riders on her back.

The renegades were less than a hundred yards away as they started up the rise. Cole figured they would have to stop near the top and make their stand.

The icy rain stung like bees, attacking their faces and hands. Then Shorty appeared at the top of the rise again and waved them on.

"What the hell's he doing?" Will shouted.

Cole urged the bird on. She gave all she had and took them to the top where they saw the walls of an old cabin at the bottom of the slope.

"It ain't exactly Fort Abraham Lincoln," Shorty shouted through snapping ice rain, "but it'll do!" Then jerking his Winchester free from his saddle scabbard, he began firing at their pursuers while Cole raced the bird down the slope.

They made the walls of the cabin just as the band of renegades reached the top of the rise, Shorty coming in behind them. Several rounds slammed into the cabin's walls as they took cover.

"Thank the son-of-a-bitch who built this cabin," Will said, taking up a position alongside a window.

"Yes, but he could have left a roof on it," Shorty said with a relieved half grin.

"Who do you reckon those peckerwoods are?" Will asked, peering around the sill long enough to have two more rounds slam into the walls.

"From what I could see," Cole said, "they looked like Sioux. But then, I'm not an expert on Indians."

"Maybe once we whip them, we can ask them," Shorty said, ducking around an opening long enough to rapid-fire his Winchester. The renegades had slipped back beyond the rise, no doubt holding a powwow as to how they were going to smoke them out.

"Do we try and make another run for it?" Shorty asked after some time had passed with no further sign of the renegades.

"Two horses, three men?" Cole said. "You figure out what our chances are."

"Maybe they got tired and left," Will said. "You know how damn' funny Indians can be about waiting around for something to happen."

"You want to take a walk up that hill and find out?" Cole asked.

Will looked sheepish at the suggestion.

"I wish it would at least quit this damn' freezing drizzle on us," Shorty said. "I could stand a smoke."

"I wonder what did happen to the roof," Will said, looking up as he shielded his face with one hand. "Somebody steal it?"

The walls were still in good order, though they sagged at the northwest corner. All the glass was gone from the windows.

"Maybe a big wind came and blew the roof off," Shorty suggested. "Sometimes they get cyclones out in this country and they blow roofs off places."

"That's probably what happened, all right," Will said. "A cyclone came along and blowed off the roof and blowed out all the windows and whoever was living here had to leave." Will pulled out his bottle and added: "Least this didn't get broke in all the commotion." He took a pull before passing it to Shorty and Cole.

"What about those Indians, John Henry, you see any more of them up there?" Will asked.

235

Cole looked but didn't see anyone. Then came a roar that sounded like rolling thunder and they all looked at one another. Then twice more the sound came.

"That's a Big Fifty," Will said. "Sharps buffalo gun."

"What the hell!" Shorty said, taking a peek through one of the missing windows.

"I used to hunt buffalo on the plains. I know a Sharps when I hear one," Will assured them.

"You reckon one of those peckerwoods has a Sharps with him?" Shorty asked.

"If he does," Cole said, "what's he shooting at?"

"As long as it's not us," Will said, "I don't care. Any gun that can kill a buffalo at five hundred yards ain't something I want aimed at me."

Several more shots from the big gun crashed through the air, then forty minutes passed without a sound.

"I'm getting damn' tired of sitting here, freezing my backside off," Will said.

"Well, I don't see how that's going to change any," Shorty said. "Unless this ice rain stops or you go and build a new roof and put it on over us."

"Screw this!" Will said, and stepped outside the walls of the cabin. "Let me borrow your horse."

Shorty said: "Go right ahead. Just don't get him shot, OK?"

"I'll go with you," Cole said. "I'm tired of the damned ice, too."

"I'll wait here, and cover you boys," Shorty said. "I'm a damn' sight better hitting what I aim at if I ain't on the back of a horse."

Cole rode with his self-cocker in his right hand, Will rode with Cole's Winchester resting across the horn in front of him. They took it slow up that hill just in case the renegades were still there waiting for them. It was hold your breath time.

What they found when they reached the top caused both of them to pull up short. Four of the Indians were dead, their faces gray under the formed ice. Each had holes blown through them the size you could put your fist through. The rest were nowhere in sight. Will and Cole looked at each other.

"What the hell went on here, John Henry?"

"I don't know."

The realization was slow in coming, then they looked again at each other.

"Leviticus Book," Cole breathed.

Will nodded. "Must have been."

CHAPTER TWENTY-TWO

"How'd you explain it, John Henry?"

"Damned if I know."

They sat their horses and stared at the dead renegades. They had the markings of Sioux braves. The thing was, they were ragged, thin, the soles of their moccasins torn. The ice glazed their faces, causing them to look ghostly in death.

"You notice?" Will said.

"Yeah," Cole said. The dead were all young men, not one looked older than nineteen. "Kids," he said.

Will nodded. "Still, they would have killed us, given the chance."

"I know."

"Why'd he do it, John Henry? Why'd Book hang around and kill these bucks? It don't make no damn' sense."

"Nothing makes any sense."

Will looked around, his gaze scouting the mist. "Jesus, he'd've had to have shot these boys from over yonder in that little stand of trees. Must be better'n five, six hundred yards and through a hard rain."

It seemed impossible for anyone to make a shot like that. To make it four times seemed unreal. They could barely make out the ghostly stand of distant trees.

"I still can't cipher it, John Henry. Why'd Book do it?"

"He wants us to know he's out there," Cole speculated. "He wants us to know he's not going anywhere . . . that he's not running from us."

Will kept shaking his head in disbelief. "Gives me the chills worse than this ice rain, John Henry."

"I caught the feeling, too."

"Why don't he just come out and fight us if he ain't going to run any more?"

"He wants to do it his way, and in his time. He's not worried about us catching him, Will. He knows we can't."

Will wiped the wet out of his eyes and busted off bits of ice from his long mustaches. "The hell we can't!" he exploded. "I'll not only catch him, I'll cut his damn' head off and take it back to Fort Smith in a gunny sack if I have to."

"You know something?"

"What?"

"He could be sitting in those trees right now, sighting us with that Sharps. All he'd have to do is squeeze the trigger and we'd be dead men, just like these poor ragged boys."

Will looked out toward the soft outline of the ghostly trees, staring hard through the silver sleet. His face knotted up. They both felt it then, the death waiting for them.

"Let's get the hell back down to the cabin," Will said.

They rode back to the shack and dismounted.

"What's up?" Shorty asked.

"We got company," Will said, handing the reins of Shorty's horse back to him.

"Who?"

"Leviticus Book, that's who."

Shorty squinted from under the caved-in brim of his hat. "How you know that?"

"He killed several of those Indians that were chasing us," Will said. "They're laid out just the other side of that ridge with holes in 'em big enough to see the ground through."

"The buff' gun we heard?" Shorty said.

Will nodded. "Shot 'em from a good five hundred yards, maybe more and through the dang' ice rain. Those Indian boys never knew what hit 'em."

"It don't make no sense." Shorty snorted.

"You got that right." Will reached for his bottle, saw it was almost empty, took a hit, passed it to Shorty.

"You want a try at this first?" Shorty said, holding the bottle out to Cole.

"No, you go ahead."

Shorty swallowed the last of the mash and set the empty bottle on a window sill. "Here's to the old boy who put up this cabin and saved our sorry hides."

Will stared at the empty like it was a sweetheart, leaving town.

"So it ain't so much we're chasing him as he's chasing us, that it?" Shorty said, licking his half frozen lips.

"That seems to be the case," Cole said.

"Then why not just sit right here and wait for him to come to us?" Shorty said.

"I ain't sitting out in this damn' ice rain any longer'n I have to waiting for some crazy son-of-a-bitch to show up so's he can put a hole through my guts," Will declared. "You want to sit around and wait, go right ahead."

"Damn, I wish it would stop raining ice on us so I could make myself a cigarette, my nerves are so up," Shorty said.

"Yeah, well you better figure out a way to smoke it wet," Will said, "because you might not get the chance later on."

Shorty shifted his gaze to Cole, who held the bird's reins, then to Will, and then back to Cole. "What's he saying?" he asked Cole.

"Nothing. Let's get going."

"Where?"

"Anywhere but here."

They cautiously mounted. Will took turns riding double with Cole and Shorty. The ice storm didn't let up until later that afternoon when it turned to snow.

Will glanced up at the sky, then tucked his chin into the top of his slicker and said: "I didn't think it could get any colder or more miserable, but I was wrong."

"I think there is a place ahead of us called Whiskey Hill," Shorty said.

"That sounds like a good bet to me," Will said. He was riding behind Cole.

"At least I recall there being a town with that name," Shorty added. "It could have a different name by now, or a cyclone could have come along and blown the town away like it did the roof on that cabin."

Will tossed Shorty a hard look. "Well, I hope it's still there," he growled, " 'cause I could stand a drink and some dry clothes and a plate of grub to go with it."

Shorty's memory proved to be accurate, because an hour later they hit the town of Whiskey Hill, only the signpost had the name crossed out and a new name painted below it: PAINT TOWN. What they saw were a few low-slung log huts, several large tents, and a few old Conestoga wagons that had been converted into living quarters. A kid with a good arm could have thrown a rock from one end of the town to the other.

"Look there!" Will said, now riding behind Shorty and pointing toward one of the buildings.

There were at least a half dozen hand-painted signs like the one on the edge of town. They had been nailed to the front of the largest of the log structures.

ROY BEAN, ATTY AT LAW
COLD BEER HORSES BOUGHT & SOLD
NO CREDIT LAND FOR SALE
JUSTICE OF THE PEACE

"Whoever that Roy Bean is," Will said, "he's got the market cornered on enterprise in this town."

"I wonder does he fix hobbled legs, too?" Shorty said with a sly grin.

"Let's hobble inside and find out," Will said. "Even if he can't fix a hobbled leg, at least we'd be out of this miserable climate."

They dismounted, tied off, and ducked inside under a low doorway. Two men were playing dominoes in a corner with an upturned pork barrel for a table. Another man was asleep in a chair, a black and white dog sleeping near the man's feet. The dog had its paws pointed toward a potbelly stove and his head resting between them. A woman with tired features leaned against the plank bar and stared at them like they were goats.

Sitting in the center of the room was a man paring his toenails with a pocket knife. He wore a plug hat and a shirt missing the collar. He needed a shave and maybe a bath, judging by the looks of his condition. He had the stub of an unlit cigar clenched between his teeth. He seemed genuinely pleased by their arrival.

"You gents look half froze. Won't you step up to the stove and warm yourselves?"

"Your sign outside says you sell cold beer," Will said. "That mean you sell whiskey, too? I sure don't want to drink anything cold on a day such as this."

"Sorry." The man shrugged. "My whiskey man ain't come by this week. It must be the weather that's holding him up. You want anything to drink, it'll have to be beer."

"I was hoping for whiskey," Will said, plainly disappointed. "Beer's best on a hot day, not a cold one."

The man closed up his pocket knife and examined the yellow horn of toenail he'd been trimming before pulling on a long gray sock over his foot. "Whiskey's hard to come by this far out from civilization," he said, "even on the best of days. What was it, Lum, last July when that one whiskey peddler was found shot full of arrows? I believe it was July, wan't it?"

One of the men playing dominoes looked up and said: "Uhn-huh."

"OK, make it a beer, then," Will said. "I guess a beer is better'n nothing."

"How 'bout you boys?" the man asked. "You want a beer, too?"

"Not me," Shorty said. "I'd as soon run naked and jump in a rain barrel on a day like this as drink a cold beer. You sell tobacco and papers?"

"Sure, cigars, too."

"No, I just want some makings so's I can roll myself a shuck."

The man pulled the beer tap and filled a glass for Will, then reached under the counter and laid some makings on the counter for Shorty. "How about you?" he asked Cole. "You want a beer, some tobacco, maybe?"

Cole had taken a position by the potbelly stove, trying to warm himself and dry out his clothes. He took notice that the two men playing dominoes were well armed with Hopkins and Allen revolvers, as was the sleeping man. It didn't mean much sometimes in that country for a man to go about armed, but you never knew whether it meant anything or not until the time came. "No, I'll just catch a little of this heat, you don't mind."

"Sure, help yourself, heat's free. Maybe when you warm up a little, you'll be in the mood to purchase something."

Shorty rolled himself a cigarette while Will drank his beer. The click of the dominoes was about all that could be heard for the next few minutes.

"I'm Roy Bean," the man behind the counter finally said. "Who might you boys be?"

"We're not from around here," Will said, ignoring the question. "You want to pour me another beer?"

Roy Bean pulled the beer tap again, filling Will's glass, then used a paddle to scrape off the head before sliding it across to him. "Like I said, my name's Roy Bean. I'm sorta the big dog here in Paint Town. Not that that means a hell of a lot."

"That give you permission to ask a man his business?" Will said sourly over his beer.

Roy Bean blinked. "Just that I ain't never seen

none of you boys around here. I like to know who comes into my town."

"You own the whole town," Shorty asked, the smoke of his cigarette curling up into his eyes, "or just this here?"

"What's worth owning, I own," Bean said. "The rest is up for grabs."

"We're just passing through," Cole said, knowing that as cold and wet and miserable as Will was feeling, it wouldn't take much to goad him into a fight, and the one thing they didn't need right at the moment was another fight.

"Passing through," Bean said, as though he had to think about what that meant. "Did I also mention I'm the mayor and chief of police?"

"Mayor?" Will said, looking up from his beer. "What sort of mayor pares his toenails in front of a lady?" Will glanced over at the woman, leaning against the end of the bar. So far, she had not said a single word. But when Will said the word "lady", she laughed.

"Mister, you must have me confused with someone else. Hell, a lady is the last thing you'll find in Paint Town."

"Pardon me all to hell for the mistake," Will said.

"You want to go to the back room with me?" she asked Will. "It'll cost you two dollars, but it'll be the best damn' two dollars you ever spent."

"I guess I didn't stop here to buy a woman."

She looked at Shorty. "How about you?"

Shorty looked around the room, saw that she was talking to him. He straightened up from the way he'd been slouching with the smoke of his cigarette curling up into his right eye. "Two dollars, huh?"

She smiled in a tired way. She looked like she hadn't gotten much sun in her life.

"I reckon I could do that," Shorty said, then he looked at Cole. "We got time?"

"I guess until we can buy another horse and get dry clothes, we're not going anywhere."

Shorty dug into his pockets and came out with the money. "Two dollars," he said, handing her the money. "Lead the way."

He followed the woman to the back and beyond a curtain.

"How about another beer while you're waiting for your friend to get his business done back there with Cleopatra?" Roy Bean said.

"Cleopatra?" Will said. "That her name?"

"Her real name is Dot, but she prefers to be called Cleopatra. Says Dot ain't a very exotic name for a whore."

Will slid his empty glass back across the bar and waited for Bean to fill it. "I knew a whore in Durango called herself the Queen of Sheba," he said. "Cleopatra, huh?"

Bean grinned. "Heard you say you're in need of a horse," he said as he filled the glass, then swiped off the head with his paddle before pushing it across to Will. "What happened, did you boys lose one?"

"Some renegade Sioux jumped us half a day's ride from here," Will said. "They shot my horse out from under me."

That seemed to get everyone's attention, including the man who'd been sleeping in the chair. "Sioux?"

"I don't think you have to worry much about them," Will said. "Four of the bunch that jumped us have gone to the Happy Hunting Ground. The other two are probably halfway to Canada by now."

"You certain about that," Bean said. "That those Indians run off?"

"Certain as anyone can be about an Indian," Will said.

The domino players went back to their game and the man sitting in the chair closed his eyes once more.

"Oh, well, that's good news that you boys put a little hurt on those heathen reds."

"I suppose it is," Will said. "Have you seen any strangers around here besides us?"

Bean licked his lips. "There was a big Negro cuss through here the other day. Had a sweet little Negra gal with him, and a man riding a mule."

Will and Cole traded glances.

"What he do while here in town?" Cole asked.

"He was looking for a little poker playing. Said

248

he was needing to kill a little time while he waited for some friends of his to show up. He won forty dollars in that card game."

Will rolled his eyes. "That son-of-a-bitch."

"You the friends he was waiting for?" Roy Bean asked.

CHAPTER TWENTY-THREE

Will Harper settled into getting as good and drunk as he could on beer while John Henry Cole stood by the potbelly stove, letting his clothes dry. The two men playing dominoes concentrated on their game, and the man sleeping in the chair remained that way, as did his dog.

Roy Bean played several tunes on a mouth harp while Shorty and Cleopatra were making themselves scarce in the back room.

"Play 'A Cowboy's Lament'," Will said to Bean. "You know that one?"

"I believe I do," Bean said. "And after that, I'll play 'The Roses Bloom in Spring'. How'll that be?"

"If it's sad, I'd like to hear you play it," Will said. "Right now I'm feeling blue and would like to stay that way for a time."

Bean began to play the ballad. A mouth harp can be a mournful instrument to begin with if played the right way. Hearing "A Cowboy's

Lament" only made it sound all the more mournful. By the time Roy Bean finished playing that sweet sad ballad, and the one about roses blooming in spring, Will looked like he might bawl in his beer. "Play those two again, would you?" he requested. Bean happily obliged.

Nearly two hours passed before Shorty and Cleopatra emerged from behind the curtain that led to the back rooms. They had their arms around each other and Shorty's eyes looked dreamy. When Will asked what had taken so long, Shorty acted as sheepish as a schoolboy that had gotten caught playing hooky.

As soon as Bean finished playing his mouth harp, Shorty ordered beers for everyone in the room, then he and Cleopatra found themselves a private table.

"I'm as happy as I've ever been," Shorty announced.

Will looked at him. "About what?"

"Lord, Will, ain't you got eyes?" Shorty said. "Cleo's an outstanding woman."

Will blinked several times. "Maybe it's because this beer is warm that I feel so terrible in my skull," he said.

"Maybe so," Shorty said.

The lateness of the hour forced Bean to go around the room, lighting lamps. "You boys plan on spending the night? I could rent you a room for three dollars."

Will continued to stare at Shorty and Cleopatra. The wind outside rattled the windows.

"Snow's gotten awful deep out there, boys," Bean announced, checking the weather conditions as he passed by one of the windows. "A man on a small horse was to run in one of them snowdrifts, wouldn't nobody find him till spring. You boys ought to consider staying out of this storm."

Will looked at Cole and said: "How you reckon that black devil is gonna make it out there in this storm? Sitting out there with no shelter of any kind, him and that skinny little gal and poor old Bart?"

"I don't know, Will."

"It may just be that he won't make it," Will said. "Maybe he'll freeze to death. Maybe this storm will do what we ain't been able to . . . end the bloody trail of Leviticus Book."

"That's a possibility," Cole said.

Will did not seem convinced. "He'll figure out something, I'd damn' well bet on that."

The man, sleeping in the chair, finally opened his eyes, looked around, then nudged the dog awake. "Come'n, Jeff Davis, time we went home and had our supper."

When the man pushed open the door and nudged his dog out ahead of him, a blast of cold air and snow rushed into the room like an unwanted guest. The two men playing dominoes looked irritated.

"Damn fool!" one of them said.

"How 'bout that room, boys?" Bean repeated. His eyes seemed to glitter with the prospect of doing business.

Will walked over to the window, looked out for a long hard moment, then walked back to the bar. "I don't reckon there is a real hotel nearby?"

"Not for a hundred miles there ain't," Bean said.

Will reached into his pocket.

Shorty said: "Don't pay extra for me. Me and Cleo have made our own arrangements for the night."

"Is that why you're so damn' happy?" Will said.

"Wouldn't you be?"

"Which way is the room, mister?" Will grunted, slapping $2 on the bar.

"Room's normally three," Bean said, eyeing the money before putting it in his vest pocket. "But looks like there ain't nobody else will be wantin' it, so I guess you can have it for two." He grabbed a lantern, then struggled into a bear coat, and led them out the back door to a small shack. "In here," he said. "I'll get a fire going."

There were four cots along the walls and a wood burner in the center. It wasn't the Inter-Ocean, but it was a whole lot better than cold ground and a blanket of snow. Cole volunteered to take care of the horses. Bean said he could put them up with his next door at his livery. He said that, come a break in the weather, he'd be happy to sell them a good horse for Will to ride.

Will said: "I'll bet you would. Is there anything you don't have the market cornered on?"

"Not in this neck of the woods," Bean said with a wide grin. "See you boys in the morning. Breakfast is a dollar . . . all the hoecakes you can get down your gullet if you get to the table before they run out."

Cole fought his way through the windy snow and gathered the horses—Shorty's roan and the bird—and led them over to the livery and grained and curried them. He regretted having left them outside so long. Then he went back to the shack and crawled onto a cot and drew the blankets over him.

Will had been sitting there in his underdrawers and socks, staring at the little wood burner; it glowed like a cherry. Then he reached out and doused the lamp's wick. The room grew dark except for the cherry glow of the wood burner.

"I got a bad feeling about this business," Will said. "I almost wish now I'd gone down to New Mexico and hunted me a killer rather than this devil, Book."

"He's no different than anyone else," Cole said. "He can get caught the same as any other man." Cole said it, but wasn't as convinced as he made it sound.

"I've chased lots of men in my life," Will said.

"But I never chased one like this one. Most men will run. Those that don't will stand and fight. I never had one do both."

"He hasn't really fought us, Will," Cole observed. "He's just played a cat-and-mouse game with us so far."

"You know how you reckoned he shot and burned Ike up?" Will said. "I think he'll probably do that to us if he gets the chance. That, or worse."

"He's just one man, Will. There's three of us."

"One man!" he snorted.

Cole could tell by the way he slurred his words that he had managed to get drunk on the beer. "We'll get him, Will."

"That was a sad thing," Will said, "the way Roy Bean played that mouth harp. Made me feel bad down to my bones. Made me think of when I shot Flora."

"You said it was an accident, Will."

"It was, but I still feel bad it happened. That and other things I've done in my life. A man does certain things he can't ever get over."

"You said she came out of it OK, that she went off and got married and had kids."

"Oh, it ain't so much I shot her. It's we didn't end up together. I think I loved her about as much as I can love a woman."

Cole heard him stretch out on the bed, heard the way the dry shucks in his mattress shifted when he lay down.

"Hard for me to think of Flora with my bullet in her and her with another man right this very minute . . . lying in bed next to him . . . him maybe . . . well, you know."

"I would think getting shot by your sweetheart would have a bad effect on a romance," Cole offered. "Maybe if you hadn't shot her, Will, it might have worked out between the two of you."

"I guess you're right about that. But I don't think that was what made her go off and marry another fellow. I think there was something more to it than that. Something about me she couldn't abide the thought of for the long haul."

Cole thought of what Ella had said about needing a man full-time in her life. "We've all made mistakes."

"Some of us more'n others."

Cole wondered if maybe Ella was spending the evening sitting in her parlor with Tom Feathers right this moment. He could almost hear the sound of her laughter, feel the touch of her hand on the back of his wrist, smell the sweetness of her perfume along the curve of her neck.

"Cleopatra," Will said.

"What about her?"

"I should have taken her up on her offer before Shorty did. If I had, it'd be me lying in a cozy bed with her right now instead of him."

"Like I said, Will, we all make mistakes. Time to get some shut-eye."

"It's the damnedest feeling."

"What's that?"

"Knowing Book could squeeze the trigger on us anytime he takes a notion, knowing he's out there somewhere, keeping an eye on us. What sort of killer hunts the men who're chasing him? We could step out the door in the morning to make water and he could do it then. With that damn' buffalo gun, he could take us off at the neck and we'd never know it until it was too late."

"Think of it this way, Will. If that's what his intentions were, he probably would have shot us by now. I think he's got something else in mind for us."

"I don't know why I let Shorty beat my time with that whore, Cleopatra. . . ."

His voice sounded distant, then Cole heard him snoring and was left to think his own thoughts, about a sweetheart left behind, and a quick killer on his trail, and neither thought brought him any comfort.

CHAPTER TWENTY-FOUR

It didn't stop snowing for three days and, when it finally did, snow was piled up to the roof tops.

"We'd need horses with wings to get through the drifts," Will said morosely.

Shorty said: "I don't mind the snow so much."

"Of course you don't," Will declared. "You got somebody to keep you warm at night."

Shorty smiled as Cleopatra brought him a cup of coffee for his breakfast, then sat on his lap while he sipped it. "Well, I can't help it I was smart enough to know a good thing when I saw one," he said. "She asked you first, but you turned her down. Don't blame me for having good horse sense."

"Horse sense," Will grumped.

"Well, at least the sun's finally out," Roy Bean said, peering through one of the frosted windows he had wiped with the palm of his hand. "That's one thing in your favor."

Cole had just come back in from checking the horses. It was cold enough to make all the old wounds and injuries he'd ever suffered come alive. Bits of ice clung to his mustaches.

"How is it out there?" Will asked.

"How does it look?"

"That's what I thought."

Cole helped himself to some of Bean's coffee and smoked a cigarette along with it. They were all getting restless, except for Shorty—he was acting more like a lovesick man every day. Will said it would take a stick of dynamite to get the smile off his face.

"So you own a business over in Cheyenne?" Cole heard Cleopatra ask Shorty as he sipped his coffee. "What sorta business?"

"A restaurant," Shorty said.

"You must do all right for yourself then," Cleo said. "Being a business owner, I mean."

"I make a living. Got a little four-room house, friends, it's a good life."

"How about some more sugar in your coffee, hon?"

"Thing is," Shorty said to Cleo, "I can use me some permanent help. It's hard to find a good waitress these days . . . one that'll stick with you. They're always running off with the first cowboy that asks them. I guess they think ranch life is a whole lot easier than waiting tables."

"Waitress, huh?" Cleo said.

"Well, it wouldn't have to be a waitress exactly. It could be more'n that if I could find the right person. I was to find the right gal to throw in with me and help me out, she could even be like a partner to me . . . you know, someone to tote the books, handle the business side of things."

"What you figure you'd pay for someone like that?" Cleo asked.

"Depends on who it was." Then with a wink, Shorty added: "What sorta qualifications she might have."

"What kinda benefits might a job like that have, besides the pay, I mean?" Cleo said.

Cole could hear Shorty swallow some of his coffee.

"I reckon the benefits would be worthwhile the right person came along," Shorty said.

"Hmmm . . . ," Cleo said.

"Well I'll be damned," Bean declared as he stood, looking through the window.

"Damned about what?" Will asked.

"There's someone coming, trudging through the snowdrifts. Must be a damned crazy man to be out, walking through the snow as deep as it is."

"He's walking?" Will said. "Not riding a horse?"

"He's walking," Bean said. "If that's what you want to call it."

Will got up and went over to the window and looked out. Cole took up a position at the other window. There, far out on the sea of snow, a small dark figure floundered in the drifts.

"You know that man?" Will asked. "He from around here?"

"Can't tell," Bean said. "He's too far away."

They watched the man fall several times, only to rise again, take two or three steps before falling again. He was the only thing moving out on the frozen wasteland and his efforts seemed pathetic.

"I don't believe he's going to make it," Bean said. "Look, every time he falls down, it takes him a little longer to get up again. He'll probably just fall one of these times and not get up. It's not uncommon for a man to freeze to death in a blizzard and not be found until spring. One of the damned cruel aspects of this northern country. Weather'll kill you as quick as anything."

Shorty and Cleopatra came over and stood next to Cole at the window.

"Poor man," Cleo said. "He looks like a wounded bird that fell from the sky."

"He might have fallen out of the sky," Shorty said. "Where else would he have come from?"

"Well, he sure didn't fall out of the sky," Will said. "Whoever heard of a man falling out of the sky?"

They watched the lone figure continue to struggle and it was evident that he wasn't going to make it without help.

"You have snowshoes?" Cole asked Roy Bean.

"In that pile over there behind the counter," he said.

Cole went over and strapped them on. They weren't the easiest contraptions to maneuver in, but he pushed out through the door with his hat pulled down tightly over his ears and the collar of his coat turned up against the wind. He struggled to get purchase atop the deep snow, and found to his amazement that the snowshoes kept him from sinking. He looked back once at the four faces watching him through the frosted glass, then started in the direction of the man who'd now fallen and hadn't gotten up.

It took Cole a good twenty minutes to reach him. When he did and rolled him over, he was surprised to see the frozen face of Bart Bledsoe. His eyes were frosted shut and his lips were blue. Cole slapped Bledsoe's cheeks until his eyelids fluttered.

Recognition came slowly, but it did, and he offered Cole a weak smile. "Mister . . . Cole."

"How the hell did you get out here?" Cole asked.

Bledsoe muttered something, pointed off in the distance, then fell silent. He was nearly frozen stiff and completely exhausted. They were both lucky he was a small man, easy to carry. Cole got him over his shoulder and started back toward the distant buildings of Paint Town with him. It was like carrying a bull calf, and twice he had to stop to rest.

Will and Shorty scrambled out to help as soon as Cole got near Bean's place. When Will saw who it was, all he could say was "Jesus!"

They got Bart inside and stripped him of his cold wet clothes and wrapped him in blankets and put him next to the stove. Will thought they should pour beer down him.

"What for?" Shorty said.

"So's we could warm him up from the inside," Will said.

"Beer don't warm you from the inside the same way whiskey does," Shorty said. "Unless you heat it first."

Cole suggested hot coffee instead.

"His lips are as blue as a Montana sky," Cleo said. "And feel how cold his skin is." Cleo said she would fix Bart some beef soup and Shorty offered to help her.

"I sure wish I had some whiskey to give him," Roy Bean said. "But it looks like now that the real snow has come, I won't have any whiskey until spring. Unless we get an unexpected thaw."

"How do you reckon he escaped from Book?" Will asked.

"That's a good question," Cole said.

Bart fluttered his eyes and saw Will leaning over him. "Why . . . Mis-ter Harper," he stuttered.

"That's something," Will said, "you escaping from that black devil and making your way through this blizzard."

Bart waggled his head back and forth. "Not . . . es . . . caped. Let . . . go."

"What?" Will said.

"I think he's saying Book let him go," Cole said. When Will gave him a confused look, he said: "I know. It doesn't make any sense."

Bart's teeth began to chatter, then Shorty and Cleo returned with a bowl of beef soup, and Cleo fed the soup to Bart a spoonful at a time, saying: "Careful, hon, the soup will burn your tongue you don't blow on it first."

"How'd he get here?" Shorty asked.

"Says Book let him go," Will said.

"Let him go?" Shorty said. "Well, if he let

him go, why'd he steal him in the first place?"

"If I knew that, the son-of-a-bitch would be in irons already," Will said, pacing the room.

"Lookit my Cleo," Shorty said proudly. "She's nursing him back to life."

Cleo had Bart's head propped on her lap while she spooned him soup; he was staring up at her like she was an angel. In a short time, Bart was nearly back to normal.

"Tell us about Book letting you go," Will said, stopping the pacing.

Bart rolled his eyes, reluctant to take them from Cleo. "He just turned me loose is all," he said, then returned his gaze to Cleo.

She smiled and said: "You want some more soup?"

Shorty noticed how Bart was watching her, and acted a little put out by all the attention.

"Just like that," Will said, "he turned you loose?"

Bart nodded. "It was cold and getting colder and we had very little shelter except for an old Army tent that the three of us could barely fit into. It was quite intimate, the three of us huddled inside that tent together. I guess that may have been the reason Mister Book pointed me in the direction of this place and told me I was free to go, because of how small and intimate it had become there in the tent for the three of us."

"Did he hurt you in any way, torture you?" Will asked.

"No. In fact, he proved very agreeable in every respect. He enjoyed sitting around a fire at night and telling tall tales and ghost stories. He enjoyed singing, too. He has quite a nice baritone voice."

"Ghost stories . . . singing?" Will said.

"It was all very entertaining," Bart said.

"What about your mule?" Will said. "That black devil was so agreeable, why'd he steal your mule and leave you afoot in weather such as this?"

"He didn't exactly steal my mule," Bart said. "We ended up having to eat it."

"You ate your mule?"

"We had to . . . we didn't have anything else to eat." Bart seemed a bit shaken by the memory.

"Did he mention the reason why he kidnapped you in the first place, Bart?" Cole asked.

Bart finally took his gaze from Cleo and looked in Cole's direction. "He said the reason he took me that night was to insure that you and Mister Harper would not kill him if you caught up to him. That he would trade me for his freedom if it came to that."

"Well, there you go," Will said. "I guess Leviticus Book ain't such a saintly fellow after all, is he? A man that would trade your life for his?"

"Oh, he said he wouldn't kill me unless it was absolutely necessary," Bart countered. "He seemed quite clear on that point. And I believe he would have kept his word."

"You could have died out there in that snow, frozen to death," Shorty chimed in. "I think Will's right, this Book ain't quite the patron saint he'd have you believe."

"No, I'm afraid I disagree. He said that he would watch me through his gun scope until I reached the safety of this town. He said, if it looked like I would fall and not get up again, he would do what was necessary so that I wouldn't suffer. He said freezing to death wasn't as bad as some might think."

"Well, that was mighty damn' generous of him, don't you think?" Will said sourly.

"What about Jilly Sweet?" Cole asked. "Is she all right?"

Bart sighed, tilted his head, and said: "She and Mister Book are much enamored of each other. They are like happy children, with the exception, of course, that they know you are after them and will try and capture him."

"Well, he's right about that," Shorty said. "That's why we've come all this distance and put up with this miserable weather, so we can capture him."

"This damn snow!" Will exclaimed, starting to pace again. "Soon's it's melted down to a tolerable level, we're going after him."

"Oh, I almost forgot," Bart said, reaching inside

his coat and bringing forth a letter. "He asked me to give you this."

Cole took the piece of paper and unfolded it. Written in pencil were the words:

I ain't guilty

"What's it say?" Will asked, stopping his pacing long enough to look over Cole's shoulder.

Cole handed him the note and watched the strain in his face as he read it.

"The hell he ain't," Will said, wadding up the piece of paper and throwing it into the stove.

"You spent some time with him Bart," Cole said. "Why didn't he just keep running when he had the chance?"

Bart shrugged his shoulders. "He said that he was tired of running from white men."

"Then why doesn't he stand and fight?" Will interjected.

Bart looked up at him, licked his lips. "He said he doesn't have any quarrel with you. I think he's hoping that you will get tired of chasing him and give up."

"Well, he's wrong!"

"He is very crafty," Bart said. "I think you should know that."

Will leveled his gaze at Bart. "Sounds like you and him became bosom pals, Bledsoe."

"He treated me kindly when he could have just as easily slit my throat if such was his intent. I find it hard to wish bad things on a man who shared his meals and stories and tent with me, given the hardships."

"Yeah, well . . ."

"I think he's trying to prove that he's better at this game than we are," Cole said to Will.

"So far he has been," Will acknowledged grudgingly. "But that don't mean he's gonna continue to beat us like a drum."

"What do you have in mind, Will?"

"Lead a man to believe in one thing, then spring the truth on him from another angle," Will said. Then turning to Roy Bean, he asked: "What's the nearest place other'n this that a man could get himself supplied?"

"Bender's Fork," Bean said. "More'n a hundred miles from here."

"So a man sitting out there in the cold with his belly crawling against his backbone might just as soon come riding into here as to travel another hundred miles, wouldn't you guess?"

Bean nodded.

"But Book won't come here as long as he knows we're here," Will said. "So the trick is to make him think we left."

"Short of leaving," Cole said, "how are we going to accomplish that?"

"Simple," Will said. "We will leave . . . or at least most of us, anyway."

Will laid out his plan to stay behind while

Shorty, Bart, and John Henry rode out. "Book can spot that speckled horse of yours from a mile off," Will concluded. "He'll figure we've either given up on him, or quit the town, then he'll come in. And when he does, I'll be here, waiting for him."

"It's a weak plan at best," Cole said.

"You have another?"

Cole admitted he didn't.

"Then we'll make a big show of it," Will said. "Leaving."

Cleopatra said to Shorty: "That mean you ain't coming back?"

"I hope that's not what it means," Shorty answered.

"Well, it could mean that if your plan don't work out, couldn't it?" Cleopatra said.

"It's not my plan," Shorty said. "It's Will's plan."

Cleopatra seemed genuinely disappointed that Shorty would be leaving as soon as the weather permitted. Shorty's face looked as sad as a hound's. "I was hoping you and me would get around to discussing more about that waitressing job in Cheyenne," Cleopatra said. "I'm mighty tired of the whore business . . . especially 'way out here in the middle of nowhere where there ain't that many men who come by in the first place. It's one thing for a girl to whore, it's quite another to sit around a week at a time waiting on trade. How am I ever going to save enough money to become independent at that rate?"

Now it was Roy Bean's turn to look disappointed. "Cleo, you're the only whore I got. If you leave and go to Cheyenne, I'll be forced out of business. Cowboys don't want to ride all the way out here just to drink a beer and play dominoes and stare at Homer's dog."

"Those cowboys have all but worn me out with their cheap and unschooled ways, Roy," Cleo said. "They can make moon eyes with each other for all I care. Or, with Homer's dog, if they want."

"Aw, Cleo." Bean was thoroughly disgusted with Cleo's remarks.

"Why don't we go on in the back room and discuss the future?" Cleo suggested to Shorty. "You still got plenty of time before the snow melts, don't ya?"

"Well, sure," Shorty said. "Why not."

Will watched Shorty and Cleopatra head for the back room. "I should have been the one she'd be discussing her future with," he said.

"Well, maybe the next time a whore asks you to go into the back room with her, you won't be so picky," Bean remarked. "Maybe, if you had taken Cleo up on her offer, she wouldn't want to leave me and go wait tables in Cheyenne with that restaurant owner. Now you, on the other hand, don't even own a horse. I doubt Cleo would leave me for a man who don't even own a horse."

Both men looked equally glum. Cole's thoughts centered around Will's plan to lure Book into a trap. If the outlaw was half as smart as he'd proved to be so far, he wouldn't allow himself to be taken so easily. Cole had a lot of faith in Will Harper's abilities as a manhunter, but even Will had admitted he had never run up against anyone like Leviticus Book before. Cole didn't like the plan, but Will was his own man. He couldn't force Harper to change his mind. They were as close to Book as they had gotten so far—too close not to take every opportunity to nail him. Will had been right about one thing. With his Sharps Big Fifty, Book could have taken them off at the neck from half a mile away and they'd never have known it until it was too late. In that open country, they were sitting ducks. As plans went, Will's wasn't much, but at least it was a plan.

Chapter Twenty-Five

Roy Bean called the warm winds that blew over the country the next two days a Chinook. "Happens," he said about the unusually warm weather. Water dripped from the roof, trickled into wood rain barrels Bean had set out. The warm winds melted a lot of snow over the next two days—enough snow that they could make a show of leaving.

Cleopatra had talked Shorty into taking her with him in spite of Bean's protests. At first, Will was against Cleo's going as well, but when Shorty argued that the more of them there were, the more of a show they could make of it, Will relented and said: "I hope you two will be real happy serving burned eggs and cleaning up spilled milk." Cleo said it beat getting rode like a Quarter horse at the races once a month and paying all her earnings out to Bean in bed and board.

Bean said his business enterprise would be ruined and that he would probably be forced to pack up and move to Texas where he heard there was a great need for cold beer. Cole told Bean that Texas already had plenty of cold beer, but that there was probably still room for him if he decided to go and be a justice of the peace.

Ab and Lum, the two domino players had put in their first appearance since the snowstorm began. They didn't say much, just sat down near the stove and began playing dominoes.

"Where you goin', Cleopatra?" Ab asked when he saw her carrying a hatbox and Shorty carrying out one of her trunks.

"To Cheyenne," she said.

"What's in Cheyenne they ain't got here?" Lum asked.

"Honest work for one thing," Cleo replied.

"Oh," said Lum. Then both men went back to their domino game as if there was nothing unusual about the town's only whore leaving for a far-off place like Cheyenne.

"They don't seem too upset about your departure," Will said, watching Shorty tie Cleo's hatbox to his saddle horn.

Cleo said: "If I had to depend on either one of those two to earn a living, I would have starved to death years ago. They're just a pair of cheap old ranchers who wouldn't know a woman from a sheep. Lord knows, they probably prefer the sheep."

Shorty grinned at that and said: "Are you about ready, hon?"

"Soon's I get my other dress trunk," Cleo said. "Can you give me a hand with it?"

Shorty followed her back inside Roy Bean's.

Will Harper was watching the distance.

"He's out there somewhere," Cole said.

"Let's hope he's watching," Will said.

"I'll ride for a day, then circle back," Cole said.

"No need, John Henry. I can handle him."

"As insurance," he said. "Just in case."

"What about Shorty and Cleo and Bart?"

"I'll send them on to Cheyenne. Shorty's in love and wouldn't be much good to us anyhow now that Cleo's running his show."

Will half smiled. "For the rest of his natural life, the way it looks," he said.

"Yeah, well, I guess as long as Shorty is willing to pay the fiddler, he'll get to enjoy the dance."

"Glad it's him and not me," Will said.

"You sure changed your mind in a hurry."

"I've had time to consider it. I'd just as soon not

be seen with a hatbox dangling from my saddle."

"Or anything else for that matter, is that it?"

Will grinned, and then they stepped back inside Roy Bean's. Will proposed to trade his hat and coat with Bart Bledsoe, only Bart's hat and coat were too small for him.

"Why do I have to trade you my hat and coat, Mister Harper?" Bart asked, looking out from under the brim of Will's hat, which set low on his head because of its large size.

Will explained how he wanted Leviticus Book to think they were all riding out of Paint Town together. "Book's got good eyes," Will said. "I want him to think you're me. Wearing my hat and coat will add to the ruse. Even with his good eyes, he can't see that good to tell it ain't me wearing them duds of mine."

Bart sighed heavily and tried to push the hat out of his eyes as he put on Will's greatcoat.

Bean made one more offer to Cleo in order to get her to change her mind about leaving: "I'll bump up your cut to sixty-five percent. And I'll even cut the price on your room and board, if you'll stay."

"You can bump it up to a hundred percent, Roy, and feed me fried chicken on a blue plate, and I'd still be leaving. A few more years of hanging around this place and I'll be as useless as Homer's dog."

Bean rested his chin in the palm of his hand, his

gaze full of dejection. "I'll probably go to Texas and be murdered by some mad-dog gunman," he said. "It'll be on your conscience, if I am, Cleo."

"Nobody said you have to go to Texas, Roy Bean," Cleo said. "You could go to California or Ohio if you wanted to. What is the big attraction about Texas?"

"I think there is more opportunity in Texas," he said. "That's where I'll go, unless you change your mind. I guess, if some gunman does get me, it will be because of you leaving."

Cleo rolled her eyes and gave him a kiss on the cheek and said: "If I was you, Roy, I'd go somewhere where there ain't any gunmen that mean. I'll write you a letter when I get to Cheyenne."

"Good luck in getting your man, Will," Shorty said, offering Will his hand. "I hope there is no hard feelings about me winning Cleo away from you."

Will shook Shorty's hand. "No, there ain't. Sometimes things have a way of working out for the best."

"Well, I never expected to go after a killer and come back with a sweetheart," Shorty said out of the hearing of Cleo who had gone into the back room for something. "I guess I'm as surprised as anybody."

"Most men would be," Will said. "All the times I've hunted for desperados, I never once came back with a sweetheart instead."

Cleo appeared, carrying a yellow parasol and a pair of high-button shoes. "You think there is room enough on the back of your horse for these?" she asked Shorty. "I hate to leave them behind?"

Shorty rolled his eyes and said: "Is that about the last of it?"

Cleo offered him a pout, then a peck on the cheek. "I just want to look my best when I walk the streets of Cheyenne. Wearing high-button shoes and having a parasol to keep the sun off is what real ladies do."

"It's just a lot of extra things to carry is all," Shorty said half-heartedly.

Cleo gave him a look that wilted the rest of his resistance.

"Be sure you make a good show of it," Will said to Cole as he got ready to leave with the others. "I want that black scoundrel to believe that we've all left and are not coming back. I want him to think he can waltz in here and get a full belly and a peaceful night's rest without having to worry about one single thing. Then, I intend on stepping up behind him with one of these big Colts of mine and surprising him."

"Don't misjudge his ability," Cole cautioned.

Will offered Cole the knowing look of a man who had spent his lifetime hunting down hardcases and desperados. "Like I said, John Henry, it ain't necessary, you doubling back."

"I'll be back," Cole said. "You can count on it."

Will remained inside while the four of them mounted up, looking for all the world like they were quitting the town and quitting the chase. And in a way, they were. Cole told Shorty to lead the way, followed by Cleo, then Bart. Cole brought up the rear. He wanted them strung out so that, if Book was watching, he could easily count their number. Like Will, he wanted him to feel completely confident the town was his.

"The weather is very pleasant," Bart commented as soon as they had cleared the town. "I find it hard to believe that just a few days ago I nearly froze to death in deep snow."

"That's the way this country is," Shorty said. "One minute everything is hunky dory, and the next you're froze stiff as a board in some snowbank. You are a very lucky man, Bart."

The sky was so bright and blue it hurt to look at it. Cole had a feeling crawling up his spine that they were being watched. He could almost feel Book watching them through the scope mounted on his Sharps. He didn't look back or act in any way concerned even though he knew it was likely Book had his sights trained on Cole's back.

They arrived at a creek by midmorning and rested there. Cleo said she was getting chafed from riding and went off into the bushes with a tin of salve to rub on her thighs.

"She's more delicate than you might imagine," Shorty said, staring off toward the bushes.

They hunkered long enough to give the horses a blow, and Cole smoked a cigarette and kept thinking he should be back in Paint Town with Will. The fact that Will had been bested by Book once already kept nagging his thoughts, that and the fact that Will had a tendency to drink heavily gave him the urge to climb aboard the bird right then and ride back to the town. The only reason he didn't was the fact that they hadn't been gone long enough, and a man with a scope in open country could spot a jack rabbit if he were watching. He'd just have to wait long enough for Book to drop his guard, then hope like hell he could make it back before it was too late.

When they remounted, Cole spurred the speckled bird alongside the dusty bay Bart was riding, one Will had purchased from Roy Bean. "Tell me what you think, Bart," he said.

Bledsoe looked at Cole from under Will Harper's big hat. "About what, Mister Cole?"

"About Leviticus Book," he said. "Tell me what you think about him."

"As I told Mister Harper," he said with a shrug of his slight shoulders, "Mister Book seemed a pleasant enough fellow and treated me well."

"That's plenty strange."

"How so?"

"It doesn't fit with what I've heard about him.

The man is accused of a lot of bad killings. Why would he let you just walk away? Doesn't make sense."

"I've thought about that, too, in light of what you and Mister Harper have told me. In point of fact, he could have killed me easily. In fact, he was big and strong enough to have snapped my neck with his bare hands. But he never even once threatened me."

"He had a higher purpose for you."

"Yes, I agree, to carry the note proclaiming his innocence."

"I don't put much stock in that, Bart. Every man in a state prison claims to be innocent. I've never known a man to admit his guilt yet."

"He was very compassionate and kind to the girl as well," Bart said. "She seemed to dote on him."

"Jilly Sweet."

"There's no doubt she's as in love with Mister Book as much as Shorty is with Miss Cleo."

"I guess, as they say, Bart, love is blind."

"I can only guess that it is. I've never had the experience of being in love myself. Though, Miss Cleo is quite attractive, don't you think?"

Under that big hat he looked rather dopey to Cole, dopey and forlorn and out of place in this hard country. But he had pluck and was willing. Cole had to give him that much.

They rode along across the wide sweep of valley

that was still white in places, brown in others from the melt off. In the far distance the Blue Mountains rose against the pale edges of sky, and a hawk caught the warm air rising up from the ground and rode it on stiff, outstretched wings as it scouted for a winter hare or field mouse.

They camped at noon by a stand of cottonwoods, the limbs and trunks darkly wet. Shorty made a meal out of some smoked beef packed in tin cans that he had purchased from Bean before they had left—smoked beef and crackers and peaches.

"I figured we'd at least eat well on the trip home," Shorty said.

Cleo sat next to him on a blanket and said: "This reminds me of a picnic I once went on when I was married."

Shorty said: "I didn't know you were married, hon."

"I was once," Cleo said. "But you don't have to worry. My husband was killed in a train wreck."

"Train wreck?"

"He was a engineer on the Rock Island railroad back in Illinois and his train went off a bridge and killed him."

"That's a sad story," Shorty said.

"It left me a widow and me not yet twenty," Cleo said. "I guess after it happened, I just sort of lost my way for a time. That's how I ended up in the *life*."

Shorty cleared his throat. Plainly he was uncomfortable with Cleo's public revelations about her past. "Well, you'll just have to tell me all about it sometime when there is just the two of us," he said.

"It's damned hard for a gal to make a living and be on her own in this country," Cleo continued, undeterred by Shorty's suggestion that she refrain from further details of her past. "When Eldon died in that train wreck, all he left me was seventy dollars and a house with rent due on it. Why, what was I to do? I didn't know no skills such as sewing or cooking or teaching. I was young and pretty. Those were my skills."

"Yes, well . . . ummm," Shorty said.

"I'm surprised that an attractive woman such as yourself didn't remarry," Bart said with avid interest in Cleo's tale of woe.

Ever since they had carried him in from the cold that day back at Roy Bean's and Cleo had spoon-fed him soup, Bart had had a difficult time keeping his eyes off her. He took every opportunity to speak with her and share her company, though Shorty made sure he never left Cleo alone for very long in Bart's presence.

"Why, yes, darlin', I had plenty of marriage proposals," Cleo said, perking up a bit now that she had two men showing a great deal of interest in her. "But the more I thought about marrying again," she continued, working her words around a slice of peach, "the more I realized that there wasn't a thing in the world to keep the next man I might marry from plunging off a railroad bridge with a thousand tons of steel on top of him just like the first one . . . or something equally disastrous. I'd just be putting my fate back into the hands of undependable and unreliable men if I was to marry again without any more skills than what I had . . . being young and pretty. I have since learned that men are weak creatures and can be killed in any number of ways. I have been a widow once and do not recommend it."

Shorty was squirming on the blanket as Cleo related her views on marriage and men. "Maybe this conversation is better suited for another time, sweets," he muttered.

But Cleo paid no heed. Instead, she leaned a little closer to Bart and said: "It ain't that I don't like men, you understand. I do. I like 'em about as well as a woman can like anything. But marriage? No, sir, I'd just as soon pass on that subject."

"I suppose I can easily see your point, Miss Cleo," Bart said.

"Of course you can," Cleo declared, patting Bart on the knee. He nearly swooned from her touch.

Shorty gritted his teeth at the gesture. "Maybe we should stretch our legs for a bit before we get back on our horses," he suggested to Cleo, rising.

"Naw, you go on ahead, hon. I think I'll just sit

here and rest. My thighs are chafed from riding. I don't feel much like walking . . . it'd just chafe me more."

"Well, then maybe I'll just sit here as well," Shorty said, plopping back down beside her on the blanket.

Cole saw the hope that Shorty would take a walk by himself and leave Cleo unattended quickly fade from Bart's expectant eyes. Cleo was enjoying the attention and the peaches equally. It caused Cole to think briefly of Ella Mims and Tom Feathers, and the way he'd felt about them sharing company, and he realized that Shorty Blaine and Bart Bledsoe weren't the only men in this world who knew the bitter taste of jealousy. He walked over to the speckled bird and stroked her neck and checked her hoofs just for some-thing to do. Then he jerked the Winchester from its boot and checked its loads before seating it again.

He rolled himself a fresh cigarette, watched as the little party sat around eating peaches and vying for one another's attention. He was a long way from home, wherever that was, and wasn't getting any closer. He was tired of being out-foxed and sleeping in cold, lonely places, and missing the company of a good woman. He wanted to put Ike Kelly's death to rest and bring his killer to justice.

"This is where I turn around," he announced.

They all looked at him.

"You want me to go back to Paint Town with you?" Shorty asked.

He was a good man, but his heart was no longer in the chase. One of the reasons it wasn't was sitting beside him on the blanket. Cole couldn't really blame him for wanting what any man wanted. "No, you three go on to Cheyenne. Will and me can handle this now that we know where Book is."

"I hate to quit on you like this," Shorty said.

"You're not quitting on me," Cole told him. "Go on back to Cheyenne."

"Yeah, well . . ."

Cole walked over and shook hands with Shorty to assure him it was all right.

Bart lifted Will's big hat from his head and said: "Here. Take this back to him and tell him it's too big for me. He probably misses not having his hat."

"I'll see that he gets it, Bart."

"I wish I had a bottle of my patent medicine to send along, too," Bart said. "Mister Harper seemed to be very fond of my patent medicine."

"Maybe next time we meet, you'll be back in business," Cole said. "Then Will can buy a bottle or two from you."

Bart hunched his shoulders. "Maybe."

Cleo said: "When you see Roy Bean, tell him I'm truly sorry that he feels like he has to go to

Texas on account of me, and that I hope some gunman don't kill him."

Cole told Cleo he'd pass along her message as he swung up on the bird and turned her head toward Paint Town. He wasn't exactly sure what, if anything, a horse thinks about, but it wouldn't have surprised him if the speckled bird was thinking she'd seen that same country before. He hoped to be back just after dark.

CHAPTER TWENTY-SIX

From a slight rise in the land, Cole could see the town's lights spread out in the distance, twinkling in the deepening dusk like flecks of gold glittering in the bottom of a miner's pan. A chill wind was blowing out of the northwest, down from the far Blue Mountains, and a coyote barked from some-where off to his left.

He crooked a leg over his saddle horn and rolled himself a shuck, waiting for full night to descend before riding the rest of the way into Paint Town. His fingers were stiff from the increasing cold and the wind picked at the tobacco he curled inside the cigarette paper before he could twist the ends closed. He struck a lucifer off his belt buckle and cupped the flame between his hands to shield it from watchful eyes.

The smoke felt good as he drew it deep into his

lungs and tasted its heat. Sitting on the bird like that, smoking a shuck, reminded him of his trail-herding days when he would ride night hawk and spend his time between looking up at the stars and waiting for the herd to jump off its bed into a full-out stampede. Longhorns were the spookiest, most unpredictable creatures God had ever put on this earth. Between them and the wild Mexican cattle, it gave a man pause and tested the nerves. He was glad that time was behind him now.

There were a lot of bad things about herding a thousand head of beef up a trail for three months at a time. Stampedes and too little sleep were some of the worst. Throw in river crossings, thieves, bad grub, and too little pay, and you just about described the entire experience. It was almost all bad, but there was some good. The good came from making friends of men you could rely on to save your sorry hide the minute your horse got pulled under by a wild river or was gored by some rank longhorn steer. It was having the company of someone to drink with and whore with and sit around the fire with. Men you knew well enough to swap stories and lies and memories of women you loved and women you lost and the ones you hadn't yet met but hoped someday you would. It was listening to some old waddie play his mouth harp at night or to the wind or the call of a hoot owl that made you understand the Big Lonely and why men became drovers. It wasn't the cattle or the horses you rode or the trails you went up or back down again that made cowboying the memory it was, it was the men you rode with and fought with and buried along the way. Men like Shorty Blaine and Will Harper and Ike Kelly. The kind of men, it seemed to Cole, they weren't making any more.

The speckled bird shifted her weight, and Cole pinched out the smoke and let tobacco and paper scatter in the wind. Then he uncorked his leg and touched spurs to the mare and walked her down the slope toward Paint Town.

Halfway there, he pulled the Winchester and rested it across the pommel of his saddle. He felt the press of the self-cocker against his left hip, and the slight weighty tug of the Colt Lightning .41 he carried in a shoulder rig under his coat. The Lightning was a backup that he'd bought several years ago down in the Settlements where he'd worked a short time as a deputy U.S. marshal. It had once belonged to a Cherokee policeman whose wife had used it to kill him in a fit of jealousy over another woman. Then she'd pawned the pistol in a hardware store to pay her man's funeral expenses. "Ain't love grand," the clerk had said who had sold him the gun. It had pearl handles and good balance, and Cole had paid $25 for it, knowing the price was too much for a bird's-eye-handled Colt, but some things you can't put a price on.

The town's short street was deserted, quiet as church on Monday. The soft plop of the bird's hoofs in the half frozen mud was the only sound Cole heard besides that of his own breathing and the creak of cold saddle leather. He neared Roy Bean's establishment with as much caution as he could manage. It didn't seem likely there would be trouble waiting, but that's when it always comes—when it doesn't seem likely.

Cole checked the reins and sat there a minute in front of the store, trying to see through the panes of frosted glass. All he could make out was yellow light coming from inside. He walked the bird around to the back of the building, dismounted, propped the Winchester against the rear wall, and pulled his self-cocker. If he was going to do close-up work, he wanted to do it with a revolver.

He touched the smooth porcelain knob on the door, gave it a turn, and pushed the door open just enough to slip inside. Up the short hall and to his right was Cleo's old room. It still had a woman's scent about it. The door was partly ajar, and Cole checked to make sure no one was inside. It was cold and empty and dark. Up ahead, at the end of the hallway, a curtain separated the back part of the building from the main room. A light shone on the other side and along the bottom where the curtain didn't quite reach the floor.

He took a deep breath, pulled his other gun,

thumbed back the hammers of both, and stepped to within a few inches of the curtain. Using the barrel of the Lightning, he moved the curtain far enough to see into the main room.

Roy Bean was sitting on a chair, holding his head.

Cole stepped out into the room and said: "Bean, where's Will?"

Bean looked up. His eyes were red and miserable, his face flushed red. He mumbled something.

"Were you injured? Did someone come and crack your skull?"

He shook his head, a pained expression etched his features. *"Nnnnnnuh . . ."*

"Will," Cole said. "Where's Will?"

Bean weakly pointed toward the front door. *"Neerrr . . ."*

"Speak up, make some sense!"

"He . . . gone," Bean muttered.

"Was it Book?" Cole asked. "Did Book come here and take him?"

Bean said something Cole couldn't understand.

"Damn it, Bean! Tell me what happened here!"

"Maah tooth," he moaned. "It's maah tooth. Infected."

"To hell with your tooth! Where's Will?"

Bean reached down at his feet and lifted a pair of pliers and held them out to Cole. "Gotta . . . pull . . . it." He touched his fingers to his swollen jaw and gave a yelp. *"Owwww!"* A single tear leaked from his right eye.

"You tell me about Will," Cole demanded. "Where is he?"

"Went . . . after . . . the col . . . red. Oh, sweet Jesus!"

Now tears leaked from both eyes. Bean was in plenty of misery. Too much misery to tell Cole what he needed to know about Will's disappearance.

The man, Homer, the one with the dog that trailed him everywhere, came in the store just then. "What's wrong with you, Roy?" he asked. "Somebody sock you in the jaw?"

Bean looked in too much pain to explain it.

"Take up those pliers and pull his tooth," Cole said.

"What?"

"Pull his tooth!"

Homer looked uncertain, looked at his little spotted dog. "I ain't no dentist. I'm a bachelor."

Cole pointed at the pliers with the barrel of the self-cocker, then brought it down hard across Bean's skull. He tumbled to the floor like a sack of potatoes.

"You broke his skull!" Homer said. His little dog yipped and pranced around on its paws.

"Just cold-cocked him so you could pull his tooth, now get on with it."

Cole holstered his guns, rolled a shuck, and

smoked it as Homer proceeded to pull Roy Bean's tooth. He cranked and pried and finally pulled it out, a bloody piece of bone that he dropped in a beer glass.

Homer was sweating hard. "He might want to keep it for a souvenir," he said, watching the tooth sink to the bottom of the beer glass.

Cole walked outside and busted ice from the top of a rain barrel and filled a bucket with the cold water, then doused the prostrate Bean with it. He came to with a start, sat up, sputtering and waving his arms. "Holy Mother of God!"

"Now tell me where I can find Will Harper," Cole ordered.

Bean blinked several times, felt his jaw, winced, worked his tongue inside his cheek, and said: "You pulled it out?"

"It was me," Homer said.

"Oh," Bean said. "I didn't know you knew how to pull teeth."

"This fellow here had to cold-cock you," Homer said. "You would never have stood the pain."

Bean felt the back of his head, winced again, spat a bloody flume, and said: "Now I hurt in two places."

"You'll hurt in more than two places if you don't tell me about Will," Cole said.

He pulled himself off the floor and staggered behind the bar. "The big Negro come," Bean said, pulling the beer tap until his glass flowed over with foam and dark brown beer. "You want one?"

Cole waved him off. Homer said he'd have a beer and so would his dog. Bean poured them each one. Then Bean took a sip of the beer himself, spat again, wiped a sleeve across his grizzled mouth, and took a long swallow.

"Only he didn't come alone," Bean continued, filling his glass again. "He had that little Negra girl with him. She's the one that actually came in. Will was sitting over there, drinking beers as fast as I could pour them. I guess he was a little off his game when that Negra girl came in."

"Go on."

Bean took another swallow of his beer, made a face. "Feels better, that rotted tooth not being there. Homer, maybe you are a dentist. Maybe that's your true life's calling."

Homer shrugged his shoulders and patted the top of his little dog's head. "Maybe so, Roy. Maybe I could start charging everybody that wanted their teeth pulled."

"What do you think, Mister Cole?" Bean inquired. When he saw that Cole wasn't in the mood to discuss dental problems, he offered him a sober stare. "Like I said, that little gal came in, looked around, and, when she saw Will, she walked right over to him. Said . . . 'How do.' . . . and tried to sit on his lap." Bean hacked, coughed up more blood, then swallowed the last of the beer.

"Finish telling me about the girl," Cole said.

"Will asked her where her sweetheart was hiding and why didn't he come in with her. She said he had left her, dropped her off right outside the town limits. Will said he didn't buy it . . . a fellow like Book leaving his sweetheart behind." Bean wiped at the corners of his mouth, inspected the watery blood. "The Negra gal said Will could believe what he wanted to, but it was the God's truth. Will said . . . 'Where is that son-of-a-bitch? I've come to arrest him and take him back to Fort Smith so's he can dance at the end of a short rope.' But the girl stuck to her story of being abandoned." Bean paused and looked around nervously. "Then suddenly, there he was. Came in the back, same way like you did. Had a big buffalo gun trained on Will, said if Will even thought about moving or going for his piece, his name would be in tomorrow's newspaper in the obituary column. I guess that Negro buck didn't know we ain't got a newspaper in this town."

"Get on with it."

"I think if Will hadn't drunk as many beers as he had, there might have been one damn' bloody fight and I'd be mopping up brains. But Will knew he'd been bagged . . . at least he acted like it. It was smart of that Negro to send in that Negra gal first and throw Will off like he did."

"Cut to it!" Cole demanded.

"The Negro said he was an innocent man and

didn't understand why Will kept chasing him all over half the country. Said he was tired of running from the law and bounty hunters like Will. Then Will said . . . 'If you ain't guilty of anything, why are you running?' And the Negro said . . . 'I'm running because you keep chasing me. But I'm warning you here and now . . . I ain't running no more.' " Bean had to pause long enough to draw himself another beer and taste it before continuing. "Then it happened."

"What did?"

"Will tried to pull his piece, only the girl grabbed hold of his arm, scratching and clawing like a wildcat, and both men's guns went off, only Will missed the mark and the darky didn't."

"Will's dead?"

"Dead as anyone can get," Bean said, shaking his head. "He's out in back in that little shack you boys slept in the other night. I had Ab and Lum come and carry him over there."

This was a piece of news Cole hadn't wanted to hear. "Book and the girl?" he said. "What about them?"

"They left," Bean said. "That Negro kept saying how Will had brought it on himself, the killing. That he never meant to kill Will, just talk him out of chasing him. Said he was sorry about the trouble, asked me if I would sell him some grub to take with them. That and an extra coat for the Negra gal because of how cold it was." Bean hunched his shoulders. "What could I do?" Then he spat a bloody gob into the spittoon near his feet and looked at Homer's spotted dog, and wagged his head as though he and the dog knew some-thing the rest didn't.

Cole took a lantern out to the little shack in the back. Lying on a cot, his arms folded across his chest, was Will Harper, one of the last good men Cole knew. His head was cocked slightly to the side, his features gray as stone. His mustaches and unshaven whiskers were black against his bloodless flesh; his lips were slightly parted so that a little of his teeth showed. He could have been a man simply taking a rest from the world. Only this time the rest would last forever.

Cole took a blanket from one of the bunks and drew it over Harper. He noticed the red flowered stain across the front of Will's shirt and Cole's fingers brushed against the cold skin. He wondered why Will had done it, tried to pull his pistol with a loaded rifle pointed at him? He had to have known what the results would be. Cole pulled a chair up next to the cot and sat there with Will Harper for a while and smoked a cigarette. The thought crossed Cole's mind that maybe Will had felt he'd simply run out of options, that if he didn't try and take Book while he could, that he was never going to take him. Maybe Leviticus Book wasn't the only one tired of the chase. Sometimes a man gets so tired and worn out, he will go for something that's not there and it ends up costing him. Cole said good bye to his old friend one last time, then walked back into Roy Bean's store.

Bean pushed a cigar box across the counter. "I collected his personal effects," he said. "Thought you'd want to have them."

Cole opened the lid of the box. It contained $80 in script, $10 in silver, a dented pocket watch, a straight razor with a yellow bone handle, a note pad, and stub pencil.

"Here's his pistol, and saddlebags, too," Bean said, laying them next to the cigar box. The ivory-handled grips of the big pistols were worn and smooth. Some of the bluing was worn from one cylinder. The saddlebags were soft, heavy. They contained an extra shirt, two boxes of cartridges, and a set of wrist irons with the key still in the lock.

Cole handed script to Bean along with the pistols: "See he gets a decent burial." When Bean nodded, he said: "Now tell me, which direction did Book and the girl go when they left?"

CHAPTER TWENTY-SEVEN

John Henry Cole was forced to wait until day-break before starting after Book and Jilly Sweet. Chasing after them at night would have been futile. Even though Bean had indicated they were heading west when they left his place, they could have veered off in any of a hundred directions along the way. At first light, he should be able to track them easily enough across the thawing, muddy ground.

Bean fell asleep atop his counter and Homer and his dog eventually left once the beer barrel was tapped dry. Cole slept as much as he could in a chair most of the night and thought about the last several weeks of his life, ever since he'd received Ike Kelly's letter down in Del Rio. One minute he'd been a lawman in that dusty little border town, and the next he was on his way to Cheyenne to work for his old friend in a small detective agency that Kelly had begun. Detective! It seemed about as strange a notion to Cole as being a stage actor, according to Bill Cody, had been for Wild Bill Hickok. Funny where life leads, he thought as he sat there with his eyes half closed, listening to the wind creep along the eaves of the store and Bean's snoring.

Cole's life in that sleepy little Texas border town had been fairly simple, an easy way for man to earn a living. The winds were warm, the women pretty, and the mescal freely flowing. Then, as they are wont to do, things changed. A Mexican bandit named Francisco Guzman—a man with whom Cole had become friends and a drinking companion—grew jealous over a sloe-eyed *señorita* in which they both had taken an interest. He should have known better. Whiskey and women shared between friends never have a happy ending. Francisco Guzman ended up pulling his pistol on Cole and Cole had shot him. It didn't sit well with the mayor or town council or the many cousins Francisco had just across the river. He had left for Cheyenne the same day Ike's letter had asked him to come and join the detective agency. Hell, what did he have to lose but his life?

Then after he had arrived, Kelly asked him to go to Deadwood and that's where he had met a woman named Lydia Winslow, and she and the murdering mob there had nearly become his undoing. By the time he had arrived back in Cheyenne, he had been ready to look for a new line of work. But Ike Kelly's murder had changed all that. So here he was, sitting in a chair, listening to the creeping wind and the snores of a man named Roy Bean and waiting for another cold sunrise. It left a metallic taste in his mouth and a throbbing pain behind his eyes. Between fits of sleep, he counted the dead and missing of his past—his late wife Zee, his son Samuel, Ike Kelly, Francisco Guzman, and Will Harper. Lydia Winslow, Ella Mims, Bill Cody—they were among the missing. And there were others as well.

The world with which he had long been familiar was changing a lot faster than he wanted it to with each passing year. He told himself that once he caught Leviticus Book and delivered him to Fort Smith, he would go and find his own peace, a place where the wind didn't howl so much and a man didn't have to walk around with two pistols on his person, a place with a porch where a man could sit and have his morning coffee and watch the world go by. And a woman like Ella Mims, sitting there on the porch with him, didn't hurt the image any. He'd had enough of the hard life. There had to be better ways of living than tracking down killers and hardcases.

Daylight broke and a rooster crowed and Bean sat up and stretched his arms and back. "I guess you'll be leaving now that it's light enough to see," he said, testing his jaw bone.

"I'd like to stay around and see that Will gets a proper burial," Cole said. "But maybe now that Book thinks he's not being followed any more, he won't have his guard up."

"I'll see your friend is treated properly," Bean assured. "Then I think I'm going to pack up and head for Texas." He looked around. "Without Cleo here to entertain the cowboys on pay day, I'll go bust in two, three months."

"Good luck to you down in Texas," Cole said, and shook his hand.

"How are the *señoritas* down that way?" he asked. "Pretty, I hope?"

"Be careful of the pretty ones, Mister Bean. Find yourself a plain-looking woman and you'll be OK."

"I'll keep that in mind, Mister Cole."

Bean stepped out on the porch and watched as Cole saddled the speckled bird, then mounted up.

"That is an unusual color for a horse," Bean commented. "I'll give you fifty dollars for her and even throw in that long-necked bay out yonder in the corral."

"No, thanks, Mister Bean," Cole said. "I think I'll stick with what brought me here."

He grinned. "That's good advice, whether it's horses or women."

"I agree."

On the trail Cole found that the tracks were fresh, dark clots of mud thrown against the patchwork of snow following the road westward toward the Blue Mountains. Tracking Book and the girl should be easy.

He followed the tracks all that day. They stopped once by a little stand of pines and had a lunch of sardines and crackers, judging by the empty tins lying around. Cole stayed long enough to chew a strip of jerky and have a smoke before continuing after them.

As the day drew to a close and the light turned blue-silver in the east and smoky rose to the west, Cole topped a rise and saw a single light flaring up out of the growing dusk down below him. He knew it was their camp.

He dismounted and waited. There wasn't anything to do but wait. He waited a long time.

Then, when he figured they were settled into their blankets for the night, he decided it was time to take them down. He jerked the Winchester from its boot, took Will's set of wrist irons he had been carrying in his saddlebags, and ground-reined the bird before starting the long walk down the hill toward the camp.

He took his time, bending low so that he wouldn't stand out against the skyline. It took him close to half an hour to reach the outer edge of their camp. There he squatted and listened. He was hoping to hear the heavy breathing of sleeping, only that's not what he heard.

Cole stepped into the ring of fire light and said: "That'll have to wait!"

Book jerked bolt upright. Jilly Sweet was beneath him, her naked breasts small, exposed to the dancing light of the fire.

"If you go for your weapon," Cole said to Book whose eyes shifted toward the Sharps leaning against a saddle, "I'll kill you here and now."

Jilly Sweet pushed herself to a sitting position, bringing the blankets up to cover her naked-ness. "It's him," she said to Book. "That's one of the mens was with Will Harper."

"Cole . . . in case you forgot, Jilly, the name's Cole."

"What you got to do with all this?" Book said. "You after reward money, that it?" He was a big man, muscular. The light danced off his black taut skin; his eyes glittered like wet coals.

"Will Harper was a friend," Cole said. "So was Ike Kelly, the man you shot and burned up back in Cheyenne."

"Whoa up!" Book said. "I ain't never shot and burned no man. Cheyenne or no place else."

"Yeah, well I guess you can plead your case in front of Judge Parker in Fort Smith. I don't care to hear it."

There was a long drawn-out instant when he thought Book might reach for the Sharps and try Cole, just as Will had tried Book back at Roy Bean's. Right at that moment, it didn't make that much difference to Cole if he did. He was tired and could still see the stone-cold face of Will Harper, lying on that little cot back at Bean's place. If Book was foolish enough to force Cole to take his life, then he was more than willing to oblige.

"Please don't shoot my man!" Jilly Sweet pleaded. "He ain't never hurt nobody!" She clung to him, her small thin arms gathered around his thick shoulders.

Cole saw the heavy look of defeat in his eyes, the fear in hers. "What's it going to be, Book? You want to do this the hard way or the easy way?"

"You let her go," he said, "and I'll go back peaceful."

"She can go where she wants," Cole said. "I've got no business with her."

"Go'n, Jilly," he said. "Scat on outta here. Take one of them horses and the money in my pants and go'n."

"Ain't leavin' you, Leviticus."

His eyes jerked in his head, twisted to the side to look at her. "Gal, do what I tell you . . . this here ain't nothin' but trouble."

She shook her head. "Ain't goin', can't make me."

His stare slowly came around to Cole again. "I ain't killed nobody, mister. This's all been a bad mistake. What you doin' is makin' it worse."

"You killed some friends of mine. Tell me you didn't."

"It was his doin', not mine. All I did was ask him to leave off on me. He jerked his piece. I did what I had to do."

"He's dead, Book. That's what I know."

He slowly shook his head, his eyes lowered. "Ain't nobody understands nothin'," he said. "Specially no white man, I guess."

Cole picked up Book's Sharps, kicked over the blankets, saw no other weapons. He took the buffalo gun by the barrel and brought the stock down hard against a large rock and flung the pieces off into the dark. Then he tossed the wrist irons toward Book and they landed near his feet.

"Put them on. One around your wrist, the other around your ankle."

Book picked them up slowly, cautiously. Cole

saw something painful come into his eyes as he looked at the manacles. "Been chained afore," he said.

"Price you pay for your crimes."

He swallowed hard, blinked. "Like I told you, mister, I ain't committed no crimes."

"That's for Judge Parker to decide, unless you want me to right here. Put them on."

"White men . . . that's all that's in them courts . . . that's all what them judges are . . . white men."

"Save the lecture. I can take you back or bury you here. You chose which white man you want to deal with, me or the judge."

He locked the irons onto his right wrist and ankle, stared at them, then lifted his gaze to Cole once more. "You doin' a wrong thing here, mister."

"I don't think so, Book. Two of my friends are dead because of you. I've had lots of time to think about that."

"He didn't do nothin'!" Jilly Sweet cried.

"You ought to put some clothes on," Cole commented. Then he gathered their horses and started back up the hill to where he'd left the bird.

"You just leavin' Leviticus an' me here?" Jilly Sweet asked. "Him all chained up like a dog . . . you jus' leavin' us here?"

"Going to get my animal and a little rest. I suggest you do the same. I'll be back down in the morning."

She started to protest but Book told her: "Hush. Go'n do what the man says, Jilly."

Cole looked at him; his stare was unflinching.

"It's a long way back to Fort Smith, mister," Book said.

"Yeah," Cole replied, "plenty of time for a man to talk himself into trying something dumb."

Cole walked their horses back to where the bird was ground-reined and tied them all off before spreading his blankets on the ground. He could see the dwindling campfire down below. He wasn't worried about Book and Jilly Sweet going anywhere the way Book was cuffed. He made himself a cigarette and smoked it, and wondered why he wasn't feeling very victorious at having captured him. Maybe it was because it was like Book said—there was still a long way to go until they reached Fort Smith. It flashed through his mind as briefly as dry lightning that there was maybe one chance in a thousand Book was telling the truth about his being innocent, but Cole thought to hell with that notion. Still, the way Book had looked at Cole when he had told him to put the cuffs on, that was a hard thing to do, to look into a man's eyes who had been chained before.

Cole told himself he was tired, worn out from the chase, and that was why he was letting things creep into his mind that had no right being there. The most dangerous man in the world is the one who can make a lie seem like the truth. He drew both pistols and would sleep with them at the ready that night. He'd come too far to make a mistake. When he finally stubbed out the smoke and closed his eyes, he closed out all thoughts of any possibility that the black man was innocent.

CHAPTER TWENTY-EIGHT

Cole saw the bloody scrape marks around Book's wrist and ankle where he had tried to pull free from the irons. "That's cold steel," he said, and reached into his saddlebags and found a tin of salve and tossed it to Jilly Sweet along with the key to the irons. "Unlock him and rub some of that salve on his wounds. Then, when you're finished with that, make some breakfast unless you want to travel on an empty stomach."

Cole sat and smoked a cigarette with the Winchester across his knees while Jilly Sweet tended to Book's wounds. She was delicate in her treatment of him even though he tried to get her to forego the efforts.

"Don't need treatin'," he muttered as she dipped her fingers into the salve and smeared it across the cuts.

"Does, too, Levi. Those cuts'll get all infected, poison your blood."

"So what if they do? You think that white man gonna care if I suffer a little bit?"

She glanced around at Cole, her fox brown eyes filled with hurt. "Leviticus, tell it true what he say about white men bein' so hateful against a black man."

"Finish up little sister, we've got a long ride ahead of us," Cole urged.

He had no interest in engaging in a conversation with either of them about what white men and black men thought of one another. He'd fought for the North during the war and there had been plenty of good brave black troopers who had fought and died with the rest of the Union boys. When a man is hugging the ground under the withering fire of lead shot and chain, it doesn't matter much what color his skin is, because the color of his blood is exactly the same, and so is his fear. As though he had read Cole's thoughts, Book looked directly at him and said: "You fought in the war, didn't you?"

"What does that have to do with anything?"

"Johnny Reb," he said. "You fought for ol' Marse Lee."

"No, I was on the other side, one of Grant's boys."

His gaze shifted slightly. "You sayin' that 'cause they lost, or 'cause it's true?"

"Like I said, what difference does it make?"

"What outfit was you with?"

Cole glanced at the rising sun. "It's getting late." He asked Jilly Sweet again: "You want to fix that breakfast or travel hungry?"

She finished applying the salve, then handed back the tin before digging around in a gunny sack next to their saddles. Cole watched her take out a thick slab of salt pork and a can of beans along with a small bag of Arbuckle's coffee and a blackened pot. He rolled another cigarette and smoked it. Book never took his eyes from him. "I was with the Tenth," Book said.

"That where you learn to shoot that long-range gun . . . with the Tenth?" Cole asked.

Book half smiled, but it was more from bitterness than amusement. "Learned a lot of things in that war. Killin' was jus' one of them."

"Killing white Southern boys? That give you pleasure, did it?"

Book's gaze shifted from Cole to Jilly Sweet who was bent over the fry pan, the sound of the bacon beginning to sizzle. "I did what I had to," he said. "What they ordered me to do, I did."

"Judging by the way you killed those renegades the other day, I'd say you were good at it."

"I can shoot, if that's what you mean."

"Why'd you shoot those renegades?" Cole asked, his curiosity renewed. "Why didn't you just let them take us on at that run-down cabin? You could have ridden away. Fact is, you could have ridden away plenty of times . . . why didn't you?"

"Tired of runnin', mister," he said. "Tired of bein' chased."

"Still doesn't explain why you shot those renegades."

He took a long deep breath, let it out. "Wanted to prove I was innocent case it came to that."

"I don't get it. How did shooting those Indians prove anything?"

"I figure you and those other men catch up to me, I explain it . . . why I kilt 'em. Then you see I ain't guilty of no murders of no white men."

"You've lost me, friend."

"Those bucks killed a white woman and her man over near Bridger two weeks back. Slit her throat after they used her. Cut the man's eyelids off so's he'd have to watch, then drove a stick down his throat. They were just a pack of starvin' red trash."

"You hear that, about them killing the woman and her man?" Cole shifted his look again to Jilly Sweet, who had paused to look at the two of them.

"Didn't hear it," Book said. "Saw it. Come up on it less than an hour after it happened. The bodies were still warm."

"How do you know the ones that attacked us at the cabin were the same ones that killed the white couple?"

"Mister, I fought Indians all over the plains with the Tenth after the war. They called us Buffalo

308

Soldiers. They hated us and fought us . . . but they feared us, too. I learned to tell sign of the different tribes. I learned to track, too. It was them."

"So you figured to do a good turn for the white man?"

He shook his head. "Don't you understand nothin'?"

"Explain to me what I don't understand, Book."

"I had a chance to end the misery they were spreadin', and I took it. Then I thought to myself, was you and those other men to catch me, I'd explain it so you'd see I ain't no cold-blooded killer. I'm just me. Just a man been accused of doin' wrong. I figure maybe if I show you and the others the truth . . . you see I ain't guilty of nothin'. Maybe you let me alone . . . let me go on. I guess I was a damn' fool for thinkin' it."

"It's a hell of a story, I'll give you that."

He lowered his gaze. "Don't matter no more," he said. "Might just as well hang as to keep on runnin' like a damn' rabbit bein' chased by a pack o' hounds."

Jilly Sweet sat down beside him while the bacon fried and the coffee boiled. She put her slender arms around his neck and said: "Don't worry Levi honey. I ain't gonna let him take you back to Fort Smith."

Cole looked at her. "A man appreciates a woman's strong love, but don't test me, child." Then he saw it—the same look in each of their eyes, a look that let him know he couldn't possibly understand what they were feeling toward each other or toward him, or white folks in general. He picked up his plate and forked out a few strips of bacon from the pan, then poured himself a cup of coffee, and sat back down again. "Eat while you have the chance. We won't be stopping again until noon, and then only briefly."

It was a somber meal under a somber sky. Gray clouds were bunched together like one large rumpled blanket and it threatened to snow again before the day was through. Cole told himself not to let the fact that Book was an ex-Union soldier who had fought for the same side he had get in the way of his judgment. Everything pointed toward Book's guilt, and that guilt included the killing of two of his friends, not to mention all the others he was accused of murdering. He guessed Book had been a good man at one time, but war has a way of changing a man, and maybe it changed Book from whatever he once was into a killer. Cole knew plenty of men who had come away from that war with a taste for blood, the same way they had a taste for opium or whiskey or women. There never was much good found in any war, but it did teach you one thing—survival. So that was what a lot of men had done after the war—they had survived the best way they knew how. For some, it was robbing trains and banks. For others, it was wearing a badge or hiring out as stock detectives. For the more independent-minded, it was bounty hunting, or cattle rustling. Just about anything they could do to earn a living with the gun skills they'd learned. And it didn't hurt any if the line of chosen work had a little spice to it, for a lot of what happened after the war seemed mighty boring at times. Cole could only guess the ways the war had changed a man like Leviticus Book.

They finished their meager breakfast and scraped out the tin plates and tossed them back in the gunny sack along with the pot and the Arbuckle's.

"It don't mean nothin' to you?" Book said, "that I shot those renegades, maybe kept you and your friends from bein' slaughtered? Don't mean nothin' that I sat here and told you the Lord's truth about I ain't never killed no white men like they say?"

"You killed Will Harper."

"He pulled his gun. He was goin' to kill me."

"He had reason to."

"No, he didn't."

"Get on your horse," Cole said.

Book looked at the wrist irons lying on the ground. "You goin' to chain me again?"

Cole looked at them, too. "No. You ride ahead of me, don't try to run."

Book helped Jilly Sweet gain her seat in the saddle, then put himself on the back of his horse while Cole mounted the bird.

"Lead out, that way," Cole said, pointing to the east.

"Why that way?" Book asked. "The Nations and Fort Smith are south of here."

"We're going to Cheyenne," Cole explained. "Take the train from there. Easier than riding the whole way back."

"Faster, too," Book said. "That way, you'll get to see me hung a whole lot quicker . . . ain't that it?"

"That's not what I was thinking. But if that's what you choose to believe, feel free."

Book's skin looked blue-black under the sunless sky. Cole noticed the soles of his shoes were peeling away and the cuffs of his pants were frayed. The coat he wore was too small for his large frame. Whatever his crimes had been, they sure hadn't paid well.

Cole gave a nod for Book to lead off. Book looked at Cole a moment longer, then turned his face away and tapped his heels to the ribs of his bay. Jilly Sweet was riding the smaller sorrel and she clicked her tongue and slapped its withers with the ends of her reins until it trotted along-side Book's horse. Cole fell in behind them.

He didn't care if they talked to each other while they rode. Cole wasn't worried about them plotting an escape even though Jilly Sweet had sworn she wasn't going to let Cole take Book back to Fort Smith. He didn't figure there was much he needed to fear from a ninety-pound lovesick girl, and Book already knew what his options were. She looked small, riding next to him, like a child. And now and again, she would tap her reins over the withers of the little sorrel, forcing it to keep up with the longer stride of the bay.

The wind swept sand and tumbleweeds across the open land. Cole could feel the bite of it, like the sting of a scorpion against his ears and face and the back of his hands. He thought of the warm winds of south Texas, how a man could close his eyes and be caressed by them in a way that was nearly as comforting as a woman's touch. The taste of tequila and mescal floated into his thoughts. So, too, did the sounds of a lively mariachi band and the clicking heels of dancing *señoritas* whose dark flashing eyes dared you to imagine the pleasures they possessed.

He shifted up the collar of his coat around the back of his neck with cold stiff fingers, trying to cut the wind. Del Rio and those warm nights seemed a lot longer away from Wyoming Territory than they actually were. A red-tail hawk flapped mightily against the buffeting wind, its body and wings dark against the ashen sky as it sought the refuge of a distant stand of pines, or perhaps some winter prey against the patches of snow and frozen sage. Cole thought if he were an old hawk, he'd be flying away to Texas to sit in the warm sand and wait for spring to come again. The hawk gave a single shrill cry that sounded like pain, and the sound shivered through Cole as neatly as did the icy wind. Ahead of him rode a small slight girl who knew only life's indecencies and the unrelenting love for the big black man next to her.

Cole remembered an old *pistolero* named Bat Belgraves who he'd met down in a New Mexico gambling den. He had liked to drink shot glasses of whiskey in his beer and brag that he killed thirty-one men and swore an oath that: "If they take me back to Texas, they won't take me back alive!" A one-armed deputy marshal ended up shooting Belgraves through the lungs over a $2 debt. Belgraves died a slow and pitifully painful death, but they never did take him back to Texas.

Cole wondered if Leviticus Book had similar thoughts about going back to Fort Smith, and, if he did, which one of them might end up like Bat Belgraves—bleeding and suffering his last hours away on some lonesome and faraway spit of land. He tried not to let himself think of the answer as he watched the hawk suddenly dive and disappear behind a ridge, a rabbit or a mouse no doubt on the other side, cowering amid the sage, unaware that death was coming on this cold gray day that was bleak and without hope.

Then, without warning, Jilly Sweet turned her little sorrel around, trotted back to where Cole was riding the speckled bird, and, when she came to within five or six feet of him, she brought her right hand out from inside her coat. Something small and silver flashed in her hand. It took Cole a second to realize it was a Derringer. Then she pulled the trigger and something white-hot flashed inside his skull.

Chapter Twenty-nine

The little gun popped like a whip crack. The slug punched into Cole's ribs, carrying him from the saddle. There was an instant of free fall, then the ground came up and slammed him hard and he felt the rush of air from his lungs.

"What you gone an' done, girl?" Book's voice sounded far away.

"Couldn't jus' let him take you back to Fort Smith, Levi," Cole heard Jilly say, her voice as plaintive as the hawk's cry.

Cole felt himself sliding down a long dark tunnel, the voices of Book and Jilly Sweet growing rapidly more distant. He tried rolling over to get to his hands and knees, but he was having difficulty just trying to breathe. He tasted bile in the back of his throat. If he was shot in a lung, he was going to die that same painful prolonged way Bat Belgraves had died. He fought as hard as he could not to die, but he was falling faster and faster down that dark tunnel.

And then a distant howling brought him gradually to the light, a yellow flame of light that danced up from the ground. "You ain't kilt him, Jilly!"

It took a moment for Cole's eyes to focus fully on the dancing flames of the campfire and in the distance he heard the mournful call of a coyote in the surrounding darkness. The blue-black face of Leviticus Book hovered above him, the edges of his eyes egg-white, his teeth smooth and slightly rounded, gleaming like sea shells behind his parted lips. "I thought maybe Jilly kilt you sure," he said.

Cole's throat was so dry he could barely swallow. Book put a canteen to Cole's lips and said: "Drink it slow." Some of the water trickled down the sides of Cole's mouth as he tried to get his throat to work. A dull ache crawled up through his core, and, when he tried shifting his weight, it felt like someone was twisting a knife blade against his ribs. The pain turned suddenly sharp and snatched his breath away, and he fainted.

"You lost some blood," Book said once Cole had regained consciousness. "I did the best I could to stop it."

Cole was presently focused enough to test the wound with his fingertips. A cold wet bandage covered the area.

"Tore up a pair of Jilly's clean drawers," Book said. "It was all we had to make a bandage with."

Cole pulled his fingers away, saw the smear of blood on them. "The bullet's still in you," Book said.

"Why didn't you take off when you had the chance?" Cole rasped.

"Jilly wanted to. She thought for sure she kilt you." Book looked down at the bloody bandage, then back at Cole. "I ain't guilty," he said. "And I ain't gonna start being guilty of anything now. If you die, then so be it. But it ain't gonna be because I just left you out here to bleed to death."

Cole noticed the butt of his self-cocker sticking from the waist band of Book's pants. "That's my pistol," he said.

Book looked down at it. "I'm holdin' it for you."

"That's mighty kind of you."

"There's been enough gun play," he said. "You up to eatin'?"

Jilly Sweet appeared with a plate in one hand, a fork in the other. She knelt down beside Cole, stared at him, said: "Brought you some beans, a biscuit. Ain't much, but it's gonna have to do."

Cole tried to take the plate from her, but the effort was more than he could stand. Just the movement alone sent a wall of flame through him.

"Better let me," she said. Cole opened and closed his mouth around the forkful of beans she fed him. In spite of the pain, he felt half starved, half sick. "I jus' couldn't let you take Leviticus to Fort Smith," she said. Her gaze was defiant. "I di'n't want to shoot you."

"Then why did you?"

Cole saw her shift her gaze to Book.

"He's my man, you di'n't give me no choice."

Cole ate a few more forkfuls of beans before the retching started. Whatever had gone in, came back up. His skin felt hot and damp like the air over a Southern swamp. He could feel a fever growing in his blood. Maybe the bullet hadn't killed him outright, but, if the wound became infected, there was still a better than even chance he would die. It was another lesson the war had taught him—the bullet didn't always kill you outright.

Book came back over and squatted next to Cole. "Either finish me off, or get me to a doctor," Cole said.

Book saw the beaded sweat covering Cole's face. He knew the same thing Cole knew. "I'll ride off to the north," he said. "There's pines up on that far slope. I'll cut some poles, make a travois. Go soon's it's light."

"Whiskey," Cole said. "You got any whiskey?"

"Mash. Got a little bit o' mash."

He left, his boots crunching on the frozen ground, returned in a few seconds with the bottle. "Try this," he said.

Cole drank what he could, trying to put a fire in his belly to fight the one in his brain. He thought of Bat Belgraves, the way he'd died, the time it had taken. He didn't want to die like that, slow, a minute at a time. He wanted it to be quick, not eaten up by a fever-fueled blood infection.

"Go on, drink the rest, you want to," Book said, as Cole tried to hand him back the bottle. "You need it a whole lot more'n me."

Jilly Sweet's wide-staring eyes softened from the defiance they had held earlier. She looked like she wanted to say something to Cole, but realized there were no words that would change anything. Her face recessed into the shadows.

"She's feelin' bad about what she done," Book said. "You want me to make you a cigarette?" He didn't wait for an answer, but reached inside his pocket and pulled out paper and tobacco, and began rolling a shuck. He twisted off the ends and handed it to Cole, then struck a match off the heel of his boot, and held the flame to the tip. Cole drew in a lung full of smoke and it felt good, a small comfort from the pain.

Cole watched as Book rolled himself one. "Learned lots of bad habits in the Army," he said. "The use of tobacco was one. Liquor was another." Then he looked over his shoulder, into the deep shadows where Jilly Sweet was sitting. "Loneliness," he said. "That's another thing a man learns about in the Army. Learns to crave a woman just as much as he craves whiskey and tobacco once he's gotten himself a taste for 'em."

Book struck a second match to light his own cigarette and the flame flared against his coal-black features. Twin flames danced in his dark eyes for a moment before he snapped out the match.

Half of Cole's brain was buzzing with the low hum of the fever slipping through his bloodstream. Book's deep, resonant voice rode the edges of his consciousness and he tried to stay with what he was saying. "Guess the whiskey and tobacco and women ain't so bad, though," Cole heard him say. His face was tilted toward the stars and Cole wasn't sure if he was talking to himself or to Cole. "That was all the Army ever taught me, I'd be a happy man." He looked down at Cole, his face a black moon, his eyes glitteringly wet. "I know you probably like most white men, thinkin' wan't nothin' better for a black man than to be able to shoot them Rebel white boys and get away with it." His eyes became fixed on Cole, like he was trying to see inside his skull. He shook his head slowly. "I never took no pleasure from it, seein' a boy get shot in the face, have his legs and arms blown off, hear him screamin' for his mama and the Lord Almighty. Ain't nobody human can take pleasure from somethin' like that."

It felt like demons were crawling over Cole's skin. He closed his eyes. Book was saying something about being forced to hide in trees and about a Rebel officer who had a long wiry beard and played the fiddle. None of it was making much sense to Cole because the buzz in his blood had grown as loud as a hundred cicadas and it felt like his veins were stretched taut as piano wire. The ground beneath him began a slow spin that grew faster and faster until he felt his fingers digging into the cold earth, trying to hold on. Then he knew with all certainty that he was going back down into that dark tunnel again, only this time he wasn't sure he would be coming back up.

Something bright pressed against Cole's eyelids and he opened them just enough to see slits of blue sky overhead. Jilly Sweet came into view.

"I made coffee. You able to sit up and drink some?"

Sometime during the night the fever had raged and brought Cole murderous dreams and a sick feeling that rotated in his belly. He nodded, and she put a tin cup of coffee in his hands, which shook so badly the coffee sloshed over the edges and she had to take the cup away from him.

"Levi's off cutting some poles to make a travois," she said. Cole saw her staring toward the distance. "Gone up to where them trees is at. Told him watch out some big ol' bear don't get him. He laugh and say . . . 'Jilly don't fret all the time.' But I do." Then she turned her head just enough to look at Cole out of the corner of her eye. "So much trouble," she said, then turned back again to watch the distance.

Cole slipped in and out of consciousness several times. At one point, he felt himself being lifted and placed on a blanket. He opened his eyes and saw Book's face high above him. "That should do," he said. "Leastwise we can travel with him till we find someone to heal him or bury him."

Every inch of Cole's skin was on fire, and every jolt over a rock or rut in the landscape brought him untold misery. He began to pray for death. It seemed ludicrous that such a small gun had brought him so much misery. He slept in fits, woke in starts, bit the inside of his cheeks until he could taste blood. It all seemed so unreal, that he would die at the hand of a slight, brown-skinned girl whose only two possessions were her fierce loyalty and a hidden Derringer. As he rocked and bounced along on the travois, he felt like death was following along behind them, like some lean and hungry wolf just waiting for the right opportunity. He wondered what Ike Kelly's thoughts had been in those final seconds of his life. Did he even have time for final thoughts, like Cole was having now? He closed his eyes and prayed that, when it was time, he would face the old wolf honorably and without fear.

The sky turned sullen, the sun lost behind a blanket of gray smudge. Cole felt the sting of hard snow against his face and eyelids. He opened his mouth and let the snow touch his tongue. He thought it an omen, that it was snowing, that the sun had gone out. He watched the fading landscape, sought the old wolf.

CHAPTER THIRTY

Droplets of wet snow like cold tears slid down Cole's cheeks and collected in his mustaches and tasted cool against his tongue. The gentle sway of the travois, the scraping sounds it made as the ends of the poles cut lines into the frozen ground, the swish of the horse's tails—these were sounds and events he remembered as he drifted in and out of consciousness.

Then, finally, the journey came to a halt. Cole heard Book's deep voice call out: " 'Lo, there in the cabin!" It was followed by the rusty sound of hinges. "Got a wounded man here!"

For a long time there was nothing said. Then a woman's voice said: "How'd he get that way?"

"My gal shot him."

"Why'd she shoot him?"

"He was taking me to jail. She didn't want him to take me to jail. That's why she shot him."

"Maybe you better keep moving, then," the woman said.

"Can't. We do, he'll die. He's almost dead as it is. What with this snow and cold and the hole in him. He don't die one way, he'll probably die another. Freeze to death, maybe bleed out."

More silence.

"What was he taking you to jail for?" the woman said.

"Murder. He thinks I killed some men."

"Did you?"

"None that mattered to him."

"I let you in, maybe you might kill me, too."

Book said: "Don't it stand to reason that, was I a killer, I wouldn't be haulin' him around, goin' to all this trouble, him tryin' to take me to jail?"

Cole heard steps in the snow, then a shadow came into view. She was holding a twin-barrel shotgun that looked too heavy for her. She was plain and tall. What Cole could see of her features through the oval of a wool scarf tied about her head and face were her ruddy cheek bones and light green eyes. She had a wide, thin mouth and pale, colorless lips. She was bundled in a Mackinaw and wool trousers that were stuffed inside stovepipe boots.

"You're right," she said. "He is near dead. Better take him inside."

Between them, Cole was lifted from the travois and half dragged, half carried inside a low-slung cabin with icicles hanging from the eaves.

"Put him over there on that cot," the woman said.

The cot was near a stone fireplace and the heat

from its fire felt immense after all day in the cold. Cole felt the ice particles in his mustache melt and drip onto his lips and chin. The best thing about being in the cold was that it had partially frozen the pain in Cole's side. Jilly tugged off his boots and Book removed Cole's coat and the woman handed them a blanket with which to cover him.

The woman said: "He might not last till evening."

Cole could feel the heat of the fire against the side of his face, then felt it begin to melt the stiffness in his joints. Then it released the frozen pain in his side as well. But it was the sort of comforting heat that made him drowsy, made him long to close his eyes and drift to another place. He wondered, as he felt himself slipping away, if dying would be as bad as he'd imagined.

Cole didn't remember dreaming. He awakened to a room that was dark except for the dancing flames of the fireplace. He saw the blanket-covered shapes of Book and Jilly Sweet on the floor not far away, the glow of fire on their passive faces. He wondered where the woman was. He tried to move, but the pain stitched in his side. He sensed someone stepping from the shadows, crossing in front of the fireplace, then pausing next to the cot.

"You've not passed on?" the woman asked.

"No. I guess this is going to take longer than I thought." Cole's voice was barely above a whisper.

"I guess you can thank me for that," she said. "I cleaned out that mess of a wound. Lanced out the sickness, put some ointment on it. But that bullet is still in you somewhere. I imagine it broke some of your ribs is what it done."

As tall as she was, her face was recessed by the shadows, but her hands hung visibly at her sides. They were large hands, red at the knuckles.

"I could stand a drink," Cole whispered, trying to speak around the dryness of his tongue that felt like it might snap off.

She slipped away. He heard the soft pad of feet on the puncheon floor, then she returned with a dipper that had droplets of water falling from it.

He forced himself to a sitting position. She held the dipper while he drank. His own hands were unsteady. The water was sweet and cool and he asked for more. This time he cupped his hands over hers as she held the dipper for him.

"You still got a fever," she said. "I can feel it through your hands."

Cole leaned back and felt the rough logs behind him. "I'll probably die here in your house. I'm sorry you had to be the one."

"Folks have died in this house before, I reckon," she said. "You won't be the first."

"I've got some makings in one of my coat pockets. A shuck would taste good."

She found his tobacco and papers and made him a cigarette without saying anything until she'd finished. She rolled the smoke like she'd had practice at it. Then she handed it to Cole and scraped a match over one of the fireplace stones. "First time I made a cigarette in two years," she said. "I hope it's to your liking."

"It's fine," Cole said as she touched the match to the end and he drew in some smoke and let it back out again. She brought the match close to her face and blew out the flame. Cole saw in that brief moment that her hair was undone, hanging loosely in a long pigtail as thick as a rope. Her hair was the color of winter brown.

"She really the one that shot you?" she asked. "That young gal?"

"She did."

"You don't look like a man that would let a bitty girl shoot you. Fact is, you don't look the sort of man that'd let anyone get close enough to shoot you."

"I wasn't expecting it. But how can you tell just by looking at me?"

"By the way you dress. That backward-turned holster on your left hip. That shoulder rig you're wearing. You're not just some 'puncher off one of the ranges."

"You're right, I'm not."

"So how did it come to pass that you let that little gal put a bullet it you . . . a man in your profession?"

"I made a mistake."

"What sort of mistake?"

"I trusted that she wouldn't shoot me. I was wrong."

"I guess you'd know that better than me."

"My name's Cole . . . John Henry Cole."

She didn't say anything, but Cole could tell she was staring at him from the shadows. "Mattie," she said. She didn't offer a second name. "Mister Book said you was taking him to Fort Smith."

"Cheyenne, then Fort Smith. That's correct."

"He says he never killed anybody, except that he had to. That he is an innocent man."

"What would you expect him to say?"

"Don't act like any killer I ever met."

"Have you met many?"

"A few. Better get some sleep. It's late."

He tossed the last of the shuck into the fireplace and, for that brief act, it felt like a hatchet was buried in his ribs. He sank down on the bunk and stared at the flames. Maybe there was a time when he thought dying was the worst thing that could happen to him. Now he wasn't so sure it wasn't living with a bullet between his ribs.

The fever flared from the center of his body, then began to crawl through his blood like a hundred hot snakes, and the rest of that night he fell from one twisted dream to the next. When he heard sounds of muted conversation, it was movement through the thick fog in his head. He heard the sounds of boots knocking against the floor, then the opening and closing of a door, accompanied a rush of cold air.

When he was finally able to open his eyes, he saw the woman, Mattie, sitting alone at a table at the far end of the room. Pewter light was coming through a window above her, lighting the edges of her face. It was a strong face. She must have known he was watching her, for she slowly turned her head toward Cole and set down the tin cup she'd been holding between her hands.

"You up to some breakfast?" she asked.

"I don't think so. Where's Book and the girl?"

"Gone," she said. "I sent them for what passes as a doctor in this country. Doc Jellicoe, lives up near Beaver Valley. He mostly doctors animals when he feels up to it and isn't drunk. I don't know he can do you much good, but, if you ain't passed over by the time he comes, I figure he can't do you much harm, either." Her clothes rustled when she stood up and came over to the cot. "You best try and eat something," she said.

"No appetite for it," Cole said.

"Coffee and sugar," she said. "Dip some bread into it. It's easy on the belly. Least try."

She helped him to sit up, then brought him the

coffee and a chunk of bread to dip into it. He managed a few bites.

"You still look peaked," she said. She laid her left hand across his forehead. "Still carrying that fever, too."

"I don't know what's keeping me alive. It must be from trying."

Her hand felt cool and smooth as marble against his skin. "Best thing for a fever is a cold bath," she said.

He offered a weak smile.

"You're hotter than a stove," she said.

"That's OK if I am." The thought of a cold bath caused parts of Cole to draw into a clench.

"No. It would be less than Christian of me not to do what I know works."

"No. Maybe another smoke would help just the same."

"Foolish man," she said, and stood up.

Cole watched as she pulled a large wooden tub from behind a curtain and set it in front of the fireplace. Then she put on her Mackinaw and began carrying in buckets of water from outside to fill the tub.

"Creek runs right past the house," she said, when she saw the look on his face. Every time she went out and came in again, snow fell off her boots and a swoop of cold air came in with her.

Cole was too weak to do anything but watch. When she judged that she had filled the tub adequately, she came over and said: "You want help getting undressed?"

"I'd as soon die of the fever as sit in a tub of cold water."

She began undoing the buttons of his clothes. He tried to stop her. "Don't make this any harder than it has to be," she said, and brushed aside his hands.

The room was beginning to slip out from under Cole as she peeled off the last layer of clothing and helped him to his feet.

"I can't do this," he said.

"It won't be as bad as you think. Just get in and sit down all at once. That's the best way."

He had no strength to resist or argue. He let her help him step into the tub. The water felt like fire as he lowered into it. He gasped, his heart felt like it would lurch out of his chest, and his knuckles turned white, gripping the sides of the tub.

"Stay with it," she said.

He shivered and shook and his teeth chattered uncontrollably. She dipped some of the water up over his head and shoulders and he thought he would come clear out of his skin. And then, after a time, the torture seemed to ease and he felt the fever beginning to shatter inside like glass hit with a rock.

She took a bar of harsh yellow soap and said: "I might as well wash your hair as long as you're already wet and willing." She commenced scrubbing his skull. Her fingers were strong, but gentle, as she worked at his scalp, and it felt good to the point that he closed his eyes. Then she kneaded the muscles of his neck and shoulders, and he felt a release of old pain that had been knotted there for years dissipate under her knowing hands.

"You about ready to get out now?" she asked, after she had finished rubbing his muscles.

His skin felt warm and glowing where her hands had been. "I'm not sure."

She helped him to stand, then dried him with a scratchy towel, rubbing it over his skin until it reddened, then wrapped the towel around his middle, and helped him back to the cot. She combed his hair straight back and put a fresh bandage over his wound, then drew a blanket over him.

"How do you feel now?" she asked.

"Better," he admitted.

She laid the palm of her hand once more on his forehead. "Fever feels like it's broke some," she said.

He asked her to help him with a smoke and she did, and he sipped a little more of the sugar-sweetened coffee with it and felt halfway normal for the first time since he'd been shot.

Then, suddenly, he began to shiver. She brought him more blankets but nothing seemed to help. It felt like he was being held in the jaws of some large invisible beast that was trying to shake the life out of him. The room started spinning out of control. His bones felt like they were shattering at the same time his flesh was being peeled away. He heard sounds coming from his mouth, but not words. The sounds were guttural, like an animal makes that's trying to survive.

His only coherent thoughts were that death had finally decided to come and was trying to shake him loose from his earthly bonds. Then in the midst of everything, he had a fleeting vision of wife and son, waiting across a wide river, their arms outstretched toward him. He wanted to go to them, but something was holding him back, clawing at his soul. Abruptly he felt like he was being wrapped in the arms of grace and a slow comforting heat began to penetrate through the icy tomb that encased him. Slowly, ever so slowly he was pulled back from the nether world of lost souls and found himself once more in the room of the cabin. When at last his limbs ceased to shake and the last traces of cold crept away, he slept in a silken shroud of sleep, the stillness in him complete, the rest undisturbed by dreams or ghosts or gnawing death.

When Cole awakened, Mattie was sitting there at her table, a tin cup held between her large hands, her sea green eyes fixed upon him. "You're better now?"

"Yes, I think so."

"Nearly lost you."

He nodded. "It felt like all hell was breaking loose."

She tilted her head, the tail of hair lying over her right shoulder a soft brown against the linsey-woolsey shirt she wore.

"It was a strange ride," he said. "I've never been so cold. It was like my bones were breaking from the inside."

"You talked crazy talk," she said. "Gibberish."

"I was freezing, and then I felt a warmth. A strange and wonderful warmth."

"Fever, that's all. It does you like that. One minute you're freezing, the next you're burning up."

"No, it wasn't like that. This was different."

"You want me to make you a cigarette?"

"No."

"Don't know why Doc Jellicoe hasn't come yet. Maybe Mister Book and that girl got lost."

"Maybe they just kept on riding," Cole said. "Maybe a doctor isn't what they went to find."

She blinked. "Mister Book didn't strike me as the type to leave you high and dry. I think if he was going to do that, he'd've done it before he brought you all the way here."

"Maybe it wasn't his idea," Cole said.

"You mean the girl talked him out of it?"

"She loved him enough to shoot me."

"Well, if he hasn't come by this evening," she said, looking toward the window with its failing light, "I'll go for Doc myself come morning."

"I think maybe you did a good thing," Cole said.

She turned to look at him again, the cup still between her hands, the steam lifting against her face. "What do you mean?"

"Getting into bed with me," he said. "Sharing your warmth, taking my cold into your own body."

She said: "I better get supper started, in case they come. Maybe you could stand to eat something." She stood, her back toward him.

"Mattie."

"The fever makes a body crazy," she said.

"I know what I know."

"I better get supper ready."

Cole had realized what she had done only midway through their conversation. A flash of it came to him, the warmth of her bare flesh pressed against him, her plain face there before his, inches away, the soft sweet breath of her mouth against his eyes. At first he thought it a dream risen out of the stark cold of his nightmare. But now that he recognized the reality of what had happened, he recalled time and time again awakening and feeling her arms around him, her legs entwined in his, wrapping him with her body until the aching cold was replaced with the warmth of summer winds. He wondered why she would deny it. Then he realized there could be a thousand reasons and not one of them was any of his business if she didn't want him to know. She had saved him.

"What's your name?" he asked.

Keeping her back to him as she fed kindling into the stove, she said: "Mattie. I thought I told you. Did you forget?"

"No. I remember it was Mattie. I'd like to know your full name."

"Mattie Blaylock," she said.

"You have a man, Mattie Blaylock?" he asked.

She hesitated in her feeding of the stove. "A sometimes man," she said.

"What does that mean exactly?"

"Mean's he comes and he goes. Right now, he's gone."

"When's he coming back?"

She picked up another piece of kindling, shoved it into the stove, into the hungry flames. "I don't know if he is coming back. You'd need to ask him." Then she turned and looked at him, the wide-set light green eyes filled with something akin to old sorrows. "Trouble with men," she said, "is you can never count on them. They're always finding ways to leave you."

"How many ways are there?" Cole asked.

"Enough to fill a woman's heart with regret and her soul with broken promises."

"He just rode off, your man?"

"This time, and a half dozen times before."

"But he always comes back?"

"No, not always. Sometimes I go and find him. If he don't come back by spring, I reckon I'll probably go and find him again. Like I did the last time he didn't come back."

"Maybe this time he'll come back."

"Maybe he will." She seemed to grow smaller as she talked, like the weight of talking about him was shrinking her. He watched her touch the back of her wrist to her cheek. "Getting warm in here," she said.

"It's the warmth I'll remember."

She gave him a narrow look. "One man gone and one half dead. Some gals just don't have any luck at all."

"Thank you for what you did."

She looked out the window and said: "They don't come soon, they'll miss supper."

"This man you're going to find in the spring if he don't come back before then," Cole said. "What's his name?"

"What difference would that make to you?"

"I just thought, if I ever ran across him, I'd tell him what a damned fool he's been."

She stared out the window at the dying light, then turned again to look at Cole and he saw the same dying light in her eyes.

CHAPTER THIRTY-ONE

Just as evening light turned to an almost dusty rose, Cole saw Mattie look up from her coffee cup. She went to the window, looked out, and said: "They're coming."

He heard feet stomping on the porch, then the latch of the door lifted, and they came in—Book and Jilly Sweet and a short, heavy-set man wearing a stovepipe hat with a bent crown.

"Mattie," said the man.

"Doc."

"That him?"

She nodded.

He looked in Cole's direction. "Shot you in the brisket, eh?"

"Close," Cole said. "More like the short ribs."

"Damn," he said, "that must've hurt like hell."

"It did. Still does."

"I'll bet."

He set a leather bag down atop the table. "You got more of that coffee, dear?"

"Plenty," she said. "You know me and coffee."

"Good, I'll have a cup to warm my innards, it's damnable cold out there."

"How about you, Mister Book?" Mattie said. "You and the girl want some coffee, something to eat?"

"Yes'm. Coffee and victuals would do just the trick," Book said, glancing at Cole.

Jilly Sweet kept her gaze lowered, avoiding Cole.

"You look a sight better," Book said, noticing that Cole was sitting on the side of the cot, maybe noticing his hair was combed and washed.

"You were expecting maybe I'd be dead?" Cole prompted.

Book glanced toward Jilly, then said: "Didn't know."

Dr. Jellicoe removed his coat and hung it over the back of a chair. He was wearing a patchwork vest over a collarless shirt. His black trousers were shiny from use. He went over and stood in front of the fire and rubbed his hands together. The fire seemed to glow red in his chubby cheeks.

Mattie gave him a cup of coffee, but before he drank any of it, he went to his leather bag that was on the table and took out a silver flask of whiskey and poured some into his cup. "How about you, Mister Book, you want a taste of this?"

Book nodded, held out his cup, his lips parted slightly as he watched Dr. Jellicoe pour the coffee in.

"Mattie?" Dr. Jellicoe asked, holding forth the flask, the firelight glinting against the metal.

"No, Doc. I've seen what a thief whiskey can be. I won't allow it to steal my mind."

Dr. Jellicoe grinned, showing a double row of

gapped teeth. "Good for you, ol' girl. It's the worst insult a man can do to himself . . . get drunk as a pole-axed mule and go about showing the world what a fool the devil sauce has made him." He took a long sip of the coffee and licked his lips.

Mattie set the table with a meager meal of fried pork, biscuits she'd prepared in a Dutch oven, pinto beans, and some turnips she'd taken from a burlap sack next to the stove and cooked in a pot of water. She fixed Cole a plate and brought it over.

"Can you do this on your own, or do you require my help?"

"Let me try it on my own," Cole said, glancing at the others who had seated themselves around the table. "You've done enough already. Sit down and eat your meal."

She looked at Cole for a moment longer than was necessary, then joined the others at the table.

Cole still didn't have much of an appetite. The bullet lodged in his side had wounded his desire to eat as much as it had his flesh. But he tasted some of what was on his plate, taking small bites and holding them in his mouth a time before swallowing. He watched Dr. Jellicoe eat. He went at his food with dogged determination, his forefinger pressed on the back of his knife as he cut into his pork, his jaw moving in a steady rhythm as he chewed, his eyes never leaving what was on his plate. And when he'd finished the last scrap, he took one more biscuit and swiped it back and forth across the drippings and ate that as well. Finally he lifted his whiskey-laced cup of coffee and washed everything down with it before wiping the tips of his fingers across his vest.

"Damn' wonderful meal, Mattie. Worth the ride out here."

"Glad you enjoyed it, Doc."

He had the look of a wanting man, but Mattie's gaze was unyielding. He fumbled around in the pockets of his vest and shirt fronts and found what he'd been searching for—a small black cheroot that he promptly fired up, then blew a ring of gray smoke that lifted and broke against the ceiling.

Book and Jilly Sweet were still working on their meals, as was Mattie, but she seemed less interested in food than did the others. "You figure on getting around to looking at the patient sometime this evening, Doc?" Mattie wondered. "Or did you just ride all this way for a taste of fried pork?"

"Oh, I ain't forgot," he said. "Just that I got plum famished on such a long ride. And a meal ain't really a meal until you've had a good seegar to go with it."

"And maybe another cup of that whiskey coffee?" she presumed.

"Point taken, madam," he said, and stood from the table. Taking up his leather bag, he walked over to the cot Cole was sitting on.

"Pull back your shirt, son, let me see that bung hole that young gal put in you."

Cole could smell his sour breath. "Mattie tells me you do most of your doctoring on animals," he said.

"Animals, cowboys, and shot-in-the-brisket gunfighters," he clarified. "Whatever comes along and needs doctoring. In this case that'd be you. Now pull back your shirt and let me look."

Cole did as he ordered, figuring that it didn't really matter what sort of doctor he was, or wasn't. Someone had to try and take that chunk of lead out of him.

Dr. Jellicoe brought one of the lamps in close and examined the wound with the tips of his fingers after he'd peeled away Mattie's bandage. Then he opened his bag, took out a long metal probe, the kind Cole'd seen surgeons use in hospital tents on the battlefields at Shiloh and Lookout Mountain and a lot of other bad places. "You might want to lean back and think about something else," he suggested.

Cole stared at the ceiling and clamped his jaws shut until his teeth ached while the doctor poked and prodded with the probe.

"Think I feel it," he said at last. Cole was sweating, his hands were damp and cramped rom making fists with them. "That or a piece of bone," he added, straightening and blowing out a stream of blue smoke whose smell caused Cole to want a cigarette.

The doctor took out a metal pan, laid the probe in it, then took out a long, slender instrument that looked like thin pliers and placed it in the pan next to the probe. Then he removed a bottle of rubbing alcohol and poured it over both instruments. The blood from the probe swirled pinkly in the pan as it mixed with the alcohol. He waited a few seconds, then took up the thin pliers. "This is gonna be a little uncomfortable. Better take a drink of this," he said, handing Cole his whiskey flask.

"I'll wait for a drink until after you take the bullet out," Cole said, declining the offer. "I suspect it will taste better then."

"Suit yourself, son. You don't mind if I have one, do you?"

"Go ahead."

Cole watched the lump of the doctor's throat in the loose sack of his unshaven neck as he took a swallow from the flask, then screwed the cap back on, and slipped it back into the same side pocket of his jacket he'd taken it from. "Here goes. I'll try to make it quick, if not painless."

Surprisingly for Cole it didn't hurt much more than the probe had, until he caught hold of the bullet and began to retract it. That's when it felt like someone was driving a railroad spike into him. It took Book and Mattie to hold him still long enough for the doctor to bring out the object he'd grabbed onto.

"Bullet," he declared, dropping the small, partially flattened piece of lead onto the table. It clattered around like penny. "Now this is gonna burn," he said as he poured some of the alcohol directly into the wound. It burned enough to make Cole's eyes water and sting. Then the doctor asked Mattie if she'd mind dressing the wound since she'd done such a fine job of it before. "You ready for that drink now, son?"

Cole took a swallow, then a second one before handing the flask back to him.

"Lucky it was a small caliber," he said, eyeing the slug of lead on the table. "A Forty-Four-Forty might have blowed out your insides, liver, intestines, all that good stuff. I think what happened was that round bounced off a couple of your ribs and just run out of power to do you much damage. I once had a man got himself shot in the skull but all the bullet did was bounce off. Knocked him cold as a pickle, but didn't kill him. 'Course, such things are rare."

"Well, I guess we were both lucky," Cole said.

The doctor grinned his picket-fence grin. "I guess maybe so."

"Thanks," Cole said.

The doctor shifted the cigar from one side of his mouth to the other. "If it hadn't been that those two friends of yours come and got me, you would've ended up dead of lead poisoning. It's been known to happen."

Cole looked across the space of the room to Book. His gaze came up from his plate and met Cole's. "Yeah, I guess I owe them a debt of thanks as well," Cole said.

"You going to stay the night, Doc?" Mattie asked.

"No. Marfina Goodlaw is expecting twins anytime. Got to get back and see how she's holding up. I know sure as anything if I'm down here, she'll have those twins 'way cross the valley. Best get going. Thanks for the supper."

"How much do I owe you for the call?" Cole asked.

"Ten dollars ought to cover it."

"Would you take a good Winchester rifle instead?" Cole asked.

"Another busted hand," the doctor said. "Ain't never met a drifter yet had a nickel to his name."

"I'll pay for his care," Mattie said.

"No, Mattie, I'll count the supper and your company as payment," Dr. Jellicoe said.

"You come out for a chicken supper some Sunday," she said.

He nodded. "Some Sunday for sure, Mattie." He set his hat on his head and gave them all a final look before closing the door behind himself.

Mattie tried to watch him from the window

but it had grown dark outside, so she set to bandaging Cole's wound.

Jilly Sweet stretched her arms and said she was tired, then took a blanket and curled up on the floor in front of the fireplace.

Cole asked Book to make them a cigarette, and by the time he finished, Mattie had finished with the dressing. She began clearing the table as Book handed Cole one of the shucks he'd rolled.

"Tell me the details on Will," Cole said.

Book looked through the haze of blue smoke from his cigarette. "I thought I already did."

"There wasn't any other way than that you had to shoot him?"

He shook his head. "No, sir, there wan't any I could see. I didn't ever think he'd try pullin' his piece with my Sharps on him, but he did. Whole thing happened so fast, wan't nothin' could be done about it. Man had to know one of us was goin' to end up dyin'."

"What about the man in Cheyenne?" Cole asked.

"What about what man in Cheyenne?"

"You shot and burned a man in Cheyenne. He was another friend of mine."

Book's eyes lifted slowly. "Didn't kill no man in Cheyenne."

"You were there."

His head bobbed. "I was there. Stopped long enough to get some things to keep goin' on . . . some flour and sugar and bacon."

"A woman I know says she saw a black man running away from where my friend's office was just before it started burning," Cole lied. "I reckon that'd have to be you."

Cole could see Mattie, standing there, the stack of dirty dishes in her hands, waiting, listening.

Book took the shuck from his mouth, held it between his fingers, the smoke curling up around them. "I was goin' down back of that alley, when I heard somethin'. Somethin' like glass breakin'. I was tryin' to keep to myself account o' I know Mister Harper be trailin' me. I heard the glass breakin'. I look inside one of them buildin's where it come from. I see a man done busted a kerosene lamp on the floor." A sheen of sweat glistened on Book's broad forehead. "Seen another man, down on the floor, look like he dead. Face in a ring of blood. Then I seen the yellow-haired man strike a match and toss it down into that kerosene from the busted lamp. I ran, mister, 'cause I know it's trouble what I seen."

"Yellow-hair man?" Cole asked.

"That's what I seen . . . tall, skinny man, well-armed."

Cole knew only one man that fit Book's description of the killer: Long Bill Longly. It took him a full minute to adjust to the news. Somehow, knowing it was Longly, made it even harder to accept. Longly wasn't worth half a spit compared to a man like Ike Kelly. Cole felt his anger grow white hot.

Book squatted there on his heels, staring at Cole.

"Will told me about another man he said you killed, then burned," Cole prompted.

Book shook his head. "No. I already tol' you, I ain't killed no innocent folks. They got me mixed up with a freed nigger named Kimbo Luke. I know Kimbo Luke. Fact is, I was chasin' him until I found out Mister Harper was on my trail. I had to break it off and deal with Mister Harper. I ever find Kimbo Luke, I'll kill him myself. Kimbo Luke and me're from the same section of the Settlements. Only Kimbo Luke is low-down, a low life. That's the man what done the killings of all them folks . . . not me."

"Then how come you're the one caught the blame?"

"To most of them white lawmen, us colored're all the same."

"More to it than that."

"No. No, there ain't."

It wasn't just his words that convinced Cole that Book was telling the truth; it was his eyes. "I'll take my weapons back now."

Book looked at him a long time.

"You and the girl are free to go," he said.

Book turned his head to look at Jilly Sweet, lying asleep on the floor.

"You givin' up on takin' me back to Fort Smith?" he asked.

"That's what I'm saying."

"What about her? What about that she shot you?"

"She did what she thought needed doing. I won't hold it against her."

Book looked at his burned-down shuck, then tossed it into the fireplace before handing Cole back the self-cocker and the Colt hide-out pistol.

"I guess me and Jilly'll get goin' first light," he said. "Still ain't too late to find Kimbo Luke an' kill him."

"You want my advice, Mister Book?"

He studied Cole's face.

"Let someone else take care of Kimbo Luke. Sooner or later, someone will kill him. Take the girl and go to Texas. Lots of pleasant places down along the border where the weather is warm and a man and a woman could grow a garden and raise a brood of kids. There are worse things in life."

All the tension seemed to go out of his dark face at once. "Maybe so," he said. "Maybe so."

Everyone settled in and the light of the fire danced around the room and up the walls and for the first time since Cole had been shot, he wasn't having to fight the rages of the fever. He felt weak and his mouth was dry, but he knew he wasn't going to die, at least not just yet, and in a few days he'd be up to riding again. New losses, old pain. That part was never going to change. But he felt a sense of renewal and was grateful to be alive. As much as it worked around the edges of his mind, he didn't let himself think about vengeance or Bill Longly. Not for the last few hours of the evening. There would be time aplenty for that come morning. He lay there in the darkening silence, and finally fell asleep.

CHAPTER THIRTY-TWO

The next morning, Cole was able to stand on the front porch of the cabin and watch as Book saddled his and Jilly Sweet's horses. The weather was cold, but clear. The sky was like blue silver and the sunlight sparkled along the surface of snow.

"I's sorry I shot you, mister," Jilly Sweet said as she came out of the cabin and stood next to Cole.

"No more sorry than I am, little sister."

"I's glad you-all lettin' Leviticus go. He says we's goin' to Texas where it's warm."

Cole nodded.

Her gaze flicked away, off toward the corral. "You think any more white mens be comin' after him?" she asked.

"I'll send word back to Fort Smith that he's dead," Cole said.

Her eyes grew wide. "Dead?"

"Do you think they'd believe me if I told them the real story?"

Then her face softened with understanding. "I guess they wouldn't."

"Maybe later, when all the dust has settled and someone kills Kimbo Luke, the truth will get told. For now, being considered dead might be the best thing."

"Yas, sir."

"Jilly."

"What?"

"He's a good man."

Her face brightened. "I knows he is."

Book finished saddling the horses and came striding toward the cabin. He had a wide smile and his teeth showed white against his blue-black face. The two things happened almost at the same time. The sound, like rolling thunder that shook the air, and Book's being lifted off his feet—his arms flung wide apart, the easy smile replaced with a twisted mask of pain and surprise. His large body slammed to the ground, a flower of blood turning the snow beneath him crimson.

Jilly Sweet screamed and ran from the porch. Mattie threw open the door of the cabin, her wrists and hands dusted with flour. "What is it? What's wrong?"

"Get back inside and get down!" Cole shouted, and went for Book. The wound in his side made it seem like he was dragging an anvil as he crossed the open stretch of ground. But he managed to reach Book, and, when he did, he saw the same look in his eyes he'd seen in the eyes of other men who had taken a killing shot. His hands were twitching and his mouth was gasping for air, causing his chest to rise and fall like a bellows.

Cole was about to try and get him to his feet when the thunder of the big-bore gun shattered the air again. An explosion of snow stung Cole's face and eyes. "Get back to the cabin!" he yelled at the girl. But she wasn't listening. She was lost somewhere in her own shock and grief.

Cole bent and lifted Book under the shoulders. He didn't have enough strength to carry him, but maybe he could drag him. But when he lifted his body up, Book's eyes sprung wide open and he mouthed a single plea: "No."

A bloody plume of foam spilled from the corner of his mouth. His gaze shifted from Cole to Jilly. Then he said his final words: "Kimbo Luke."

Before she could protest or scream or cling to him for another second, Cole had her by the waist, half carrying, half dragging her toward the cabin while the hole in his side burned like a hot coal. Twice more the air was shattered by the big gun and snow kicked up around them, but Cole didn't stop or slow down until they had reached the cabin.

Then they were inside, lying on the floor, Jilly Sweet next to Cole, his breath coming hard, sweat soaking through his shirt, the stitch in his side tearing at his nerve endings. Mattie was crouched behind a wall.

"What is it, John Henry? Who's out there?"

"Kimbo Luke," he said.

She looked at Jilly. The girl's expression was frozen into a mask of disbelief, her hands glazed with the blood of her man.

"Watch her," Cole said, and crawled to the corner where his Winchester was propped near the foot of the cot. The heavy splatter of rifle slugs slamming into the outer walls of the cabin sounded like metal rain.

"Mister Book?" Mattie said as she put her arms around Jilly. "He's . . . ?"

Cole shook his head negatively. Mattie put her right hand up to her mouth, then reached down and stroked Jilly Sweet's wet face.

Cole took up a position at the window, checked the lay of cover out beyond the cabin. There was a stand of pines maybe a hundred yards distant. That's where Kimbo Luke had to be. Cole flipped up the tang rear sight on the Winchester and peered through it and sighted down the long, blued barrel, and brought the front sight in line. He scanned the tree line, hoping to catch a glimpse of movement, a flutter of shadow in among the narrow shafts of sunlight dancing through the trees—anything that would give him a target. Kimbo Luke was smart enough to know that even a puff of smoke would be detected, and so he had ceased firing at the cabin. Now it would turn into a waiting game, at least until someone got tired of the waiting.

"Can you see him?" Mattie asked.

"No."

She took a deep breath, let it out. "How did he know?"

"There is only one way," Cole said. "He's been trailing us." He saw the look of confusion on her face. "Maybe because Book was after him. Maybe he decided to turn the tables."

Jilly began to rock back and forth in Mattie's grasp. A soft moaning sound keened from her throat like a low wind that comes before a winter storm. Cole turned his attention to her for a moment. He'd been there himself—lost in the head—when Zee Cole and their son had died. He knew her need to run, to escape the reality to cry and curse everyone including God for the pain that you couldn't describe if you had a thousand years to try.

A sudden explosion blew out the window near Cole's face just as he started to turn his head again. Shards of glass sliced his cheek, and one drove a splinter just above his right eye. A trickle of warm, sticky blood clouded his vision for an instant until he wiped it away with his sleeve.

Mattie was holding her breath, staring at Cole, at the tiny cuts that razored his face.

"Stay where you are," Cole said.

"He'll come, won't he?" Mattie said. "When it gets dark, he'll come and burn the cabin with us in it."

"He'll try." Cole could see the next question form itself in her eyes. "I'll need to kill him before it gets dark." He pulled off his bandanna and dabbed at his face and pulled out the sliver of glass sticking like a needle in his eyebrow.

"Damn him!" Mattie cursed.

"Damn him to hell!" Cole said. He brought the Winchester back up, rested the barrel on the remains of the shattered casing. Judging by the destruction, Kimbo Luke was using a Big Fifty, like the one Book had carried. He had probably had it fitted with a brass telescope as well.

Again Cole scanned the tree line, searching for something, anything that would give Kimbo Luke away. He had to get him before nightfall. Mattie was right. Kimbo Luke would come after it got dark and burn the cabin. And with just the one door, those of them that didn't burn, he would shoot as they came out.

Cole held his breath and drew the front sight of the Winchester in a line even with the front row of the pines. He picked a spot, then squeezed off a round, then cleared the window just in case.

"Did you see him?" Mattie called. "Is that why you shot?"

"No. I just wanted him to know I was looking for him."

She let her breath out, offered Cole a disappointed look. "We don't stand a chance, do we?"

Jilly Sweet had a vacant look; she was staring into a world that lay somewhere beyond the keening of her grief. She sat on the floor next to Mattie, her arms locked around her drawn-up knees.

Another round hit the cabin.

The stress was taking its toll on Mattie. Every time one of the rounds slammed into the outer wall, she flinched like she had been slapped. Cole noticed blood was leaking through his bandage; the side of his shirt was sticky from it. But a leaky wound was the least of his problems.

He picked sections, ten, twenty feet apart, and fired rounds into the tree line. If nothing else, maybe he'd get lucky just once in his life and kill someone by accident. In between shots back and forth, there were long silences, then the roar of the big gun and another slug slammed into the outer wall. But Cole was never quick enough or lucky enough even to catch a glimpse of the smoke from Kimbo Luke's rifle.

The rest of the day they sat and watched the sunlight that angled through the shattered window cross from one side of the room to the other. Cole went through the options over and over again in his mind. Finally he knew what he had to do. It was by then less than an hour until the sun would set beyond the Blue Mountains.

"There's just one way," he said.

"What?" Mattie asked.

Cole pulled the Colt Lightning from his shoulder rig and handed it to her.

"What's this for?" she asked.

"In case I don't make it back," he said. She blinked, uncertain. "For you and Jilly. If he makes the cabin and starts it afire, better this than being burned alive."

Mattie swallowed.

"I'm going to try and make the horses. If I can make the horses, maybe I can make the tree line."

Mattie looked at the pistol now in her hand. "I don't know if I can," she said.

"You might not have to," Cole tried to assure her.

He moved to the door, the Winchester in his right hand, crouched there for a moment, then lifted the latch. With the pain throbbing through his side, he wasn't going to be able to move fast, but, if he stayed low and kept moving, he might make one of the saddle horses. He gave it a silent count of three, then ducked out the door. It would take two or three seconds for Kimbo Luke to try and put a sight on him. Cole figured he'd have to be lucky, or he'd be unlucky and be hit with the first shot.

Cole had just cleared the porch when the roar

reached his ears and a spray of snow kicked up in front of him. He quickly changed direction, heard the thunder of the second shot, didn't see it hit anything, but heard a slapping sound behind him. The horses were nervously prancing inside the corral. They were maybe thirty more paces.

Boom! Jilly Sweet's little sorrel reared, tossed sideways, and went down. Kimbo Luke had read the plan.

Cole kept moving, hoping he could reach Book's mount before Kimbo Luke could put a sight on it. His boots sloshed through the soft icy snow. His breath came hard in short bursts of vapor that clouded in front of his face. He was within a few feet of the horse when the thunder rolled again, buckling the forelegs of Book's mount. It went down, its muzzle digging into the wet snow, its eyes rolled white, then the rest of its body toppled over, the shod hoofs flailing the air.

Cole cursed as he turned toward the speckled bird that stood, unsaddled inside the corral, her ears pricked. Then the roar of the big gun, and Cole went down, flinging aside the Winchester as he toppled. He was down to one last possibility— that of faking his own death. Kimbo Luke was too good a shot to continue to miss. He had to make him think he was a tad better than he was.

For a long time Cole lay there on the cold snow-covered ground under the unyielding silence. The icy wetness soaked through his coat and shirt, and he wasn't sure how long he could lie there without moving. He'd made sure to pull the self-cocker as he was falling and lay with it under his body, holding it in his right hand. He lay with his face turned to the side. Through slitted eyes, he could see the red sun touching the tips of the Blue Mountains. The sky was the color of brass. He waited for Kimbo Luke to come and burn the women inside the cabin.

More time passed before he heard the sound of footsteps crushing the wet snow, coming closer. Cole had to make sure his timing was right, that he would get to within pistol range before he made his move. Anything less and he would burn the women.

At one point, he heard the steps pause. He listened, then figured he had stopped to inspect his work on Book. Cole heard the sound of his breathing, like a whistle of air through his teeth and nose. He tried to hold his breath.

Kimbo Luke took his time. Cole guessed he was going through Book's pockets. Then he heard him grunt and the crush of boots on wet snow again. They came close, then stopped.

"White man," Kimbo Luke said, almost as a grunt, "I'll take you and put you in the cabin along with that nigger yonder and them two women, and burn you all up. Fust, let's see what you got in them pockets."

Cole felt Luke's hands going through his jacket

pockets, pulling out his Ingersoll watch, his tobacco and papers, the book Lydia Winslow had given him, the one about Don Quixote, the one he hadn't finished reading and maybe never would. Kimbo Luke's breath was hot against the back of Cole's head.

"What's this?" he snorted. Cole could hear him turning the pages of the book. Then Cole could feel his breath again as his hands gripped Cole's shoulders and turned him over.

"Big mistake," Cole said, then fired.

The first shot knocked Kimbo Luke backward. Cole came up and fired again. The second shot spun him around and put him to one knee. He had the look of a man who'd just lost everything he had in a single hand of poker, and in a way he had. He fumbled with the Sharps, and Cole saw his third shot shatter the top button of Kimbo Luke's coat. The pages of the book fluttered near his outstretched hand along with Cole's nickel-plated watch and makings. He picked them up and put them back in his pocket along with the book about an old man in search of his life.

Cole noticed, looking at him, that Kimbo Luke was a lot shorter and thinner man than was Leviticus Book. His color was lighter, too. It made Cole wonder why the law down in the Settlements had mistaken one man for the other. Then he remembered what Book had said about white lawmen and white man's justice, and he understood why the mistake had been made.

Cole picked up the Sharps lying nearby, brushed the snow from the brass scope and from around the trigger guard. It was quite a hunk of heavy iron. Then he gathered up his Winchester and walked back to the cabin to let Mattie know she wouldn't have to use his other handgun, after all. Kimbo Luke would do no more burning, except maybe in hell.

CHAPTER THIRTY-THREE

It snowed that night. There was a white ring around the moon. Cole sat at the table across from Mattie. They drank coffee and listened to the broken sobs of Jilly Sweet as she slept a fitful sleep on Mattie's bed. Mattie had some laudanum in a blue bottle that she gave Jilly to help her sleep. Mattie said her man had bought her the laudanum in Colorado Springs, when they were there, because her nerves had been acting up.

"It wasn't my nerves," Mattie said. "It was the way we weren't getting along. In between the good times, there were a lot of bad." Mattie went on to say how the laudanum had put her mind in a fog whenever she took it. "Things'd get rough between us and I'd find myself in that fog, just wandering around, feeling all loose in my joints, like I wanted to float off the earth. After a time, it got to where I wanted to be in the fog more than I wanted to be anywhere else. It didn't help matters between us, so I finally put the bottle up in the cupboard and left it there. For a time after, I had cramps because of it."

"The things we do to each other," Cole said.

She smiled sadly. "Yes. I wonder sometimes if a man and woman were meant to live together. Don't know many that have ever done it well."

Cole thought of Zee and wanted to tell Mattie that there were people who could live together and love each other, but the woman who sat across from him had her mind full of her own troubles, so he kept the thought to himself.

Earlier, Mattie had helped Cole wrap the two dead men in blankets and carry them to the lean-to.

She had looked at him and said: "They will freeze stiff left out here. We should bury them."

"The ground's frozen," Cole had told her. "The burying will have to wait until spring."

She had looked horrified.

"What about wolves?" she had said. "Won't the wolves come and get at them?"

"Tomorrow, I'll take a rope and pull them up on the roof of the cabin."

"Dead men on my roof!" she had exclaimed.

"Unless you want them in the house."

"There's no other way?"

"It's a sorry place to have to die," Cole had

said, "Wyoming in the winter. Maybe a cowboy will come by with a wagon and you can have them taken into the nearest town and they can be put in storage until spring. If you had a wagon, I'd take them with me to Cheyenne."

"I suppose I should be grateful instead of complaining," she had said. "We could have all been burned up by Kimbo Luke."

Now she looked tired, her eyes weary over the rim of her cup. "That was a brave thing you did to save us all," she said.

"It was a necessary thing. There was little that was brave about it."

She rubbed the upper parts of her arms as though she suddenly felt chilled. "If you hadn't been here . . ." She didn't finish the thought.

"If I hadn't been here, then most likely, neither would Kimbo Luke," Cole put in. "You can look at it either way."

"We can only guess," she said. "He might have come along sooner or later and burned us anyway."

"If you want, you and Jilly Sweet can go with me to Cheyenne," Cole said.

She stared at him for a moment, her green eyes dark as jade in the low light. "No. My man might come while I'm gone. I better wait for him in case he decides to come back. . . ."

"I'll ask Jilly in the morning if she wants to ride back to Cheyenne with me."

"She can stay here with me if she wants."

"That's kind of you, Mattie."

"Not so kind as you might think," she said. "It would beat staying here alone with dead men on my roof."

"I suppose it probably would."

"She might want to stay at least until spring when we can give Mister Book a decent burial," Mattie said.

"Well, we can ask her what she chooses to do first thing in the morning," Cole said. "I think I'll spread my blanket on the floor. You take the cot."

The next few days, they rode out the winter storm that piled snow up to the bottoms of the windows. Mattie mended Cole's shirt and he brought in buckets of snow to melt into water for washing and drinking. Jilly Sweet talked to herself, talked to her dead lover through the ceiling like he was up there on the roof, listening to her.

Cole cleaned and oiled his weapons, fed the speckled bird and the lone jack mule that belonged to Mattie. He didn't know who her man was, but he suspected he would not be coming back ever.

He read portions of *Don Quixote* to them at Mattie's insistence, and she found it to her liking. Even Jilly would stop talking to Book long enough to listen to the misadventures of the old *don* and his manservant, Sancho Panza. It was a good way to pass time and let Cole's wound heal, reading about the noble old warrior who thought sheep were armies and windmills were the foe.

"That true, about that fellow?" Jilly asked at one point. "He really crazy like that?"

Cole didn't want to tell her it was a work of fiction, that Don Quixote and Sancho Panza were not real people. Perhaps it was partly because, if they weren't real, they should have been. "They're as real as any of us," he told Jilly. "And I'm not so sure the old man is as crazy as he seems."

She smiled. "Them two sound like me and Levi, traveling all over."

Mattie's gaze met Cole's. "I've got a man does the same thing," she said. "Always getting ideas in his head and chasing after them. I guess men are just born with itchy feet and crazy notions floating around inside their heads."

Jilly laughed, and Mattie laughed with her.

On the fourth day, the sun came out and began to melt the glassy icicles hanging from the eaves. Cole felt up to riding. Being in the company of women made him think more than once of another woman—one he'd left up in Nebraska. The sooner he finished what he'd begun—finding Ike Kelly's killer—the sooner he could try and get his life back to something better. Maybe that meant returning to Ogallala and seeing if Ella Mims was still interested in a man who'd gotten tired of riding the Big Lonely.

"I'm pulling up stakes," Cole announced at breakfast.

The eyes of the two women were on him.

"You must feel perky," Mattie said.

"Perky enough to ride to Cheyenne and finish some business," he said.

"You-all gonna leave?" Jilly said. "You-all gonna jus' go off an leave us?"

"I want you to have this, Jilly," Cole said, handing her the book.

"But I don't know how to read much," she said.

"Maybe Mattie can help you with it."

Mattie patted the girl's arm. "Sure. You and me will read the covers plum off that book. And when we're finished, spring will have arrived."

"Tell you what," Cole said. "Soon as I've taken care of my business in Cheyenne, I'll ride back this way and check in on you. And if you're still here, we'll have a picnic."

Jilly seemed uncertain, and so did Mattie.

"I'll swing by and tell Doc Jellicoe to check in on you in the meantime," Cole proposed.

"Tell him to bring a chicken and we'll have that supper I promised him," Mattie said. "You like fried chicken, don't you, Jilly?"

Cole gathered his gear, his Winchester and saddlebags. Mattie handed him the Colt pistol he'd given her the day he'd shot Kimbo Luke.

"You keep it," Cole said.

"No, I'm no shootist," she said. " 'Sides, I still got that old double buck I keep under the bed. I guess if I was to have to depend on hitting anything, I'd most likely hit it with that double buck than this little *pistola*. You take it. I've a feeling the business you're going to Cheyenne for will require you to be well heeled."

"Maybe you're wise beyond your years," Cole said.

"Surely am."

He put on his coat and hat, and stepped out into the brilliant sunlight that was made even more brilliant by the way it glared off the snow. He saw the speckled bird prick up her ears as he approached the corral. She knew they were leaving. The muscles under her hide rippled with anticipation.

"Don't bite me and don't buck me off just because I haven't ridden you in a week," Cole said as he laid the blanket on her back, then set the saddle down atop it.

She snorted through wet black nostrils and tossed her head. He stroked his hand along her neck and spoke a little Spanish to her as he reached under her belly and grabbed the cinch strap. She pawed the snowy ground as impatient as a saint in a saloon, waiting to get going. He put the bit between her teeth and adjusted the bridle, then led her out of the corral. Mattie came from the cabin. Cole could see Jilly Sweet standing in the doorway.

"I put some chuck together for your ride," Mattie said, handing him a burlap sack. "I don't reckon there are many restaurants between here and Cheyenne."

Cole tied the sack to the horn of his saddle. "You and Jilly going to be all right?"

"We'll make out until my man gets back," she said.

"I'll ask Doc Jellicoe if there's someone who can come with a wagon and get those corpses off your roof and take them to town to be stored."

"It'd make me rest easier," she said, "knowing I don't have dead men on my roof."

"Mattie."

"What?"

"Your man doesn't deserve you."

"Hell, I know that. But what's it got to do with the way I love him?"

"I finish up my work in Cheyenne, I'll swing back by."

"You do that," she said. "And if we're not here, you'll know he came back and got us."

"I hope he does."

"So do I."

"Would you mind so much I gave you a kiss on the cheek?" Cole asked.

"On the lips would be better," she said. "The only way a man should kiss a woman is on the lips. Kissing on the cheek is for women to do."

He kissed her on the lips. It was a dry, light kiss that sealed their friendship and respect for each other.

Cole put a foot in the stirrup, then found himself in the saddle for the first time in more than a week. It felt odd, like he was ten feet up in the air. He heeled the bird over to the porch.

"I'm counting on you to help Mattie out here," he said.

Jilly was holding the book in her hands.

"You learn to read, everything else will be easier for you. Go with Mattie if her man comes to get her. Things have a way of working themselves out, Jilly. You'll see."

She blinked and her lower lip quivered. " 'Bye," she said. "Thank you for the book."

"You're welcome."

Cole reined the bird's head around and spurred her into an easy trot. She didn't seem to mind the snow and took to it like she'd been born in a barn on Christmas day.

He didn't look back. He didn't have to. He knew both women would be all right without him there, that life would catch them up and carry them on to whatever destinies awaited them.

CHAPTER THIRTY-FOUR

The weather remained remarkably good, with only an occasional spitting of snow mixed with alternating sunshine and clouds. Cole stopped by Dr. Jellicoe's yellow clapboard house in a little settlement halfway up a valley surrounded by craggy snow-covered slopes. The doctor's was the only house that wasn't built of logs and you could spot the yellow paint from a half mile off. Mattie had given Cole directions and had told him about Dr. Jellicoe's penchant for the unusual when it came to paint. The air over the valley was smudged with wood smoke drifting out of blue metal stovepipes poking through the shake roofs. Except for the occasional bark of a hound too lazy or cold to show itself, the valley was as peaceful as a graveyard.

Cole knocked on the door of Dr. Jellicoe's place and stamped the snow off his boots while he waited for someone to answer. In a few seconds the door opened and there was Jellicoe, his walrus mustaches hiding most of his mouth, his eyes rimmed red. Cole could smell the liquor on his breath; it came out warm and sour when he spoke.

"I know you from somewhere?" He squinted at Cole as though he were trying to see him through the bottom of a whiskey glass.

"You dug a bullet out of my side back at Mattie Blaylock's," Cole said.

Then the knots of uncertainty fell out of his lumpy face and his big shaggy mustaches lifted in a lippy grin. "Oh, yeah," he said, "that's right. Looks like you lived in spite of my operation."

Cole could hear the phlegm rattle around in his throat as he laughed at his own sense of humor. "So far I'm still walking around, as you can see. You mind if I step in for a minute?"

"No, come right ahead. Mattie come with you?"

"No. Matter of fact, that's the reason I stopped. I'd like you to check on her in a few days."

"She ailing?"

"No. She's fine. It's just that I'm on my way to Cheyenne and she and the girl are out there all alone."

"You mean that little tan child?"

"Yes."

"Where's the big colored fellow, that friend of hers?"

"He's laid out on Mattie's roof."

"Roof! What's he doing up on the roof?"

"He was shot and killed."

"How'd that happen? You shoot him, did you?"

"No, another black man named Kimbo Luke shot him."

"He seemed like an all right fellow to me. Why'd this Luke shoot him?"

"It's a long story, one I don't have time or inclination to go into."

"I still don't understand him being on the roof."

"It was the only way we could make sure the bodies didn't get molested by wolves."

"Bodies? There's more than one?"

"Kimbo Luke's laid out on the roof, too."

"Sounds like I left from out there just in time," Jellicoe said. "Who knows, if I had stayed the night, I might be on the roof along with them other fellows."

"So, you'll make it a point to go out and check on Mattie and the girl in a few days?"

He nodded.

"One more thing," Cole said. "If there's someone around here who has a wagon, maybe they could go out and bring in the bodies. Mattie doesn't much care for having dead men on her roof."

"Don't blame her. That's an awful thing to have on your roof, corpses are."

"Thanks for everything, Doc. I promised Mattie I'd stop back this way. I'll bring you the ten dollars I owe you for the care."

He looked skeptical but offered his hand and told Cole to keep an eye on the wound in case it got infected again.

Cole camped that night by a little stream where the water shimmered with blackness against snowy banks. He boiled water and threw in a pinch of coffee from the sack of chuck Mattie had fixed him and cut a slice of dried beef and put it between some crackers. Afterward, he smoked a shuck and drank the rest of the coffee as he sat, cross-legged, on his soogans and listened to the deep silence. The night was black with stars and the moon still had a circle around it. Then from nowhere, he heard the long, mournful call of a gray wolf just as he tossed out the dregs of his coffee and stubbed his smoke. The wolf sounded as lonely as Cole felt.

Cole hoped to make Cheyenne in two or three days of steady riding. He wished then, that Mattie would have thought to slip a pint of mash whiskey in the gunny sack to help ward off the cold and silence, but wishing didn't make it so. He didn't much miss liquor, but there were times when he did, and this was one of them. Wind swept down from the Blue Mountains and he didn't get a lot of sleep that night what with thinking of the coming days. He kept his head on his saddle and his feet toward the fire and managed as best he could.

The next day dawned bright and clear and he rose early. His back and legs felt stiff enough to break if he moved too quickly. He didn't bother with breakfast.

Late that afternoon, he came to a settlement of sorts. It was just a few homesteads, four or five little log structures. A man was chopping wood out in front of one of the homesteads. He looked up as Cole checked the reins of the bird. He was solidly built with a face full of burnished whiskers.

"Is there a place here I could get a meal?" Cole inquired.

"Depends," the man said. He had the heavy drawl of a Southerner.

"Depends on what?"

The man looked at Cole, the speckled bird, the trappings. Then his gaze drifted to the stock of the Winchester and back up to Cole. "You a lawman?"

"Would it make a difference if I was?" Cole asked. "About getting a meal?"

The man's tongue came out and licked at his lips, the moisture freezing on the tips of his wiry beard. "Step on down," he said.

Cole followed him inside the log hut. A woman sat nursing a baby in one corner of the room. She looked up when they entered but made no attempt at covering her breast. The baby had a pale head with veins as blue as ink. The infant made a sucking sound, then sighed, then started nursing again.

"Maylou, man here lookin' fer a meal."

She was as pale as the infant, like neither of them had ever seen sunshine. She had a thin face, high cheek bones, and hollow eyes, like the infant had sucked most the life out of her.

"There's beans," she said. "That's it. Just that pot of beans. Got a little sow belly in it."

"Look," Cole said, "I don't have any money, but I have a good watch I'll give you. Maybe it would fetch three or four dollars from someone that needs a good watch." He reached into his pocket and took out the Ingersoll and laid it on the table. He'd bought that watch in Laredo from a man with a clubfoot who was selling them on a street corner one summer afternoon. It kept better time than half the railroads.

Neither one of them said anything. The man took a plate down from a plank shelf and ladled out some beans from the kettle hanging in the fireplace. He set the plate down next to the watch. Then he picked up the watch and examined it.

"Say it keeps good time, does it?"

Cole nodded. The beans had little taste, but they were hot and warmed his belly and that's about all he could ask for. He didn't encourage conversation, concentrating instead on the plate of beans, figuring to eat and get on his way.

The man said: "That a Colt pistol you're wearin'?"

"Remington," Cole said. "Forty-Four-Forty center-fire. Self-cocker."

"Had me a good pistol once. Big Navy. Thirty-Six caliber. Had pearl grips."

"You in the war?" Cole asked. "That where you come by the Navy?"

"Rode under Mosby," he said. "Some of us had Navies. Cap and ball models. I ended up having to trade mine after the war for a mule to plow my ground with. The mule died before I could plant. Ever'thing went plum to hell the day that war ended. I wish now I'd never traded my pistol for that mule."

"It was a hard war in lots of ways," Cole said.

"You don't sound like you fought for the gray," he said. "The way you talk, I mean."

"I didn't."

Something bitter and hurtful flashed in his eyes like he had suddenly opened up a drawer filled with tintypes of dead loved ones. Then he snorted and said: "I shot a lot of you Yankees in that war with that Navy of mine. I'd still be shootin' Yanks if Marse Lee hadn't turned over his sword to that little hide tanner, Grant."

"Yeah, well," Cole said, "I guess that war's been over a long time."

He grunted. "Some of us is still havin' to live with it."

Cole knew what he meant.

"You want another plate of beans?"

Cole nodded. His belly had been scraping his backbone all day. The woman was watching him. Her hair was the color of dusty wheat, long and stringy and uncombed.

"That pistol," the man said, setting the plate of beans in front of Cole. "You be willin' to trade it?"

"No."

"You ain't heard what it is I got to trade fer it," he said.

"I have need of my gun, mister. It's not for trade."

He swallowed. Cole could see the fever of excitement burning in his gaze. "Trade you a turn with Maylou for that pistol," he offered, his voice hoarse. He wiped a knuckle under the tip of his nose.

"Like I said, the pistol's not for trade."

He jerked his head around, glanced at the woman. She simply stared back.

"How 'bout whiskey, then?" he said. "You got a jug in your saddle pockets? I'd trade you a turn with her for a jug."

"No whiskey," Cole said, feeling a knot form in his stomach. "You make it a habit of trading your wife to strangers for pistols and whiskey?"

"She ain't my wife," he said. "Sister-in-law. Least she was till my brother died. Hit hisself in the leg with a axe choppin' firewood. Gangrene set in. Died from it. Left her with a belly full of kid. Took her in is what I done. She needs to earn her keep same as the rest of us. Hard fact, but that's the way things is out here."

"That war must have done something to you it didn't do to the rest of us," Cole said.

His brows knitted. "You was a Yank," he said.

"How would you know what that war did to us who lost?"

"I wouldn't," Cole said. "But don't insult me again."

"You ain't invited here no more!" he flared.

Cole laid the fork down and stood up. The woman continued to stare. The infant at her breast had fallen asleep, its head tilted to the side, the small lips pursed. A pearl of milk lay in the corner of its mouth. It didn't look like it would survive the winter. Maybe in that way, Cole thought, it was lucky.

He still had two days of riding ahead of him before he reached Cheyenne. There wasn't much he could say or do to a man who had lost everything in the war including his soul. The woman would have to figure it out at some point and make her own decision. The Rebel had been right about something. It was a hard life.

Cole mounted the bird. The saddle leather creaked from the cold.

The man said: "Don't come back 'round here, mister!"

Cole touched his spurs to the bird. The sooner he got to Cheyenne and finished his business with Bill Longly, the better.

CHAPTER THIRTY-FIVE

Shorty Blaine was sitting at a table with Cleopatra and Bart Bledsoe when Cole came in. It was an hour past sunset and, except for the three of them, the only other person in the diner was Wayback Cotton. He was eating a bowl of mush with molasses poured over it.

"Mister Cole!" Bart said. He was the only one unoccupied at the time. Shorty and Cleo were busy counting the day's receipts, and Wayback was staring into his bowl of mush like it was a crystal ball that held the future of the human race. As soon as Bart announced Cole's name, the others looked up.

Shorty squinted through the curl of gray smoke coming off his cigarette. Cleo had her hands full of loose change.

"God damn!" Wayback declared, bits of wet mush clinging to his mustaches. "Look what the cat drug in!"

It had been a long ride. Cole must have looked like death warmed over. Certainly that's the way he felt.

Shorty stood up and hobbled over and extended his hand. "Glad to see you made it back, John Henry. What the hell took you so long?"

"For steak and a cold beer, I'd be happy to tell you," Cole said.

"Where's Will, outside tying up the horses?" Shorty asked.

"Will didn't make it," Cole said.

"Book?" Shorty said. "Was it Book that killed him?"

"Yeah. But it wasn't the way you might think."

Shorty's forehead knurled into fleshy ridges. "Hell, I don't see how that could be." Then he looked toward the window. "I don't see Book, neither . . . you kill him?"

"I didn't. Someone else did."

"Well, I guess it don't matter who killed who as long as Book got his. Leastwise, he won't be doing any more slaughtering and burning."

"He wasn't guilty," Cole said. He could hear Leviticus Book's words echoing in his head.

"Say what?"

"We chased down the wrong man. Book turned out to be innocent."

"Shit, John Henry. You got me more confused than a Chinaman."

"Bart," Cole said, "I'd consider it a favor if you would take my horse down to the livery and see she gets put up."

"Sure, sure," he said, putting on his coat. Cole noticed he was wearing an apron. "Just a little something to tide me over till I can save up for another mule and a wagon," he said almost apologetically.

"He needed work, I had work," Shorty explained. "I seen better at waiting tables, but he's steady. Now you want to tell me how it is Book ended up killing Will but ain't guilty of anything?"

Cole sat down at the table across from Cleo. Wayback picked up his bowl of mush—carried it like it was the last gold out of the Black Hills— and joined them. Shorty threw a steak the size of a dinner plate on the fire and drew Cole a beer.

Cole explained what had happened, how Will had made a fatal mistake, and how he'd tracked down Leviticus Book and Jilly Sweet, and the part about her shooting him. He told them about Kimbo Luke and the rest of it. When he finished, Shorty leaned back on his chair and said: "I'm a son-of-a-bitch. Then it was Long Bill that killed Ike?"

"It looks that way."

"I ain't surprised," Wayback said. "But why'd he do it?

"That's what I came back to find out," Cole said.

"He was in here eating supper an hour ago," Shorty said. "Him and Leo Foxx. Eating and belching up their food like a pair of shoats."

Cole started to reach for his watch to check the time, then remembered he had traded it.

"They're probably over to the Blue Star," Shorty said. "Foxx runs him a faro game and Long Bill sorta hangs around, lapping up Foxx's crumbs."

"You take on one," Wayback said, a spoonful of

mush gripped in his left hand, "you'll have to take on both of 'em."

"I've thought of that," Cole said. "Maybe it doesn't have to come to that. Maybe Foxx is smart enough to stay clear of a fight that's not his."

"I'll go over with you when you're ready," Shorty said.

"No. But I do appreciate the offer, Shorty."

They both knew that Shorty wasn't a gunfighter. And even if he lacked fear, he was no match for men like Leo Foxx and Long Bill Longly.

"You want me along," Wayback said. "I'll go find me a god-damn' shotgun and assassinate the sons-a-bitches while you palaver with 'em. I'll sneak up behind 'em and blow out their backbones."

"Tell you what, Wayback. Why don't I borrow a dollar from Shorty, and instead of you going to find a shotgun, you go get us a bottle, so, when I get back, we can do a little serious drinking?"

"Shit," Wayback said, "if that's what you want."

"I smell that steak burning, Shorty," Cole advised.

"Did Roy Bean go to Texas?" Cleo asked. "Or did he find himself another whore?"

"He was still trying to decide whether he should go or not when I left," Cole answered. "But he didn't find himself another whore. That's all I know for certain."

"He's too far out in the tules to do much business, anyway," Cleo said, "even if he had him a hundred whores. Ain't but one or two cow outfits out there." She was stacking the loose change in front of her into little silver towers. "Roy's an enterprising soul," she added. "He just gets dopey-eyed sometimes. Dreams of someday meeting an actress and becoming famous his own self. Man sure can dream big."

"He talked of practicing the law," Cole said.

"Whatever gave him that idea?" Cleo wondered.

"He thought maybe he would be good at it."

"Humph!" Cleo snorted. "Knowing that man, he'll probably go practice the law some place there ain't nothing but rattlesnakes and scorpions and outlaws and end up running some little rum joint in the middle of bejezzus."

"He sounds like my sort of man," Wayback said. "I don't care much for towns, neither. Maybe I'll get to Texas sometime and look him up. You say his last name is Bean?"

"You ain't never going to Texas, Wayback," Shorty said.

"Why ain't I?"

"Because it's too damn' far to walk and you're too poor to buy a horse. And even if you did buy a horse, you're too old to ride it. You might just as well stay here and forget about going to Texas."

"You know, this mush could use a little more lick," Wayback said. "Pass me that maple syrup, would you?"

Cole ate the steak with a hunger long ignored

and washed it down with the glass of beer Shorty had drawn him. Then he made himself a shuck and smoked it.

"That chuck looks like it's brought all the life back into you," Shorty said. "You walked in, I thought you was a ghost. You want another steak?"

"No, that one was plenty."

They sat there in silence for a time while Cole smoked the cigarette. It got so quiet you could hear the paper burn and Shorty's Regulator clock ticking above the door.

"Time I pay a visit to Long Bill," Cole said when he'd finished the smoke.

"You sure you don't want us to go with you?" Shorty said.

"Yeah, you sure?" Wayback asked. "I can get us that bottle of whiskey after I assassinate them sons-a-bitches."

"No. It's better I go alone."

Bart Bledsoe came in, knocking snow dust from his hat and shoulders. "Starting to snow again," he said. "It's pretty, but awful cold. Do you think spring will ever come to these parts again?"

Cole checked the loads in his pistols, then stepped out into the night air. It was time to finish his business.

He walked down to the Blue Star. The lights from its windows lay on the snow in yellow squares. He opened the door and went in.

The place was doing a good business. On a snowy night, there isn't much for men to do except drink and gamble and proposition working girls. Judging by the crowd, they were mostly cowboys, although one or two of them could have been bull whackers or prospectors, waiting out the winter so they could go back up into the Black Hills come spring.

Cole worked his way through the crowd, looking for Long Bill. The sawdust floor was puddled with melted snow from wet boots and a blue smoke haze floated in the air. There was the loud mixture of voices, of men talking to one another on various subjects such as the weather and cattle and horses, and, of course, women. The cowboys were mostly young, pink-cheeked boys with little or no hair on their faces. But there were a few old cowpunchers among them, men whose gazes were fixed on their own images in the big mirror of the backbar. They were men who'd long ago run out of idle conversation, men who saw in their own reflections the grizzled faces and tired eyes that held a string of bittersweet memories of lost opportunities, squandered wages, and a lifetime of drifting. And somewhere inside those memories, too, were the sweethearts they'd left behind, and the ones they were still hoping to find. Those eyes knew more than they were telling. They knew of long winters that were getting longer each new season, and a trail that was soon coming to an end. They knew lots of things they weren't telling, thoughts that weren't given to idle conversation.

Cole saw Leo Foxx dealing faro amid a heavy haze of smoke from the players ringing his layout. A chubby young woman stood next to him with her hand resting on his shoulder. Cole could see the silver-plated Policeman's model pistol lying on the table next to Foxx's right hand. The badge pinned to his vest was the size of a liberty dollar. It looked out of place on a man like him. But it wasn't Foxx he'd come for.

Cole continued to look through the crowd. He gave half a thought that Long Bill might be out, making rounds, then discarded the possibility. Long Bill wasn't the sort of man to do any honest work. He went to the bar and ordered a beer, figuring he'd give it a few minutes to see if Longly came in.

He kept watch by looking at the mirror in back of the bar. And in a single reflective moment, he thought to himself that he wasn't much different than the old hands who stood alone, their bellies pressed up against the bar while they sipped their beer and thought of lost sweethearts and trails they could have taken but didn't. Something caught his eye. He turned in time to see Long Bill coming down the stairway, still buckling his belt. Cole looked along the upper hall, saw the prostitute, Cimarron Cindy, leaning against the jamb in an open doorway. Her eye was nearly swollen shut.

Cole stepped away from the bar, pushing his way through the crowd, taking the self-cocker out of his hip holster and dangling it along his leg as he moved to the foot of the stairs.

"You're under arrest, Longly!" he said loud enough for Long Bill to hear him above the din. Longly looked up, his hands still fumbling with his belt buckle. He stopped three steps from the landing.

"What the hell you talking about, Cole?"

His hair was lank and stringy, his face shone with sweat. Cole noticed the knuckles on his right hand were red.

"The murder of Ike Kelly," Cole said.

Longly raised the hand with the red knuckles to his mouth and swept his shaggy mustache with his thumb and forefinger. "Well now, you got some proof of that, do you?"

"An eyewitness," Cole said.

"Eyewitness, my ass! You better let go of something you're not up to. I could kill you in a heartbeat."

"If you were armed, maybe you could," Cole said. "Trouble is, the only weapon you got is what you're tucking into your pants. Let's go!"

Cole still hadn't lifted the self-cocker, but he'd thumbed the hammer back. He could see Longly's gaze drift downward to the blue metal barrel.

"This is horse shit!" he said.

"I didn't come here for a discussion. Let's go!"

The room had gotten quiet. Cole heard someone cough and the sound of a chair scraping across the floor. It was like everyone was holding his breath, waiting to see if Cole was going to shoot Bill Longly and give them something to talk about for the next ten years.

"Put your piece away, Cole!"

The voice was Leo Foxx's somewhere behind them.

"Don't get into this, Leo," Cole said without turning around.

"Why not? It's my town, Longly's my man. You come in starting trouble, what'm I supposed to do, just stand around with my thumb up my butt?"

"You'd be better off if you did, Leo," Cole said.

"No, you're wrong, Cole. You see, to take me on would mean you'd have to turn around and raise that iron you've got hanging at your leg. Me, all I got to do is pull the trigger on this Police Colt. You figure out what the results would be."

"One more chance to back away, Leo. That's what you've got."

"Fuck you!"

Cole spun around, bringing up the self-cocker. Their two shots sounded like one. Cole felt Foxx's bullet rip through the sleeve of his coat. His bullet took Foxx mid-chest and carried him across a table where there was a pile of loose coins that fell on him like silver rain as he crashed to the floor.

Long Bill jumped on Cole's back and began pummeling him with bony fists, knocking the pistol from Cole's hand as his weight pushed Cole to the floor with him atop, swinging those long arms. Cole felt the pain in his side flare up like fire as he could feel the old wound tearing apart.

Longly's right fist crashed into the side of Cole's head and his left glanced off Cole's cheek. Longly's eyes were glassed over and his teeth were bared behind the shaggy mustache. Then his hands went around Cole's throat and clamped down like a vise, shutting off the air. Cole's left arm was pinned beneath him, beneath Longly's weight on top of him, and he tried separating Longly's hands from his throat with his free hand.

Longly's wrists were knobs of hard bone and sinew and he put all his weight behind the strangling grip, trying to squeeze the life out of Cole. Cole's free hand gave up trying to tear Longly's hands away from his throat as he fumbled to pull the backup from his shoulder rig, but one of Longly's knees bore down against the pistol and Cole couldn't reach in and jerk it free. The strength in Longly's hands flowed out of his arms and shoulders and came to a choking confluence at Cole's windpipe. Cole could feel his own strength starting to lag as his lungs screamed for air.

"I told you, you ain't up to me! I told you I'd kill you in a heartbeat!" Longly's shouted threat came in a spray of sour breath as the beads of sweat from his forehead dripped onto Cole's face.

He worked his hands harder still and Cole could feel himself starting to slide down a dark tunnel that held no light at the end. The fleeting thought that Longly was going to kill him flashed through Cole's mind. The strange thing was, Cole wasn't afraid—he was mad. Longly had killed Ike Kelly, and now he was going to kill Cole and get away with both murders! Something terrible went through Cole in a flash of hatred and anger like he'd never felt before. Like a bolt of raw lightning, he swung his free hand with everything he had and crashed it into the center of Longly's face, feeling the bone and cartilage of his nose shatter into a spray of blood.

Longly's hands released their grip and went to his face. Cole pulled the backup pistol from his shoulder rig and pressed it to Longly's gut, thumbing back the hammer as he did. "You want to finish it?" Cole said.

The blood leaked through Longly's fingers as his eyes nearly crossed, looking down at the cocked revolver.

He rolled off, onto his knees, as Cole pushed himself to his feet and stood over Longly. "Let's go!" Cole said.

"Where?"

"Where do you think?"

Longly staggered to his feet, and Cole marched him outside, his head still throbbing from Longly's blows.

"You taking me to jail?"

"Not before you tell me why you did it?"

"To hell with that."

Cole shoved him into an alley, pressed the barrel of the pistol to a point just below Longly's left eye. "I don't have any reason to save you for the hangman," he said. "You want, I'll shoot you in the face!"

Longly swallowed behind the mask of blood. "He got a wire on me. Kelly did."

"Wire?"

"Some work I did up in Montana."

"What sort of work?"

Longly's muddy eyes shifted in their sockets.

"What sort of work?"

"Killed a kid . . . a rancher's kid. Man named Jensen. He put out a ten-thousand-dollar reward on me."

"You've done other work," Cole said. "Similar."

Longly's head darted side to side. "Not like this. The kid was ten years old."

"You shot a ten-year-old boy?"

"It was from a long way off," he said, flecks of blood sputtering from his mouth. "Shot him from a quarter mile off. I was up there, doing stock detective work. I thought the kid was a rustler."

"So Ike got a wire on you and was going to arrest you and take you back for the reward?"

He nodded his head. "I wasn't going back to Montana, let that man hang me. It was a god-damned accident I shot his boy! I wasn't going to let him hang me over no god-damned accident!"

"Why didn't you just get the hell out of town instead of killing Ike?"

A dull look compressed itself behind his eyes. "I di'n't think to."

"Foxx know about the wire?"

"He knew. Shit, he di'n't care."

Cole brought the barrel down hard across Longly's collar bone and stepped back as he slumped to his knees.

"Jesus!" he yelped, the tears welling in his eyes.

"It's going to feel worse than that when you're standing on the trap waiting to hit the end of the rope," Cole said. "Another thing. After they hang you, I'm going to send a wire to Jensen up in Montana and let him know."

CHAPTER THIRTY-SIX

Long Bill Longly was hanged on the 15th of December under a wintery sky with most of the town turned out for the event. A circuit judge named Flagg sentenced Longly, and, when he had

392

heard the judgment, he had looked at Flagg and said: "This is one hell of a Christmas present you've given me. I hope you know that!"

Flagg had hammered his gavel down hard and said: "If I could hang you twice, I would."

John Henry Cole didn't go to the hanging. He went to Shorty's Diner instead and had a cup of coffee and smoked a shuck.

"See you didn't go?" Shorty said. "Me, neither."

"It's not something I would take any pleasure in, seeing a man hang," Cole said. "Even if it is Long Bill's hanging."

"I guess they'll drop him through the trap whether me and you are there or not," Shorty said. "I think Wayback went."

"Where's Cleo?" Cole asked.

"Buying herself another dress," Shorty said. "Woman sure has a thing for dresses."

"You thinking of getting married?"

"You think she'd have me?"

"She could do worse."

Shorty squinted through the smoke of his cigarette. "Hell, I reckon she could." He grinned.

"I hear tell the town committee is considering hiring Bart Bledsoe as the new city marshal," Cole said.

"That's another thing," Shorty said. "I think he'd do all right, but I sure do hate to lose a good waiter like him. Man's conscientious."

"Life goes on."

"Sure does. What about you? What're your plans?"

"Thinking of going up to Nebraska, see Ella."

"Huh!" he grunted. "I ain't surprised. But I thought you told me there was some local joker up there, looking to horn in?"

"Who knows? Maybe she's married by now. Thought I'd just go and see what's up."

"You thinking of coming back this way?"

"It could happen," Cole said. "But with Ike dead, there's not much here for me."

"Friends," he said. "You got friends here. Me and Cleo and Bart to name a few. Friends is an important thing to have."

Wayback came through the door, stomping the snow off his boots. "Well, he's gone to perdition," he said. "Long Bill is probably dancing with the devil in hell right now. Good hanging. You boys should've been there."

"Do you want some coffee?" Shorty asked.

"Could you lace it with a little sour mash?"

Shorty spilled some whiskey into Wayback's coffee and pushed it across the counter to him. Wayback tasted it, smacked his lips, and said: " 'At's good. Where's Cleo?"

"Buying a dress."

Wayback's face screwed itself up. " 'At's too bad. I like lookin' at her when I come in."

"Don't look too hard," Shorty said. "Say, you ever waited tables before?"

Cole shook hands with Shorty and Wayback and went to the room he kept at Sun Lee's. He was looking over some of his things for the trip to Nebraska when Sun came in.

"You leave again, Mistah John Henly?"

"This time, maybe for good, Sun."

"Oh, that's too bad. I solly to see you go. You funny man, I gonna miss you. Maybe I keep the room fol you case you come back."

"Keep what's still here for me. If I don't come back, sell it for my rent."

Cole shook hands with him. Sun Lee was a warm, friendly man with a gentle spirit and the right outlook on life. He would miss his company.

Cole walked down to the livery.

Harry Slaughter, the liveryman, was repairing a bridle. "Come for that off-color horse, did you?" he asked.

"Came to see if you were interested in buying her," Cole said.

"Hmmm. How much you want?"

"Eighty dollars," Cole said, "and I'll throw in my Dunn Brothers saddle."

"Eighty's a lot," he said.

"Take it or leave it."

"Done," he said, and pulled a roll of scrip out of his pocket.

"I'd rather it was in gold," Cole said. "Double eagles."

"I'll have to go up to the bank if you want double eagles."

"I'll wait. The train doesn't leave for an hour."

Slaughter left.

Cole went to the stall where the bird had a mouthful of hay. "This is where we part company," he said.

Her ears pricked up and her big dark eyes came around to look at him.

"You sure turned out to be a hell of a horse." She tossed her head as though she half understood what he was saying. He spoke a little Spanish to her and reached in his pocket for some lumps of sugar he'd taken from the diner. He held them in the palm of his hand while she sniffed them for a second, then the soft muzzle dipped down and lapped them up.

"I guess you've given up trying to bite the hand that feeds you," Cole said. "It's a lesson a lot of us hardcases should learn to appreciate."

He took a brush and a currycomb and worked it over her hide.

Slaughter came back with the gold coins in his hand.

"Here's your double eagles," he said. "Eighty dollars, four double eagles, just like you wanted."

"I've changed my mind," Cole said.

"What? You trying to hold me up for more money?"

"No. I've decided not to sell."

He looked sorely disappointed. "The saddle, neither?"

"No, I'll need the saddle if I keep the horse."

"Well, I guess it's your horse and saddle to do with what you want," he said.

"Sorry for the inconvenience."

They shook hands and Cole threw a lead rope over the bird and hefted the Dunn Brothers saddle in his free hand, and walked down the street.

"You don't know how bad I could have used that eighty dollars," he said to the bird.

She walked along behind him like she was worth a thousand. Cole was heading back to Shorty's Diner. He didn't want to, but he was broke and had to ask Shorty for a loan, even if it meant he had to swallow his pride.

He was almost there when Bart Bledsoe came running up the street, calling after him. He had a piece of yellow paper in his hand.

"Mister Cole. I've a wire just came for you," he said, nearly out of breath.

Cole put down the saddle and took the telegram.

"Pretty nice, huh?" Bart grinned.

"Damn right it's pretty nice."

"Hell, you earned, I'd say."

The telegram was from Montana Territory. It said simply:

Justice has been done. My boy can rest in peace now. Have sent the $10,000 reward money to the bank in Cheyenne to be deposited in your name. Thank you for letting me know that Aaron's murderer has been captured and will be hanged. Respectfully, Ethan Jensen

Cole, still holding the telegram, looked at the bird and said: "For a couple of hardcases, *we've* done pretty good."

ABOUT THE AUTHOR

Bill Brooks is the author of twenty-three novels of historical and frontier fiction. After a lifetime of working a variety of jobs, from shoe salesman to shipyard worker, Brooks entered the health care profession where he was in management for sixteen years before turning to his first love—writing. Once he decided to turn his attention to becoming a published writer, Brooks worked several more odd jobs to sustain himself, including wildlife tour guide in Sedona, Arizona where he lived and became even more enamored with the West of his childhood heroes, Roy Rogers and Gene Autry. Brooks wrote a string of frontier fiction novels, beginning with *The Badmen* (1992) and *Buscadero* (1993), before he attempted something more lyrical and literary in the critically acclaimed: *The Stone Garden: The Epic Life of Billy the Kid* (2002). This was followed in succession by *Pretty Boy: The Epic Life of Pretty Boy Floyd* (2003) and *Bonnie & Clyde: A Love Story* (2005). *The Stone Garden* was named by *Booklist* as one of the top ten Westerns of the decade. After that trio of novels, Brooks was asked to return to frontier fiction by an editor who had moved to a new publisher and he wrote in succession three series for them, beginning with *Law For Hire* (2003), then *Dakota Lawman* (2005), and finishing up with *The Journey of Jim Glass* (2007). *The Messenger* (Five Star, 2009) was Brooks's twenty-second novel. *Blood Storm* (Five Star, 2011) was the first novel in a series of John Henry Cole adventures. It was praised by *Publishers Weekly* as a well-crafted story with an added depth due to its characters. Brooks now lives in northeast Indiana.

Center Point Large Print
600 Brooks Road / PO Box 1
Thorndike, ME 04986-0001 USA

(207) 568-3717

US & Canada:
1 800 929-9108
www.centerpointlargeprint.com